REAPER

A NOVEL

TIMOTHY J. VANBRANDT

In Memory of Everett L. Dupree
1966 - 2016

Love you and miss you, my friend.
Say hi to Jesus for me.

PROLOGUE

Original Timeline – July 1980

As he sat in the backseat of the family car en route to Freedom Cathedral for church services on a warm, breezy Sunday morning in early July, Malcolm Anderson felt as though he were on his way to a birthday party. For the first twelve years of his life, Malcolm, or Mal, as everyone called him, along with all of the other kids who were deemed too young or too fidgety, had been confined to the basement of the structure for Sunday school while the adult service was going on above them.

This was okay for a while, thanks in part to the efforts of Mrs. Crawford, the church secretary and Sunday school teacher who did her best to keep them occupied, if not entertained, until they heard the worship team, with its closing song, bring their sequestration to a merciful end. But by the time he had reached the age of eight or nine, Mal found himself yearning to join the older kids and adults in the sanctuary for the main service. He did not know why, exactly, as his parents had warned him that he would probably be bored to death listening to the pastor's message. Nevertheless, he was intrigued by the idea of hearing someone speak with authority about what he had thus far found to be the most baffling, profound, heart-wrenching, disturbing and absolutely incredible book he had ever read – the Bible.

Mal had loved reading the children's Bible he had first received in kindergarten. Its colorful pictures and descriptions of faraway places and long ago times had fascinated him. As he got older and was given increasingly more advanced versions, he came to realize that the *real* Bible was not all fast-paced adventures and happy endings. There was a good deal of plodding narrative and scholarly commentary, of history and culture, and of tragedy and sorrow. With each passing year, however, he came to love reading the Bible even more. He read from it every day, and had completed a cover-to-cover reading every six months for the last four years. In fact, without even being aware of it, he had become something of an expert on its content, at least within their family; his parents, though they faithfully attended church every Sunday, never read the Bible, nor did his older brother Mitchell. Thus Mal never had anyone to discuss scripture with, and as a result he was ignorant of his own sizeable reservoir of knowledge.

Mal's father parked the car in the small lot behind the church, and as the four of them walked toward the rear door of the sanctuary, they also passed the door that led to the basement. Despite his growing anticipation, Mal felt a twinge of nostalgia ripple through him. It was true that most Sundays in the church basement were monuments to boredom, but on the plus side, he had made some good friends during the past few years. Some of them, of course, being older than Mal, had gone ahead of him, and he looked forward to seeing them once again every Sunday. But there were also a few who were younger than him, most notably Danny Henderson, who still had about six months to go until his 12th birthday, when he, too, would join the ranks of the "Bigs", as the two of them had nicknamed the upstairs crowd.

The kindness and charm of Mrs. Crawford notwithstanding, it was the occasional daring scheme or hilarious prank with Danny that had made their basement years even remotely bearable. For example, there was the time that Danny had hidden in the broom closet inside the girls' restroom, and when seven year-old Betsy Farrington came in to answer the call of nature, he whispered from the darkness in his raspiest, most evil voice, *"Your soul is mine!"* It seemed to Mal that Betsy's scream of terror echoed throughout the building for at least the next thirty seconds . . . just about the time that several alarmed Bigs came hurtling down the steps to investigate the ruckus. Danny later said that he could not sit down for the next two days on account of the thrashing he had received for that little gem of a stunt.

But the crown jewel of treasured memories – though it was terrifying at the time -- would always be their adventurous foray into the woods adjacent to the church property. There was a trail that led into the woods just off the parking lot, and Danny and Mal had often talked about exploring it sometime. They both lived about six miles from the church, which was too great a distance for them to plan an after-school or Saturday morning hike, so they were resigned to merely dreaming of it. But on one Sunday the previous year, an absolutely glorious early June morning, Danny was waiting anxiously for Mal at the bottom of the church basement steps when he arrived.

"Let's do it!" Danny whispered excitedly as he yanked Mal out of earshot from the others. "Let's go check out that trail!"

Mal stared stupidly at his friend, trying to gauge whether he truly meant what he was saying.

Danny quickly affirmed his sincerity. "Come on, come on!! We've got to go right now! We have to be back here in an hour!"

"But Mrs. Crawford will notice we're gone, and come looking for us," Mal protested. "When she doesn't find us, we'll be in more trouble than we've ever seen before! I can already feel the sting of my dad's belt on my butt! And *you'll* get it even worse than you did the last time!"

"We won't tell anyone where we've been," Danny countered, "we'll just say we went for a walk around the church property to get some fresh air and exercise. We'll get in some trouble, no doubt, but it won't be that bad. Come on, you big chicken! Just think, in a month, or six months, or a year from now, nobody else will remember, but we may have a memory that will last a lifetime!"

Mal again hesitated, fixing his gaze upon the dust particles that hung suspended in the ray of sunshine that had managed to penetrate the filthy window at the top of the basement wall. He extended his hand into the bright shaft of light, feeling its warmth upon his skin, and an instant later, he made up his mind. "Okay, let's go!" he said.

As casually as possible, they glanced around the room at Mrs. Crawford and the other children. Seeing that she was busy getting them started on the activities she had planned, they meandered over to the stairway, took one more look behind them to make sure they were not being watched, then darted up the steps as quietly as they could. At the top of the stairway, Danny opened the exterior door just a crack and peered out into the parking lot to see if there were any late arrivers to the service. Seeing no one, he nodded at Mal, and they slipped out through the doorway and closed it softly behind them. Their adventure was officially underway.

As there were no windows at the back of church through which someone may have seen them making their escape, they sprinted confidently across the parking lot and entered the woods. The service typically lasted an hour and fifteen minutes, so they agreed that they would be back at the church in one hour, which would, if luck were on their side, give them time to re-enter the basement and mingle with the other kids for a few minutes before the service ended. Additionally, if someone did notice they were gone, and upon their return inquire as to where they had been, those extra minutes might be enough for their cover story to be heard and accepted, and the whole incident forgotten, by the time their parents came to get them.

They decided that they would run, rather than walk, for the

entire first leg of the journey, which would maximize the distance they could cover and thereby improve their chances of finding something interesting. In theory, they could run for thirty minutes, then turn around and run back. But instead, they decided that it would not make sense to run for more than twenty minutes. If they found some lost civilization, or hidden caverns, or wreckage from a thirty year-old plane crash containing a payload of stolen gold bullion, they would have some time to explore their discovery before having to run back to the church. On the other hand, if they encountered nothing worth stopping for in those first twenty minutes, they would have forty minutes to get back to the church, which would give them the option of walking rather than running. That would allow their bodies a chance to cool down, and their shirts, which would no doubt be drenched in perspiration after a twenty-minute run, a chance to dry out.

The boys ran down the trail at a brisk though not breakneck pace, enjoying the sights, sounds and smells of this late spring morning, and before they knew it they had approached their predetermined turnaround point. But Danny wanted to press on for just a few minutes more, and Mal hesitantly agreed.

Another three minutes passed uneventfully, and by now, Mal was getting very nervous about the time. "Alright Danny, we've got to go back now. We're already going to be cutting it close."

"Wait, just a little further!" Danny pleaded. "Look, there's a bend in the trail just ahead. We'll turn around up there."

As that bend was only about fifty yards ahead, Mal figured that one more minute would not seriously jeopardize their chances of returning on time, so he continued on with Danny in the lead. When Danny reached the point where he could see around the bend in the trail, however, he let out an enthusiastic *whoop!* and sprinted on ahead, much to Mal's dismay.

The trail came to an end just a stone's throw past the bend, and the opening in the trees provided an alluring glimpse of what lay beyond: a lush, green meadow dotted with wildflowers, birds and butterflies of every imaginable color. This clearing in the midst of the woods was three, maybe four acres in size, and was surrounded by a seven-foot tall chain link fence. At the left side of the meadow stood a grove of pine trees, with half a dozen towering sycamores scattered throughout, and in the center of the clearing was a small pond, about one hundred yards across. A white sand beach, eight to ten feet in width, encircled the pond, and on the far side was a small rowboat that was tethered to a short dock. This was not your typical slimy, putrid green pond, but rather was crystal-clear, apparently well-maintained, and highly inviting.

Danny was standing at the fence, grinning from ear to ear, when Mal arrived a few seconds later. "Wow! Isn't this the coolest thing you've ever seen? Kind of like an oasis in the desert, only in the forest instead!"

While generally not as excitable as his friend, Mal, too, was impressed. "Yeah, it is," he said, nodding. "I wonder who owns this?"

Danny shook his head. "Probably somebody we know, since this town isn't very big, but I lost my sense of direction with all of those twists and turns in the trail. Whoever it is, they must want to keep it a secret."

"Can't say I blame them. You could go on a vacation almost in your own back yard! Pitch a tent on the beach, cook hotdogs and marshmallows over a campfire, just get away from everyone for a few days!"

They stood silently for a few moments, both of them mesmerized by the peacefulness and beauty of the place, when suddenly Danny began to climb the fence. "Let's go see how the water feels!" he shouted.

"No, we have to get back! We'll be late!" But even as he spoke the words, Mal knew there was no stopping Danny at this point. He shook his head, sighed, and began to scale the fence.

Once on the other side, the boys jogged the short distance to the edge of the pond, slipped off their shoes and socks, and stepped into the water. It was freezing!

"Well, it's only the beginning of June," Mal observed. "Give it another month, and this'll feel like a swimming pool."

"Yeah, next time, we'll wear our trunks under our pants and go swimming!" Danny squealed. "Only problem will be putting our pants back on over our wet trunks. The water will soak through our pants, and people will know we were up to something."

Mal had walked back across the narrow beach and was swishing his feet through the damp grass in an effort to remove the sand that had stuck to them. "We'll figure that out later. Right now I'm more worried about people knowing we were up to something *today*, especially if we're late getting back. Come on, get your shoes on, we've got to leave right now!"

Danny nodded, crossed the narrow beach and began to clean his feet in the grass as well.

They had pulled on their socks and shoes, and were just about to retrace their steps back to the fence, when they saw something dart out from behind the grove of pine trees to their right. The tall vegetation made it impossible to ascertain what it was, but they could make out a fluffy white head bouncing just below the tips of the tallest grasses. Moments later, they saw another, taller creature emerge from the trees in pursuit of the first one, and they could tell from the shape of its head and from its short, black, curved horns that this one was a goat. They watched with amusement for a minute or so as the two animals appeared to be playing a game of tag; the goat accelerated and caught up to its grass-shrouded playmate, after which, in an apparent reversal of roles, both animals turned and ran in the opposite direction.

On the next turn, the fluffy white-headed animal moved toward the sandy beach, where the vegetation was shorter and sparser, and it finally revealed itself to be a sheep. Whether it noticed the two of them or not, they were not sure, for it simply ignored them and trotted merrily on its way. But when the goat emerged from the tall grass, it stopped dead in its tracks and fixed its gaze upon them. And kept it there.

Neither Danny's nor Mal's families were farmers, but they lived in a farm community, so they had both been around goats on a handful of occasions before this one. They knew the animals could be aggressive if there was food at stake, but they had never heard of a goat being dangerous. And yet they were both immediately aware of something peculiar in this particular animal's demeanor, something that made it seem menacing, perhaps even hostile. It was in the way that the goat regarded them with its yellow eyes; not with the curiosity that would have been expected, but rather with anger and indignation. In unison they began to back away, initially more out of uneasiness and uncertainty than fear. To their dismay, the goat began to follow them. They turned their backs to it and accelerated their pace to a fast walk. Looking behind them, they found that the goat was keeping pace. Again they increased their speed, and again the goat followed suit. Their uneasiness was beginning to give way to something more like alarm.

"Let's run back to the fence!" Danny whispered, as though he were concerned that the goat would not only *hear* him, but also *understand* what he was saying.

"No, not yet," Mal responded. "We're too far away. If we run now, it'll catch us before we get there, if that's what it wants to do."

"What *does* it want, like, to eat our faces off or something?" Danny asked with a nervous laugh.

"I don't know, but just keep moving at this pace. As long as it keeps the same distance until we get to the fence, I'm fine with that."

The next time they looked round, however, they realized that the goat must have sensed what their strategy was, for it had increased its pace to a trot and had begun to close on them. The boys looked at each other, and both of them could now plainly see the fear on the other's face.

"On the count of three, we run for it," Mal said.

Danny nodded.

"One . . . two . . . three!"

There was a humorous saying that Mal had heard two years before, when his family spent their summer vacation in Yosemite National Park. It was said that if you were ever chased by a bear, you did not have to worry about outrunning it . . . . you only had to outrun the guy you were with. And while he and Danny were being chased not by a 400-pound black bear with one-inch claws and two-inch canines, but rather by a 150-pound goat with hooves instead of claws and with teeth that were probably not sharp enough to penetrate their clothing, Mal could not help but think of that saying. And to consider its merits. For while he was lean and athletic, Danny was a bit on the portly side, thus it took only a few seconds before he began to pull away.

"Wait for me, Mal!" Danny pleaded.

"JUST RUN!" Mal screamed. He looked back again and saw the goat nearly upon his friend. The tall grasses and wildflowers were slowing the two of them down, but it had little or no effect on the goat, which was able to leap over the knee-high flora in great bounds rather than having to charge through it. "RUN, DANNY!" Mal screamed again, for there was nothing else he could do. He swiveled his head back around and now saw that they were quickly approaching the chain link fence . . . thirty yards away . . . now twenty-five . . . now twenty. But because it was too tall to be scaled quickly, and because their pursuer was so close behind them, it seemed that the fence was only going to hinder their escape rather than aid in it.

And then an idea came to Mal. He had noticed when they first climbed the fence that beneath it, and all the way around the perimeter, lay a bed of river stone about two feet wide, a foot on either side, apparently placed there as a means of keeping the fence clear of vegetation. It was the larger variety of stone, each of them three to four inches in diameter; in other words, large enough to make a formidable self-defense projectile.

Mal reached the fence, grabbed two of the stones with his left hand, and one more in his right. He whirled around and cocked his arm back, ready to hurl the first stone at the goat in hopes of deterring it just long enough for Danny to reach the fence and for the two of them to scramble over it. Seeing that his friend was directly in the line of fire, he took three steps to his right to give himself a proper angle with which to see and attack their opponent.

But when the goat became visible to Mal, he nearly dropped his arsenal from sheer terror and shock; it was running almost blindly behind Danny, having lowered its head as though to ram, or even *impale*, him with its horns. Mal had never heard of such crazed behavior from a goat, and he wondered if it might be rabid.

Mal's hesitation was short-lived, however, and he flung the stone with all of his strength at the exposed head of the goat, praying that he did not misfire and hit Danny instead. His aim was true, and the stone struck the goat on the top of its skull with a resounding *whack!* The animal stopped dead in its tracks, threw its head back, and issued forth an unearthly sound, something between a roar and a scream. A fresh wave of terror cascaded through Mal when he heard that shriek, but this time he did not hesitate.

"GET OVER THE FENCE!" he shouted at Danny, as he hurled another of his missiles at the goat, this time aiming for the flat spot right between its eyes. His throw was off the mark just a bit, but still an effective one as the stone struck the beast on its left shoulder. The goat stomped its hooves and bellowed at Mal once again, but the bombardment seemed to be serving its purpose for the time being, as it did not advance forward any further.

Mal glanced behind him and saw that Danny was nearing the top of the fence. He waited a few seconds longer, holding another stone in the ready position to keep the goat at bay while his friend completed his getaway. When Mal heard Danny's feet hit the ground on the opposite side of the fence, he dropped the stone, turned and leaped as high upon it as he could. The chain link was already hot to the touch thanks to the intensity of the mid-morning sun, but it would have taken the heat of a branding iron to get him to relinquish his grip, for instantly he heard the pounding of hooves as the goat sprinted after him in a final, desperate burst.

Mal reached the top of the fence just as the goat rammed into it inches below his feet, and gripping the top rail, he launched himself up and over it, falling the seven feet to the ground and landing on his side with a sickening *thud*! The impact drove the wind from his lungs, and for the next sixty seconds he lay paralyzed, frantically seeking that elusive next breath. During that time, the goat screeched and thrashed, urinated and defecated, and hurled itself repeatedly against the fence, mad with rage at having lost its opportunity to .... to do whatever it had planned to do. It was also during that brief face-to-face encounter that Mal noticed its eyes; they were no longer the yellow color that he had seen when it first emerged from the tall grass near the pond, but rather a fiery red. In fact, it was not just the irises that were red, but also the pupils.

As he stared into those eyes, Mal had the unnerving feeling that the intense light they were emitting was searing through his skin, his bones, and into his very soul. And there was something else as well, something that would haunt him for the rest of his life. It was not merely animal instinct. It was intelligence, calculation, deception .... and *evil*. Yes, evil, of the purest kind. Mal knew that of all God's creation, only human beings were made in His image, thus only human beings possessed a soul, and only human beings possessed an understanding of both good and evil. But somehow, this goat, this *thing*, also possessed a soul, one that had been spawned in the very depths of hell.

When finally the breath returned to Mal, and he was able to

tear his gaze away from the demonic eyes of the goat, he stood up gasping and motioned for Danny to follow him. They ran back into the woods and kept running, stopping only when they reached the trailhead near the parking lot of the church. By then, Mal was bursting at the seams, waiting to hear Danny's reaction to their encounter with the goat.

"Did you see them? Did you see its eyes?" Mal blurted out between gulps of air.

Danny was even more winded than Mal, and stood bent over with hands on knees for no less than a minute until he finally had enough breath to respond. "What about them?" he huffed.

"What *about* them? They were glowing *red*, that's what about them! Did you look at its eyes, or not?"

"Yes, I looked at its eyes! How could I not have looked at its eyes when it was standing three feet away from us? But what are you talking about, *red*? They were yellow, like every other goat I've ever seen."

Mal shook his head adamantly. "They were yellow at first, but when we got to the fence they turned red. How could you not see that? And what about that scream? Did that sound like a goat to you?"

Danny looked at Mal as though he were seeing a human being for the first time. "I don't know what you're talking about. I saw yellow eyes, not red, and I heard a goat bleating its fool head off because it has rabies or something. I think you're suffering from post-dramatic stress delusion!"

Mal started to respond, but then simply offered a dismissive wave of the hand. It was apparent that, for some unknown reason, Danny had not seen what he himself had seen, so there was no point in prolonging the argument. "Okay, whatever. And it's post-traumatic stress disorder, not post-dramatic stress delusion."

"Huh?"

"Never mind. I hear music and singing inside the church. I

think we made it back just in time, but we'd better get down in the basement and quick."

They quietly opened the door of the church basement and proceeded down the steps, with Danny in the lead. Near the bottom, he stopped, turned around and said, "It was just a rabid goat. Right?"

Mal nodded, but only to appease his friend. He knew what he had seen and heard . . . and that rabies did *not* do that to an animal.

That unforgettable adventure was thirteen months ago, and between themselves, Mal and Danny spoke of it often (though Mal always left out the part about the red goat eyes). And though they saw each other every day at school, and frequently spent Saturdays together as well, Mal was going to miss hanging out with his friend on Sunday mornings. But a new chapter of his life was about to begin, and he was looking forward to it just about as much as he was regretting having to leave Sunday school behind.

Mal walked alongside Mitch and behind their parents into the sanctuary and up the center aisle, to the family's usual spot in the fourth row on the left side. Here and there along the way, a few heads turned, and smiles were offered, from those who were aware that it was his first time among the Bigs and wanted to make him feel welcome. He smiled politely in return, feeling his face flush from the unexpected attention. Shortly after that, the worship team came out onto the platform and the service began. The lyrics of each song were projected onto large screens on either side of the platform, and Mal cheerfully read them and sang along. At the conclusion of the worship segment of the service, Pastor Pete Miller strode up to the podium to begin his sermon.

"Well, friends, today we're starting a new series called *Divine Utilization: Allowing God to Use You as He Sees Fit.* Throughout the series we'll talk about things like releasing your grip on the steering wheel of life, so to speak, so that God can take control of it, and about discovering your spiritual gifts and how to put them to use to glorify Jesus Christ. But first things first. At the head of any trail that leads down a path of servitude lies the inescapable need for us to empathize with those we want to help. In short, we must have compassion. We must heed the words of Robert Pierce, the founder of World Vision International and Samaritan's Purse, who saw widespread hunger while on a mission trip to China and wrote in his Bible, 'Let my heart be broken with the things that break the heart of God.' A broken heart is a compassionate heart, and without a compassionate heart, there would be no motivation for us to spend four months traveling across Asia spreading the gospel and feeding the hungry, as Pierce did, much less for acts like shoveling your elderly neighbor's driveway after a snow storm, or dropping money into a Salvation Army bucket. In fact, without a broken, compassionate heart, it would never occur to us to do the simplest, least expensive, yet most valuable thing of all, which is to pray for those in need. About Pierce, Pastor Richard Halverson, former Chaplain of the United States Senate, once wrote, he 'prayed more earnestly and importunely than anyone else I have ever known. It was as though prayer burned within him . . . Bob Pierce functioned from a broken heart.'

"It may seem counterproductive to live life with a broken heart. After all, why would a nonbeliever want to become a disciple of Jesus Christ if he sees Christians as a brooding lot of doomsayers, worry warts, and party poopers? The Bible itself tells us, in Proverbs 15:13, 'A happy heart makes the face cheerful, but heartache crushes the spirit.' Think about it from a secular standpoint; are you attracted to people who always seem downcast and depressed, or would you rather be around people who smile, have a sense of humor, and seem to love life?

"Well, I think we can begin to understand this sort of paradox by looking at what Paul said to the church in Corinth in chapter seven, verses eight through eleven of his second letter to them. He wrote, 'Even if I caused you sorrow by my letter, I do not regret it. Though I did regret it – I see that my letter hurt you, but only for a little while – yet now I am happy, not because you were made sorry, but because your sorrow led you to repentance. For you became sorrowful as God intended and so were not harmed in any way by us. Godly sorrow brings repentance that leads to salvation and leaves no regret, but worldly sorrow brings death.' And so the kind of broken heartedness we ought to feel should come not because our boyfriend or girlfriend broke up with us, or because our favorite sports team lost to their archrival, but because we grieve for the loss of our innocence, and for how it damages our relationship with God. Once we become broken hearted for ourselves, it leads to repentance and salvation. And only then we can become broken hearted for the suffering of others.

"The prophet Jeremiah is a good example of this. He was called 'the weeping prophet' because his heart broke over the plight of his people. You recall that Judah had turned its back on God, instead worshipping money, power and idols, and forming alliances with pagan nations. Jeremiah relentlessly preached repentance, warning that if Judah failed to do so, the country would be invaded and destroyed by Babylon, and the people would be held captive for seventy years. Unfortunately, as we all know, the people didn't listen, and Jeremiah's warnings would eventually come to fruition. His words in chapter 31, verse 15, although not literal in that they referenced the symbolic mother of the northern tribes of Israel who had died roughly 1,300 years before, give us a sense of the devastation inflicted upon Jeremiah's people: 'A voice is heard in Ramah, mourning and great weeping, Rachel weeping for her children and refusing to be comforted, because her children are no more.' That verse is also found in the gospel of Matthew, when he recounts King Herod's horrifying edict to slaughter all of the boys in Bethlehem that were two years old and under, after Herod had learned that he had been outwitted by the Magi and was unable to find and kill the baby Jesus. The terror and grief of the mothers in

Bethlehem must have been unimaginable.

"And so we must become like Jeremiah, feeling not worldly sorrow, which is really a nice way of saying 'to wallow in self-pity,' but Godly sorrow, which again, subsequent to our own repentance, is directed at others and is a result of the physical, emotional and spiritual suffering that we see people going through. Letting our hearts be broken in this way will lead to a desire to serve . . . "

Mal had listened intently to Pastor Miller's words for the first few minutes, but then finding that the sermon was not as fascinating as he had hoped it would be (as foretold, he also realized, by his parents), he had gradually allowed his mind to begin to wander away from the sanctuary, to his friends, his family's upcoming vacation to Disney World, the Major League Baseball Game of the Week, and other such worldly diversions.

But when the words "Rachel weeping for her children" touched his ears, though he was not necessarily consciously aware of having heard them, his attention snapped instantly back to the message like a lion tamer's whip. He immediately knew, somehow, that those words were of tremendous significance, not merely within their historical context, nor with respect to the pastor's sermon. No, there was some deeper meaning to them, something prophetic, perhaps even life-altering.

As he pondered this, the room began to feel warmer, and things around him began to shimmer, as though it were all morphing into some strange sort of mirage. Then Pastor Miller's words began to fade away, or rather, were increasingly drowned out by the sound of Mal's own heart hammering in his ears as his pulse quickened.

His head began to throb, his fingers and toes went numb, and his stomach had that jittery, queasy sort of feeling like when he plummeted down a steep drop on a rollercoaster. And while these feelings scared him, they were nothing compared to the horror he felt a few seconds later, when he glanced at those around him and saw ragged, gaping wounds suddenly opening up on their heads, felt a few seconds later, when he glanced at those around him and saw ragged, gaping wounds suddenly opening up on their heads, faces and necks, as though they were being mauled by an invisible beast. Even more shocking, however, was that somehow, they were all unaware of being brutally savaged, for they did not react, not even so much as a flinch. Mal wanted to scream at the sight of this, but paralysis had suddenly gripped him, clamping down like a vise from his toes all the way up to his throat.

And then, bizarrely, something else happened; the memory of that day in the woods thirteen months before came flooding back to him. Perhaps it was some kind of self-defense mechanism, his brain forcing itself to focus on something other than what was now transpiring around him to prevent his body from going into shock. But that did not make a whole lot of sense, because his run-in with the red-eyed goat had been nearly as terrifying as what he was now witnessing. No, there was a reason that that memory had re-emerged at this precise moment, and Mal instinctively knew it was because it was somehow connected to this gruesome scene.

Seconds ticked by, then minutes, and still no one spoke, or cried out in pain, or fell over dead from loss of blood. Their expressions and body language remained the same, even that of old Mr. Jamison, who was sitting in the row in front of them and a few seats to Mal's right. Mitch had once told Mal that like the sun rising in the east, Jamison was guaranteed to nod off halfway through the sermon every week; and true to form, his lids now fluttered sleepily, but this time over empty sockets, his eyes having been gouged out by the invisible creature, while his mangled chin occasionally dropped down to his chest before bobbing back up again. And all the while, the goat incident kept replaying in Mal's head to the echoes of Pastor Miller's words, as though they were part of the soundtrack to a movie: *"Rachel weeping for her children, refusing to be comforted, because her children are no more."*

Gradually Mal's breathing and heart rate slowed, as he began to recognize that this episode and the goat incident both pointed to some sort of vision . . . a premonition, in fact. The demonic goat -- perhaps the most universally recognized symbol of evil -- represented a coming horror, a monstrosity like nothing the world had ever seen. The mauling of the church people depicted the exact intentions of this unspeakable abomination. And lastly, the verse from Jeremiah 31 was symbolic not of grieving Israelite mothers, but of grieving mothers *everywhere*. Indeed, not just of mothers, he realized, but of humanity in general. People of all ages and nationalities, to suffer and mourn like at no other time in recorded history . . . and ultimately, to be silenced forever.

PART ONE

THE VISION

"For God does speak – now one way, now another – though man
may not perceive it. In a dream, in a vision of the night, when
deep sleep falls on men as they slumber in their beds."

Job 33:14-15

Original Timeline – August 1990

I t was times like these that a tiny part of Mal wished he had not turned his life over to Christ when he was a boy. The woman sitting across from him at Dinky's Italian Restaurant, inside the Victory Hotel in Chicago, was absolutely stunning; long, wavy, natural blonde hair, oceanic blue eyes, sensuous lips, athletic but curvaceous figure, and funny and smart to boot. And what was killing him the most was that she wanted him. *Badly.* He knew it long before they had left the hotel's conference center an hour ago.

Mal had been one of the speakers at the parapsychology conference, and this woman had approached him during a break, under the guise of wanting to understand more about his profession. But she stood much too close to him, her face not ten inches from his, so close that he could smell the cinnamon Altoid she had obviously just popped in her mouth moments before she approached him. And her *perfume* . . . dear Lord, her perfume! He had no idea what kind it was, but it might as well have been named "Pure Pheromones", because it made him want to ravage her right on the spot. Mal did not know what it was about being a psychic that was such a turn-on to women. But there was no mistaking it, for he had begun to notice it ten years ago, shortly after the incident at church when he had seen his family and fellow churchgoers ripped apart by an invisible creature and realized that it was a vision of things to come. In the following days, his psychic abilities began to blossom rapidly, to the point where he was frequently seeing future events, usually unfortunate ones, and was able to help those involved to steer clear of the circumstances that would have otherwise led to their demise.

Of course, there were plenty of skeptics, for often times there was no evidence that his intervention had prevented injury or loss of life. For example, a person who would have fallen to his death had he gone ahead and climbed that tree in his backyard, or hike up that slippery mountain trail on his Appalachian vacation, would have no way of proving that Mal had saved his life by telling him to shun those activities.

But there were a handful of occasions when there could be no disputing Mal's ability, such as the time he advised a farmer who lived down the street not to work in his barn that day, as the man normally did. It was a very windy day, the barn was old and poorly maintained, and the structure collapsed at around 2:00 in the afternoon, a time when the farmer almost certainly would have been inside. When word got out about these incidents, not only did adults come flocking to see if he could tell them something about their future (regrettably, it did not work that way; he could not peer into a crystal ball and selectively see the future, but rather, the visions simply came to him randomly), but the girls also came flocking because they thought it was cool. Throughout middle school and high school, Mal received calls almost nightly from young ladies who were smitten by him. Sometimes, two, three, even four would call in a single evening. The fact that he was a charming, handsome fellow certainly did not hurt, either.

Now that Mal was 22 years old, it was grown women – anywhere from eighteen to as much as forty-five years old in some cases – who threw themselves at him incessantly. Of course, it was no longer just the fascination of being in the presence of someone who could see future events; he was also well known within the psychology and parapsychology circles, having written numerous magazines articles and spoken at conferences like the one he had just attended. And most of all, it was because he was extremely wealthy – one of the wealthiest young men in the country, in fact.

Mal's parents, Vincent and Barbara Anderson, had opened a small machine shop 25 years earlier, and the company had steadily grown and diversified until it became a major manufacturer with annual revenues exceeding $1 billion. The company had been sold four years ago, and the Anderson family now had investment and trust accounts valued at over $500 million. Vincent and Barbara had retired to Switzerland, and Mitch and Mal had each been given $25 million on their 20th birthdays to essentially do with they wanted, though they had been raised to be responsible and ambitious, and neither had any intention of squandering his fortune or of living a slothful life. Indeed, Mitch had graduated near the top of his class at Stanford, and was now a software engineer for a Silicon Valley firm. Mal had attended Northwestern for a couple of years but had dropped out after receiving his inheritance, his career as a writer and speaker having already begun to take off.

Despite some of the women, like Sandy, for instance, looking as though they ought to be gracing the cover of a magazine or up on the big screen, Mal had never given in to the desire for a one-night stand. He longed for a true relationship, one that involved meaningful conversation, laughter, discovery, and growth, not merely torrid sex. And even though he knew it was unlikely he would find all of that in a woman he met at a conference, he often asked them out to dinner afterwards on the off-chance that one of them would prove to be different . . . to be looking for the same thing he was. That was why, despite her obvious desire for him, Mal had invited Sandy to Dinky's – hoping that if they got to know each other a bit over dinner, she might prove to have some substance and be interested in him on a personal level.

Mal ordered his favorite Italian fare – chicken parmesan -- while Sandy, not surprisingly given her fantastic figure, ordered a grilled chicken salad that had fewer than 500 calories. They chatted casually throughout dinner about the usual topics: their careers (she was an assistant to a clinical psychologist at a Dallas-based practice), their families, recent political events, sports, and so on. And while the conversation was friendly enough, the closer they came to finishing their meals, the more the tension escalated between them. Sexual tension, to be precise. The way she looked at him. The exaggerated manner in which she licked her lips. The way she arched her shoulders back slightly, but enough to thrust her breasts out noticeably further.

"It's getting noisy in here," Sandy suddenly announced. "I'm having a hard time hearing what you're saying." She had been sitting across from him at a four-person table, and she got up and moved to the seat on Mal's left. Then she slid the chair even closer, so that their knees were touching beneath the table.

Yes, she was setting him up, moving in for the kill.

He could feel the perspiration beginning to prickle his forehead, as his heart hammered away in his chest. This had obviously been a mistake, and he wished furiously that he could wind the clock back one hour and do things differently.

And yet . . . . why was he being such a prude? They were two consenting adults, after all, who had the right to enjoy themselves, and each other, as they saw fit. Sure, he would love to meet a nice girl who he could have a serious relationship with, but that obviously had not happened yet, or he would not be sitting here with Sandy. So in the meantime, why not have an evening of fun with her? She would be leaving in the morning, and they would almost certainly never see each other again. No strings, no painful goodbyes, just a pleasant memory that they could each hold onto for as long as they liked.

Careful, Mal, it's just the perfume messing with your head. He could almost hear the conflicting whispers, one in each ear, and if he were to turn his head in either direction, he felt certain he would see the tiny versions of himself, one with a halo and one with horns, perched atop his shoulders.

"Can I interest you in some dessert?"

Mal's inner struggle was interrupted briefly with the question posed by their waitress.

Sandy responded before Mal had the chance. "Yes, we'll have two orders of the chocolate mousse cake and a bottle of your best dessert wine sent to room 618. And put the entire bill on that account, along with a 20% gratuity. Thanks so much." She smiled warmly at the waitress, but in her eyes was a hint of something that said, "That'll be all, you are dismissed."

The young woman picked up on the hint, nodded, said "Thank you, enjoy your evening," turned and was gone.

Sandy looked back at Mal, leaning in closer than ever, and said, "Now, let's continue this fascinating conversation over dessert and a nightcap up in my room." She stood up, and waited expectantly for him to follow suit.

The room seemed to spin around him. He swallowed hard and took in the biggest gulp of air that his lungs would allow. It was time to make a decision. *Go home, or go with Sandy, go home, or go with Sandy . . .*

"Well? What are we waiting for?"

God forgive me, but she's got me under her spell. He stood up and allowed Sandy to take him by the hand and lead him out of the restaurant, toward the hotel elevators. There was no one sharing the elevator with them, so the second the door closed, Sandy nestled up against him and began to purr like a kitten. Then she began kissing him on the neck and running her hands through the hair on the back of his head. It was apparent she had done this many times before and knew exactly how to get a man excited, and it was working yet again. Mal's heart rate rose to new heights as he envisioned what he would do with Sandy when, after what was beginning to seem like an eternity, they finally reached the privacy of her room.

But the second he heard the bell signal that the elevator had arrived at the sixth floor, a startling sensation suddenly rippled through Mal, like a wave rushing up on the beach. He felt a strange and powerful desire, almost a *need* in fact, to leave the hotel immediately, drive home and go to bed. As in go to sleep. Alone. It was not that he felt tired. And it certainly was not that he had lost his nerve about having sex with Sandy. In fact, that was part of what made it so strange, as his desire for her seemed as though it was multiplying by the second. Nevertheless, he felt a rapidly growing sense of urgency to sleep, even though Sandy's advances had him so electrified right now that he could not even imagine being able to close his eyes, much less fall asleep. But the need was undeniably there, and had grown to the point where it now surpassed his burning desire for Sandy.

The elevator doors opened, and Sandy released him from her clutches and stepped into the hallway. When Mal did not follow her, she turned around and looked at him quizzically. "Well, come on handsome, what are you waiting for? Don't tell me you're one that likes to play hard to get? I'd say we're a little too old for that, wouldn't you?"

"Uh . . . I'm sorry, Sandy," Mal said. He was as embarrassed as he had ever been in his life. "I'm afraid I have to leave. There's, uh, something I realized I have to do."

Sandy stared at him, speechless for a moment, then burst into laughter. "Okay, you got me! You had me going for a minute! But come now, though I love the occasional juvenile prank, it's time for some grownup fun."

Mal shook his head and gave her what he thought was his most apologetic expression. "Look, Sandy, you're an incredibly beautiful and sexy woman, and I can't think of anything more I would want than to . . . uh . . to be with you tonight. But there really is something important that I have to do right now, though I'm not sure I can explain it to you. Call it one of my psychic episodes."

She stared at him again, utter shock and anger now contorting her face. It was obvious that she had never been turned down by a man before. "You've gotta be kidding me! You're turning *this* down?" She swept her hand from in front of her face down to her thighs, like the models on the game shows did when they were displaying prizes to the contestants. In this case, Mal was the contestant, and Sandy's body itself was the prize, though like all of the others that had come before, it was one that he would have to forfeit.

"I'm really sorry, Sandy," Mal said again, and with all sincerity. "Have a safe trip back to Dallas."

Before she could say another word, he hit the button for the main floor on the elevator keypad, and the doors slid shut. Immediately he felt her siren-like grip on him broken.

"Thank you, Jesus," he muttered to himself. He did yet not understand what this bizarre beckoning to his own bed meant, but as he had been about to succumb to his most primal desires, against the wishes of his Lord and Savior, he was grateful for the intervention despite the fact that it was completely inexplicable.

Mal left the hotel and hurried to his car outside. He lived in a spacious condominium in Winnetka, about fifteen miles and twenty minutes away. Normally a commute of that length would have allowed him time to think deeply about a number of different subjects, but on this night, in his trancelike state, and with the aid of a force that seemed to reach out and yank him across that distance, he arrived at his home before he even realized he had left the hotel parking lot. He still felt no fatigue or drowsiness whatsoever, yet that same force pulling him towards sleep was unrelenting.

Mal had only the vaguest notion of stripping off his clothes, still reeking of Sandy's perfume, and tumbling into bed. He was out cold even as his head touched the pillow, and within seconds plunged into a dream world the likes of which he had never entered before.

Three days later, he pecked away furiously on his laptop, trying to record every last detail of the dream before it slipped away.

2

*T*he dream begins with me standing on the edge of a cliff, overlooking a valley, in the dead of night. Despite the darkness, I have a sense of my surroundings because the light from a full moon is reflecting off snow-covered peaks around me, and because I can see distant lights twinkling in some small, unknown town on the valley floor far below me.

I am also immediately aware of the fact that I am dreaming, which, as I recall, is known as a "lucid" dream. This is incredibly exciting, because I have never been a lucid dreamer before, even when I have had other visions and premonitions in my sleep. I simply awoke and then realized I had had a vision inside of a dream, though I was not aware of it while it was happening..

I am fascinated that the dream seems so real – the sting of the cold air upon my skin, the smell of pine forests around me, and the sound of the wind whistling through the trees -- but then again, because I know I am dreaming, I suppose that I have some degree of control over my environment and can therefore enhance its vividness. And yet I also realize that while I am aware that I am dreaming, I am powerless to direct the events that are about to unfold. I can only sit and watch.

A short time later, the sky begins to brighten to one side of the horizon, I presume the east, as I have no sense of direction in the dream. I have never seen a mountaintop sunrise in real life, and I am awestruck as the increasing level of light reveals a gorgeous spectrum of color splashed across the sky. The night breezes slip *away through the trees, the air becomes still and begins to warm, and birds commence their morning choruses. And yet I cannot fully appreciate this tranquil scene, for it somehow feels like an illusion (and not simply because it really is an illusion, it being only in my head). I sense there is something coming, something that will swallow up all beauty and purity with ugliness and evil, something that makes me anxious and afraid.*

Soon after, the sky begins to darken again as rain clouds stampede in from the west. Lightning pierces the darkness every few seconds, with the accompanying booms of thunder ricocheting off the granite peaks around me. With the wind beginning to buffet me, I decide that I do not like being so close to the edge of the cliff, even in a dream, so I turn away from the precipice and sit down on a rock a few yards away. Seconds later, a boy walks out of the trees and sits down beside me. I judge him to be around ten, maybe twelve years old. He does not acknowledge me at first, but rather studies the swirling skies above, as though he is looking for some hidden revelation scrawled across the seething black clouds, or in the jagged fingers of lighting.

Finally, the boy turns to me and says, "You'd better get started. You'll want to see as much of this as possible before they come get you."

Certainly he knows that I have no idea what he is talking about, but does not offer anything more, so I ask him the obvious: "What exactly will I be seeing? Who is coming to get me? And may I ask who you are?"

"To your last question, my name is Randall Wilhelm, and I was chosen for this task just like you have been chosen for yours. That's all I can tell you about myself. To your second question, it would be anyone who might realize you had been gone too long. And to your first question, you are about to see things that have not yet come to pass, but will in due time. You must act upon what you see without hesitation or doubt. If you do not, the world as you know

it will end. For ten years now, you have known this. You did not know exactly how it would come about, or that you yourself would play a key role, but now it is time that you do."

Randall's responses to my questions are mostly cryptic, and therefore I wonder: who is it that might realize I am gone, and furthermore, gone from where? Is this boy a real-life person with a real-life task, or just a dream character with a dream task? And what is my task, exactly? These things confuse me, but with respect to his assertion that the world as I know it is coming to an end, and that I have known it for the last ten years . . . I know exactly what he is referring to. The memory of that day in church, when I saw the horribly mangled bodies around me, and when I made the connection between that vision and the one I had had thirteen months prior to that, the day that Danny and I had been chased by the goat, had steadily faded over the years. But it never left me completely, always lurking in some dark corner of my mind, until the time came for the 'hows' and 'whys' to be revealed to me. It seemed that that time was now, despite the fact that the messenger is someone I would have least expected. And so I ask him, "where will I see the things you speak of?"

"Not here, but somewhere near," Randall answers, then stands up and walks to the edge of the precipice. "There is a storm coming," he observes.

I suppress the urge to laugh at his statement of the glaringly obvious. The storm is not coming, it is already here.

"No," he says, apparently reading my thoughts. "Not that storm. That one." He points down into the canyon at something I cannot see. "Come here," he says.

As the wind has continued to intensify, however, I elect to remain seated.

"COME HERE!" he commands, with a surprising tone of authority.

This time, I grudgingly rise and walk up beside him. "What are you looking –", I begin, but before I can finish my question, he pushes me off the edge of the cliff, and I fall screaming and flailing into the gaping void. I seem to be falling a very long time, long enough to remember a low budget science fiction movie I had once seen about people who were murdered in their dreams and how it caused them to die in real life. If that could actually happen, would the fact that I am aware that I am dreaming be enough to save me, or would my heart implode within my real body in the split second that my dream body splatters upon the canyon floor?

Fortunately I do not have to learn the answer to that question, for my pinwheeling body suddenly straightens itself out and slows its descent, and I touch down gently upon the ground much like a skilled parachutist might have done. I find myself standing in the middle of a quiet street in an apparently middle-class residential neighborhood, for there are modest but well-maintained houses lining the avenue on either side. I assume I must be in the town I had seen from up on the cliff, though I cannot wager a guess as to exactly where in the world this might be, for the vehicles parked in the driveways are of makes and models that I have never seen before, and the houses, while attractive, have rather bizarre angular features that are also unfamiliar to me.

I am not sure what to do at this point, so I take a moment to reflect upon the words that Randall had spoken. I am supposed to see something, and to act upon what I see. I assume that that "something" is not just a pleasant but mysterious neighborhood in some faraway town, but I do not know how to proceed from here. And apparently time is a factor here, because I need to see this before "they come get me", though I still do not know what that means.

I become more engrossed in these thoughts than I realize, for I do not hear the car approaching from behind me, until it is too late and the car hits me. Or rather, passes through *me, as if I am, or it is, some sort of apparition. Again I briefly recollect movies I*

34

have seen, where a person dies and his ghost lingers, passing through any solid object he encounters, from walls to furniture to living people. But of course this is not analogous to my situation, for I know that I am still very much alive but simply dreaming. Thus my state of being is more akin to that of Ebenezer Scrooge in A Christmas Carol *than to Patrick Swayze's character in* Ghost *(at least I think so; the movie came out last month and is number one at the box office, but I have not seen it yet).*

As the car moves away from me and gets smaller, so too does the road noise it produces become fainter, and I eventually become aware of the sounds of muffled yelling and screaming. I listen closely and realize the noise is coming from the house directly to my left. I approach the house and try to peer through the front window, but the glare on the surface of the glass prevents me from seeing into the room on the opposite side. I think about knocking on the front door, but then I remember that this will not work, and that I am not restricted to the traditional means of entering structures. So I simply walk through the brick and glass wall of the house and find myself standing in the living room, watching a terrible argument taking place. Or, to be more precise, a terrible berating *taking place.*

There are a woman and a young boy cowering on the floor, while a man stands over them screaming all manner of threats, insults and obscenities. The man is so furious that his face is bright red, the veins on his forehead and neck are nearly splitting the skin, and he shakes violently from head to toe. After a few moments, it becomes clear that his tirade contains no discernible message, and it is then that I notice several empty whiskey and beer bottles scattered about the room. I know this is a drunken rant, probably brought on by something as trivial as a light left on in the bathroom or a toy left lying on the floor. I also judge by the variety of holes punched in the drywall and gouges in the furniture that this is a regular occurrence. While I am fortunate to have never known an abusive alcoholic, as this man obviously is, I know the type, and I wish I could solidify myself and bash him over the head with something hard and heavy, like a bulldozer, for example. But I am coming to grips with the fact that I can only observe these happenings, not participate in them, so I do my best to emotionally detach myself.

In two or three minutes, by my estimation, the man's fury is spent, and he collapses onto the sofa and passes out. The woman and boy remain on the floor for a short time, the latter sobbing quietly while the former cradles his head and gently shushes him. Then suddenly the room goes black.

Almost immediately, the light returns and I find myself in a bedroom, this time alone with the woman and boy. In terms of their ages, they look the same as they did before, but I figure this to be another day, because they are both dressed differently, and there is a nasty purple lump on the boy's forehead. Again he is crying, and the woman is comforting him, but this time they are having a discussion.

"What did I do, Mommy?" the boy wails.

"You didn't do anything, sweetie," the woman responds. "Daddy just isn't himself when he drinks that awful drink."

"Then why does he do it? If it's bad, why does he drink it?"

The woman momentarily struggles for an answer, though I am certain she has been asked this question by her son before. "Well, he has a very difficult job, you see, and if you drink only a little of that drink it can help you relax and take your mind off things. But Daddy doesn't realize he's drinking too much of it until it's too late, and it has made him angry and want to . . . to punish us for things that we really didn't do. So what we need to do is try to forgive him when he does that, and most of all, we need to pray that God will help Daddy to see that what he is doing is not right. Do you understand?"

The boy is silent for a while, blinking away tears and gazing

36

thoughtfully out the window and into the back yard. I am looking directly into his face, into his eyes, and I am struck by the contrasting aspects of his countenance. He is a physically beautiful young boy, his blond hair and blue eyes giving him a sort of Scandinavian look. But now his face is contorted with anger, and it creates an impression that starkly opposes his normally angelic appearance. I can also see there is a struggle going on inside of him, as that unnatural anger duels with the loving, forgiving tendencies that are typical of a young child. In a moment, his face brightens, and he turns back to his mother with a smile.

"Yes," he says, "let's pray for Daddy. I just know God will change his heart if we pray really, really, hard!"

His inner turmoil has been resolved, and he has chosen righteousness over rage. For now.

*O*ver the course of the next several weeks (in dream time), I observe several other incidents similar to those I had seen at the outset of the vision, but also a few that do not involve yelling, hitting, or throwing of objects, and which in fact seem mundane and trivial at the time. I learn that the man's name is Carl Zintak, his wife's name is Sherry, and their son's name is Brian. I know that the boy is six years old, for there is a discussion about his seventh birthday party that is coming up in a few weeks, and he is asked which of his friends he would like to invite. He mentions half a dozen or so names, presumably classmates or neighbors, and his mother prepares the invitations and mails them out.

I learn other things that are more surprising, such as the fact that the year is 2086 . . . which is 96 years into the future! To a certain extent I had known this to be true from the beginning, based on the unfamiliar automobiles and architectural styles I had seen, as well as the highly advanced television, computer, and home appliances that the Zintaks possess. There was also the fact that Randall had said that I would be seeing things that had not yet come to pass. But when I see the date on a newspaper one morning, I am shocked indeed! I had thought perhaps 10 or 20 years into the future, but not 96! And then I see TV shows and pictures in magazines that feature people zipping around in personal hovercrafts and jetpack-type apparatuses, and I am even more amazed!

Despite the advances in technology, however, one area in which society seems to have retained the status quo is in its class divisions – there are still upper, upper-middle, middle, and lower-middle classes. The Zintaks seem to be somewhere in the middle, possessing a handful of nifty gadgets while at the same time being relegated to more traditional conveniences, such as a land-based vehicle instead of a hovercraft, and a manually-operated vacuum cleaner instead of the robotic housemaids which no doubt exist in this time as well.

Brian's birthday arrives, and that afternoon, so do his young companions along with one or both of their parents. For a while, the party progresses much like any other involving children of that age: there is running, laughing and playing at the outset, followed by pizza delivery, then birthday cake, candles, a birthday wish, and ice cream. I find myself enjoying the party, though of course I cannot participate, but at the same time I feel anxiety burning in the pit of my stomach, for by now I have witnessed enough of these scenes that I understand there is likely to be a dramatic and unpleasant conclusion. And indeed, shortly after the cake and ice cream have been served and consumed, that final dreaded event transpires.

The birthday gifts are brought out, and one by one Brian opens them. There is a remote-controlled spaceship, a futuristic soldier costume, three or four video game cartridges, a basic tablet-type device for a child, and a few other items. Brian seems genuinely delighted with each gift, and after they are all opened he politely thanks every one of his friends, as well as the parents who are in attendance. Sherry beams with pride upon this show of gratitude, and even the normally stern-faced Carl, while not going so far as to crack a smile, does at least nod his approval.

Moments later, one of Brian's male friends engages him in a discussion about one of the video games that Brian was given. The boy explains that he had received the same game for his own birthday a couple of months before, and how he had figured out how to do such-and-such, and had already advanced to level this-or-that.

While this discussion is ongoing, another boy, with Brian unaware, opens the box that contains the soldier costume and begins to put it on. At this point, the parents are involved in their own discussions, and the other children have gone back to their earlier activities. No one notices the boy putting on the soldier costume, until he dons the helmet and picks up the laser rifle, which then elicits some "Aw, cool!" comments from a few of the children who finally take note.

When Brian hears this, he turns to see what his friends are so enamored with. He sees the boy wearing the soldier costume – HIS soldier costume – and the politeness and gratitude in his expression are replaced with fury and hatred.

"THAT'S MINE!" he screams, and snatches the rifle away from the other boy. "Take that off, NOW!" Brian stands nose-to-nose with the suddenly terrified boy, his face reddening and his fists clenched. The sounds of laughing and talking cease immediately, and everyone in the room stares at Brian in stunned silence, including Carl and Sherry, until Brian repeats his command. "I said, take that off, now!"

"Brian!" Sherry finally exclaims. "You know what we've told you about sharing with your friends! Now tell Sawyer you're sorry!"

But he never gets the chance. Carl has now emerged from his state of shock as well, and his wrath has been awakened. He strides quickly across the room and grabs Brian by the front of the shirt. "WHAT IS WRONG WITH YOU?!?" he bellows, as he shakes his son violently. "YOU KNOW BETTER THAN THAT!" He shoves, indeed nearly hurls Brian backward, toward the entrance to the hallway. "NOW GET IN YOUR ROOM! THIS PARTY IS OVER!"

Now it is Brian's turn to be terrified, as his short-lived episode of rage is dwarfed by that of his father. "No, Dad, I'm sorry!" he cries in vain. "Sawyer, I'm sorry! I didn't mean it!"

"I SAID GET IN YOUR ROOM!" Carl shouts, even louder than before. Then he turns to face their guests, making a Herculean effort to calm himself momentarily. "I'm sorry everyone," he says with a faint, fabricated smile. "I'm afraid Brian's misbehavior has ruined the party. These darn kids, you know, they're so unruly." Something resembling a staccato cough is ejected from Carl's mouth. It takes me a second to realize that he has attempted to laugh. "Thank you all for coming," he finishes, then turns to glare at Brian once again. The boy is standing in the hallway, tears pouring down his bright red cheeks, looking beseechingly at his mother in hopes that she might intervene and find a way to salvage the party.

Though she, too, is clearly afraid of her enraged husband, the anguish she is no doubt feeling at seeing her son's heart broken over his party coming to such an abrupt end gives her just enough courage to speak out. "Carl," she says gently but imploringly, "I think if we just send him to his room for a few minutes, it will teach him a lesson about --"

Carl detaches his hateful gaze from his son, whirls around and fixes it upon his wife. She is silenced instantaneously. By this time, some of the parents have already begun to gather their flocks and make for the front door; those who are still sitting, upon seeing Carl's fury now directed at someone other than his son, immediately follow suit. Within one minute the house has been vacated, save for its regular occupants.

As soon as the front door closes, Brian turns and runs down the hallway and into his room, with Carl right on his heels. I elect not to follow them, for I have no desire to witness this scene yet again. Instead I watch Sherry standing in the kitchen, tears leaking from her closed eyes, wringing her hands and praying silently as she always does during these "lessons." Her face contorts in sheer agony as the first of Brian's screams pierces the air.

4

A fter one of the many incidents I witness in which Brian receives a beating from his father, followed by comfort and compassion from his mother, I remember a paragraph from Hugo's Les Miserables (*it suddenly strikes me as odd that I am having* real-life *memories inside of a dream, but again, this is no ordinary dream), describing the gradual transformation of the soul of Jean Valijean from one characterized by natural goodness, to one of wickedness and utter disregard for the well-being of others while he was in prison. It read: "Thus during nineteen years of torture and slavery, this soul mounted and at the same time fell. Light entered it on one side, and darkness on the other." It is abundantly clear to me that the light entering one side of Brian Zintak is from his loving, kind-hearted mother, while the darkness entering him from the other side is from his hateful, self-centered father. And while I am not normally a pessimistic person, I cannot seem to stymie an increasingly-strong conviction that unlike Valijean's soul, which ultimately expunged the darkness and became a brilliant beacon of light, Brian's soul is destined for just the opposite.*

That is why I am at times angry at Sherry – though it may seem irrational -- for not doing more to protect Brian. She is a slight woman, while her husband, comparatively speaking, is a virtual hulk, but it seems to me that she could arm herself with something, stand between Carl and her son during the former's rampages, and defend the boy with extreme prejudice, if necessary. Or she could simply take Brian and leave one night after Carl has reached his alcohol limit and passes out on the sofa. But I know that she will never take up arms against her husband, for it is apparent that she does not have the capacity to harm another person. And to leave him would be just as unconscionable, for it would mean discarding the vows she had once taken and still holds sacred. This "stay the course" attitude of hers, while noble, seems increasingly futile and destructive to everyone involved. And so I wait, once again, for the approaching tsunami that will dwarf these relatively weak tidal waves I have seen thus far.

⅄　　⅄　　⅄

It is during Brian's conversations with his mother (he seldom speaks to his father unless first being spoken to, and even then his responses contain only as many words as are absolutely necessary) that I begin to realize how intelligent this boy is. He uses words like "articulate", "immaterial", and even "serendipity" (I am not even sure I could define that word), and he mostly reads adult newspapers and magazines in lieu of the children's books that line the shelves in his bedroom. He also seems to have a grasp of how one's actions today can have repercussions on what comes next week, or next year, or a decade from now, which in my experience is unusual for a 7-year old. Of course, he is prone to emotional outbursts like the one he had during his birthday party, when he momentarily forgets about the consequences that inevitably follow when he loses control. But aside from that, he always seems to be planning, calculating or assessing something or other. He even smiles and nods when his mother, like most mothers do, teases him about one day wanting to kiss and date pretty girls. Most boys his age would have been indignant and repulsed at the very thought of their lips touching anyone else's but their mother's. While perhaps not yet embracing that idea, he at least seems to understand that such desires are an inevitable part of growing up.

As I see the boy developing mentally at an astonishing rate, it occurs to me that the combination of these natural gifts with the harmful effects that his abusive father is no doubt having on his *psychological and emotional development make for a very ominous outlook on his life. This formula – great intelligence combined with a tumultuous childhood – has produced many diabolical fiends throughout recorded history. I had studied Hitler's life in school, and I remember some of the details of his childhood. Hitler's relationship with his father was marred by frequent, intense conflict due to Adolf's refusal to conform to the strict discipline of the state-owned school that he originally attended. Hitler's younger brother died of measles when Adolf was 10 years old, and he soon changed from a popular, engaged, and studious boy to one who was bitter, detached, and constantly fought with teachers. There was no question that Hitler had the mental capacity to be successful, and indeed, in his autobiography* Mein Kampf, *he revealed that he had intentionally done poorly in school in the hopes that his father would let him pursue his dream of becoming an artist, rather than trying to force him into a career in the customs bureau, thus following in the elder Hitler's footsteps. Finally, though there were other detrimental incidents along the way, the death of Hitler's father when he was 13, and his mother when he was 18, seemed to seal his fate as becoming one of the most evil and destructive men who ever lived.*

I had also read many articles about the life of Ted Bundy, the renowned 1970's serial killer who was executed about a year and a half ago. Bundy's circumstances made him a prime candidate for monsterhood from pretty much the day he was born. Unlike Hitler, the identity of Bundy's father was never known for certain, but it was speculated by some that he was the product of incest between his mother and her abusive father. Until he was three years old, Bundy and his mother lived with her parents, but not as mother and son. In order to avoid the stigma associated with birth outside wedlock, Bundy and all of the other family members were told that the grandparents were actually his parents, and that his mother was actually his older sister. Bundy was never told the truth by either his mother or his grandparents, but eventually discovered it on his own, though exactly how that happened was uncertain. In any event, he harbored resentment toward his mother thereafter, for first lying to him and then never revealing the truth to him. Bundy had told interviewers that he respected and identified with his grandfather, who aside from having potentially raped his own daughter, was reportedly volatile, tyrannical and bigoted, with a hatred of blacks, Jews, Catholics and Italians. It was no surprise that by the time he was a teenager, Bundy was picking through trash barrels throughout his neighborhood in search of pictures of naked women, or prowling the streets late at night hoping to see women undressing behind undraped windows. After high school, Bundy's intelligence was evident during stints at the University of Puget Sound, University of Washington, Temple University, and again at Washington, from which he eventually graduated with honors. He was accepted into the law program at Puget Sound and attended classes for about one year before dropping out . . . just about the time that young women began to disappear in the Pacific Northwest.

Brian has one thing going for him that Hitler and Bundy did not, which is a powerful positive influence in the person of his mother. Nevertheless, though I still do not know for certain how this dream will end, I am increasingly convinced of the direction things are heading.

5

*T*he dream continues with several consecutive scenes that occur in the Zintak living room, and involve only Sherry and some unknown man, apparently a friend of hers, whose name, I learn, is Jerry. I listen closely to their discussions, but they always seem inconsequential; they talk about the Bible, about the weather, about gardening, cooking, politics, and sports. Sometimes Jerry talks about his wife, and when he does, it is always in a very negative light, saying that she is cruel, manipulative, unappreciative, and materialistic. And occasionally, he asks Sherry questions like "how are you doing . . . how are you really doing?" I realize that Jerry is aware, on some level at least, of the abuse that Sherry and Brian are being subjected to at the hands of Carl Zintak. This man seems to have genuine concern about the two of them, and I wish that Sherry would open up and tell him everything, so that someone, anyone, would know the truth and do something to help them. Invariably, however, she flushes with shame at those questions, gives brief, evasive answers, and changes the subject. The visits always end at about 2:30 in the afternoon, as Jerry gets up to leave for work. He always becomes very nervous and hesitates at the door, as though there is something he wants to do or say before he goes. But he never does; he always leaves with a simple "goodbye Sherry." I notice as I watch him through the front window after he leaves that he is always on foot, which suggests that he lives nearby.

After several of these scenes, I cannot help but wonder how they fit into the overall picture, since Brian seems to be the focal point of this vision, with Carl and Sherry playing only secondary *roles. Then one day I see Sherry enter through the front door of the house, no doubt just returning from her daily walk as I observe that she is wearing her running shoes. She has a puzzled expression on her face as she looks down at an envelope she is holding in her hand. She opens the envelope, removes the letter that it contains, sits down at the kitchen table and begins to read. Assuming there is some significance to this letter, I move around behind her so that I can read it over her shoulder. The letter reads:*

Dear Sherry, first of all, let me apologize for telling you this in a letter. I have tried many times to tell you during our visits, but just couldn't find the courage. I finally decided to tell you in a letter, since I could no longer keep it to myself, but also could not tell you in person.

I can't even begin to describe how much I have enjoyed getting to know you these past few months. You have become a source of light to me, when my life is otherwise dark and dreary (*I guess I am not the only one who has read* Les Miserables *or has come to recognize Sherry as a ray of light*). I have told you about my marriage and how unhappy it makes me, but after I spend a few hours with you, it lifts my spirits to the point where I can face the darkness for another day. And just about the time I feel hope and joy slipping away again, I am able to spend another day with you, and once again I feel rejuvenated.

But I know this cycle can't continue, nor do I want it to. It's time to put an end to it, to banish the darkness once and for all, and to make hope and joy my daily bread instead of the occasional feast. It's time to tell you, finally . . . that I love you, Sherry Zintak. I love you more each time I see you, in fact more each time I think of you. And I think you love me, too, even if you have not admitted it to yourself. I am always amazed at the loyalty you show to your husband, despite the way that he treats you (yes, I know about that, even though you've never opened up to me. I can see the sadness in your eyes, the loneliness, the longing for something more). Your loyalty is one of the things I love most about you, as it shows the depth of your love, your grace, your devotion. But it has also cost you an opportunity to have a happy life, not to mention that it has -- and please forgive me for saying this – put Brian in jeopardy. As much as you love God, and trust in His Word, I don't believe he would want you to stay with Carl if it meant that it might result in harm to your son. I know the Bible says that a person should only divorce their spouse in the case of marital unfaithfulness; but didn't Carl vow to love and cherish you, all the days of your life? Isn't he being unfaithful by failing to do those things?

I want to take you and Brian away from Carl – this very day!! Please, won't you let me? I don't mean run away, I know that would be foolish, as you would be accused of kidnapping. I only mean that I want to take you to a safe place nearby, and we can both begin the process of ending our miserable marriages, while we also heal together. We will get a restraining order placed on Carl, so that you and Brian don't have to worry about him hurting you. And when it's all over, the three of us can go anywhere we want to go, and live the life of hope and happiness that we deserve. I know how scary this all sounds, but I hope you will trust me . . . . I hope you will trust in God, for I feel in my heart that this is what He wants us to do.

I will see you very soon, and we can discuss this face to face. I will be counting the seconds until then, when I can once again see your lovely face and bask in your warm glow!   All my love, Jerry

Sherry seems surprised by the letter, though I am not. Jerry's feelings for her had become apparent to me during their past few living room discussions, and his nervousness each time he got up to leave was a dead giveaway. But Sherry's unmatched humility made her blind to the fact that there was at least one other man, and very likely lots of other men, besides her husband who were attracted to her. Of course, most of them would not pursue a married woman no matter how strongly they felt about her, but Jerry had now decided it was worth attempting to overcome that obstacle. And I, for one, was rooting him on.

But I also feel much sympathy for Sherry. After reading the letter, she lays it on the table and stares straight ahead for several minutes, a tormented expression on her face. Whether it is because she is tempted by Jerry's offer despite her moral convictions, or because she is contemplating the best way to let him down gently, I do not yet know. But I will soon find out, as there comes a knock at the door. She hesitates for a moment, then walks to the door and glances through the sidelight to see who is there. Her head drops and she pauses yet again, and I begin to think that she may elect not to admit her visitor. But then she opens the door, and lo and behold, it is Jerry. He is visibly shaking, and has such a pathetically terrified look on his face that I am certain he is going to vomit right on her doorstep.

"Come in, Jerry," Sherry says with a tone of resignation. It is clear that she knows she must deal with this situation . . . . one way or another. "Sit down, please."

Jerry nearly runs to the sofa, his rubbery legs threatening to fail him before he even gets there. "So you . . . you got my letter?" he asks timidly.

"Yes, I just read it."

"I'm sorry I couldn't manage to tell you any other way, and for coming over here so soon afterwards and not giving you a bit more time to think about it. I just had to see you. I . . . had to know. I've taken the day off work, so that we could . . . I mean, in case you . . . say 'yes'."

Sherry wrings her hands and stares down at the floor, anguish still clouding her face. Finally, she begins. "Jerry, you are a wonderful person, and you have become a very good friend. Maybe my best friend, if I may be so bold. But you and I are both married, and we need to love our spouses unconditionally. They both have many faults, but don't you see, that's exactly why they need us in their lives! God can change their hearts, and I believe He will, but for Him to do that, we must remain faithful to them."

"But at what cost?" Jerry protests. "Your safety? Brian's safety? Maybe even your lives?"

Sherry pauses, looking down at her hands folded in her lap. "I believe . . . that God will protect us."

"Are you willing to put that to the test? And are you telling

me you have no feelings for me? That you're staying with your husband, and that's what you really want?"

"I didn't say I had no feelings for you, Jerry. What I'm saying is, I made a commitment to my husband, and I intend to keep it. I can't give you what you want. I'm sorry."

Jerry vigorously shakes his head. "I can't accept that. It's not right! God does not expect us to willingly subject ourselves to abuse and mistreatment!"

"Yes, that's exactly what He expects, if need be. After all, His only Son subjected Himself to far worse than anything you and I have gone through. And He warned us that our lives would be full of challenges and heartaches. But He also promised us that He would be with us every step of the way, and carry us through the darkest of times. No matter how long it might take."

There can be no mistaking Sherry's conviction, but Jerry will not take "no" for an answer. He continues to argue and plead with her, becoming increasingly agitated, and I begin to wonder if I have been wrong about this man. He is not simply in love with Sherry, he is obsessed with her. It is clear that he had convinced himself that this story would end happily, just as he had written it in his mind, but now that it had taken an unexpected twist, he was not able to cope with it. I am getting more and more concerned about this situation, to the point where I fear that Jerry may become violent, when suddenly the sound of the overhead garage door opening brings the argument to a halt.

"Oh my God, it's Carl!" Sherry gasps.

Jerry is equally alarmed. "But it's only 2:00! Why would he be home so early?"

"I don't know! Sometimes he comes home early. It just depends on how his day is going. You have to leave, now! He can't see you here, he won't believe we're just friends! Don't go out the front door, he might see you through the front windows of the garage. You have to go out the patio door and walk around the

other end of the house. Please, go now!"

Jerry jumps up, hurries toward the patio door, and slides it open.

"Jerry?"

He stops and turns to look at her.

"I've given you my answer. You must accept it. And please . . . don't come back here ever again."

He stands frozen, staring at her in shock as the finality and firmness of her tone begins to register with him. Then we all hear the sound of a car door slamming in the garage, and it brings him out of his trance. He steps through the opening, slides the door shut behind him, and is gone.

Sherry watches him leave, then gasps as her eyes are drawn to the letter on the table. She dashes forward, grabs the letter, and has only enough time to bend over and slide it under the edge of the area rug beneath the table before the door to the garage opens, and Carl walks in.

"Hi honey!" Sherry calls out as cheerfully as she can. Her cheeks are flushed, and she is slightly out of breath. I pray that her nervousness only seems apparent to me, since I know what just went on, and not to Carl, who does not.

Carl approaches the table and stares at her coldly. My guts do a flip-flop inside me when I see that expression, for surely it means that he knows.

Sherry, of course, can do nothing but continue her bluff. "What's wrong? Did you have a rough day at work? Ah, silly me, of course you did, that's why you're home early! Why don't you relax and I'll get you a snack and a beer?" She does not wait for his response, but instead turns and walks toward the refrigerator.

Carl stares at her for a few more seconds, while I hold my breath. Then he turns, walks into the living room and sits down on the sofa. He still looks angry, but given his volatile temperament, if he was aware of, or even suspicious of, Jerry's presence here, he

51

would have certainly unleashed his fury on Sherry in a way that I had not seen before. So the fact that he did not do that means that just maybe his current emotional state really was due to a bad day at work. Just maybe.

*T*he next sequence occurs a short time after Carl had nearly walked in on the discussion between Jerry and Sherry -- I am guessing maybe 3 or 4 days later. It is on a Saturday or Sunday, I know, because the entire Zintak family is relaxing in the living room. Carl is checking emails or surfing the internet on his tablet, Sherry is reading the Bible, and Brian is building something out of what looks like an erector set, only more sophisticated. All of a sudden, Carl looks up from his tablet and makes a surprise announcement.

"We're going on a vacation!" he says cheerfully.

Sherry and Brian look up at him, then at each other, with a combination of shock and confusion. It is apparent that they have not taken many, if any, family vacations before.

"Well? Aren't you going to say anything, like 'where are we going'?"

"Well that's great, honey!" Sherry finally says. "Where are we going?"

"Glacier National Park!"

"Glacier?" Sherry asks. "Why Glacier? Aren't all of the glaciers gone?"

At first I think that Sherry is confused, because while the glaciers are disappearing, they are not entirely gone. But then I remember again that the year is 2086, and certainly by then, all of the glaciers will be gone.

Carl rolls his eyes and shoots his wife a condescending look. "Of course the glaciers are gone, but the mountains aren't! The lakes aren't! The wildlife isn't! There's still plenty to see there. And *plenty to do, also. We can go hiking, fishing, camping, or just drive around and take pictures."*

"Well . . . okay, then!" Sherry says, though she still looks perplexed, no doubt wondering if her husband had been captured by aliens and replaced with a lookalike. Then she turns her attention to Brian, who had been sitting quietly on the floor. "What do you think, Brian? Does that sound like fun?"

"Yeah!" he says, breaking into a huge grin. "I've seen pictures of Glacier National Park, and it looks awesome! When are we going?"

"A week from today," Carl responds. "I've got all the arrangements made, and I have the okay from my boss to take a week off work. We'll fly up there, rent a big SUV for the week, and buy or rent all of the gear we'll need when we get there. It's going to be great!"

The discussion goes on for quite some time, Brian excitedly asking his father a million questions, Sherry beaming with joy at the idea of her family taking what is very likely their first vacation together. I even see her eyes glisten with moisture, and I suspect that she is silently thanking God for working to warm and soften her husband's cold, hard heart. But when I look at Carl, though he is laughing and smiling and at first glance enjoying the moment, I get the unnerving impression that it is just a façade . . . and that there is some ulterior motive hidden beneath. The fact that the Zintaks already live next to a mountain range, and that Carl has selected a vacation destination that will be similar to their everyday surroundings, does nothing to alleviate my anxiety.

I hope I am wrong about this, that it is simply Carl trying to get comfortable with a different attitude, a different outlook, than what he is accustomed to. I expect I will find out, one way or the other, very soon.

⋏   ⋏   ⋏

"Come on, I think we're almost there!" Brian yells.

Those are the first words I hear as the next scene begins. I am a few steps behind Carl and Sherry on a trail winding through a dense forest – no doubt, somewhere in Glacier National Park. They are walking hand-in-hand, each wearing a day pack, with Brian skipping merrily along about thirty yards ahead of them. It is a beautiful day, with sunlight filtering through the trees, and the air a bit crisp but plenty warm enough for hiking. I can see the edge of the forest about 200 yards ahead, with a canvas of pale blue behind the trees. That must be their destination, the end of the trail.

"Brian, slow down and wait for us!" calls Sherry, though it does little good, as Brian maintains his pace and if anything, pulls even further ahead.

The three of us emerge from the forest onto a smooth plateau that overlooks a deep, wide canyon. Jagged peaks thrust upward on the opposite side, as far as one can see in either direction, with a few tendrils of snow snaking through the upper reaches of the range. Directly across from us, about halfway down from the top, there is a large pocket nestled into the side of the slope, and at the bottom of that pocket is a small, turquoise mountain lake dotted with chunks of ice that are glittering in the sunlight. Quite simply, the view is absolutely spectacular, despite the absence of glaciers.

The distance from the edge of the forest to the edge of the plateau appears to be about eighty yards. Brian is standing perhaps twenty-five yards from the drop-off, scanning the surroundings with utter incredulity.

"WOW!" Sherry says what we obviously all are thinking. "This is amazing!"

"You see!" Carl responds. "I told you it would be worth the walk. The best places are almost always off the beaten path."

His words – "off the beaten path" – make me realize there is no one else around. I suppose it is not unusual to find solitude in one of the country's more remote national parks like Glacier, unlike the most popular ones like Yellowstone, the Grand Canyon, or the

the most popular ones like Yellowstone, the Grand Canyon, or the Great Smoky Mountains, but nevertheless I find the absence of any other visitors to be . . . . unsettling. As before, when Carl first brought up the idea of this vacation, I get the feeling there is something disingenuous about his intentions.

"Come on, let's get a better look," Carl casually suggests.

They walk forward, towards the edge of the cliff, with Carl continuing to lead Sherry by the hand. When they approach Brian, he begins to fall in behind them, but Carl prevents him from following.

"No, why don't you stay here, buddy. We're just going to walk up ahead a few more steps to get a look into the canyon. Do me a favor and keep an eye out for any bears or mountain lions that might be prowling around."

Brian is startled at the sound of the words "bears" and "mountain lions", and looks up at his father to gauge how serious he might be. But Carl gives him a smile and a reassuring wink, causing Brian to laugh off his momentary nervousness.

"Carl, did you have to say that?" Sherry admonishes. "Now he'll be scared!"

"Ah, you worry too much. I was just having a little fun with him."

When Carl tells Brian to stay behind, I am surprised for a moment, as I can see little harm in the boy accompanying them a bit further, until I realize that this whole thing is playing out like a script. And my uneasiness suddenly escalates to something between alarm and panic. I want to rush forward, screaming, kicking and clawing as I burst through the barriers of the dream and into reality, to save the day. But again, I understand that I cannot do that, and that I must remain as calm as possible so that I do not miss any details that may prove to be important later on. And so I follow Carl and Sherry as they approach the precipice. When they are about fifteen feet from the edge, Sherry abruptly stops.

"I don't think I want to go any closer," she says. "You know I don't like heights."

Carl turns to her and smiles. I can see him squeezing her hand very tightly. "It's okay, babe," he says. "I've got you. And you see? It's safe all the way to the edge. No loose rocks or anything that might cause you to lose your footing. If it were dangerous, they would have put up guard rails."

That last statement, I know, is complete nonsense. To put up guard rails along every foot of dangerous drop-off, in every national park in the country, would cost tens, maybe hundreds of millions of dollars, and probably take decades to complete. And yet, it is enough to convince Sherry to set aside her fears and proceed forward alongside her husband. They cover the last fifteen feet and stop mere inches from the edge, where they can see straight down into the canyon below.

It then occurs to me that my back is toward Brian, and I suspect that for these next few moments, I need to be at a vantage point where I can see all three members of the family at one time. So remembering that I have at least some element of control over my environment, I move past Carl and Sherry and step out into the void, walk a few steps on nothing but air, and turn back to face them. Now I can clearly see all three of them.

"It certainly is beautiful," Sherry says, looking at the mountains surrounding them, and then down into the canyon.

For the first time, I glance down as well, and estimate that it is at least two thousand feet to the bottom. When I look up again, I notice that Brian is still standing in the same place, but now with his back toward us, staring at something in the trees or further up on the mountain.

"Yes, it is," Carl replies. "And so are you."

He releases her hand, causing her to gasp at being so close to the edge, and now without her tether. But Carl quickly places his arm around her shoulder.

"Shhh, don't worry, I've still got you."

She smiles and relaxes once again, then looks up into his eyes. "Oh, Carl," she says. "This is so amazing. I have been praying so hard for you. I knew the man I married was still in there somewhere, but if he could just find a way to set aside all of the worries and vices, he would once again be the kind of husband and father that he was meant to be."

He smiles back at her, though it has that same mask-like quality that it had a week ago in the Zintak living room. Then he glances behind them at Brian, casually, as though he is merely checking up on him. Brian's back is still turned toward us.

"It's funny you should use the word 'vice'," Carl says, now whispering. "Kind of hypocritical, don't you think?"

Sherry looks at him with surprise and confusion. "What do you mean?"

"Did you think I didn't know about the Jerry and Sherry show?" he hisses, and with that, any pretense of pleasantry is gone. His face is now contorted with anger. "Did you think I was that stupid?"

The surprise on Sherry's face is now replaced by shock, the confusion by terror. She shakes her head and is about to say something in response, but never gets the chance. Carl removes his hand from her shoulder and slides it to the middle of her back, then shoves her off the edge. She pitches forward into nothingness, arms and legs flailing, and is about halfway to the bottom before she even lets out a scream.

There is no time for Carl to celebrate his newfound freedom. He understands that the show must go on. He falls to his knees and leans out over the edge, reaching as though he could pluck Sherry from the air and save her life. "OH MY GOD, SHE FELL!!" he screams. "OH DEAR GOD, SHERRY!! NO, NO SHERRY!!" He does not look back toward Brian, not yet, even though he knows the boy would have spun around the moment he heard his father yelling.

He must be patient, just for a few seconds, until he hears Brian screaming, too. Until then, Carl has to make it look as though he were momentarily oblivious to his son, like any man would be after just witnessing his wife's tragic death. But what he does not know is that, seconds after he had glanced over his shoulder at Brian, the boy had lost interest in whatever it was that he had been looking at, and had turned back toward his parents . . . just in time to see his father murder his mother.

I focus now on Brian. Seconds tick by, yet he does not make a sound. I can see the horror on his face, as I would have expected, but to my surprise, it is quickly replaced by an expression of sheer hatred. And not just momentary hatred, either; hatred that has no doubt metastasized for years, and now, with this final impetus, it geysers forth with power that belies the physical stature of the one who harbors it. He takes a step forward, then another, very quietly, while his father continues his falsified weeping and wailing sounds. Then Brian is running at full speed, and covers the twenty-five yards in just a few seconds.

Carl cocks his head slightly as he hears the pounding of footfalls when Brian is still a few steps away, but there is no time for him to react. Brian drops his shoulder and slams into Carl's back, and though Carl weighs perhaps four times more than his son, Brian's momentum and rage generate enough force to send Carl plunging into the abyss, just like his wife.

Brian stands on the canyon rim for a long time, staring down at the two tiny specks far below, still seething with rage. Eventually, however, his anger dissipates, and is replaced by feelings more along the lines of what one would expect – grief, terror, exhaustion, and loneliness. He turns and stumbles a few steps towards the trail leading through the woods, but then collapses and bursts into a sobbing wail. I levitate back onto solid ground, walk over and sit down next to him, though of course I can be of no comfort to him. After a while, three hikers, two men and a woman, emerge from the woods, *and when they hear Brian's cries and see that he is alone, they come running toward him.*

"What's wrong, little guy?" they ask. "Are you okay? Are you lost? Who are you with?"

Brian does not answer immediately, as he is still crying uncontrollably. After several minutes of soothing reassurances from the hikers, he finally calms down just enough to say, "They fell. Over there. My mom tripped and stumbled toward the edge, and when my dad tried to grab her, they both went over."

I realize instantly that Brian must have been far more composed, at least on the inside, than what he had appeared to be on the outside, for he had recognized the need to come up with a story to conceal the fact that he had been responsible for his father's death, even if it had been justified. And this shows that he is not only composed, but cunning and resilient as well.

The hikers look at each other with alarm, then one of the men says, "Kelly, you stay with him. We'll go see."

The two male hikers hurry over to the edge where Brian had pointed, and both look down into the canyon with their binoculars.

"Oh my God," one of them says. "He's right. That must be them."

The two men run back to Kelly and Brian. As there is no cell phone signal out here, one of them offers to go for help, while the other stays with the woman and the boy. The man is gone for perhaps two hours, during which time the two adults try to keep Brian's mind occupied by asking him about things like school, his friends, his favorite TV shows and movies, and anything else they can think of.

Finally, as dusk begins to fall, we hear the sound of a helicopter approaching. Kelly and the man lead Brian to the edge of the trees to allow the helicopter to land on the plateau. Two paramedics disembark, briefly examine Brian, and then help all three of them climb aboard. As they are taking off, I see a second helicopter come in above the mountains on the opposite side of the canyon, then drop down and disappear from sight below the rim. The people in that chopper have apparently drawn the grim duty of scraping the remains of Carl and Sherry Zintak from the canyon floor.

7

I *am left standing alone in the deepening twilight, pondering the events of the day. It has been emotionally draining, to say the least, and though I know I am still asleep, I almost feel as though I am physically exhausted. I have seen more than I want to see already, and I know there is more to come.* Much more. But *somehow I need a break from this, without rousing myself completely from the dream. I decide to try something . . . . an experiment of sorts. This is, after all, a lucid dream, and I know that I have some degree of control over it. So I close my eyes, and imagine myself being transported from that mountaintop, to the one where this dream first began. When I open my eyes again, I find to my satisfaction, if not delight, that I am indeed not only back at the starting point, but that Randall is sitting alongside me.*

"I'm not really surprised to see you," he says, "even though I warned you that you have only so much time before they come looking for you. I've been watching these events unfold, and it sickens me, just like it does you."

I glance over at him and see the anguish on his face, and I know he means what he says. In fact, I realize that it may be even more traumatic for Randall to watch than it is for me, since I have had roughly twice as many years as he has to become desensitized to this sort of thing. That is, if he is a real person outside of this dream. Not that I have ever witnessed anything like this firsthand, but I have certainly seen more of these stories on TV than he has, and it has no doubt helped me to steel myself against the atrocities I am now observing.

"I guess it doesn't do any good," I respond, "to ask why such horrible things happened, or will happen, to be more precise, to a little boy and his kind, loving mother. It's a cursed world, and in it, 'you will have trouble', as Jesus Himself said. But I'm still trying to understand what this has to do with me. And you, for that matter."

"As I told you, I have been chosen for my task, and you for yours. We might one day understand the reason God chose us, but then again, we may not. 'It is what it is.' Isn't that what you grownups like to say?"

I look at him again and smile. "I myself try to stay away from trite expressions, for the most part. But you're right about one thing. God usually does not explain Himself. You'd think He'd be a much more popular guy, so to speak, if He did. Especially when tragedy strikes. If we could somehow understand why God chooses not to intervene, it would be a whole lot easier to trust and follow Him, don't you think?"

"I think that's the whole point," Randall responds. "It would be too easy. Imagine the skies opening up, and a booming voice from above saying, 'This is God, and here's why I allow thousands of innocent people to die tragically every day.' Assuming He could provide an answer that people would find acceptable, and that wouldn't just make them even angrier, they would have no choice but to put their trust in Him. Or at the very least, to acknowledge His existence."

"I suppose you're right," I say. "It wouldn't take a whole lot of faith to believe in Him if you had that kind of evidence."

We sit quietly for a few minutes, here in the eye of the storm, no doubt, as I think we both know that the worst is yet to come.

"By the way, I'm Malcolm," I finally say.

Randall turns to shake my hand. "Yes, I know. It's a pleasure to meet you," he says, "even in these bizarre circumstances."

"It's a pleasure to meet you as well. So how did a boy your age acquire such wisdom?"

He shrugs and says, "Who's to say I'm really this wise? It's a dream, after all. And since God Himself is the one directing it, He very well could have given me gifts that I don't have in real life, just so I could play my part in this thing."

"Possibly. But if we really are talking about events that could change the world, then I suspect that He chose you because of what you already had. You were the right person for the job."

"And you as well. Your role requires compassion and courage, in addition to your telepathic abilities."

"Not really," I counter. "I'm just a bystander, after all."

"You're a bystander now," he says. "But I told you that you will have to act upon what you see. In real life, not in the dream. That's where many of your traits and abilities will come into play."

"I suspected as much," I say, nodding. "I guess if that's true, then I'd better get back and see what more there is to see." Then I smile and add, "And don't worry, you won't need to push me over the cliff this time."

He briefly returns my smile before his expression turns melancholy. "That's something we've both seen enough of, haven't we?"

*B*rian remains in the care of social services for the next several days, after which he goes to live with his Aunt Cindy and Uncle Ron Spears, Sherry's sister and brother-in-law, at their secluded fifty-acre estate that I gather lies a few miles outside the town. During that time, the police come to visit him on several occasions, asking him the same questions over and over, yet wording them differently to see if it will confuse the boy into providing conflicting responses, which might indicate that he had some involvement in his parents' deaths or at least knew more than he was saying. I do not think they suspect him of foul play; they are simply using standard interrogation techniques to rule out that possibility. Finally they are satisfied that the deaths of Carl and Sherry Zintak are accidental, and the case is closed.

For the first several weeks after his parents' deaths, Brian does not do any reading whatsoever, as he used to, but instead spends many hours each day just staring at the walls of his new bedroom, at a picture of Sherry that he has removed from one of Cindy's photo albums, or out the rear windows of the house into the Spears' massive backyard. Indeed, the entire house is massive, for I learn that Ron has made a fortune building a medical equipment company that has customers all over the world. He reminds me of my own father; energetic, passionate, determined, demanding – the consummate self-made mogul.

Because of his professional responsibilities, Ron is typically gone for several days at a time, but Cindy is always at home and *does her best to engage Brian in conversation and activity. Her efforts are often futile, however, and by mid-afternoon she has usually given up on them for the day. This is always a disappointment for me to witness, because Ron and Cindy have no children of their own, so at present Brian has no playmates besides Cindy. Still, I am at least glad that Brian seems to be safe for now, and that his aunt and uncle are kind, generous people who are looking out for his best interests.*

As one would expect, Brian's varying expressions and demeanors make it clear that he is struggling with a wide variety of emotions, from denial to resignation, from love (for Sherry) to hatred (toward Carl). But there are also signs that the deductive machinery within his amazing mind is running as smoothly as ever, and I have the growing sense that there will come a day when he experiences some kind of personal epiphany, one that will alter the course of not only his own life, but quite possibly the lives of those around him as well.

And indeed, one afternoon a few months later, after Brian has returned to school and his life seems to be migrating towards some degree of normalcy, he suddenly begins to work furiously at his computer, downloading books and articles, speed-reading, scribbling and typing notes. And all the while he is doing this, he keeps the picture of his mother close by and glances at it frequently. I stand behind him while he works, reading the titles of the materials he has acquired, and his rapidly rising pile of notes, in an attempt to figure out what he is doing. The books and articles are on a variety of topics in fields such as physics, chemistry, mathematics, and mechanical engineering . . . in short, areas that I never studied, and even if I had, I would have probably not recognized any of the theories presented in these materials, given that they are nearly 100 years beyond anything I would have ever seen. I suppose that I should not be so surprised by the complexity of the subject matter, for it has now become apparent that Brian is not merely very should not be so surprised by the complexity of the subject matter, for it has now become apparent that Brian is not merely very intelligent, he is a bona fide genius.

Among the books is one on astrophysics that catches my attention, and while it is also far too technical for me to fully understand, I am able to grasp a few of the basic concepts of one chapter that Brian seems to focus on – black holes. I learn, for example, that a black hole is formed when a giant star burns through the last of its hydrogen fuel, causing its core to collapse inward upon itself in an indescribably violent reaction that produces temperatures in excess of 100 billion degrees. The end result is a speck of matter that is almost infinitely tiny, but the density of which is almost incalculable. The gravitational pull of this object is so powerful that nothing in the universe can escape, once it strays too close and crosses the "event horizon," which is the point of no return. Beyond that line, even rays of light are drawn in, creating the appearance of a blank spot, or "black hole", in space.

I also learn about the bizarre relationship between black holes and time. The force of gravity actually slows time, as can be demonstrated by placing an extremely accurate clock on each floor of a skyscraper, and observing that as you descend from the top floor to the bottom – in other words, as you get just slightly closer to the center of the earth where gravity is strongest -- the clocks tick at progressively slower rates. This effect is multiplied to a staggering degree in a black hole, making them virtual time machines. If you were to approach the event horizon of a black hole, time would slow to the point where spending one minute there might equate to the passing of a thousand years on Earth. Such powerful gravitational pull would suppress anything and everything else, including time itself.

It is not long after this that Brian's interests expand to include a fascination with his uncle's medical equipment business. It would seem that contrary to the assertions of some of the doctors, pharmaceutical companies and manufacturers of durable medical equipment in my time, a century of additional research and technological innovation will not bring about the end of disease, deformation and death. Thus Ron's business is booming, and Brian seems to want to become a part of it when he grows up. And with Brian now being his adopted son, with apparently no other designated heir to the Spears empire, Ron seems delighted at the boy's sudden interest. Brian begins tagging along with his uncle to the office on Saturday mornings, or on weekdays when school is not in session. He is a big hit with Ron's staff; they find him to be polite and humorous, and are of course awestruck by his amazing intelligence.

All the while, Brian continues to accumulate and study more scientific and technical material in his bedroom. I want to believe that these are in essence the prerequisites that he might be taking if he were enrolled in college, that they will provide the fundamental knowledge that he will need if and when he takes over Ron's business one day, but most of the topics just seem to be too loosely connected to manufacturing, if connected at all. And then there is the fact that he has always taken precautions to make sure his aunt and uncle do not find any of the materials that he keeps in his bedroom and on his computer, which would not make sense if the two courses of study were related. No, it seems clear to me that he has some ulterior motive with respect to the technical information, but for the next several years of his life, his intentions elude me.

Y ears pass by, and Brian turns eighteen. Ron and Cindy spare no expense in throwing a huge backyard party for Brian and his friends, with a pig roast, chocolate fountains, multi-tiered cakes and other confectionary treats, alcoholic beverages of all kinds, an incredible fireworks display, and a private concert with a band that I gather is known throughout the country. With all of its sights, smells, and sounds, the party is a veritable avalanche to the senses, but all things considered, the evening is rather uneventful.

The next day, however, things get interesting very quickly. After the three of them have finally awakened sometime after noon, Ron and Cindy call Brian into the study for a surprise revelation. Ron informs Brian that his father had taken out a very sizeable life insurance policy on his mother, "coincidentally, just days before the accident," Ron says. Brian is completely unaware of the insurance policy, though of course, he and I both know that its timing was not a coincidence, given Carl's plan to murder Sherry and claim it was an accident. The point, however, is that as of midnight the previous day, Brian's eighteenth birthday, he is suddenly worth hundreds of millions of dollars (an amount that I suppose is equivalent to perhaps tens of millions in my own time. Not enough to put one on the Forbes list of the world's wealthiest people, but certainly enough to live comfortably for the rest of one's life).

Ron and Cindy also inform Brian that he is now the owner of the house that he and his parents had lived in, to do with as he pleases. Ever since Carl and Sherry's deaths, the Spears had had a *housekeeper vacuum and dust once a week, a lawn service company do the mowing, trimming and weeding during the summer, a snow plowing company clean the driveway and sidewalks during the winter, and a handyman service patch drywall holes and cracks, replace missing shingles and leaking gutters, and make other repairs as needed. Aside from that, the house had not been touched. The furniture, draperies, carpets, bedding and decorative items were all just as they had been the last time the house was occupied. Ron and Cindy felt it was not their place to redecorate or to dispose of anything, but rather to preserve it in order to give Brian full control over if and how he wanted to update the house, or whether to keep it at all. They did not expect him to actually choose to live in the house, but that he would sell it or perhaps rent it to someone else while he was away at college.*

But they were wrong. The very next day, Brian thanks Ron for giving him the opportunity to one day take over the family business, but then states that now that he is an adult and has ample resources of his own, he has decided to go in a different direction with his life. Ron and Cindy are devastated and try to convince Brian that there is no need to rush into a decision, that he can take plenty of time to think it through. But Brian is adamant that he has other plans and that they should begin to devise an alternative succession plan for their company. He thanks them again for all they have done for him, packs up his clothing and personal items, and moves back into the house he had grown up in. The fact that he can afford a much more luxurious home than this seems not to matter to him at all. It is clear that he is exactly where he wants to be.

There are numerous pictures of Brian and his parents adorning the house, and he quickly disposes of any that include his father. He then goes out and has several copies made of the picture of his mother that he has been keeping in close proximity to himself for all these years, and puts at least one copy of this picture in every room. *And when he is satisfied with the appearance of the house, he boots up his computer, gets out his notebooks and scientific journals, and goes back to work.*

⅄   ⅄   ⅄

Days and weeks go by. Nothing changes. Brian works feverishly at his computer day and night, constantly downloading new materials. He stops only to eat, use the bathroom, exercise, and sleep for a few hours each night. He occasionally goes out to purchase groceries, but mostly he has his meals delivered. As always, he glances at his mother's picture frequently while he works, and on those infrequent occasions when he does leave the house, he invariably takes a copy of it with him.

Finally, there is some unusual activity. It begins on the computer. Brian seems to be mostly finished with reading, studying, and absorbing, and his focus is now on creating. Graphically, that is. He has an incredibly sophisticated software program that allows him to easily (at least, he makes it look *easy) and rapidly design . . . something. It seems to be a sort of cylindrical chamber from what I can tell, connected to several control panels, which in turn are wired to, and seem to be drawing power from, something that vaguely resembles a drill press, though that is a very crude comparison. I have no idea what this device is, though as I watch him work on it hour after hour, day after day, I occasionally feel as though I am on the verge of some sort of revelation as to what his creation – indeed, what his new purpose for living – might be. But then it slips away from me and I am as baffled as ever before.*

A few weeks later, a truck pulls up in front of Brian's house and delivers several large boxes that are brought inside the garage, most of which appear to contain chemicals and lubricants. The next day, there is another delivery, this one of thin aluminum panels, angled steel bars, and all sorts of different fasteners (note, I use familiar metals like "steel" and "aluminum" to describe these items, though I suspect they are probably made of far more futuristic materials that have not even been invented in my own time). There are more deliveries the next day, and the day after that, some in containers, some wrapped in plastic. I do not know if there is more coming or not, but at that point, Brian apparently decides he has enough on hand to begin working on whatever it is he has in mind, for he begins to unpackage the items. There is wire and conduit of many sizes, electronic panels, crystal LED lights, copper and flexible tubing, various colors of fluid, small tanks with hoses connected to handheld tools that look something like the phaser guns from the original Star Trek series, and lots of other items that I could not begin to identify.

The Zintak garage is not huge but has plenty of space for Brian to lay out the materials on the floor. He begins to assemble them in accordance with his design, first bolting the angled steel, then donning protective clothing – mask, gloves, boots and apron – and fusing the seams to create a sturdy frame (I use the word "fusing" rather than "welding", because he employs the phaser-like tool to complete this task, and the process bears only a vague resemblance to the craft of the iron and steel workers from my time). This takes the better part of two days, and on the third day Brian turns his attention to the aluminum panels. While fusing the angled steel, the phaser-tool had been set to produce a very narrow, orange beam, but now Brian adjusts it to yield a wide, reddish-colored pattern, then sweeps the beam across the panels, heating them to make them pliable. He then uses another tool, much like a large rolling pin, to give the panel an arced shape. After checking the dimensions of the panel with several precision measuring instruments, he adjusts the phaser-tool yet again so that it emits a blue, cooling beam that returns the panel to its original hardness. And lastly, he mixes up a batch of a transparent liquid using a variety of chemicals and other fluids, and applies several coats of his concoction to the panels, making sure that every square inch is covered.

About halfway through this process, I realize that he is fabricating the outer shell of the cylindrical chamber, and that he intends to build this device entirely within the confines of his garage. In looking at the design on the computer screen, I had gotten the impression that it was a larger device that he would build in separate modules within the garage but then move to a more spacious facility. I was not sure of this, however, because in Brian's time, they use a measurement system that is neither English nor metric, so I could not decipher the dimensions of the cylindrical chamber and other components as they are shown on the screen. Now I know that this garage is big enough to house the entire contraption, which means that Brian intends to operate it here as well.

Over the next few days, as the device slowly but steadily materializes, looking more and more like the rendering on the computer screen, I can feel myself inching closer to the revelation that has thus far eluded me. It is like a picture inside my head, blurry but becoming ever more focused, and my excitement grows along with my confidence that Brian's intentions will soon become clear.

And then, finally, it happens. Brian is sitting at his computer, tweaking some ridiculously complicated formula that, to me, may as well be written in Chinese. The descriptions of the numerous variables appear along the top of the spreadsheet, with the actual formula appearing below the variable descriptions. I have studied this particular spreadsheet many times during the past several weeks as I stand over Brian's shoulder and watch him work. But there is one word at the bottom of the list of variable descriptions that now catches my attention, one that I had somehow overlooked before; that word is "years". I watch as Brian changes the quantity of one of the variables, and the formula recalculates to yield the number "11.72957". He changes another variable and the recalculated result is "11.48947". I realize that the result of the formula is in number of years, and when I do a quick mental calcu-

lation, I gasp as the revelation finally comes. It has been somewhere between 11 and 12 years since Sherry Zintak – who was unquestionably the center of young Brian's universe -- was ripped away from him without cause or warning. The pieces of the puzzle – this bizarre machine, Brian's fascination with topics like black holes, quantum physics and the theory of relativity, and his obsession with his mother's picture – have assembled themselves at last.

Brian is building a machine that will send him back in time and allow him to save his mother's life.

10

*W*ork continues. The cylindrical chamber slowly takes shape and is eventually enclosed with hinged doors that are made of the same material as the walls, and coated with the same chemical solution. Control panels are painstakingly assembled and wired, and eventually cover an entire wall of the garage. The drill press-looking device is constructed from the floor up, and when it is finished, connected to the control panels.

As I watch all of this, I gradually develop what I believe to be a rudimentary understanding of how the time machine works. The upper part of the drill press-thing has what looks like an inverted laser beam, which I think is actually some kind of neutron emitter. Just below that is a small, flat compartment that will hold a tiny amount of nuclear fuel, which I do not think Brian has yet obtained and which I have no idea from where he will get it (unless in this time, like the professor quips in the movie Back to the Future, plutonium is readily available at any convenience store. I rather doubt that, though). The neutrons will enter the compartment and bombard the fuel, creating fission that will release an enormous amount of energy. That energy will be channeled into a metallic canister -- a compression chamber -- which is mounted on a vertical shaft beneath the flat compartment. The nuclear energy will power the compression of matter within the chamber to such an incredible density that it will form a tiny black hole. In outer space, black holes are not only enormous, but are essentially round and draw in matter And light from all directions. Incredibly, Zintak has figured out a way to not only create a black hole on a minute scale, but also to control its direction, as though it were a flashlight beam, but with the added ability to terminate the beam at a precise location. This will enable him to establish the event horizon exactly where he wants it to be, in close proximity to whomever or whatever is to be transported back in time. Within that small area, the passage of time will slow to a crawl, while further away, time will move forward at its normal speed.

While this more or less makes sense, I also realize that it does not explain how the person or object near the event horizon actually moves backward in, rather than simply being suspended in, time. I suspect, however, that among the myriad of absurdly complicated formulas that fill the pages of Brian's notebooks, there are some that relate to a law of time that is similar to Newton's third law of motion: for every action, there is an equal and opposite reaction. If that is true, then the force of time moving away from one positioned near the event horizon must create equal propulsion in the opposite direction, causing him to move backward on the timeline rather than being glued to the same spot. It would stand to reason that that backward inertia could, in theory, continue indefinitely until the time traveler winds up back at the very creation of the universe, but in reality, will be halted at such time as the machine burns through its fuel supply, or is powered down when the traveler reaches his pre-programmed point along the timeline.

The other thing that baffles me is the purpose of the cylindrical chamber with the aluminum-paneled shell. Initially, I had thought this to be a necessary part of the machine, in the way that a rocket ship is needed to transport an astronaut through the Earth's atmosphere and into outer space. But I was able to discern from reading Brian's notes that that is not the case; his calculations and computer simulations had established with nearly 100% certainty that there was no enclosure needed to protect himself as he traveled into the past. Essentially the machine would create a tunnel through time, and the traveler could move through that tunnel with no more ill effect than if he were walking down the hallway of his home. Nevertheless, it is clear that Brian's intention, when his work is finished and he is ready to leave, is to enter the cylindrical chamber and for the machine to send the entire capsule back in time. I hope that further observation will allow me to identify the purpose of the chamber.

As Brian moves ever closer to realizing his vision, there are a number of potential flaws in his time travel plan that enter my mind, and I cannot help but wonder, even though he is a genius, whether these have occurred to him. For example, what will he do once he has saved his mother's life? I assume this will be accomplished by killing his father again, at some point in time that is prior to the trip to Montana. Once that is done, will he remain in the past and watch over his mother and his younger self from a distance, acting as a sort of guardian angel for the rest of their lives? Or would he attempt to explain to them that he is Brian from the future and has come back to protect them, in hopes of having some sort of a strange relationship with the two of them? Which of these two options he might choose could be decided, in part, by whether or not there would be harmful effects resulting from two versions of himself meeting face-to-face at the same point in time. It is hard to imagine that Brian would not have considered this, though I have not seen anything in his notes or computer models that would suggest he has solved that problem, if in fact it does exist and had crossed his mind.

It seems unlikely to me that Brian will choose option number one -- watching from a distance -- because in doing so, he will never be able to enjoy his mother's company again. I do not believe he has built the time machine merely to save Sherry's life; I believe he also wants to be with her again. Perhaps he has designed the machine to bring him back to his own time, where he can resume his relationship with his mother again after having saved her life in the past. If that is the case, however, there will be a gap of almost 12 *years from the time he last saw his mother until the day he returns to his present time. Any number of things could happen during that time, since by changing the past, he would also be creating a brand new future from that point forward. His mother might, for example, die in a car crash a week, a month, or a year after she is saved, thus making this entire exercise futile. And if that were to happen, what if young Brian himself happened to be in the car and was killed? Would the present-day Brian suddenly cease to exist the moment his younger self died (or do we each live in what Asimov referred to as an "indeviant reality" – if I was following his logic in* The End of Eternity *– a state of being that would not change even if one's past were altered)? And finally, even if Brian's plan worked and he saved his mother, returned to the present day, and his mother and younger self safely navigated the 12-year span, he would face the same issue that he would if he remained in the past, specifically how to present himself to them and be a part of their lives. Furthermore, there would also be one* new *and very significant development, which is that his younger self would in fact no longer be his younger self, but rather his* same-aged *self! Brian would have an identical twin!*

Considering all of these possibilities, both if Brian remained in the past or returned to the future, I cannot see any desirable scenario for him. The fact is, he simply cannot do what he would like to do, which is to place himself in the shoes of his younger self and have everything be just like it was 12 years ago, except without his father. Altering the past is one thing; recreating *it is something different.*

While this is all fascinating to ponder, the question that continues to nag at me more than any other is why all of this is being shown to me. Even if Brian completes the machine and successfully transports himself back to a time when he can save his mother's life, as far as I am concerned, it will not matter whether he chooses to remain in her time, or whether he returns to his own time. Either way, it will be a century or so into my future . . . meaning these events will have no impact on my life, or any part of the world as I know it. So what is the purpose? I consider going back to visit Randall again, but I know that that is a question that he probably cannot answer, and most likely would not, even if he could. Thus, I have no choice but to keep watching.

Then one day, Brian takes a break from his usual lunch delivery and decides to find something in his kitchen to eat. He removes several different fruits and vegetables from the refrigerator, along with milk and yogurt, and some ice cubes from the freezer, drops it all into a blender and purees himself a smoothie. He is drinking the smoothie and reading something on his handheld device, when the doorbell rings. He sets the device on the table but keeps the glass with him as he walks across the living room floor to the front door. He opens the door and greets a deliveryman who has brought a small package for Brian, no doubt yet another component of the time machine. The deliveryman has a handheld device of his own, which he holds up in front of Brian's face and snaps a picture of it to confirm his identity. The device beeps twice, apparently to signal that the recipient's identity is confirmed, and the man nods, hands Brian the package and returns to his truck. Both hands now full, Brian uses his foot to close the door. He turns away from it and retraces his steps across the living room floor and into the kitchen, but catches his foot on the edge of the area rug beneath the table and stumbles. The glass tips forward and its contents empty out onto the rug. Brian unleashes a few obscenities, sets his glass and the package on the counter, then slides the kitchen table onto the laminate floor and begins to roll up the area rug, I presume so that he can take it somewhere to be cleaned.

And that is when he finds the letter. It takes me a moment to realize what it is . . . the letter Jerry had written to Sherry, confessing his love for her. Once it dawns on me what this is, I am shocked to see it. I had assumed that Carl had discovered the letter, which is how he had become aware of Jerry and Sherry's relationship (though of course, he had obviously concluded, incorrectly, that Sherry felt the same way about Jerry as he felt about her, and had avenged himself of her perceived infidelity). Evidently, Carl had learned of the "Jerry and Sherry show" some other way. Brian looks at the letter with confusion, then opens it and begins to read. As he does, I sense that I am about to witness yet another turning point in this bizarre saga.

Brian reads the letter once, enters the living room and sits down on the sofa, then reads the letter a second time. And then he remains sitting for a long time, staring blankly at the wall in front of him. Finally, he turns toward the end table on his right, where the framed picture of his mother sits, the same one he has distributed throughout the house and which he has spent many hours staring at. He picks up the picture and looks at it, and his face now contorts with rage and hatred. He hurls the picture against the wall, the glass shattering into innumerable tiny fragments, and lets fly another torrent of expletives, these directed specifically at his mother. "LIAR!" he screams. "YOU BETRAYED HIM!! YOU BETRAYED US BOTH!! YOU DESERVED TO DIE!!"

And then the tirade really *begins, as he smashes or hurls everything in his sight, from decorative items, to furniture, to lamps, then into the kitchen where he does likewise with cabinet drawers, dishes and small appliances. As he vents his anger, I desperately want to tackle him, sit on his back and pin him to the floor as I explain to him that just like his maniac father, he is wrong about his mother. I want to tell him that his mother was the kindest, most loving and loyal woman I have ever encountered, and that she would have gladly given up her life if it was necessary to avoid hurting either her husband or her son. I want to tell him all of that and more, because I realize that this discovery likely means that any glimmer of light that remained within Brian has now been extinguished, and that the darkness has at last swallowed his soul.*

11

*T*he next scene is the shortest I have been shown thus far, but also one of the most dramatic. It is dark, and Brian is standing in the driveway of his house, alongside his car. For several minutes he simply stares at the house. I am standing between him and the left rear door of the vehicle, and something prompts me to look into the back seat. There are two suitcases and a laptop case lying on the seat. The way Brian is looking at the house, as though remembering all of the years he spent here, I suspect he is not merely going on a trip but rather is leaving the house, never to return. And why should he? His father was a monster, and his mother (he believes) deceived and betrayed him. There is nothing left for him here. I am guessing he has left all of the furniture and decorative items here as well, since those, too, would have memories associated with them. The only thing I am not sure of is if he has arranged to have the time travel equipment moved to a different location. I am assuming he did, because I remain convinced that this whole thing involves time travel in some way. Otherwise, it would have nothing to do with me.

I look over at Brian just as he reaches into his right front pocket and removes something that resembles a garage door opener. He points it toward the house and presses the button. I expect to see the garage door open, presumably so that Brian can take one more look inside to verify that everything of value has been removed. But instead, I hear a "whump" sound inside the house, followed a split second later by the outward explosion of most of the windows in the house. Seconds later, flames are pouring out of the shattered windows and curling up the sides of the house. Within a minute, the entire structure is engulfed.

Apparently satisfied that the house will not survive the blaze, or perhaps recognizing the need to leave the area before authorities are dispatched, Brian gets into his car, backs out of the driveway and speeds away. So much for abandoning a house when you can obliterate it, perhaps along with some of your own personal demons as well (though this I doubt).

I stand watching the spectacular blaze for a few minutes longer, until fire consumes the ceiling joists that the garage door supports and track had been mounted to, causing the door to collapse. As I had suspected, the garage is empty.

12

A s *the next scene begins, it is immediately clear, based on Brian's appearance, that a considerable amount of time has passed, probably several years. He is walking through what appears to be an enormous warehouse that I would estimate to be at least 1,000 feet long and maybe half as wide, and is empty with the exception of scattered pallets, various kinds of debris, and a row of glass-walled offices along one side of the structure. Brian is accompanied by a man who I do not recognize. They walk slowly in silence from one end of the warehouse to the other, Brian stroking his chin thoughtfully as he inspects the building from floor to ceiling. Finally, the man speaks up.*

"Do you have any questions about the facility, Mr. Zintak?"

Brian is silent for a few moments longer, then says, "What did you say the asking price was?"

"Thirty million."

"I'd be willing to pay twenty for it."

The man smiles slightly, then says, "Well, that's a start. I can certainly take your offer back to the owner, but I don't think he'll be willing to drop his price by a third."

"I should have mentioned that I will pay in cash," *Brian responds.* "No financing needed. I can provide immediate proof that I have the funds available, and we can close the deal in a matter of days. Surely the owner will come down a bit further than he had planned to, given that this will probably be the most hassle-free deal he's ever made."

The man nods and replies, "Yes, I'm sure that's true to some *extent, but probably not by ten million."*

"So you won't take my offer to him? If not, then let's go look at another property. There are plenty of them around."

"Whoa, whoa!" the man says, raising his hands defensively. "I didn't say that. I will be glad to take your offer back to the owner. But of course, you know he will counter, probably with something in the neighborhood of twenty-six or twenty-seven. Just so I have an idea, how much more are you willing to come up?"

"Not one dollar. That is my first and only offer."

The man stares into the cold depths of Brian's eyes, and I can see in his own expression that he has no doubt Brian means what he says.

"I'll get back to you shortly." *They shake hands rather awkwardly, and Brian turns and leaves the building.*

This exchange has provided no indication of what Brian is planning next, but given the size of this place, it is fair to assume that it will dwarf the scheme he had cooked up in his garage.

⅄   ⅄   ⅄

A few weeks later, I am guessing, Brian stands at one end of the same building, watching as an army of construction workers is furiously building out the interior of the warehouse. They have replaced the glass walls of the offices with framed walls, and are constructing additional spaces in a variety of sizes, some that appear to be more offices, others that are large enough to be efficiency apartments, and still others that might be meeting or recreation areas. And then there is a single, enormous space in the very center that is perhaps four times the size of any of the other areas – no doubt a workspace of some kind. The building is tall enough to accommodate a second floor, and at the far end, they have already completed the first floor, laid subflooring on top of that, and are beginning to build more rooms on the second floor.

I suppose this makeover is not much different from any other such situation where an existing building is converted into some-

thing that looks entirely different, and for an entirely different purpose. But there is one thing about this particular conversion that is VERY different, and that is the lining of the interior. Instead of paneling or drywall, as you might expect, the walls, the ceiling and even the floor, are being lined with the same aluminum-like, chemical-coated panels that Brian had used to construct the cylindrical chamber in his garage. So now I know that this new plan is very much like the old, but on a much larger scale. The other thing that is now apparent is that his plan is no longer a one-man show, but will involve other people. LOTS of other people.

What is not apparent to me, however, is the purpose for the additional structural system that is constructed on the inside of the building after the aluminum panels are installed. A steel skeleton, capable of supporting the entire structure completely on its own, is erected and bolted to the aluminum panels. I know the panels are not light, but neither did they appear to be exceptionally heavy as the workers were lifting them into place and mounting them to the exterior walls. Therefore, the logical conclusion would be that Zintak is not overly concerned about the panels causing too much strain on the original structure, but that the additional support system is needed for some other reason. Whether or not it is significant to my understanding of this vision remains to be seen . . . but thus far, I cannot think of any part of it that has not been significant. So we will see.

rian is now sitting at a picnic table, across from another man I have not seen before, in a lovely wooded area next to a narrow, trickling stream. It would seem to be some kind of a park or nature preserve. There is currently no one else around, and I quickly gather from the discussion between the two men that that was the intent.

"I'm sorry I couldn't give you more details when we spoke on the phone, Dr. Millenkamp, but you know how it is, Big Brother might be listening," Brian says.

"I understand completely, Mr. Zintak, though you gave me just enough to pique my curiosity, even though I am a genetic engineer and not a physicist. These panels you developed, these . . . . 'temporal shields', I think you called them? You say they will completely protect anyone who is inside the enclosure from any and all effects of tampering with the past?"

"That's correct," Brian says. "So let's say I travel a hundred years into the past and detonated a nuclear device in the city of Chicago, where your great grandmother happened to be living at the time. A literal example of the grandfather paradox, if you're familiar with that term, though in fact, any inconsistency in past events may be regarded as a grandfather paradox. Anyway, your great grandmother would obviously be vaporized, but if you were inside a room or a building that was surrounded by the temporal shields – completely surrounded, mind you, from floor to ceiling -- the death of your direct ancestor would have no impact on you, and you would only be able to deduce what had happened by *observing the aftereffects, if any, that remained following that one hundred-year period. So if you walked around the site of a nuclear explosion one hundred years after the fact, assuming the radiation had been neutralized and vegetation had had sufficient time to grow back, you might not know that anything had happened. But let's say you detonated that nuclear device just five minutes into the past. You had better stay inside that shielded enclosure, because if you stepped outside of it and were anywhere near the site of the explosion, you would die instantly."*

Millenkamp chuckles and shakes his head. "A temporal shield. That's incredible! And as for the time machine, if that device actually works, then it would be the greatest achievement in the history of mankind! Of course, it's one thing to simulate the force of a black hole, slowing time down just outside of the event horizon and then catapulting yourself into the past. It's another thing altogether to return to the present time. How did you manage to accomplish that?"

"I didn't," Brian admits. "It's impossible. I would never have been able to return."

Aha! I think to myself after hearing this exchange. That answers at least three of my questions, the first one being whether or not the time traveler could return to his own time. Zintak has just made it clear that that is not possible. The second question was whether or not we dwell in an indeviant reality, and this was answered when Brian explained that a "temporal shield" is needed to protect one's self from any tampering with the past. This clearly suggests that there is no such thing as an indeviant reality; that is, changes to the past do not spawn alternate realities that exist parallel to the original, but in fact, simply wipe out the original in favor of the new. And the third question was with respect to the exact purpose of the aluminum-paneled cylindrical chamber that was part of the original concept, and its successor, the encased complex where Zintak will execute his new plan. Millenkamp's last statement implies that the time machine and the temporal shields are actually independent components of the system. Strictly speaking, neither the cylindrical chamber nor the encased complex would be necessary for the time machine to function; however, the temporal shield is, for all intents and purposes, equally vital because, again, there is no indeviant reality. Anyone not protected by a temporal shield would be subject to the effects of alterations to the past . . . . up to and including nullification of one's very existence. So just for the sake of argument, if Brian could have returned himself and the cylindrical chamber to the present time after saving his mother's life, he would have been shielded from any ill fate that his mother or younger self might have suffered during that 12-year time gap. Thus, if that tragic car accident did take place, for example, the worst that would have happened is that Brian would have returned to his present time simply to find his mother and younger self dead and buried at some point in the past. But of course, Brian has just admitted that it would have been impossible for him to return to his present time, meaning he would have been stuck in the past.

That leads me to again ponder the question of what exactly Brian was planning to do – specifically with regards to his younger self -- once he arrived in the past. I think I now know the answer to that question as well, and the realization chills me to the bone. I had concluded previously that there were only two possibilities: (1) be content to watch his mother and younger self from a distance; or (2) attempt to explain who he was to the two of them in hopes of having a relationship with them. But now I realize there was a third option -- to kill his younger counterpart so that he could have his mother all to himself. To accomplish that without wiping out his own existence, Brian would have needed to lure or forcibly compel his younger self into the cylindrical chamber before killing him. Shocking though this may seem, it is the only conceivable reason he would have needed to transport the cylinder back in time, for as I have already stated, the chambers only purpose was to serve as a temporal shield and not for time travel itself.

"So now," Millenkamp continues, "you intend not to transport yourself back in time, but to send someone or something else instead. Is that correct?"

"Yes," Brian says coolly. "Finding the letter under the rug, as I was telling you on the phone, was the best thing that ever happened to me. It made me see the error of my ways. It would have been utterly foolish of me to waste the technology on a single trip into the past, to save the life of someone who got exactly what she deserved, especially when you consider the substantial hurdles I would have had to overcome in order to reinsert myself into her life."

Brian does not elaborate on this last statement, but it seems clear that he realizes his chosen course of action – killing his younger self – would have been just as deeply flawed as the other options. First of all, he would have needed to be extremely cautious and opportunistic if he were to kidnap the younger Brian without anyone seeing him. And second, it was absurd to think that he could simply approach his grieving mother and tell her that he was Brian from the future and had come back in time to comfort her. Even if he could convince her of that, there was no guarantee that she would eventually warm up to him. Furthermore, sooner or later she would realize that if this really was an adult version of her son as he claimed to be, that this horrific murder of her precious 7-year old Brian could not have occurred on the original timeline. And that, in turn, would lead her to realize that the culprit must be none other than the adult Brian.

"Now," Brian continues, "I look towards the future, and the tremendous opportunity that we have right at our fingertips. Together, your creation, and mine, will leave the future not to chance, but will instead shape it to be exactly what we want it to be. That is, if you'll join me?"

As he is speaking, I notice Brian discreetly slipping a hand into his jacket pocket. There is something inside the pocket, I cannot tell what it is, but I have no doubt it is some kind of weapon, for the pocket suddenly protrudes straight forward beneath the table top and points directly at Millenkamp's midsection. If he does not give Brian the answer he wants, it will be the last words he ever speaks, for whatever this plan involves, it must certainly need to remain hidden from the general public.

"My research," Millenkamp says after a lengthy pause, "has always been used to heal, to cure, to restore. Now you want me to use it for mass destruction. Why should I do that?"

"We both know why," Brian responds. "The man who killed your wife and daughters right in front of you was a monster, a cancerous tumor in our society that should have been cut out and disposed of. But instead, based on a mere technicality, he was let go, and is probably out there right now doing the same thing all over again. And he is just one among many. They are everywhere. The fact is, our entire society is rife with this cancer. Someone has to wipe it out. It was God who played the role of reaper a few thousand years ago, and He chose Noah to be the father of a new race. But God isn't playing favorites anymore. And that's okay, because we have the ability to do the reaping ourselves. Oh, and by the way, we get to be Noah, too."

By the time Brian finishes, Millenkamp's face is twisted with anguish, and tears flow freely down his cheeks. He looks to be several years older than Brian, though not so old that he could not have had young children. Perhaps in his mid-forties? I am guessing that the loss of his wife and daughters has occurred fairly recently, probably within the last year, and the sorrow and anger he feels are still very much like lightly-scabbed wounds that are easily torn open again.

"I . . . I still have a hard time grasping the reality that they're gone," Millenkamp splutters. "And I . . . I . . . "

"It's okay," Brian says, having donned a mask of sympathy.

90

Underneath, I know he could not care less about Millenkamp's family, or his mental or emotional state. But he certainly is good at pretending like he does. "Go ahead, tell me. Just let it go. You can't keep doing this day after day. Eventually, it will destroy you."

That is ironic, I think to myself, coming from a guy who has spent the better part of his life obsessing over his dead mother.

"And what if I want to be destroyed?"

"You don't. If you did, you would have done it yourself months ago. You have too much left to give, too much left to do. Now tell me."

Millenkamp reflects upon Brian's words for a moment. "I should have never tried to reason with that psychopath. I had met plenty of radicals like him before, people who think their view is the only one that's right and can't possibly be reasoned with. I should have known he had violent intentions."

"It wasn't your fault, Dr. Millenkamp. In your statement to the police, you said that when he broke into your house, he hadn't even pulled the gun out yet. He was not violent at first, explaining to you very calmly why he felt your particular science is an offense to God and to nature. Since you didn't know what his intentions were at that point, and you didn't want to alarm your family, you tried to engage him in a logical debate, to show him how genetic modification and cloning can be used for good things like wiping out disease and correcting deformities. It was a perfectly reasonable approach. In fact, it was the only approach you could have taken, until he pulled out his gun and his intentions became clear."

"Yes, but it wasn't his demeanor that should have given him away, it was his eyes! They haunt me to this very day! Even now, I can see the evil, the hatred in them. And as he stood looking down at me while the four of us sat at our kitchen table, that unwavering stare locked upon me, I knew what he was going to do. I knew he must have something under his jacket, some kind of weapon that he

intended to use. I could have punched him or tackled him right then, before he pulled the gun, and either subdued him or at least given my wife and daughters a chance to get out of the house and run to the neighbor's. But I didn't. I tried talking him down, though I knew it wouldn't work, and because of that, my family is dead."

Having blurted this out, Millenkamp breaks down sobbing. Brian reaches across the table, with his left hand, and gives him a soothing pat on the forearm. His right hand is still inside his jacket pocket, and his weapon is still pointed toward Millenkamp.

"Yes, your family is now in a better place," Brian says consolingly, "but their deaths don't have to be without meaning. In fact, if they hadn't died, you wouldn't even have agreed to meet with me today, much less consider my proposal."

There is silence for a while. Brian has made his pitch, and Millenkamp is considering it.

"My heart is telling me I shouldn't do this, while my head is telling me I should," Millenkamp says at last.

"Forgive me for saying this, Dr. Millenkamp, but it was your heart that led you to talk to that man, while your head was telling you to take action. And look what ended up happening?"

Instead of being offended, Millenkamp merely nods. He has apparently come to the same realization . . . and to a decision as well.

"Alright, I'll join you, Mr. Zintak. May God have mercy on us both if we're doing the wrong thing."

Upon hearing this, Brian casually slides his right hand out of his jacket pocket and extends it across the table. Millenkamp grasps and shakes it.

"Think of it as the lesser of two evils. Do we sacrifice a mostly depraved human race, with the exception of a few elite members who are handpicked in order to ensure that only goodness survives, or do we simply stand by and watch as that depravity ultimately consumes the little bit of goodness that still remains?"

Millenkamp again ponders Brian's words, then lets out a huge sigh. "You're right, of course. But you may have to occasionally remind me that we're working for the greater good."

"I most certainly will," Brian says with a smile.

14

*A*fter the scene ends, I think about the exchange between Zintak and Millenkamp. It is clear that the traumatic experiences these two men have endured have caused both of them to lose all faith in humanity (not to mention their sanity as well), which has then led to this fantastic plan to send some sort of genetically engineered life form – a "reaper", as Zintak characterized it – back in time to wipe out virtually all of the human race, with only a few handpicked "good" people being protected from changes to the timeline and thus surviving the apocalypse. Up to this point in the vision, I had continually wondered what all of this had to do with me, as I would be dead long before the occurrence of these events. But now I am beginning to understand why this reaper must exist in a time that is very different from their own . . . my time, as it would now appear. For one thing, whatever form this reaper might take, it apparently will not be capable of wiping out billions of people in a short period of time. It would seem instead that the task will take decades to accomplish. Secondly, while it was not mentioned during their discussion, I suspect that Zintak and Millenkamp will not be able to control or destroy the reaper, so they cannot simply turn it loose in their own time, even if it was capable of killing billions of people in a matter of days or weeks. Thus, while the two fiends and their "master race", as I have dubbed them, will be safely tucked away inside the temporal-shielded enclosure, they will eventually have to step outside of it. And when they do, they will have to live in a world that has been affected – for better or for worse – by the reaper. In fact, they may actually have to face reaper itself, *if it happens to have a lifespan that is greater than a hundred or so years. If my assumption that they cannot control or kill reaper is true, then a face-to-face encounter with it is something that Zintak and his recruits will certainly want to avoid if at all possible. Therefore, it seems plausible that reaper must be engineered to have a lifespan that is long enough to accomplish Zintak's goal of destroying the human race, but not so long that it will still be alive when the master race emerges from the shielded complex.*

As I piece all of this together and grudgingly acknowledge the inevitable appearance of reaper within my own time, the big question that has yet to be answered is exactly what hellish form reaper will take. Will it be a virus? A massive swarm of killer bees? Maybe a horde of reanimated corpses? (I admit here to being a fan of zombie movies, but I am only being quasi-facetious, as I have no idea yet what Millenkamp is planning to create. For all I know, he may just end up being a 22nd century version of Dr. Frankenstein.). I can only guess at this point, but whatever it is, I know that I have the obligation, if not the strength and wisdom, to try to stop it from carrying out its terrible mission.

⚔ ⚔ ⚔

The building construction continues, as does the assembling of Zintak's team. He recruits young men and women who are not only extremely intelligent, but who, for the most part, are physically stunning as well – the women are beautiful, the men are handsome, and all are strong and athletic. There are a handful of elderly and/or average-looking individuals, who I assume were recruited because they possess knowledge or skills that are essential to the project, but for the most part this group certainly has the outward appearance of a master race.

As he is assembling this group, Zintak's utter ruthlessness and descent into madness are very apparent. I witness scenes where Zintak holds a private meeting with a potential recruit, like the one with Millenkamp, except that it has an undesirable outcome – spe-

cifically, that the answer to Zintak's proposal is "no". Of course, he cannot allow anyone who is not to be part of his group to know about their plan, so in these situations he withdraws the weapon from his pocket and fires it at the unsuspecting recruit. The weapon makes no sound whatsoever, nor does it jump in Zintak's hand like a pistol would, nor emit any visible projectile or beam. But there is no question that it works, because it instantly burns a hole of about three inches in diameter all the way through the victim's body. At point blank range, Zintak invariably hits the left side of the victim's chest, thus killing him or her upon contact. He gets up and leaves immediately, but within minutes a crew of three other men arrives to dispose of the body and eliminate all physical evidence from the scene.

Eventually, Zintak's confidence and perceived loyalty toward him by the group members grows to the point where he can administer severe punishment to those who fail in their tasks without fear of abandonment or retribution from the others. For example, one day as the team is busy equipping the laboratory that had just been completed, a man drops a piece of equipment on the floor, smashing it to pieces. With six other group members looking on, Zintak briskly walks over to the man, withdraws his weapon, and blasts a hole through the man's forehead. There are gasps and cries of shock and horror, but no one makes a move toward him.

Calmly, Zintak explains his actions. "Clumsiness and buffoonery, though not quite as damaging as greed, lust and hatred, are nevertheless detrimental to society and will therefore not be tolerated. Please use this as an example of the consequences of such careless behavior from this point forward."

I am not surprised that I do not observe any additional acts of "clumsiness and buffoonery" after that.

Å   Å   Å

The laboratory/control room – the "cockpit", as the group calls it -- constructed within the warehouse is immense, measuring perhaps two hundred feet on each side. But this does not really strike me as peculiar so much as what is being constructed inside this room – an enclosure that I would regard as a cage, not because it is made with bars but because it is made of a transparent material that is every bit of eighteen inches thick. Furthermore, there is not one but two of these cages being built – one inside the other. Both inner and outer cages are circular, with the inner cage -- which is located exactly in the center of the outer cage -- measuring approximately twenty-five feet in diameter, and the outer cage measuring about one hundred feet in diameter. Both inner and outer cages are twenty feet in height, with a roof over the entire structure that is constructed of the same transparent material as the walls are made of. There is a single door in each of the cages, also made of the transparent material, and I notice that the hinges on the door of the inner cage are on the inside, while those on the door of the outer cage are on the outside. Both doors are controlled remotely, so there is no handle or keypad on either of them. In short, the cages would seem to be impenetrable and inescapable, and it seems clear that this is where reaper will reside until it is sent back in time.

There is something being constructed inside the inner cage. After a few days, when it begins to vaguely resemble the same drill press-like device that Zintak had constructed in his garage, I realize it is a larger, apparently more sophisticated version of the time machine. I listen to the cockpit technicians discussing many of the same principles and design concepts that I had read about in Brian's notes or deduced from observing him. It uses fuel derived from radioactive material, and compresses a tiny amount of matter so densely that it creates a singularity – the center of a black hole. I had already learned that the event horizon surrounds a black hole, and that time slows down as you approach the event horizon . . . but whatever crosses the event horizon is destroyed. Therefore, for someone or something to be sent back in time, they must approach the event horizon but not cross it. It follows, then, that the event *horizon must fall within the walls of the inner cage, to guard against anyone or anything inadvertently crossing over it. Similarly, the outer cage must be located on the edge of the area in which reaper would be pulled backward in time once the device is activated – the "temporal zone", as the technicians call it.*

The question that keeps nagging at me is: why are the walls of the cages so thick? I had been leaning toward some sort of virus as the agent of humanity's destruction, but such a massive enclosure – which I myself have characterized as a "cage" – would obviously not be used to contain a virus. And then I remember the vision I had had as a 12-year old boy, the one that I had in church when I saw gaping wounds inexplicably opening up on everyone present. No virus could ever do that, and it becomes clear to me that the reaper is, in fact, something much different. Something extremely powerful. It should not be long before I find out exactly what that something will be, for while Zintak is directing the construction of the time machine and the transparent cages, Millenkamp is beginning development of the reaper.

15

*T*he first hint I receive at what Millenkamp is planning is the embryos that begin to grow in jars in the cockpit. They are animal embryos, which I know not from their appearance, because most of them look very similar, but simply because the jars are labelled, and there are dozens of them. They include a variety of marsupials, bats, birds, lizards and turtles, as well larger animals like gorillas, lions, bears, sharks and dolphins, among others. And there is much talk of "genetic modification", "transgenesis", "GMOs" (which I eventually figure out is "genetically modified organism"), "recombination", and other such jargon. As is the case with Zintak's work, most of the terms related to genetic engineering are foreign to me, but in total, and used in context, they provide me with a basic understanding of Millenkamp's concept. By combining the genetic material of numerous animals, he is attempting to create an entirely unique life form that will have the abilities of each of its "CCs" - component creatures. Additionally, they are developing a process they call "geno-enhancement", which involves strengthening the attributes of each of the CCs to give reaper abilities that far surpass the sum of its individual genetic parts. For example, if elephant DNA is used to make reaper, the geno-enhancement process may give it the strength of three such animals instead of one; if dolphin DNA is used, reaper may be able to swim up to sixty miles an hour instead of twenty-five.

While this horrific thing that Millenkamp is creating is still just a blueprint, I understand now why the walls of the glass cages are so thick. Pound for pound, it will be the most powerful creature *that has ever lived on our planet.*

⅄   ⅄   ⅄

A significant period of time goes by; at least several months, perhaps a year or more. The time machine has long been completed. Zintak waits only for reaper to reach full maturity before firing up the device and sending the creature on its mission to liberate planet Earth from the "evil" of humanity and allow a small but worthy remnant to start over. The creature was moved into the cage some time ago, after it became too strong and aggressive to be restrained by any other means. Its development has, by all accounts, been a huge success. If "success" is defined by the sheer terror of one gazing upon it, then I would absolutely have to agree with that characterization.

The creature is truly like something out of a nightmare: roughly the size of a rhinoceros, but with a sleek, muscular feline body; covered with armor plating along its flanks and from the back of its neck to the base of a flipper-like appendage that protrudes from its rear end; sporting wings that are built for speed like those of a falcon and which tuck neatly into grooves in the armor plating that helps to reduce drag when the creature is swimming, running or digging; a broad, triangular-shaped head with a flat, bony forehead; double-rows of jagged teeth on the top and bottom of its mouth, like a shark; and long, straight claws on each paw, like those of a mole. Its default color is greenish-brown, but it has the ability to alter that almost instantly to blend into its surroundings. It appears to be equally suited for land (both on top of the ground and below it), air and sea.

While their teams were busy working on the time machine and the creature, Zintak and Millenkamp had been busy refining their plan. The number of years that reaper could be sent back in time is contingent upon the amount of nuclear fuel they had been able to accumulate; more fuel meant that the event horizon – and therefore the temporal zone – would be in place longer, thus the further back in time that reaper could travel. The madmen have determined that based on the amount of fuel on hand, the creature can travel 105.2 years into the past, with a margin of error of plus or minus 0.7 years. They debate whether or not they should attempt to acquire more fuel, but ultimately they decide not to, because their models and mathematical projections have shown that it should only take the creature between 86.2 and 94.6 years to exterminate the human race, depending on environmental factors and the rigorousness of human resistance throughout those nine decades.

As for reaper, since they cannot control it, and would be hard pressed to destroy it even with 22nd century weapons, they must ensure that its life is over by the time they emerge from their protective enclosure. The creature would certainly not die of natural causes by then, for like the tortoise that is among its CCs, it has a life span of two hundred years or more. But this problem is easily solved by implanting a virus, surrounded by a synthetic casing, inside the creature. The casing is designed such that it will deteriorate after one hundred years, plus or minus 1.7 years, thereby releasing the virus into the creature's bloodstream and killing it within a matter of days. Thus even if the maximum margin of error for both of the variables is realized – the time machine sends the creature only 104.5 years into the past, and the creature lives an extra 1.7 years – there should still be a gap of 2.8 years between the creature's death and the emergence of Zintak and his people from their sanctuary.

Though I now have a good deal of specific information about Zintak's plan, one thing that troubles me is that I no longer have a reliable sense of what year this is. For some strange reason, people in the 22nd century do not seem to have a need for clocks, calendars or time & date displays on their computer screens. I know it was 2086 when the dream began, and that Brian was six years old at the time. That would mean it was 2098 when he turned eighteen, but 2086 when the dream began, and that Brian was six years old at the time. That would mean it was 2098 when he turned eighteen, but since that point, long stretches of time have been skipped over, and I could hardly wager a guess as to what year it is now. Based on Brian's appearance, I am virtually certain that he is in his mid-thirties at least, but could be as old as his mid-forties. That would mean the year is anywhere from 2115 to 2125. As the creature is being sent back 105 years into the past, that would peg its arrival between the years 2010 and 2020. That will certainly be well within my lifetime, but it would be nice to have a more precise idea of when the arrival will occur. I hope to see something before this dream ends that will provide me with that information.

The other thing that is worrisome is that I do not have any idea where the creature will appear. I did learn that the creature will arrive in the past at this very same location, since it is travelling across time, not across physical space. That bit of knowledge has to be worth something, but exactly where am I? The dream had begun with me literally falling into a town that was nestled alongside what I am guessing was the Rocky Mountains, but it is certainly possible that Zintak could have abandoned his hometown after he blew up his house. Something tells me he did not do that, perhaps because he had friends and associates in the area, people he wanted to approach about joining his cause, but even so, it does not do me a lot of good knowing only that I am in a town that lies in the eastern shadow of the Rockies. It is true that while I would not have any idea how to go about fighting the creature even if I was standing there waiting to greet it, logic dictates that knowing not only when it would arrive but also where, would be valuable information indeed.

16

f inally, reaping day arrives. The master race is like a bunch of kids on Christmas Day, brimming with good cheer and excitement. If Zintak's plan works, it will be as if Santa himself had delivered their gift – an empty, purified planet to use as they see fit.

The technicians begin to arrive in the cockpit, and while they are waiting for their superiors to join them, they stand around watching the creature, which is relentlessly circling inside the cage as it always does. It had only attempted to smash through the glass a handful of times before its survival instinct apparently alerted it to the fact that such efforts were futile and would only result in harm to itself. But its mission, I now know, is branded into the very fiber of its being, and it clearly yearns for the freedom it needs to do what it was designed to do – kill every human possible, where ever and whenever it comes into contact with them. I find it disturbing that these people are studying this creature with a bizarre sort of admiration, despite knowing that it would dissect and devour them in a matter of seconds if it could.

Zintak and Millenkamp arrive a short time later and begin to bark out orders. The time machine is activated, and as it steadily powers up, the compression device begins to compact the matter that will become the singularity at the heart of a miniaturized black hole. The process seems to take a long time, minutes in dream time but perhaps hours in real time (though I cannot be sure because, as I mentioned, there are no clocks visible). Eventually, though I cannot see any evidence of changes inside the cage, a circular line representing the event horizon pops up on the computer screen displays, and slowly works its way outward from the machine. Inch by inch it approaches the inner cage, pushing the temporal zone ahead of it, getting ever closer to the unsuspecting creature.

Then, finally, as the computer display indicates that the event horizon has reached its maximum radius, a point just inside the inner cage, the creature's pacing suddenly stops. It remains frozen for a few seconds, then begins to shimmer and fade, sort of like in the old Star Trek TV series when someone had stepped into a transporter beam and slowly dematerialized. And then, the creature disappears completely.

Up to that point, save for the humming of the time machine, the room had been as quiet as a mausoleum. But when the creature vanishes, the technicians erupt into a chorus of cheers and applause. A few of them collapse into their chairs, joyful but physically exhausted from all of the grueling work that had gone into building this facility and executing their plan to regenerate the human race. I notice that Zintak, however, has not yet joined in the celebration. He seems to be the only one who has not forgotten how important it is that the machine not only perform, but perform precisely as it was programmed to; specifically, that the creature is sent far enough back in time that it will have no chance of living through that entire span and being alive on this day. After all, Zintak and Millenkamp have known all along that they could not devise a way of controlling the creature, and while it might be possible to kill it with modern weapons, it was a confrontation they wanted very much to avoid.

Zintak continues to study the instruments for several minutes, a look of intense concentration and concern on his face. But finally, the readings indicate that the time travel span has surpassed the creature's maximum life expectancy, and the relief is visible on his face and in his body language. He raises a hand to signal his team to calm down so that he can deliver a congratulatory speech.

"Thank you all for your commitment to this initiative, for

your patience, endurance, and for the sacrifices you have made in order to become pioneers in a new and better world. Each and every one of you, regardless of your role here, has been an integral part of our project and now stand ready to reap the rewards for your contribution. I do, however, want to especially thank Dr. Millenkamp, my partner and friend, for all that he has done. His ingenuity and bold vision allowed us to create something completely unique and with all of the attributes needed to reshape the past in a way that will ensure an unimaginably bright future for each of us. Now then, let's go check out our new world."

Zintak exits the cockpit, the technicians trailing behind him like ducklings following their mother. With that, the scene abruptly changes . . . and that it is when things really start to get interesting.

⚓   ⚓   ⚓

I am not sure where I am at first. But then I recognize the mountains surrounding me – just barely visible in the twilight of what seems to be an early- to mid-spring day, judging by the buds on the trees around me -- and I realize that I am very close to the place where I was when this dream first began . . . in Brian Zintak's home town. But it looks much different now, the houses being smaller, with more obtuse angles, and in general, homier-looking. Though I do not recognize this town, the familiarity of the architectural styles suggests that I am back in my own time, or something relatively close to it.

As I stand on the sidewalk alongside the street, waiting for something to happen, I see a man walking towards me, apparently coming home from work as he is dressed in slacks, a shirt and tie, with his sport coat in one hand and a satchel in the other. I notice there is a smile on his face and that he is glancing to his left, at the house that is directly to my right. I suppose that after a hard day at work, he is looking forward to an enjoyable evening with his family. As he gets closer, and I get a better look at his face, he seems familiar to me, not in the déjà vu sense of the word, but in some

105

stranger kind of way . . . as though I have never met him but nevertheless ought to know who he is. He suddenly stops and appears to be looking straight at me with a puzzled expression, which in turn puzzles me because I know he cannot see me. And then I realize what is causing his bewilderment – the air between us begins to blur and oscillate, like heat rising from an asphalt surface on a hot summer day. The blurry spot, nebulous at first, begins to take on a more definitive shape – that of a circle. And then it takes on a third dimension, that of depth, and I realize that it is forming a tunnel . . . a tunnel through time, to be precise. As I would expect, the man looks terrified by what he is seeing, at least initially. But then, amazingly, his fear dissipates and is replaced with excitement, perhaps even something approaching joy.

"Oh . . . my . . . God," I hear him whisper. "It's him! It's time!"

I have no idea, of course, what he is talking about, as he clearly believes this phenomenon to be something other than what it actually is. That is not surprising, for there is no way he can know what is about to emerge from the tunnel, and if he did, he would be running away rather than looking forward to the arrival of the most deadly foe the human race has ever encountered.

A moment later, the man finds out the hard way just how wrong he was, as the creature emerges from the tunnel and slices through his legs with one flick of its razor-sharp talons. He lies stunned on the sidewalk, the creature looming over him, and I almost look away as I expect it to slash additional members from his body. But it seems to recognize that it has already inflicted a mortal wound upon its victim, and having been designed to kill as quickly and efficiently as possible, it turns and moves off toward the man's house at a speed that utterly shocks me. Of course I knew that the creature would be several times stronger and faster than any other animal on the planet, but even so, watching it cover the fifty-or-so yards between the man and his house in the blink of an eye is some-

thing I could not have been prepared for.

I sympathetically glance down at the man, who briefly tries to raise himself up from the concrete before giving up when he becomes aware of his missing appendages, then regrettably leave him behind in order to pursue the creature. Obviously in real life I could never keep up with it, but this being a dream, I simply must choose to follow closely behind it, no matter where or how fast it goes, and it is made so. The creature crashes through the front door of the house as though it is made of paper rather than solid wood, and slaughters the man's wife and two children before they even have a chance to scream. I am horrified at the sight of this and am glad that it happens so quickly that their pain is extremely brief, notwithstanding the fact that this event has not yet occurred and thus there has been no actual suffering.

From there the creature moves on to the next house and kills its inhabitants in the same way. And then on to the next, and the next, and so on, all the way down the street. At first, there are no sirens, no policemen, ambulances, firemen or SWAT teams. The creature moves so quickly that everyone is caught by surprise and cannot react in time to save themselves or call for help. Eventually, however, it leaves behind a woman who is injured but who remains conscious. She calls 911, and minutes later, approaching sirens can be heard. The creature hears this, its survival instinct trumps its urge to kill, and it stretches out its wings and flies off into the mountains before any threat materializes. As it soars into the night sky, however, I notice that it has caught the attention of two other people who are out for a walk, a man who stands frozen staring up at it, and a woman who is fumbling with her cell phone, trying to get a picture of it. She ends up being too late, but soon the world will know of the creature's existence, for there are at least three eyewitnesses to its rampage, assuming the injured woman survives.

I continue to pursue the creature after its initial attack. Once it is a safe distance from Zintak's hometown, it lands on the ground and continues on foot, probably to use the rugged terrain as cover until it finds another populated area. But it does not behave as I expect it to, which is to attack the next available target. Instead, it travels an incredible distance before it strikes again, this time in a densely populated urban area in the dead of night, and one that I happen to recognize – Manhattan. It smashes through the front doors of a high rise apartment building that is no doubt home to some very wealthy and influential people. The building alarm is triggered instantly, so the creature remains for only a very short time, though it is still long enough to kill a few dozen people. It then exits the building and picks an escape route through darkened alleys until it reaches Central Park, swims across the Jackie O. Reservoir, hurtles down 97th street and disappears into the Hudson River. This time, as far as I can tell, there are no witnesses save for a couple of winos who would probably never report what they saw, and would not be believed if they did.

And so it continues like this – brief, lightning-fast attacks, completely random and unpredictable, and typically with few, if any, survivors or witnesses. The creature eats when it needs to (which is quite frequently, given its absurdly high metabolic rate), and its meals consist of anything convenient that contains an adequate amount of calories, from plants to animals to human beings. It sleeps only one or two hours a day, and when it does, it retreats to a secluded area, typically forested or mountainous, and if there are no caves or deep crevasses to hide in, it burrows deep into the ground where it would be virtually impossible to find. And to protect it even further, while it sleeps, its body temperature drops to just a few degrees above freezing, making it invisible to infrared scanners. Oh, and in case the reader is wondering, the creature's range is not limited to a single continent. Its ability to hunt and thus refuel underwater allows it to swim across any ocean on the planet, after which it continues its relentless assault on foreign soil. But in order to maximize its killing time, the creature generally spends several weeks on a contiguous piece of land before making the transoceanic trip to a different continent.

Weeks, months and years go by (again, in dream time), and the cycle continues, every single day. It eats and sleeps as needed, and the rest of its day is spent killing. Period. After a while, I disengage from the creature and spend some time simply observing humanity and how it is being affected . . . and I find that it is not holding up well.

People are fleeing cities and towns, having recognized that the creature primarily targets populated areas. This rapid demographic shift is having a devastating effect on business and industry, as there are no longer enough people left to produce goods and provide services. And of course, those people who are abandoning their jobs no longer have a way to provide for their families, so they are increasingly resorting to illegal methods – such as looting, robbery and assault – to obtain food and water, or the money to purchase those things.

The governments of the world are under incredible pressure to capture or kill the thing responsible for this chaos, but they are at a complete loss for answers. The creature has yet to demonstrate any discernible pattern in its attacks, so government officials do not know where to position their military assets that may be able to stop it. Martial law is declared worldwide (where it did not exist already), and armies and National Guard units are assigned to protect the most heavily populated areas. This does not deter the creature entirely, as it still manages to slip through undetected whenever it chooses to, but it does temporarily have the desired effect, as the attacks begin to focus mainly on smaller villages and pockets of people. I know, however, that this creature is as cunning as anything that has ever lived, and it is simply evolving its strategy. I believe that it senses that even the most densely populated areas cannot continue indefinitely in a state of isolation; they must have interaction with the outside world in order to obtain the goods they need to survive. By killing everything around these urban areas, thus cutting off their lifeline, the creature will eventually force them to abandon their strongholds and venture forth into what should by then be little more than a wasteland . . . and where they will stand no chance whatsoever.

I return to the creature, hoping to spot some kind of weakness that I might pass along to the authorities (those in real life, that is, after this dream has ended and I am forced to take action of some kind, in hopes of saving the world). I see nothing that remotely appears to be an Achilles heel, and so, while I certainly abhor the sight of my fellow human beings getting butchered like cattle, I find it to be slightly less depressing than watching humanity as a whole sink further into a cesspool of despair and self-preservation at any cost. So I opt to continue following the creature on its bloody rampage.

Then one day, the inevitable happens . . . though I had not thought about it up to that point (perhaps intentionally). I witness my own death at the hands – well, claws, to be precise – of the creature. It bursts in on my brother Mitch and me (I can tell it is us even though it is apparent that we are much older than we are now, in the year 1990) through a pointlessly boarded-up window. Like so many other victims who began to arm themselves even inside their own homes once word of the creature's attacks had spread, each of us has a high-powered rifle laying across our thighs as we sit on the living room sofa watching a movie, apparently trying (probably without much success) to distract ourselves from thoughts of impending doom. But as with all of the others, it makes no difference; the creature is simply too fast and strikes without warning. Even if we had been standing there pointing our guns directly at the window as the creature broke through, shooting it would be like trying to take down The Flash -- the DC Comics super-hero who moves so fast he can actually outrun a bullet. While the creature is not quite that fast, it can certainly react quickly enough to avoid being shot, even at close range.

As the creature moves toward Mitch and me, and I anticipate watching myself die, I have the same wild notion that I did when Randall pushed me off the mountain – that the moment my dream life ends, my real life will end as well. I am not certain yet whether this will prove to be true or not, because the first time around, my freefall had been halted inexplicably before I hit the ground. But finally, I receive confirmation that this fear is completely irrational, for the creature makes quick and easy work of my brother and me, and when the dream continues on, it is apparent that I have not died in real life.

The creature continually cuts down its victims with virtually no resistance. But one day, it swoops down into the city of Grayling, Michigan (I know this because I notice the "Welcome to Grayling" sign on the main route that passes through the city) and roots out a group of people that is hiding in the basement of their home. There are five people present, a man and a woman who appear to be in their late forties or early fifties, a young man and young woman in their early to mid-twenties, and a boy who looks to be in his mid- to late-teens. Presumably the older couple is a husband and wife, and the three young people are their children. As the creature moves toward them, the older man steps out front to protect his family, as any honorable man would. But his older son pulls him back and takes the lead instead. He is armed with a shotgun, and levels the weapon at the creature and fires. But as always, the creature sidesteps the blast and darts forward, knocking the shotgun from the young man's hands with one easy swipe.

I assume this will now end quickly, but to my surprise the young man screams with rage and hurls himself at the creature, pummeling its head and throat with a degree of speed and strength that is uncanny for a human being. The creature is stunned by this onslaught, and for a moment becomes defensive, rather than offensive, for most likely the first time since its arrival. It manages to *lash out with a hind leg and push the young man away, then paces back and forth, sizing up its opponent rather than instantly closing in for the kill, as it normally would. There is clearly hesitation and uncertainty on the part of the creature, which I find incredible considering that it is not up against an F-22 Raptor fighter jet or M1A2 tank, but rather a single, unarmed man.*

A few seconds later, the creature attacks, lashing out with its claws, but the man blocks the attempt and moves in close again, like a skilled boxer getting inside of his opponent's blows. He hammers away again at the creature's chest just below its armor plating, and I hear the distinct sound of a rib cracking. It roars with pain, and clamps its teeth down upon the man's shoulder. He screams in agony, and the tables quickly turn in favor of the creature. With a twist of its head, it tears the man's arm off at the shoulder and flings it aside. The young man's father and brother, finally breaking free from the grip of terror, rush in to assist, but they are easily hurled into the concrete foundation walls and crumple into broken, lifeless heaps.

My attention had been briefly focused on the father and brother, and when I look back at the young man, I would swear that for a few seconds, the exposed muscle and tissue of his shoulder was twitching and swelling . . . almost as though it was starting to grow back. But before the limb can regenerate, if in fact that is what is happening (with all that I have seen thus far, nothing would surprise me at this point), this gallant struggle at last comes to an end as the creature moves in to finish off the young man, then does the same to his mother and sister.

Though this encounter concludes just as I thought it would, I suspect there is something significant about the young man's tenacity and almost superhuman abilities. Perhaps it is the hope that there may be others like him that could pose a credible threat to the creature's reign of terror; whatever it is, I will remember the details of this scene and reflect back on them as the situation warrants.

Over time, the creature is able to take out some of the world's most influential leaders, including the President of the United States, despite him being surrounded by soldiers and high tech weaponry 24 hours a day. It sustains some fairly significant injuries during that attack, but they are not life threatening, and heal very quickly. Other world leaders then decide to withdraw from the public entirely, sealing themselves deep within their underground bunkers. The creature probably can never get to them, and they have enough supplies to last for years, but that will not matter. There are still decades remaining in the creature's lifespan, and the government officials' food and water supplies will certainly run out before then. When that happens, they will be forced to emerge from their hiding places and confront the enemy. Furthermore, by then there will be few people on the planet left to govern, and those that are still alive will have become like savages, caring only about survival and not about anything their former leaders may have to say.

Years continue to tick by. The creature must travel longer distances, and rely more heavily upon its instincts, cunning and acute senses, to locate victims. But even then, it never once wavers from its purpose. It is as relentless now as it was on the day it first arrived.

Then one day, the creature is flying over a silent, empty city, searching for signs of humans or human activity, as it would on any other day. It has been months since it last killed a human being, but again, it will never stop looking. It suddenly lets out a shriek that I have never heard from it before and seems to clutch its midsection, and I realize it is in extreme distress. The creature descends rapidly, almost in a freefall for a few seconds, and for a moment I think it is going to splatter onto the pavement below. But at the last second it manages to get its wings flapping again, just enough anyway, to avoid the splatter and reduce it to a rough, tumbling landing. In the process, both of its wings are crushed; its flying days are now over.

For the next few weeks, it drinks from dirty puddles and eats garbage, at least when it has a desire to feed, which is less and less often as its body shuts down and its appetite wanes. And incredibly, even now, though it stumbles through the city in a seemingly delirious state, barely able to stand, it searches for human prey. Right up to the bitter, lonely end.

17

*A*nd now, I fall in line with Zintak and his master race as they file out of the sanctuary within which they have shielded themselves from the effects of the events that have transpired over the better part of the last century. I step outside the building and am blinded by the intensity of the sun, but when my eyes adjust, I am momentarily surprised by what I see; not the loading docks, concrete walls and surrounding warehouses and industrial facilities that had been here when Zintak first acquired the property, but rather, the same residential area I had been when I saw the creature arrive in the past. I recognize several of the houses, including the one that had belonged to the man who was killed on the sidewalk, even though they now stand abandoned and dilapidated. There are rusting vehicles in the driveways, vegetation sprouting up through cracks in the pavement, pieces of trash tumbling down the street, and here and there a bleached human skeleton. Zintak's warehouse is the only structure left from his own time, but even that looks very different on the outside. The original exterior shell of the building is completely gone, and only the temporal shields are now visible.

And then I realize what I am seeing – the redevelopment of this area, from residential to commercial, had never taken place. Even Zintak's building itself did not exist, for those who had erected it, or more likely, their parents, had been killed long before construction began. That was the reason Zintak needed to build a second structural support system inside the complex, because without the exterior walls that the temporal shields had originally been attached to, the panels would have collapsed the moment the creature was sent back in time. It all made sense to me now.

There is another loud shout from the master race as they recognize the probable outcome of their efforts. They will need to send drones out to the distant corners of the planet to verify that it is empty, but if what they are seeing now is any indication, they have accomplished their goal of purging the "evil" from the world, leaving behind only a few seeds of "good" with which to regenerate society.

⚔   ⚔   ⚔

I pinball back through time once again, and the first thing I see, which gives me a great feeling of relief, is myself, alive and well. I know immediately that all is not lost, at least not yet. I know there is more to the story, an alternative route through time to the one that I had just witnessed. Can the world yet be saved? Does the creature have some weakness that can be exploited? Is there some weapon or strategy that can be employed to defeat it? I cannot wait to find out.

I observe myself sitting in what appears to be a branch of the Chicago Public Library, reading birth announcements on the computer. At first I wonder if I am just killing time, because I cannot imagine why birth announcements would have any relevance to my plight. But soon it becomes clear that I am searching for something in particular, so I pay closer attention to the names that come up on the screen. I do not find what I am looking for, and so I check again the next day, and the next, and so on. Finally, I seem to fixate on the announcement of the birth of one Jason Patrick Devine, born to James and Katrina Devine of Grayling, Michigan on Saturday, November 16, 1991. I do not recognize the name Devine, but the town of Grayling I certainly do. That is where I had seen the creature battling the young man who had strength and speed that far surpassed that of the average person, though ultimately it was not enough to save his own life or that of his family. I print a copy *of the announcement, place it in my pocket, and exit the library.*

The next scene shocks and disturbs me like none I have witnessed so far. I become a baby snatcher! I break into someone's house in broad daylight while mother and baby are both asleep, steal the baby from his crib, and escape before anyone knows I was there. Once back in my vehicle, with the baby strapped into an infant seat in the back, I drive through a town that seems somewhat familiar to me. And in fact, it is familiar, for as I pass the city limits, I see a sign that says, "Thanks for Visiting Grayling". Now the pieces are falling into place. Could that courageous young man and this newborn baby be one and the same person – this Jason Patrick Devine? If so, what could I have to gain from kidnapping him, if in the grand scheme of things he is to be little more than a minor annoyance to the creature? Apparently that is just the point . . . by kidnapping him, the grand scheme of things is about to change.

With assistance from my brother Mitch, I raise the boy as if he is my own – as Jason Patrick Anderson. We tell him that I am his natural father, and that my wife, his mother, had abandoned us shortly after his birth. As the years go by, he demonstrates exceptional physical and mental abilities, not so much that he appears to be superhuman in any way, but he is certainly without peer in anything he chooses to do. Furthermore, as his facial features become more recognizable, there can no longer be any doubt that he is indeed the same person who will become the courageous young man I had seen fighting the creature. I come to believe that this boy has been sent by God Himself to save humanity from the fate that Zintak would have for it, and in reaching this conclusion, my own role in this incredible saga becomes clear. If I do not take the boy away from his parents, we will all perish just as it has been revealed to me. On the other hand, if I kidnap young Jason and reveal to him his true purpose, then teach him to strengthen and hone his abilities such that they are many times greater than they otherwise would have been, perhaps it will be

117

enough to give him the upper hand when he engages the creature at some point in the future.

When Mitch and I decide that the boy is old enough, I tell him the truth about who he is. He is reluctant to accept this at first, but eventually he does. At that moment, our lives take on a singular focus – to prepare Jason for the most important battle ever to be fought by mankind, against an enemy that at this point in time has not even been conceived of. We do this by pitting Jason against the strongest, fastest, deadliest animals on earth, and though none of them compare to the genetically-enhanced creature, they provide the worthy opposition that Jason needs to strengthen the skills, and develop new ones, that may just give him a chance when that fateful day finally arrives.

I witness a few of these battles during the dream, but I have opted not to include a detailed description of them in this record for two reasons. One, they are all very graphic and have the same outcome – Jason's defeat of his opponent. And two, assuming I actually proceed according to what I have witnessed so far, which is to kidnap Jason as a boy and eventually begin to train him once he has been told the truth about who he is, then undoubtedly I will share this record with him at that point in time. I believe that an important part of his growth and development will be to learn how to fight on his own, without any advance knowledge or guidance. Thus to reveal the details of his training missions herein would be self-defeating. Also, while it may or may not be relevant, there are discussions I have with Mitch and Jason during the dream in which references are made to training missions that I have not witnessed. I have some theories as to why that might be, but the point is that I cannot record what has not been revealed to me.

At last, the final scene is revealed (though as I would soon find out, it was not intended to be the final scene). I am standing in the same spot as before, on a sidewalk next to a residential street in a lovely town nestled at the foot of a mountain -- Zintak's home-

town, though I do not know its name. The creature arrives just as I had seen it before. It attacks the same poor soul as it had on the original timeline before darting off toward the man's house. But this time, something different happens; a vehicle approaches at a high rate of speed and screeches to a halt alongside where the man is lying on the sidewalk. Two men get out of the vehicle and run over to check on the victim. It is Jason and me! His appearance is virtually the same as it was the first time I saw him in this dream, when he was killed by the creature along with the rest of his family in the basement of their home. That would put him somewhere around his mid- to late-twenties, which in turn puts me somewhere in my mid- to late-forties.

As Jason is about a hundred times faster than I am, he gets to the man first. He kneels down next to the man for a moment, stands up again, then whirls around and looks down as he hears the man say, "You . . ." But the words that follow are inaudible, drowned out by a much louder voice thundering down from somewhere above me. The words are, "Mr. Anderson? Mr. Anderson, can you hear me?"

And then the dream world fades away, and I find myself back in the real one.

⚔   ⚔   ⚔

"Mr. Anderson? Mr. Anderson, can you hear me?"

At first, the words seemed like part of Mal's dream, and if it were just words alone, he may well have been able to remain in his dream world long enough to witness the outcome of Jason's epic battle with the creature. But one of the two police officers who were standing over his bed was also shaking him, and it was a bit too vigorous for Mal to avoid being roused from sleep. As recognition of his surroundings set in, Mal remembered the words Randall had spoken during the dream --- " they will come to get you " – and he now understood what they had meant, even though he was not sure why they were here.

"What . . . what are you doing here, officer?" Mal asked. "Is everything okay?"

"We were going to ask you the same thing," the older of the two policemen answered. "I'm Officer Douglas, this is Officer Willamson. Your brother Mitchell has been calling us for the last twenty-four hours, asking us to come and check on you. He said you were supposed to call him on Wednesday, and when he didn't hear from you, he started calling you on Thursday morning and has been trying ever since. By Thursday evening he was so worried that he called us and asked to have someone sent over to check on you. But it wasn't exactly at the top of our priority list, and we couldn't get over here until tonight. So are you all right then?"

"I think so . . . . but wait! Are you saying it's *Friday night*?"

"Well . . . yes," Officer Douglas responded. "Why, what day did you think it was?"

"I got home from a conference on Tuesday night and went to bed. I thought this would have been Wednesday morning."

"And you've been asleep ever since then?" Williamson asked.

The two police officers glanced at each other with what they thought were knowing looks.

"Oh, no, it's not what you think. I had a couple of drinks with . . . an associate after the conference ended, but I wasn't intoxicated. I wasn't feeling like myself, so I actually came home a bit earlier than I anticipated, and went to bed. I guess I must have . . . come down with something, a nasty flu bug, maybe." That last part was a lie, but Mal was not about to tell them he had just had a three-day dream about a futuristic evil genius, a time-travelling genetically engineered monster, and a divinely appointed superhero that could save the world.

"Uh huh, whatever you say, Mr. Anderson," said Douglas. "As long as you're okay. Do you need anything before we go? Maybe call your brother for you?"

"No, no, it's okay, I'll call him right now. Thank you for your concern, officers. Have a good evening."

Mal put on his robe and followed them out to the living room. "Hey, what about my front door!" he said, seeing the splintered door frame and broken handle.

But Douglas and Williamson had already left the house and were getting into their vehicle. It was not important right now, anyway. Mal had to call Mitch to let him know he was okay, and then get busy writing, committing to paper every last detail of the dream that he could remember. It would be a sort of history book in reverse, and would set forth the two potential routes through time that had been revealed to him; one -- the original -- that would come to pass if he simply forgot about what he had seen, and the other – the alternate -- that would transpire if he agreed to play the part that he had apparently been chosen for.

Though Officers Douglas and Williamson had awakened Mal before he had seen the alternate timeline's ending, the fact that he *had* seen all of the original timeline and knew precisely how that one ended meant that there was really no choice to speak of. In order to save humanity, he would have to kidnap Jason Devine and raise him as though he were his own son, then one day reveal to him his true identity and purpose in life.

PART TWO

PREPARATIONS

Original Timeline – November 1991

J ason Patrick Devine was born in Grayling, Michigan on Saturday, November 21, fifteen months after Mal Anderson's lucid dream. He weighed seven pounds, three ounces, was twenty-one inches long, had a tuft of dark brown hair and a scrunched-up newborn face, and he cried when the doctor spanked him. All things considered, a very unspectacular birth, not at all indicative of the kind of life he was destined to lead.

At least, Mal *assumed* that Jason's birth had been unspectacular, judging by the fact that there had not been a throng of doctors rushing excitedly toward the delivery room – which would certainly have been the case if Jason had come out of his mother's womb throwing kicks and punches, or doing cartwheels across the floor. This was good, because it meant that Jason had not yet drawn any undue attention to himself, which would make Mal's task a lot easier.

The first thing Mal had done after he recorded all of the things he had seen in his vision was to go out and buy a large stack of books and videos on parenting. He was single and had no dependents, nor did he have any nieces or nephews; his only sibling, his brother Mitch, was also a bachelor. Thus, Mal had very little experience with young children, and none whatsoever with newborn babies, so he had spent the last year learning all he could about parenthood.

He had also recently begun telling his friends and neighbors in the Chicago suburb of Winnetka, where he lived, that he had accepted a position in Savannah, Georgia, and would soon be moving there. He said he would be living in a hotel for the first few weeks while he found a place to live, and would send them his new address once he got settled. In fact, Mal had purchased a home outside of Sioux Falls, South Dakota, where he would take Jason immediately after they left Grayling. He would never return to his home in Winnetka, having already arranged a private sale through his attorney, and would sever all ties with past associates and acquaintances. In short, he had taken steps to make it very unlikely that anyone would ever make a connection between a baby abduction in Grayling, Michigan, and a man who lived in Winnetka, Illinois and who had purportedly moved to Savannah, Georgia, but in fact had secretly relocated to Sioux Falls, South Dakota.

The property Mal had purchased consisted of a modest, three-bedroom ranch home surrounded by about 600 acres of land, located on a dirt road about 10 miles northwest of Sioux Falls. Aside from the barns and stables on the property, there was only one house visible for as far as the eye could see . . . which was exactly what Mal was looking for. Not only would they have lots of space and privacy, but they could also see for miles in all directions and would know if anyone was approaching, at least during the daytime. It was critical that no outsiders ever observe Jason performing superhuman feats such as lifting vehicles over his head, or running 80 mile-an-hour wind sprints across the open plains. This would surely bring the media, and then government, swarming in like locusts. Mal realized that this was a somewhat irrational fear, for he had not seen this in his vision, which was a pretty good indication that they would not have to deal with outside interference or similar problems throughout Jason's training. Still, it made sense to take every precaution possible to keep Jason a secret until the time came to reveal him to the world.

The birth announcement Mal had seen in his vision revealed the exact time, date and location of Jason's birth, and that was how he knew to be at the hospital on this particular day. He had no intention of kidnapping Jason from the hospital, but he wanted to be here just to see if everything went alright. After that, he would wait several days, perhaps even weeks, until an opportune moment presented itself, at which time he would remove Jason from the Devine home. He had learned that Jason's parents, James and Katrina Devine, both worked full-time and it was a safe bet that James would return to work within a few days after the child's birth. Katrina would no doubt remain at home with Jason for several weeks or months before returning to work.

Mal's plan was to take Jason during the day, while James was at work, so he would only have Katrina to deal with. He knew from the vision that he could take Jason stealthily, at a time when both he and his mother were napping, but if things did not work out the way he had foreseen and Katrina was awake when he entered the home, he would have no choice but to use a stun gun to temporarily disable her. By the time she revived, he would have already met Mitch at the rendezvous point 20 miles away, where they would transfer Jason to Mitch's rented vehicle and put a different license plate on Mal's car. Mitch would drive Jason to Sioux Falls while Mal drove alone. If anyone reported seeing Mal leaving the Devine's neighborhood and had gotten a look at his license plate, the police would be searching for the same vehicle but with a different license plate number and with no baby inside.

With Jason's birth having been uneventful, Mal left the hospital and drove back to the small cabin he had rented a few miles outside of town. Grayling was a popular recreation area among hunters, boaters, fishermen and nature lovers, due to its proximity to Lake Margrethe, the Au Sable River, and thousands of acres of forested hills. Mal had paid for his cabin rental with cash and had made the reservation using a phony ID – a top-of-the-line knockoff that most people could not afford but which was not an issue for Mal given his vast pool of resources.

As Mal pulled up the driveway to the modest, three-room cabin, it occurred to him that he was perhaps the only person in the world who could accomplish the task that lay ahead. After all, it would take someone who not only had the means to finance the training of a superhero, but also the psychic ability to have foreseen the shocking events that would unfold over the next century. Mal knew of maybe five or six other legitimate psychics in the world who had ability comparable to his own, but none of them had the financial means to simply drop what they were doing and spend the next 20 or 30 years planning training exercises at a variety of exotic locations and harsh climates around the globe.

Inside the cabin, he popped open a beer and sat down at the tiny kitchen table to review his notes and jot down a few new ideas. He would be doing a lot of that the next few days as he waited for the right time to make his move. The nervous tension he felt had been building gradually for several weeks, and would continue to do so until he had Jason safely hidden away at their new home in Sioux Falls. Although his vision had included the kidnapping scene itself, Mal had no illusions that that was a guarantee of success. The events he saw in his vision would only come to pass if he was both careful and fortunate, not only in the planning and executing of the kidnapping but of every training exercise throughout Jason's life.

What also bothered Mal was the growing sense of dread he felt at having to rip Jason away from his family. James and Katrina Devine would undoubtedly be devastated, and would probably fear that the man who stole their son would mutilate and murder the boy, as is so often the case when a child is abducted by a stranger. The only reassurance he could give them was to leave a note with a vague explanation of why he had taken the child, a note he had written months ago. He had not seen himself leaving the note in his dream, but he had decided to do it as a means of easing his conscience. It read:

> Dear Mr. & Mrs. Devine,
>
> This note is from the person who kidnapped your son. I want to assure you that I have not harmed him in any way, nor will I ever do so in the future. I will raise the boy as if he were my own, and will do everything I can to make sure he is protected and cared for. I am very sorry for taking Jason from you and causing you so much pain, but I had no alternative. Jason is an extraordinary human being who is destined to do extraordinary things, but this can only happen if he is raised under my tutelage. I wish I could explain to you how I know these things, and why I am the only person who can help Jason realize his full potential. But if I told you, you would never believe me, and I would be divulging information that might jeopardize the mission that Jason was born to fulfill. This mission, as I hope you will eventually learn, is one that simply cannot be allowed to fail. And if we are successful, I promise that Jason will return to you one day in perfect health, and looking forward to sharing many happy years with his parents. Until then, may God bless you and keep you from harm.

It had been decided that after they arrived in Sioux Falls, Mitch would then return home to Palo Alto, and remain there for several years until Jason was old enough to begin his training. After that, he would retire from his position in Palo Alto and would join Mal in South Dakota in order to provide logistical assistance or any other type of support that might be deemed necessary. Each of them hoped that focusing on their respective responsibilities would help them push thoughts of a tormented James and Katrina Devine out of their minds. If not, that would be a heavy burden for them to carry around for the next 20 or 30 years.

The Devine family lived on the edge of a housing development on the outskirts of Grayling, about a mile from the town's main highway. Outside the city limits, there were a number of lightly-traveled dirt roads that snaked off into the hills, routes used mainly by hunters and snowmobilers. Mal found such a road not far from the Devine home, and he parked his car just past the first bend he came to, so that it would not be visible from the main road. From here, he estimated the distance to the Devine home to be about ½ mile, and he could get there by walking through the woods and approaching the house from the back yard. Barring some unforeseen event, he should be able to avoid contact with people along the way.

After about ten minutes of hiking through the woods, he reached the crest of a hill and could see slivers of houses through the trees at the bottom of the slope. He took out his binoculars and scanned the area below him to see how close his path had taken him to the Devine home. He could only clearly make out the features of the house directly below him, and he could tell that it was not the one he wanted. He went further down the hill until he had a better view of the houses on either side of the one before him, but still no luck. Creeping forward even further, while trying to keep a large oak tree between himself and the windows of the house ahead of him, he reached the edge of the treeline. He scanned the row of houses to his right with the binoculars, did not find what he was looking for, then turned to his left and did the same – and bingo! The Devine residence was six houses down from his current location.

He retreated back into the woods about fifty yards and circled around behind the tidy gray bungalow. With the binoculars, he peered into the windows of the Devine house and those on either side to make sure no one happened to be watching. No one was. He sprinted across the back yard, trying to stay as low as possible, and crept up below what he guessed was one of the bedroom windows. It was about 12:30 p.m., and he hoped that both mother and child would be napping. He glanced quickly into the room, thought he saw movement, and ducked under the window again. After a few seconds without any screams or other sounds, he peeked into the room again and saw that the movement was from a spinning mobile that hung from the ceiling, and that Jason lay sleeping in his crib beneath it.

Mal moved to the other window along the back of the house, peered inside, and was tremendously relieved to see that Katrina was asleep in her own bed, a baby monitor lying on the pillow next to her. She was a beautiful woman, average in height, with exquisite features, long blonde hair, and a figure that belied the fact that she had just given birth a week before. It made Mal's heart ache, for he realized that he would probably not be able to date a woman again until he was a middle-aged man; there would be no time for such pursuits until Jason's training was complete. And that would almost certainly mean that he would never have children of his own.

Moving to the corner of the house, Mal glanced around it to make sure there was no one coming down the street that might see him going inside. The street and houses on the opposite side were quiet, so he moved quickly to the side door, found it unlocked, and stepped inside. He was in the kitchen, with the living room being located directly in front of him and a hallway to his right that led to the bedrooms in the back. His heart hammered as he tiptoed down the hallway and stepped directly into Katrina's view momentarily before turning into Jason's room. He leaned out into the hallway and studied Katrina to make sure he had not awakened her. She had not moved since he first saw her through the window, so he closed the door to Jason's room as quietly as he could and approached the baby's crib. He turned the volume on the baby monitor down to its lowest level, in case the child made any soft sounds of protest at being awakened from his nap. Of course, if he started crying loudly, neither the low volume on the monitor nor the closed bedroom door would prevent Katrina from hearing, but anything less than that would hopefully not disturb her.

Although he had never been arrested and therefore had no fingerprints on record, Mal had slipped on a pair of latex gloves before entering the house to make sure he left as little evidence as possible. He removed a microcassette recorder from his pocket, which he had used to tape his own rhythmic breathing as he slept. He hit the play button and adjusted the volume to a level he judged to be comparable to Jason's breathing, and placed the recorder next to the baby monitor. As he had hoped, Jason was sleeping on his back, and Mal gently slid his right hand under the baby's back and his left hand under the base of Jason's skull. He lifted the baby out of the crib and laid him against his chest as delicately as possible. He breathed yet another sigh of relief as the only sound the boy made was a slight whimper, after which he returned to a peaceful sleep.

Holding Jason with his left arm, Mal reached down and turned the volume of the baby monitor back up to its normal level, then walked back to the door and opened it silently. Katrina was still sleeping, so he proceeded down the hallway and to the kitchen, where he removed the letter from his pocket and placed it on the table. Out on the street, he could see the mailman was just pulling up to make his daily delivery, so he waited a few seconds until things were quiet again. Then he opened the side door, walked to the corner of the house, and headed back toward the woods. He walked slowly and softly across the yard, even though he knew it increased his chances of being seen, because he felt it was less risky than if he moved too quickly and jostled the child awake. The baby would then start crying, which would undoubtedly draw someone's attention and have the police swarming all over him before he could possibly make it back to his car.

Mal reached the woods without incident, and continued to move slowly until he figured he was out of earshot, which was maybe an eighth of a mile. He could not keep this pace all the way back to the car, because it would probably take him an hour to get there, and by then Katrina would have certainly discovered her missing child and called the police. So he paused momentarily and listened to the woods to make sure no one was following or out for a leisurely stroll. Hearing nothing, he broke into a run and continued on toward the car.

As Mal had expected, the sudden movement awakened the child, and after a moment's hesitation, he began to cry. Mal had no choice but to ignore Jason, and he kept going at a pace he never thought he could have maintained considering he was running with a baby in his arms. Twice he thought he heard the sound of sirens in the distance, but he knew it was probably just his imagination.

Several minutes later, his chest heaving and his heart about to explode, he reached the dirt road and spotted his car about a hundred yards to his left. He forced himself to run the rest of the way, knowing every second could be precious. Jason was still screaming and crying as Mal strapped him into the baby seat in back. Mal turned the car around and drove back onto the main road, wishing he could jam on the accelerator and get out of town quickly, but knowing that would be foolish. It would be a shame to have successfully taken Jason from his home, only to be thwarted by a traffic violation.

As he reached the southern edge of town near the entrance ramp to southbound U.S. 23, Mal passed the Grayling Police Station. There were no officers frantically running for their cars, nor any other unusual activity. Mal checked his watch, and saw that it had been about 30 minutes since he had left the Devine house.

Katrina had apparently not yet discovered that her son was missing, or perhaps was just now calling 911. In any event, by the time the police were able to respond, he would be miles away and the baby would be safely in Mitch's hands. The last thing he saw before merging onto U.S. 23 was the sign that said, "Thanks for Visiting Grayling".

Original Timeline – November 2001

Jason's 10th birthday party was a bittersweet occasion for the boy. On the one hand, it was the first major chronological milestone in his life, but on the other, it was a relatively small gathering with just a few friends and couple of the neighbors who had known Jason all his life in attendance. Jason made friends easily at school, but he had to leave them behind quickly because of his accelerated development – not just intellectually but physically as well. At the age of 10, he was already a sophomore in high school, and he figured to graduate in less than a year. He was five feet nine inches tall, weighed 170 pounds, and was a star athlete on the varsity football, basketball and baseball teams. Yet he was still a 10-year old at heart, and he would have loved to spend his afternoons on the playground like other kids his age, instead of running wind sprints, lifting weights and practicing free throws. It was as if he had missed his entire childhood.

Still, Mal tried his best to make Jason's birthday a happy one, especially considering that tomorrow, he would tell Jason the truth about his past, as well as his future. Until now, Jason had used the surname Anderson, and had always believed that Mal was his father. But it was time that Jason Anderson became Jason Devine – the one person who could save the human race from certain destruction.

⅄   ⅄   ⅄

The next morning, Mal and Jason attended the 10:00 service at Four Corners Church, as they did every week. It was a windy, rainy morning, a good day for staying inside and reading a book or playing a game of chess, and Jason expected that they would be turning left out of the church parking lot and heading toward home. Instead, however, Mal turned right and drove toward the outskirts of town.

"Where are we going, Dad?" Jason asked.

Mal looked at him and smiled faintly. "I thought we'd take a little drive. There's something I need to talk to you about."

Jason's expression revealed his puzzlement. "Okay, but why can't we talk at home? You don't usually like to be driving around in this kind of weather."

"No reason," Mal lied. "I just wanted to go for a drive. A little wind and rain never hurt anyone." In truth, this was going to be a very difficult conversation, and he had to be prepared to take dramatic action, if necessary, to convince Jason that his story was true.

Jason studied Mal for a moment, and then shrugged. "Okay, go ahead. What's on your mind?"

"Let's drive out to Tanner's Point while I collect my thoughts. We'll talk there."

"Uh, Dad, Tanner's Point is where high school kids go to make out. I can't say I have any desire to be seen there with my *dad*."

Mal chuckled. "I know, but I don't think there will be anyone else there at 11:00 on a Sunday morning, do you?"

Jason shrugged. "I guess not."

They drove for about ten minutes until they reached their destination, which was at the top of a hill that overlooked Sioux Falls. As Mal had hoped and expected, the place was deserted.

Mal turned off the ignition, took a deep breath, and turned to face Jason. "You trust me, don't you son?" he began. "I've never lied to you, have I?"

"Of course I trust you, Dad. And no, as far as I know you've never lied to me."

"Then you've got to trust that what I'm about to tell you is the truth, no matter how ridiculous it sounds. This is not a joke, this is very, very serious. And I am not losing my mind, although it may very well sound that way. Okay?"

Jason shifted uneasily in his seat, slightly unnerved by his father's grave demeanor. "Uh, sure Dad. I'll believe you."

Mal waited for nearly a minute, trying to overcome his nervousness, then drew in a deep breath and began. "I am not your father, Jason. I have never been married, and your mother did not abandon us after you were born. Your birth name was Jason Patrick Devine, son of James and Katrina Devine of Grayling, Michigan. I . . . I stole you from them when you were only a week old."

Mal glanced at Jason to see his reaction to what had heard thus far. The boy simply stared at him with a blank expression, perhaps already entertaining thoughts that his father *was*, in fact, losing his mind.

"It's true," Mal continued. "With Uncle Mitch's help, I took you right out of your crib while your mother was sleeping in the next room. Then I brought you back here to raise you as if you were my own child, and the story has always been that my wife decided she wanted nothing to do with motherhood and just up and left one day after you were born. Now, before you jump to the conclusion that I'm one of those baby snatchers that you hear about in the news, let me tell you why I did what I did." He paused. "And this is where the story gets a little hard to believe.

"You know all about the visions, the premonitions that I occasionally have, things that are about to happen around the world, right? Well, eleven years ago, I had the mother of all premonitions. It came to me in a dream one night, and was so lengthy and detailed that it kept me asleep for almost three days. It would have been even longer than that, except that Uncle Mitch got worried when he couldn't reach me by phone and called the police to come check on me. I was living in the Chicago area at the time, and with him living in Palo Alto, we didn't see each other that often, not nearly as much as we do now. So we would usually talk on the phone almost every day. When he couldn't reach me, he had good reason to think that something was wrong. The police broke through the front door and woke me up before the dream ended, or it may have taken several hours longer.

"Anyway, what I saw in the dream was the most terrifying thing that any human being has ever witnessed. Death and destruction on an unprecedented level. And the only person on earth who has the power to stop it . . . is *you*."

Mal paused to catch his breath and to once again try to read Jason's thoughts. The boy was looking at him with an expression of deep concern, now almost certainly wondering about his father's sanity.

"I know this sounds nuts already," Mal continued, aware of how unsteady he sounded, "but let me tell you about the dream from the beginning. About 78 years from now, there will be a child born by the name of Brian Zintak who will grow up to be as evil a man as this planet has ever seen, right up there with Stalin, Hitler, bin Laden, and a handful of others like them. He will also be a genius, and his unparalleled mastery of the physical sciences will enable him to do something that most scientists thought could never be done – build a time machine. Yes, a time machine, just like in the movies and science fiction novels. A machine that can send anyone, or any*thing*, back in time. And just like in the movies, such a device could be used to do incredibly bad things if it was in the hands of the wrong person. Brian Zintak is, or will be, such a person."

The doubt on Jason's face was now clearly visible, and his silent contemplation finally ended. "A time machine? Come on, Dad, I think you've been watching too many of those movies you were just talking about!" He reached over and touched Mal's forehead with the back of his hand. "Seriously, are you feeling all right?"

Mal slapped Jason's hand away impatiently. "I'm feeling just fine! Now you said you were going to trust me on this, didn't you? Then let me finish!"

Jason rolled his eyes and said, "Fine, I'll play along. What is Zintak planning to do with the time machine? Go back in time and wipe out his enemies, people who have stood in his way of becoming whatever he wants to be?"

"Actually, you're close, but Zintak can't personally use the machine, because there are limits to what it can do. He was *thinking* about going back himself, until he changed his plan after . . . well, never mind that now, you can read all the details in the journal I wrote right after the dream ended. The important thing is that the machine can only send someone or something *back* in time. It can't return that someone or something to their present time. So if Zintak were to travel back in time and eliminate any obstacles to his future success, he could never return to his own time to reap the benefits."

"So what good is a time machine if he can't use it to his advantage? And what does this have to do with me?"

"I'll get to your role in this shortly. As for how the machine could be used if he himself can't be the one to time travel, like I said, it doesn't have to be a person, it can be . . . something else."

"You mean like a bomb or something? That's what *I* would do, send a bomb back in time and have it wipe out my rivals." Jason paused for a moment as a thought occurred to him. "Why would Zintak need such an elaborate plan, though? Involving time travel, that is? Why not just hire a hitman to go kill your rivals in your own time? What advantage would he have by killing his rivals in the past?"

"Because his 'rivals', as you referred to them, are not merely a handful of people, as I alluded to earlier. What he actually wants to do . . . is to wipe out the *entire human race.*"

Jason glanced at Mal with raised eyebrows. "The entire human race? There is no bomb that can kill everyone on the planet, though I guess in a hundred years there very well could be. And if that's what he's planning, then I guess it would make sense to send the bomb into the past rather than detonate it in his own time. But then again, wouldn't he have to somehow shield his own ancestors from destruction? Wouldn't he be committing suicide if they were to die? A 'retroactive abortion', like they called it in *The Terminator?*"

"Obviously Zintak would have thought of that. And he solved that problem by developing a material, a temporal shield, he calls it, that protects him from changes made to the past. He has the facility where his laboratory is located completely covered with these temporal shields, and as long as he remains inside, no matter how the timeline is altered, he will not be affected. Furthermore, from his perspective, there will be no passage of time whatsoever. A microsecond after he sends his weapon into the past, assuming it works as intended, the earth's population will drop from seven billion to just 300. That's the number of people Zintak has selected to be his followers, his 'master race,' as I call it. Most of these people will be recruited voluntarily, a handful forcibly, but they will all be people with extraordinary physical, intellectual, and artistic talents. These chosen few will form the foundation of his master race. Anyway, after Zintak flips the switch, the 300 simply step outside the shielded complex and experience the changed world, whatever that may look like."

Jason considered this for a moment. "So you're saying that Zintak really *does* create the mother of all weapons of mass destruction? And he uses it to essentially replicate the Great Flood and wipe the planet clean?"

"To wipe the planet clean of *people*, not plants or animals," Mal said. "That's why he can't use a futuristic nuke or some other such weapon, because it would destroy *everything*, not just the people. Among Zintak's recruits are a team of biologists and genetic engineers, led by a man named Millenkamp, who is nearly as brilliant as Zintak. These people will develop a way to combine, and enhance, the DNA of several of the world's most ferocious animals into a single life form, the prototype of a new species, one that has no fear of human beings but rather an overriding instinct to kill them. Imagine a creature that is faster than a cheetah on land, a dolphin in the water, or a falcon in the sky. Imagine a creature that has such an advanced metabolism that it only requires one to two hours of sleep a day, can absorb nutrients from virtually any organic substance, including dirt, and never defecates or urinates because its body converts every single calorie that it consumes into energy. Imagine a creature that is like a ground mole on steroids, with powerful claws and legs that enable it to burrow deep into the ground and remain there indefinitely. Imagine a creature that has the night vision of an owl, the hearing of a bat, the smell of a bear, and is stronger than an elephant. Imagine a creature that is so cunning that it will utilize almost human-like strategies to ensure its own survival long enough to complete its mission. That pretty much sums up what we're up against."

Jason rubbed his chin thoughtfully, still not buying his father's story but nevertheless intrigued. "You said a minute ago that when the creature is sent back in time, the population would drop from seven billion to 300. Six billion is about where we are now, and the fact that you're telling me that *I'm* somehow the key to stopping it, which by the way, you have yet to explain, means that the creature will arrive sometime in the not too distant future. The way you've described this thing, I can see how it would be a handful to kill, but against 21st century technology, satellites, infrared, and so on, I don't see how it would stand a chance. So that begs the question, why wouldn't Zintak send it much further into the past, say a thousand years, when there would not only be a lot less people, but they would have little more than sticks and stones to use for weapons?"

"First of all, don't underestimate this thing. Its strength, speed and cunning will be like nothing the world has ever encountered before. Even so, your point about it being sent even further back in time is well taken. The answer is that Zintak will send the creature as far back as he can, given the amount of fuel that is available to him. The time machine is powered by some type of radioactive fuel that is very expensive and difficult to acquire. Once the machine is activated, it will continue to send the creature backward along the timeline until it runs out of fuel."

"Ok, so that explains why the creature will appear sometime in our future rather than in our distant past. And let's assume for the sake of argument that it can elude modern weapons and technology indefinitely. How is one animal supposed to kill billions of people? That would take centuries, wouldn't it?"

"Not quite. Zintak's computer simulations project it at around ninety years, give or take a few years."

"Even so, ninety years is a long time. The thing will live that long?"

"Of course, that's no problem. They used the DNA from a tortoise to make the creature. They can live to be two hundred years old or more."

"But if it lives *that* long, then it most likely will still be alive when Zintak and his people step out of their shielded complex. That means it will hunt them, too, unless they have a way of controlling it, or at least killing it very easily."

"Again, Zintak thought of that. They placed a virus inside of a capsule, and implanted it in the creature's body. The capsule was designed to dissolve right around that same ninety-year time frame. Once that happens, the creature will die within a matter of days, or at most, weeks. So unless Zintak's calculations are off or something goes wrong, the creature should be dead by the time they exit their complex."

Jason paused for a moment, then shook his head. "Not to beat a dead horse here, but regardless of what Zintak's computer simulations may have demonstrated, I just can't imagine a single creature, no matter how fast, how strong, how cunning, being able to *kill seven billion people* in just ninety years. And that number increases every minute of every day! Doesn't that seem totally impossible to you?"

"Yes, it would seem so," Mal agreed. "But the creature will have an ally, one that Zintak is not only well aware of but that he is counting on heavily to assist in his quest for global genocide. And that ally is humanity itself. We are already destroying our planet at an alarming rate. The polar ice caps are melting, lakes and rivers are drying up, fertile land is morphing into desert, plant and animal species are dying out every minute of every day, devastating storms are increasing in number, and so on. There are those who still deny that these changes will have a significant long term effect on the planet, but if they could see into the future as I have, the debate would be over in about two milliseconds. Even by itself, global warming will eventually cause our population to slow to a crawl, and then to begin to drop. And when you add the creature into the mix, you'll have what I call the 'social disruption' factor. Ever so gradually, the creature's reign of terror will disrupt the basic institutions and functions of society, including government, commerce, education, communications, and even reproduction. People will become too fearful to think about having children, and that will only accelerate our own demise. All of these variables were factored into Zintak's calculations."

There was silence for a moment as they both contemplated the grim future Mal had described.

"So what triggered Zintak's narcissism?" Jason eventually asked. "Was he born that way?"

"Well, that's complicated. I go into great detail in my jourrnal on how the monsters, both the human and animal variety, came to be, but basically it was due to the influence of his abusive father, followed by a bizarre series of events that included witnessing his father murder his mother, then Zintak exacting revenge on his father by killing him, and ultimately a misunderstood discovery he made years later that destroyed the wonderful memories he had of his mother. He ends up believing that humanity is evil and deserving of annihilation, and that he himself should be the patriarch of a new master race."

Again there was silence before Jason spoke again. "It's certainly a fascinating story, but let's cut to the chase. If what you're saying is true, then it sounds like Zintak has anticipated all of the potential pitfalls with his plan and taken steps to prevent them. So back to my unanswered question: what's all this got to do with me?"

"Because, Jason, you are the one person on earth who has the ability to defeat the creature. You have extraordinary talents that you are entirely unaware of, but which I know without a doubt that you possess because I saw you using them in my vision. Many people have already recognized what a gifted child you are, but you don't realize that you have just scratched the surface of your potential. Without proper guidance and training, however, you would have soon reached the limits of your ability, which would never have been enough for you to defeat the creature. In fact, I saw it kill you and your family in the dream. You put up an incredible fight, but in the end, you were just another casualty. That's why I had to abduct you when you were just a baby, so that I could one day tell you about your destiny and begin training you myself. If I had tried to explain all of this to your parents, they would have thought I was nuts and ignored me completely, or called the police and had me hauled away. You would have never known the truth about who and what you are, and the human race would have been slaughtered like cattle when the reaper is sent back in time."

"The 'reaper'?"

"That's what Zintak calls the creature, as that is its purpose, to cut down humanity like a farmer harvesting wheat."

Jason nodded and focused his attention on the town below them. A long period of silence ensued.

"So what do you think?" Mal finally asked.

Jason turned to face his father, the compassion and concern showing in his huge, solemn eyes. "It's pretty clear that you believe what you're telling me, Dad. But I just can't get past the fact that this premonition is like nothing you've ever experienced before. I never questioned the authenticity of the visions you've had that were related to world events in the *near* future, since they always proved to be true. And I certainly didn't doubt your psychic ability when you helped the police find that little girl who had been kidnapped and was being held for ransom. But now all of a sudden you're predicting the end of the world, in effect, and you're telling me I'm Superman and that I'm the only one who can save the human race! I mean, think about it from my perspective. Would you believe all of this if you were me?"

"I never said you were Superman. Superman is invulnerable, you're not. And yes, I think I would believe the man who raised me, the one I've believed to be my father up until now."

"The same man who just told me he's been lying to me all my life about where I really came from," Jason countered.

Mal involuntarily winced from the pain caused by Jason's remark. "Touché," he said.

Jason immediately regretted his words. "I'm sorry, Dad. You've been a great father to me, and I love you. But this story of yours . . . it's just too outrageous. I was inclined to believe you when you told me about Zintak's plan, the time machine, the creature, all of that. In fifty or a hundred years from now, it wouldn't surprise me at all if time travel were invented. And the things they're doing now with cloning make it entirely possible, maybe even probable, that a creature like this 'reaper' you described will be created at some time in the future. But the thing I'm having a hard time with is the part about me being some kind of savior. That has nothing to do with science, unlike the time machine and the genetically engineered creature. It's . . . it's just too far out."

Mal sighed and shook his head. "Well, you're right about one thing," he said. "Your abilities have nothing to do with science. In fact, the one *true* Savior, whose existence neither of us disputes, is the One you can thank for your abilities, not science."

Jason turned away from Mal and stared out the window for several minutes, contemplating. The wind had increased in intensity as they had talked, screaming about the vehicle and occasionally rocking it with violent shoves. He had the wild notion that his father's bizarre tale had been blown in by the elements themselves, descending upon them like the sheets of rain that pummeled the car. It was just too incredible for him to believe.

"Look," Jason said at last, "I have no doubt that God can do anything. He made the entire universe, so He can certainly turn me into a superhero if he wants to. But isn't His revelation complete? If I were a superhero, wouldn't that prove His existence, and make faith in Him obsolete?"

Mal shook his head. "I won't answer that question. We'd be getting into a theology debate that neither of us can win. The bottom line is, you think I hallucinated the whole thing, is that it?

Or worse yet, maybe you think I'm going crazy. Is that what you think?"

"No, of course I don't think you're going crazy. But you said yourself it was a dream . . . maybe *this* time, that's all it was, a dream. Maybe you shouldn't read anything into it. Or maybe it *was* some kind of hallucination. You said you slept for almost three days, right? So maybe you had a fever or something, and didn't realize it. If so, you could have been delirious. You know how bizarre a dream can get when you're delirious."

Mal opened his mouth to issue his next counterargument, but

then just smiled and nodded his head. "I guess I've failed to convince you," he sighed. "And I suppose I can't blame you for not believing me. It *was* a pretty wild story."

Jason reached over and patted his father's arm. "It's okay," he said. "As long as you're willing to let this go and not obsess over it, we can pretend this conversation never happened."

"That's just it, son," Mal said, shaking his head. "I can't let it go. Not now, not ever." He reached quickly into the pouch along the bottom of the car door, withdrew a .22 caliber pistol, and shot Jason at point-blank range.

4

"All right, I believe you," Jason growled. "I just wish you'd have tried a little harder to convince me before you decided to shoot me."

It was 6:00 p.m. on Monday, thirty hours after Mal had shot Jason in the left thigh. Though he still felt a mild burning, itching sensation where the bullet had penetrated (and been dug out later by Mal), there were no visible signs of the wound remaining.

"You know I waited until I felt I had no alternative," Mal countered. "And besides, even if you had said you believed me, somehow I don't think you'd have been completely convinced until you saw for yourself the incredible regenerative ability your body has. Not only that, I have always suspected that that ability would never have surfaced until your body was actually *forced* to use it, which unfortunately required the infliction of a traumatic injury."

"But you said I had other abilities as well, like great strength and speed. Why didn't you just ask me to lift something really heavy, like your pickup truck for example, or run the hundred-yard dash in three or four seconds? Anything but *shooting* me, for God's sake."

"Because you wouldn't have been able to lift that much weight, or run that fast, until you had opened your mind and fully accepted who you are. That's why your physical accomplishments thus far, though impressive, maybe even freakish, have not been unnatural. You had no idea what you were truly capable of, so your mind had subconsciously established artificial limitations upon your body that were comparable to those of your peers. I didn't think you would ever voluntarily open your mind to the truth, so I had to take dramatic action to convince you. Now do you understand?"

"Yes, I understand," Jason said grudgingly. "But answer me this. Suppose I get it done. I use all of these amazing abilities and kick this monster's butt. Kill it, to be more specific. In the future, won't Zintak realize immediately that his plan had failed? Won't he just try again?"

"I don't know," Mal admitted. "It's certainly possible. But I suspect that there might be more to this saga than what we know of it right now. Others may have a role in it as well. We can only do our part, and leave the rest to God. I have no doubt He's got it all figured out."

"Yeah, I'm sure you're right about that. Now let me ask you one more thing, and be honest with your answer. Did you see yourself shooting me in your vision?"

"Yes, I did," Mal confessed, "but when you read my journal, it won't be in there. I left that part out."

"Why?"

"Because as I was writing it, I was thinking ahead to this day, when I would have to reveal to you who you really are. At that point, I wasn't sure how I would go about telling you, whether I would discuss it with you first, as I eventually decided to do, or whether I would ask you to read the journal first and then discuss it with you afterwards. If I had chosen the second option, imagine how you would have reacted when you read the part about me shooting you. You might have bolted out the door and run straight for the police, especially if you were beginning to believe the story."

"Okay, that makes sense. Is that why you chose the first option?"

"That was a minor consideration. It was mainly because I felt I owed it to you to look you in the eye and tell you who you really are, rather than have you read it in the journal."

"Well . . . . thanks, I guess. So what do we do now?"

"Well, first of all, you need to read my journal. There's a whole lot more detail in there than what I've shared with you so far. And then we need to get you started on a training program. Nothing fancy at first, just strengthening exercises, both for your body and your mind. Once you graduate from high school, the workouts will get a little more . . . intense."

Jason was intrigued. "Intense? How so?"

"You'll know when you read the journal, at least in a general sense. And then when the time comes, we'll have a very in-depth discussion about it. But to get you started, let's go buy you a set of universal weights and some other equipment you'll need for your workouts."

"Why do we need to do that? I can just keep working out in the weight room at school, like I am now. Hey! I just realized, I'll be an even bigger star than I am now. Maybe I can get a scholarship to a football powerhouse like Alabama, Michigan, or Oklahoma!"

"A scholarship?" Mal's face clouded over almost instantly. "I'm sorry Jason, I guess I wasn't clear about something. After today, you can never again play organized sports, and you can never again work out or exercise with anyone else but me. Now that you've learned and accepted who you are, your body will develop at a very rapid pace. Within a matter of months, you will be so much stronger and faster than other high school athletes that it would be like playing against preschoolers. It would be extremely dangerous to everyone, them because of the risk of serious injury, and you because of the chance you might draw the attention of scientists, government agencies, or the media. In fact, in this day and age, it's a virtual guarantee that the media would find out. So we have to do everything we can to keep this a secret."

Jason's heart sank as he realized that he would have to endure more of the same loneliness he had felt most of his life, and that in fact, it would get even worse. "How long will I have to live like this?" he asked, and immediately wished he had not, because he feared what the answer might be.

"Well, I'm not sure," Mal said softly. He understood the despair Jason felt at having to largely forego any social life during a period that for most people is the happiest of their lives – their teens. "I don't know exactly when the creature will arrive, but it could be as late as the year 2020 or so, which means about twenty years. You're ten now, so to be safe, we should plan on training you until you are thirty. After that, you can have a family, a career, do anything you want to do."

"You mean, assuming I win," Jason said dryly.

"I believe you will win, though of course I can't be sure since I didn't see the end of the dream. But what you need to recognize is that winning, or losing, for that matter, may not factor into this lifetime. We don't know if this is the original timeline or the altered one. Up until the point the creature arrives, they are one and the same. If we are on the original timeline, then it will be almost 80 years before Zintak is born, and there will be no creature to fight during this lifetime. In that case, like I said, once you complete your training you can do anything you want to do. On the other hand, if the altered timeline lies ahead, then so does your fight with the creature. What kind of life you have afterwards, if any, will depend on who wins the fight, as you alluded to. Do you follow me?"

Jason thought for a moment, trying to make sense of the concept of time. It was like trying to focus on a single color while looking through a kaleidoscope.

"Alright, I think I follow you," he said finally. "But maybe you should have lied to me and said that I would definitely be facing reaper in this lifetime. I might have been more motivated to train hard if I had thought that I *would* have to face it in fifteen or twenty years."

"You're saying that because there's only a 50/50 chance that you will face the creature in this lifetime, that it will lead you to slack off? I know you well enough to say that's a bunch of crap.

But it's my job to make sure you work your butt off every single day for the next twenty-five years. I'll be on you like mud on a pig. And besides, just knowing that if you fail to defeat the reaper, it will mean the death of the entire human race, that should be enough to keep you motivated."

"So then there really *is* a chance I could lose?" Jason asked apprehensively. "Isn't it a foregone conclusion that I'll win?"

"All I can tell you is what I saw and I what I *didn't* see. I saw the unprepared version of Jason become a victim of the creature just like everyone else. But I didn't get the chance to see how the fully trained Jason would fare. Like I told you, I believe – no, I am *convinced* -- that God chose you for this task, and I don't know why He would have done that if you were not destined to win, whether I saw it happen or not. But since I didn't see it, I can't be absolutely certain. That's why we'll need to be fully prepared and to have faith."

"Preparation and faith are great, but I still don't get why this is a one-man job. It just seems hard to believe that a single creature, an *animal*, would be capable of killing everyone in the entire world before somebody figured out a way to stop it."

"You still don't realize what you're going to be up against. Or more to the point, what *ordinary* people will be up against. I've already told you about the creature's physical attributes, and oh, by the way, I forgot to mention that Zintak added some human brain cells to its composition to make it as cunning and creative as you or me. This creature will never engage in a prolonged attack, even if there are ample victims available. It may pop up in the middle of New York City and kill two or three hundred people, disappear like smoke in the wind, then show up an hour later in Boston and do the same thing. It will move so fast that police and military forces will not possibly be able to mobilize in time to confront it before it is gone. Though its most primal urge is to kill, if it detects any kind of Danger it will suppress that desire and run, swim or fly away long danger it will suppress that desire and run, swim or fly away long before a pursuer can get close to it. If those options aren't available, it can burrow 50 feet into the ground in a matter of minutes, slow its heartbeat down to a couple of beats per minute and remain there for days until it senses that it's safe to leave. And if that isn't enough, it can change its skin color almost instantly to match any possible surrounding. It can survive in any climate on earth, from desert to polar ice cap, and it can eat virtually anything organic, from meat to plants, even the ground itself if it contains enough nutrients. The only time the creature will be vulnerable is when it is sleeping, and even then it will not stop to rest until it is certain that there are no threats in its vicinity. So trust me when I tell you that it's extremely unlikely that any ordinary person, or group of people, no matter how many there are or how much firepower they're carrying, will ever be able to kill this creature."

Jason pondered this as he lightly scratched the mended bullet wound on his leg. "So I guess it really is *my* battle to win or lose," he finally acknowledged. "It certainly gives new meaning to the 'Army of One' slogan."

⚔ ⚔ ⚔

At the very moment that Jason Devine comes to grips with the truth about his identity and his destiny, along the banks of Alaska's Kenai River over twenty-five hundred miles away, an enormous grizzly bear stands erect and perfectly still in the crisp, damp air, save for its wriggling snout, which is operating at full throttle. It had been standing on all fours in knee-deep water, waiting for a rainbow trout or king salmon to swim by and offer itself up for breakfast. But in an instant, all thoughts of food are forgotten, as its senses focus on something else . . . something entirely new. It has no scent, no taste, and cannot be seen, this something, *but it is there nevertheless, as real as the sting of the cold river water or the smell of ripe wild berries. It is an* urge, *a feeling of being drawn toward something or someplace unknown. Not a powerful urge, at least not yet, but even now the urge is growing, becoming stronger, until one day the bear will no longer resist and will follow instinctively. It does not think these things, or understand them, for its brain does not work that way, but somehow it knows, it* feels.

At the same time, over halfway around the world on a grassy plain in the middle of the African nation of Chad, a lioness drops a hunk of zebra carcass in front of its den beneath a large outcropping of rock and spins around as if it had been startled by something. Inside the den its cubs, which had been mewling incessantly in anticipation of their evening meal, are suddenly silent. It is dark here, yet still the lioness sees . . . both with its eyes and with its mind. It, too, senses something coming, not an imminent danger but more like a speck on the horizon. The lioness is wary, but not alarmed, for its instincts tell it that this enigmatic foe has not yet arrived. After a few moments, it turns back to the zebra carcass and drags it beneath the rock ledge, where its cubs, having also emerged from their brief trance, eagerly devour their dinner.

Indeed, at that very instant, all of Mother Nature holds its breath. Creatures large and small, even the birds in the air and the fish in the oceans, pause momentarily. They all sense it . . . that their world has somehow changed, or will *be changed by things that have yet to occur. They are conscious of these things to come in a way that cannot be called understanding, for they are animals and not people. But there is nevertheless an instinctive awareness, an inherent means of absorbing their surroundings that humans do not share. Henceforth, they will be in a constant state of alertness, their keen instincts sharpened even more by a growing sense of urgency, of foreboding. Until then, they return to their eating, drinking, mating, sleeping . . . and waiting.*

Original Timeline – May 2002

S even months later, Jason graduated from Oakwood High School as expected. And although he had graduated at the top of his class and had scholarship offers from several of the top colleges and universities in the country, he had to turn them all down. Since the day he had learned his true identity, he had been zeroed in on his training, even though it was of the plain vanilla variety and typically uneventful. But now that school no longer beckoned, he was free to train anywhere – which meant training in much more creative and challenging ways. Specifically, he would begin fighting live competitors, for it was the only way to even remotely simulate the kind of fight Jason would be in for when he finally had to face the creature.

He started out small and local at first, wandering through the rocky hills and plains of South Dakota and tangling with coyotes and bighorn sheep, and eventually moving up to bison. Then they began making trips across the country, and later, around the world, so that he could engage the biggest, strongest and most dangerous animals on land.

Though Jason would certainly carry a gun when he one day came face to face with the creature, he never used them during these encounters, for the development of his fighting abilities depended upon direct contact with his opponent. And develop, he did; his quickness, hand-eye coordination, anticipatory skills, and of course his regenerative ability (he was now almost guaranteed to get mauled, given the level of competition he was facing) all improved dramatically. He realized that while he had been getting stronger and faster as a result of his home-based workouts during his school years, he had plateaued with respect to combat training. After all, he could do no more than spar lightly with Mal and Mitch, for he could have killed them with very minimal effort, and hammering away at stationary objects like boxing bags and dummies was of limited benefit.

The other thing he learned as soon as he began to train in this manner was that he absolutely hated it. He had always been a nature lover, appreciating the beauty of God's creation like few others, he believed (though he knew this was a purely subjective viewpoint and could never be proven), and having to destroy even a tiny part of it every time he went on a training mission was something he could never get used to. Even the animals seemed to despise him for it, because they were always hostile towards him; whether they were typically aggressive species, or reclusive, made no difference. In reality, Jason knew they were probably just protecting their territories or their families, but sometimes it seemed as though they really did have an axe to grind with him.

There was one animal, though, that he did not care for at all, and that was sharks. He had seen the classic shark film *Jaws* several times, as well as countless low budget movies on the cable channels, and was always glad at the end of the movie when the shark was blown up, chopped up, electrocuted, or devoured by something bigger. It seemed to Jason as though sharks, with those black, characterless eyes and insatiable appetite for raw meat, were the only truly evil member of the animal kingdom. That was not true, of course, for there was no such thing as an evil animal (not yet, anyway), but surely there was no other beast that inspired terror in humans more so than the shark. For that reason, Jason was filled with both fear and excitement when, twelve years after his first coyote fight, Mal told him one day that his training was about to rise to a whole new level. They were heading to Dyer Island, South Africa – home of one of the densest populations of great white sharks on the planet.

Original Timeline – March 2014

M al paced relentlessly across the deck of the fishing boat, checking his watch every few seconds like a teenager at the end of a school day. These training exercises had always worried him, but what he felt at this particular moment was something more like sheer terror.

"That kid is going to be the death of me! Where is he, Mitch? And why are you so calm?"

Mitch Anderson, who at 48 was two years older than his brother, was a picture of composure as he sat at the bow of the boat reading a copy of *Sports Illustrated.*

"He'll be all right, Mal," Mitch said evenly without so much as glancing away from his magazine. "And I'm calm because I realize that there's nothing we can do to help him. Even if we knew for sure that he was getting torn to pieces right now, there isn't a thing we could do about it. So I figure my time is better spent cramming a few more facts into my already voluminous brain than it is wearing a hole in the deck."

"But he's been down there for *twenty-five* minutes!" Mal persisted. "What does that tell you?"

Mitch sighed and tossed the magazine aside, finally exasperated by Mal's irrational pleading. "It tells me he hasn't seen anything yet and that he lost track of time, that's all."

Mal's jaw dropped in utter incredulity. "Are you kidding me? Would you mind telling me how someone can lose track of time when his lungs are screaming for air? No, Mitch, if he hadn't seen anything, he'd be back up here by now. Which tells *me* he must have tangled with something that was too big for him to handle."

Mitch shook his head. "It's too soon to jump to conclusions like that, Mal. The fact is, we don't know how long he can stay down there. It could be an hour for all we know. And besides, didn't you see this in your dream? Doesn't he kick some shark butt down there?"

"I've told you before, there were encounters I didn't see but knew they had taken place, like this one."

"Okay, but you did see battles that took place after this one. Doesn't that mean he can't be killed?"

Mal looked at Mitch as if he were the dumbest person on the planet. "What do you think would happen if he jumped from the top of the Empire State Building, or put a gun to his head and pulled the trigger? Do you think he wouldn't die? A premonition is not a guarantee. The end result can change if we wander too far off the path along the way."

"Then maybe you shouldn't make things up as you go, and instead, stick to what you actually saw."

"There's an element of risk and faith involved. It's not exactly like reading a script and acting it out. And do you now doubt me and my whole approach to his training? Do you think we should scrap this and go home, maybe keep him confined to the weight room again and hope that's enough?"

Mitch raised his hands in surrender. "No, of course not Mal. Would I have quit my job and moved here from Palo Alto if I doubted you? All I'm saying is, try to relax. Getting your blood pressure up is not going to help matters. And like I said, I'm guessing he can stay down there for a lot longer than twenty-five minutes."

"How do you figure that, when just last week he topped out at twenty-*three* minutes?"

"That was in a swimming pool," Mitch responded. "This is the deep blue sea, for God's sake! I'm betting the added adrenaline will allow him to stay down for at least forty-five minutes, maybe a lot more."

"So now it's forty-five minutes? Just a minute ago it was an hour! And I specifically told him to only stay down for twenty minutes at a time, so it doesn't matter how much air he's got left in his lungs. He would've come back by now if he could."

"Like I said, maybe he lost track of time. If he's got plenty of air left, he probably hasn't even bothered to check his watch yet." Mitch grinned as another thought occurred to him. "Or maybe he's intentionally defying you for keeping him on such a short leash all the time."

Mal glared at his brother for a moment, then resumed his pacing. "Five more minutes and we're going down after him."

"*Ten*," Mitch said firmly. "Give him *ten* more minutes, Mal. I guarantee he'll be back by then."

Again Mal stared icily at Mitch, his body beginning to shake not only with fear but also anger. "All right," he growled, "*ten* more minutes. But Mitch, I'm warning you, if he ends up as an appetizer for a great white shark, I'll see to it that *you* are the main course."

A   A   A

It has been roaming the ocean for thirty years, having grown to over twenty feet in length and weighing three tons. It can detect electromagnetic variations in its prey of as little as one billionth of a volt, and can smell a drop of blood in the water from three miles away. It has 3,000 teeth in its mouth, and a bite force of 4,000 pounds. It is the most notorious predator on the planet, and fears only one thing: the smell of a carcass of one of its own.

The shark glides through the water, as it does every minute of every day of its life, even when it is sleeping, for it if does not, it will die. It detects something in the water, some distance away, and feels compelled to investigate. This time, however, it is drawn not by the smell of blood, or by electrical impulses, but by something else, something not sensed but rather felt. The pull becomes stronger as the shark approaches the object, and though it has recently fed and is not hunting for food, it nevertheless feels the urge to attack.

⚓   ⚓   ⚓

When Jason checked his watch for the first time, he was amazed to find that over twenty minutes had elapsed since he had left the boat. He had been so enthralled with the abundance of aquatic life and the beauty of the coral formations that he had temporarily lost all awareness of everything else. That included not only the twenty-minute time limit that Mal had given him, but also the considerable danger that this training mission involved. What surprised him even more was the fact that he had already broken his own personal record for underwater duration, yet to this point his lungs had offered no protest whatsoever. He felt fresh, clearheaded, and energized in a way that he had never felt before.

As Jason was not usually one to disobey his father, his first thought upon realizing his tardiness was to abandon the mission and immediately return to the boat. To do so would put him only about five minutes behind schedule, enough to warrant an earful from Mal but probably not enough to cause him to go totally ballistic. But with the spirit of adventure having temporarily possessed him, and an uncharacteristic mischievous impulse having rippled through him, he decided that the time had come to defy his middle-aged mentor for the first time in his life, or at least the first time in recent memory. So he stayed.

He swam slowly along the ocean bottom for a time, studying the plants and various types of fish, occasionally looking around to see if he had drawn the attention of any sharks. That was why he was here, after all, which was something he had briefly forgotten when he had first descended into this gorgeous underwater panorama. But an attention lapse here could easily prove to be fatal, so he forced himself to focus on his mission and to scan the waters around him, instead of the scenery beneath him.

He saw nothing. No sleek gray forms darting up from the depths, no razor-sharp teeth glinting in the opaque sunlight. Nothing.

Jason checked his watch again – twenty-five minutes underwater. He felt a tiny burning sensation in his chest and knew that he was finally beginning to run out of air. But he also knew that he could stay down for another ten to twelve minutes, enough time for him to complete his mission if he could pick a fight within the next couple of minutes. Come to think of it, he was surprised that he had not already, for it usually did not take this long. He would wait three more minutes, and then he would have to give up and head back, since there may not be enough time left to tangle with a shark and still get back to the boat before his lungs involuntarily gasped for oxygen that was not there.

With no worthy adversaries in sight, Jason considered inflicting a shallow cut upon himself with the Bowie knife he held in his right hand – the only weapon he carried. But he quickly dismissed this idea, as it would no doubt draw not just one shark, but *lots* of sharks. And if the tigers and great whites in these waters were as big as in the pictures and videos he had seen, then just one of them would be a handful. No, he would have to wait for a random, unprovoked attack. Maybe a shark would mistake him for a tuna, or porpoise, or a seal, or a ---

And then it happened: a gray and white lightning bolt ripped silently through the murky water and slammed into him before he could even flinch. The shark's eyes rolled back, the flesh around its mouth receded, and in a microsecond its massive jaws had clamped around Jason's torso and pinned his right arm to his side, rendering the knife temporarily useless. Almost instantly, his visibility was reduced to zero as blood poured from the gashes in his back and side and clouded the water around him. He initially felt no pain from the bite wounds, but the pressure exerted on his midsection by the shark's jaws was phenomenal, as if he were caught in a giant mousetrap.

Although this was Jason's first underwater training session, he thought he had been prepared for it. For the past thirteen years, since he had first learned the shocking truth about his existence at the tender age of ten, Jason had worked feverishly to develop his strength, skill and stamina. By the time he reached his twelfth birthday, Jason was already the strongest human being on earth, having bench-pressed 1,500 pounds, curled over 400 pounds, and leg-pressed nearly 3,000 pounds. At fourteen, he could run alongside Mal's car for nearly 2 miles at a speed of 50 miles per hour, and could hold his breath for over fifteen minutes. And a year later, he found he could consistently hit a paint can with a baseball . . . at a distance of 150 yards. Since he had first begun training against live animals, he had fought and defeated many dangerous creatures on land: a lion, a tiger, a rhinoceros, several black bears, and even a bull elephant. He knew it would be a much different feeling fighting an animal underwater, but given his training and physical prowess, he did not anticipate it being a particularly difficult challenge.

But as he struggled to free himself from the jaws of his attacker, the last of his oxygen being forcibly expelled from his lungs, he knew for the first time in his life what it felt like to experience pure terror. This shark -- this *monster* -- that had a vise-like grip on him was without question the most powerful, most deadly adversary he had ever faced. It was like an aquatic pit bull, refusing to let go, at least until it had crushed him or bitten him in half. He had been incredibly foolish and arrogant to think that he could so easily defeat such a creature, particularly since he had never been this close to a shark before and could not have known what to expect.

Jason's terror turned to panic as he realized that if he did not break free from the shark's jaws in the next few seconds, he would either drown or be devoured. So he forced himself to set aside his fear and to recall the research he had done on how to survive a shark attack.

Nose, eyes and gills, he thought. Those were a shark's most sensitive areas. He brought his left arm up and pummeled the shark's nose as hard as he could; once, twice, three times, and finally it relinquished its grip on him. But before he could move his right arm away, the shark snapped its jaws shut again, and with one quick jerk of its huge head, it bit Jason's limb off just above the elbow.

Though his first impulse was to scream, he had regained enough control over his mind and body that he was able to fight that impulse because it would have meant spending the last of the oxygen in his lungs. He kicked his legs swiftly back and forth with all of his strength, propelling himself upward and away from the shark in a desperate attempt to escape. But he knew he would never reach the boat before the shark resumed its attack, and he reluctantly turned to face the beast again. This time, however, he had only one arm to work with and no weapons.

The shark had already devoured Jason's arm and was moving quickly toward him. As it closed in upon him, its black eyes rolled back into its head and its teeth seemed to spring right out of its mouth.

Jason waited until the last possible second, when the shark was only a few feet away, then he swung his left arm up to the side of the shark's head and pushed himself out of its path along its right flank. Before it could swim away from him and circle around for another charge, he grabbed its dorsal fin with his remaining hand, yanked himself atop the shark, and clamped his legs around it. Its girth was incredible, and Jason had to spread his legs as wide as possible and use his heels to dig into its sides.

Feeling an unwelcome rider on its back, the shark swished its tail rapidly, trying to pull away. But while Jason's stump of a right arm was useless, his legs were fully functional, and with them, he managed to maintain his hold on the shark's flanks. He maneuvered his body to the left of the dorsal fin, and slid himself forward so that he was within an arm's length of its gills. He cocked his good left arm back and balled his fist, and with every ounce of strength he could muster, he drove his hand through the shark's gills and into its body.

Had it been born with vocal cords, the huge great white would have surely screamed in pain as Jason's hand penetrated its body. It thrashed wildly, desperately trying to disengage from its would-be prey. But Jason would not let go, except to loosen his leg clamp slightly so that he could slide down the shark's side and thus plunge his arm deeper inside of it. Because his thoughts were growing fuzzy from a lack of oxygen to the brain, he could not remember where the shark's heart was located, despite all of the anatomy diagrams he had studied. So he grasped and groped and tore ferociously at the leviathan's innards, for ten, twenty, perhaps thirty seconds or more, until finally it gave up the struggle and began to sink.

Jason knew the shark may not be dead yet, that it might be sinking only because of a lack of oxygen to its lungs and that it might still have enough life left to resume its attack, but he could not wait to finish off his opponent. He had to get to the surface, and he had to do it *now*. He withdrew his arm from the shark's body and kicked upward with everything he had left, using both arms to help propel himself to the surface. As he ascended, he saw one of the strangest sights he would ever see in his life; another great white that had moved in, rather than joining in the attack, suddenly turned and fled into the depths. But he also saw other huge, shadowy forms, these with telltale spotted patterns across their backs – tiger sharks – moving in just as quickly as the great white was fleeing. And he knew that most likely, there were bull sharks in the area as well, and they were more aggressive than either great whites or tigers.

No more than a second or two before he would have involuntarily sucked seawater into his lungs, Jason exploded through the surface of the water like a dolphin doing tricks. But the only trick he cared to perform at this particular moment was getting back to the boat, which he could see drifting about 200 yards away, before losing any more appendages. He screamed at the top of his lungs to get Mal's or Mitch's attention, then began to swim toward the boat as fast as his three-limbed body would allow.

Moments later, he heard the boat's engine come roaring alive, and the small craft swung around and came toward him. He knew the boat was moving quickly and would be alongside him in just a few seconds, but it nevertheless seemed to hover on the horizon, as if it were planning to watch the bloody carnage from a safe distance. This made him even more acutely aware of the murderous hulks that were undoubtedly closing in on him from below, and he kicked forward even harder than before.

Finally, after what seemed like several minutes, the boat pulled up alongside him, and two pairs of brown, leathery hands grabbed him under the armpits and yanked him into the boat, even as a huge, spotted gray head emerged through the bloody froth.

The Anderson brothers lay their young protégé gently onto his back, and Mitch found a length of rope to use as a tourniquet for Jason's injured arm while Mal went into the cabin and returned with a blanket. They covered the boy with the blanket and gently massaged his shivering body from head to toe.

"Stay with me, Jason!" Mal urged. "Try to focus your thoughts on accelerating the regeneration process. Concentrate, boy!"

After a few seconds, Jason's eyelids fluttered, and the glazing on his eyes slowly evaporated as he regained his sense of where he was and what had happened.

When Mal saw this, and the new tissue that was beginning to sprout from Jason's injured arm, he collapsed onto his rear end with a huge sigh of relief. "He's going to be all right," he told Mitch.

Mitch nodded in agreement.

After a few minutes of silence, Mal sat up and leaned over Jason with as stern a look as he could muster given the circumstances. "What happened down there?" he gently admonished Jason. "You stayed down too long, didn't you?"

It took some effort for Jason to respond. "I . . . I felt fine up to the point where the shark blindsided me," he whispered. "I still had a few minutes of air left in my lungs."

"A *few minutes*? Jason, how many times did we go through this before you went down there? You can't pick a fight with a shark when you've only got a few minutes of oxygen left! You use a lot more air when you're struggling than you do just looking at the fish!"

"All right, Mal, ease up a little," Mitch intervened. "I think he gets the message."

"Stay out of it, Mitch!" Mal shot back. "We need to talk about this. He needs to understand how important it is that he not take unnecessary chances!"

"Stronger," Jason whispered, before Mitch could respond.

"What was that?" Mal asked.

"Stronger. The worse my injuries are, the stronger I get when I'm fully healed."

Mal had to admit that that statement was true. Jason was no stranger to injury, but there had been two occasions that rivaled this one in terms of severity; once when he fell sixty feet while climbing a rock wall in Wyoming, and the other while fighting a black bear in the Sierra Nevada range. The climbing incident resulted in over half of his bones being broken, including a cracked skull, while the black bear had raked its claws across Jason's throat and chest, causing him to lose an incredible amount of blood. But less than a week after each of those incidents, Jason was fully healed and could lift over 1/3 more weight than he could just prior to the accidents.

Still, Mal reasoned, if Jason were a cat, he would have used three of his lives already, and since he was *not* a cat, he might not have another six lives to burn. Indeed, Jason's next serious injury might very well be his last.

"You know he can't let up, Mal," Mitch said, as if reading his brother's mind. "He's got to keep pushing it to the limit, make himself as strong as he can possibly be. It's the only way he . . . it's the only way *we* stand a chance."

No, Mal thought to himself, *even then we don't stand a chance.* He had had this nagging feeling for some time now that despite all of Jason's incredible abilities, they would not be enough when that dreaded day came that would bring the arrival of the creature, and Jason found himself engaged in a battle the likes of which they simply could not replicate no matter how many sharks, bears and lions he fought. Mal had been thinking about mentioning it to Jason, mainly just to plant the seed in his brain and not because he had any theories of his own about what additional tools or tactics Jason might need to defeat the creature. Mal decided that now was as good a time as any to bring it up.

"Listen, both of you," he said. "You're right that we have to keep putting Jason in these situations. And it does seem as though the more severely he is injured, the stronger he becomes. Like a bodybuilder, working his muscles so hard that he tears them apart, and when they heal, they are bigger and stronger than before. But there's something I've wanted to tell you, Jason. Despite all the amazing things you can do with your body, your strength, speed, and regenerative ability . . . . I have this feeling it won't be enough to defeat the creature. I've always suspected there is something more inside you, some sort of untapped skill. I can't help you discover it, because I have no idea what it might be, but somehow you need to figure it out. Whatever it is – and I have been haunted by this for years -- I think it will be the difference between defeating the creature, or not."

"What makes you say that, Mal?" Mitch asked.

Mal thought for a moment before answering. "I can't say for sure. But over the years, the thought of Jason taking on the creature brings to mind the story of David taking on Goliath. At the beginning, both Philistines and Israelites alike knew without a doubt that Goliath was going to squash David like a bug. But then David produced a weapon that allowed him to kill Goliath without having to engage him in hand-to-hand combat. I wish my dream had not ended prematurely, because I have this feeling that if Jason wound up defeating the creature, it was not with sheer strength or speed but through the use of some unexpected strategy or skill. But again, without having seen the battle to its conclusion, there is no way of knowing what that might be."

"Well, with that sobering thought in mind," Mitch said, after they had all reflected upon Mal's words for a few minutes, "let's head back. Jason needs a good, hearty meal to replace all the calories he just burned, and then we could all use a good night's sleep."

"Agreed," Mal said. "But Jason, don't be overly concerned about what I just said. You'll need to figure it out when the time comes, but I have no doubt that you will. Like I keep saying, it's all part of God's plan."

7

Original Timeline – September 2016

For the next two and a half years, Jason's training continued, twelve hours a day, seven days a week. There truly was no rest for the weary, as the saying went, though in Jason's case, physical exhaustion was not really the issue, since his body regenerated so quickly. It was much more a battle of mental fatigue than anything else. He had a tough time getting out of bed every morning and preparing himself mentally for another day of the same old grind. Consequently, he found his mind wandering more and more frequently as the weeks came and went. In fact, for the past couple of months, not a day had gone by that he did not think about his parents, James and Katrina Devine, wondering what they and their lives were like.

Jason imagined his mother to be beautiful, energetic and quick-witted, with a warm smile that would lift even the lowest of spirits. He somehow knew that she was strong-willed, but at the same time respectful of her husband's position as leader of the family. She was artistic and creative, but also very active and athletic. She could appreciate a Picasso and a bottle of fine wine just as much as a football game and a pitcher of cold beer. She had a playful, mischievous side to her, but was best known for her compassion and kindness.

As for his father James, Jason had no doubt that he was as loving a man as God had ever created, eternally devoted to his wife and fiercely protective of his family. He was rugged and strong, but also sensitive and understanding. He was undoubtedly a leader, not just of his family but also at his workplace and in his social circles. He was highly intelligent and ambitious, yet he was not materialistic or unappreciative of the simple things in life. He was the rare kind of man who, when his children (if he and Katrina had had any more after Jason had been taken from them) would get into bragging matches with their friends about whose dad was stronger, more handsome, or better at this or that, the Devine children would *always* be right.

Yes, it was certainly true that Jason longed to meet his parents, to explain to them why he had been missing from their lives all of these years, and to hold both of them in his arms for a long, long time, as if to absorb all of the pain they must have endured. And yet he had no regrets about his life, no ill-will towards the man he had been calling "Dad" since he uttered his first words nearly 25 years ago. Mal had been a father to Jason in every sense of the word, from changing his diapers as a baby, to patching up his cuts and scrapes as a boy, to making sure he finished his homework every night until he graduated from high school. Indeed, although the *activities* they engaged in were unique, given the preparations they were forced to make in order that the world might be saved, the *relationship* they enjoyed as father and son was actually quite normal. That is, if there was such a thing as "normal" in this day and age . . . perhaps "non-dysfunctional" was a more accurate term.

In any event, if and when the day came that Jason was able to meet his biological parents, it would never change the way he felt about Mal. And if there were any doubts about that whatsoever, they were snuffed out faster than a candle in the wind on the day Malcolm Anderson died.

λ   λ   λ

Jason, Mal and Mitch had traveled to Alaska so that Jason might tangle with a few bears – preferably grizzly – as part of his training program. As always on these missions, the mood was somber as they drove their rented pickup down a dirt road that snaked away from the main highway through grassy meadows and up into the mountains – prime bear country, so they were told by a few locals. They could find no enjoyment in the gorgeous scenery around them, because they knew how this excursion would end – in the slaughter of some of the most beautiful animals in the world. The fact that such a sacrifice was necessary to help ensure the survival of the human race was of little consolation to them.

The trio left Anchorage and drove for more than three hours until they reached the city of Kenai. They turned onto a logging road off Beaver Loop Road and drove another two miles until they spotted the head of a barely discernible and little known trail that a local tour guide had told them about, one that ran mostly along the Kenai River. Mitch pulled up alongside the trailhead, turned off the vehicle, and they all got out to stretch their legs.

With dozens of these training missions behind them, Mal knew instinctively that Jason intended to stay long enough to only kill one bear. "Better take two or three of them," he said. "We may never get back up here again, and you can use the work."

Jason stared at the ground beneath him for a few moments, knowing he was going to hear those words but nevertheless deploring the sound of them. "Yeah, I guess so," he finally mumbled, then turned and headed down the trail.

The Anderson brothers got back into the truck and sat quietly for a few minutes before Mitch finally said, "You know he'll probably only kill one, then just wait an hour or so before he comes back to make it look like he did two or three."

"Yeah, I know," Mal replied. "I think he's been doing that for a while now. I can't say I blame him. I'd probably do the same thing if I were in his place. All this killing must seem pretty senseless by now. I can imagine there must be days when he says to himself, 'screw it, I'm done with this. I'm going to get married, have a few kids, live to be eighty years old and die a natural death.

I'm never giving this reaper crap another thought, and Brian Zintak can kiss my you-know-what.' So it's up to you and me to keep pushing him, to keep reminding him what's at stake here. If he chooses to listen to us, great, but if not, if he only does half or a third of what we tell him to do, let's just pray that it's enough."

"Yep, I guess that's all we can do," Mitch agreed.

They sat silently for a while, each man trying to focus on appreciating the awesome beauty that surrounded them rather than the solemnity of this excursion.

A few minutes later, Mal lifted the thermos that he had brought with him to his lips and took a swallow of water, then realized that there was pressure building up in his bladder from all of the liquid he had consumed on their drive out here. "I've gotta take a leak," he announced, then capped the thermos and opened the truck door. He could have stood next to the truck and simply faced away from it while taking care of his business, but he decided he would be polite enough to walk a short distance from the truck so that his brother could not hear his urine stream hitting the ground. There were a few scattered bushes nearby, the nearest about twenty-five yards from the truck, and Mal ambled off in that direction.

⅄   ⅄   ⅄

Ursus horribilis – "terrifying bear". At 1,500 pounds, standing ten feet tall on its hind legs, with 4-inch claws and 2-inch teeth, the grizzly is certainly that. This one is 23 years of age and is nearing the end of its life, its reign at the top of the food chain drawing to a close. Though its senses are not as sharp as they once were, it suddenly rears up, having felt a jolt of something it has not felt for the past fifteen years. It is something familiar, even though it lies at the distant edge of its memory. It is an urge, a beckoning, something powerful, something irresistible. The call must be heeded, the desire satiated.

Two miles away, another bear, younger and smaller, yet faster and more aggressive, also feels that same powerful pull, one that creates a primal need to explore, to pursue . . . to attack. It, too, responds to the call.

⅄   ⅄   ⅄

After Mal left to relieve himself, Mitch turned his attention to a magazine he had brought with him. So it was that he first heard, rather than saw, the attack coming: the sound of heavy thumping of feet, or paws, as it were, combined with hoarse, ragged breathing. He looked up just as a huge, golden brown mass of fur crossed the dirt road a few feet in front of the truck; a grizzly bear was making a beeline toward his unsuspecting brother.

Instinctively, Mitch threw open the truck door, jumped out and screamed as loud as he could, *"LOOK OUT MAL, THERE'S A BEAR COMING!"*

⅄   ⅄   ⅄

Mal was just zipping up his pants when he heard Mitch yell. By virtue of its sheer volume, the scream startled him, but he quickly dismissed it as a prank. After all, though he was no expert on bears, he was sure they were not in the habit of attacking a man when he was *peeing*, for God's sake! Besides, the sound of their vehicle would have surely scared any bears that were nearby into retreating at least few hundred yards. He was about to step from behind the foliage and return to the truck, when something exploded through the bushes and slammed into him like a flash flood rushing through a desert canyon. He knew in an instant that Mitch's warning had been legitimate, and yet he was so shocked by this sudden, unprovoked attack that the bear had already taken two bites of him before he even started to scream.

⅄   ⅄   ⅄

Mitch watched in horror as the bear plunged into the bushes after Mal. Though it disappeared from his sight, there was little doubt that it found its victim a few seconds later, for his brother began to scream in terror and agony. Mitch frantically scanned the interior and bed of the truck for something he could use as a weapon, but there were none to be found. Until now, Mitch and Mal had never needed, nor even *anticipated* the need, to arm themselves on these training missions.

Without so much as even a tire iron to be found in the truck, Mitch was about to go help Mal in any way he could – by throwing rocks, sticks, whatever he could find – when he realized that the best weapon available to him was not an object, but a person. He started screaming for his nephew as loud as he could, even as he felt a burning despair growing inside himself that Jason would arrive too late.

⚔   ⚔   ⚔

Jason had walked about ¾ of a mile when he came to a stop. There was a bear nearby; he could smell it, hear it, *feel* it. It was watching him, like a cat, waiting for an opportunity to strike. And then he saw it – the massive head, large enough to fill a wheelbarrow; the yellow-white fangs flashing in the gloom beneath a northern pine tree about thirty yards away; the golden-brown fur covering a body the size of a small car. It had been standing perfectly still, sizing him up, until it realized that it no longer had the element of surprise. And then it charged toward him.

When the raging bear closed to within a few feet of him, Jason leaped straight into the air, pirouetting gracefully as the bear passed harmlessly beneath him. Landing softly on the ground, he looked up and saw that the bear had already turned and was coming at him again, thick threads of drool hanging from its mouth as it anticipated a tasty meal. Jason could have easily leaped to avoid it again, but he elected not to. Instead, he engaged the bear directly and immediately, knowing full well that it would sink its deadly teeth into him and slash him with its murderous claws. With his regenerative ability, he did not fear injury, and in fact welcomed it. He had discovered some time ago that the more serious the injury, the better -- in order to force his body to work as hard as possible to repair itself. The challenge, of course, was to make sure that he did not get injured *so* severely that he was incapable of defeating his foe before it defeated *him.*

It took Jason only a few seconds to realize he was going to get as much as he could handle from this particular foe. The bear tore flesh from his body, shook him in its mouth like a rag doll, and pummeled him with its huge paws. Jason fought back, using his superhuman speed to circle the bear and pound away at it with his sledgehammer-like fists. The bear howled in pain and spun around, slashing at Jason with its 4-inch razors, its fury rising by the second. He ducked away, now trying to keep the mauling to a minimum to allow his injuries, already becoming serious, time to heal.

The two titanic foes danced around each other for several minutes, trading punches for slashes, gaping wounds for crushed bones, until at last the time came for Jason to finish off his opponent. He leaped above the bear as it closed in on him, coming down on its back. With one hand he grabbed the bear's fur at the back of its neck in order to steady himself, and with the other he pounded the animal's skull as hard as he could – once, twice, then three times before it gave in with a loud *crack*! The bear howled again and tried desperately to throw Jason off its back, but he delivered one more vicious blow to its head, and the skull completely disintegrated and was driven into the brain tissue beneath. Though it had put up a valiant effort, the mighty grizzly whined softly and fell over dead.

The second the battle ended and silence ensued, Jason heard screaming. First one voice, and then two. He did not know whether it had just started, or whether the sounds of his struggle had been masking the screams for the past several minutes. But he knew one thing for sure – it was both his father and uncle who were screaming, and they were in serious trouble.

Jason ran back toward the truck, staggering and limping along the way with his injuries still healing. Normally he could have reached a speed of over one hundred fifty miles an hour, and thus could have covered the distance back to the truck in a matter of seconds. But after the clash he had just endured, he could only muster a fraction of that speed, and it therefore seemed to take an eternity to reach his destination.

As he approached, Jason could see what all the screaming was about; a second grizzly bear had attacked either Mitch or Mal – he could not tell which one because the victim was lying on the ground, curled up in a ball trying to protect himself from the attack. Gritting his teeth and nearing the limits of his pain threshold, Jason increased his speed and hurled himself into the bear's flank; and though he was outweighed by well over a thousand pounds, his speed was great enough that it produced sufficient momentum to knock the bear onto its side. It quickly recovered and got back onto all fours, then turned to focus its attention on Jason.

Jason backed away from the bear, trying to draw it toward him while at the same time formulating a plan to kill it or at least drive it away. Given the gravity of the situation, and the fact that he had no other weapons available, Jason turned and sped to the truck, seeing Mitch standing alongside it and knowing then that it was Mal who had been attacked. He tore the tailgate off the back end of the truck with a single yank, returned to the bear and clubbed it over the head repeatedly until the tailgate was a mangled ball of steel, and the bear's head was bloody pulp.

By then, Mitch had skirted the battle and was standing over Mal, an expression of stunned horror on his face. Jason came up alongside him, and he, too, froze when he saw the extent of Mal's injuries. He was now lying on his back, and there was a large chunk missing from his lower right flank. His right arm had been all but stripped of flesh and nearly bitten off, and most of his scalp was also gone, exposing the skull beneath. The amount of blood that was pouring out onto the ground from all of his various wounds was almost beyond comprehension.

As it was the middle of September, they had brought nothing with them in the way of blankets, so they wrapped Mal in their jackets and used their shirts to bandage his head and arm, and then quickly carried him to the truck. Jason held Mal in his arms as Mitch drove the truck back to the main road. There was very little discussion as they drove, for they were both praying silently for a miracle. That is, until Mal came to and whispered something that Jason could not hear.

"Shhh, it's ok, Dad," Jason said as he fought back tears. "Don't try to talk, just save your strength. We're getting you to a hospital."

"No," Mal said, straining to be heard. "Something I . . . . need to tell you."

Jason wanted to shush him again, but there was a part of him that was grudgingly coming to acknowledge that Mal was slipping away, and whatever it was that he had to say, it was no doubt important and warranted his attention. "Go ahead, Dad, I'm listening," he said, and leaned over to get his ear up close to Mal's lips.

"I wanted to say that I am very proud of you. I could not be more proud of you if you were my own son. Not because of your strength, or skill, or speed. Because you have become a man of courage, compassion, and integrity. It's easy to see why God chose you for the task that lies ahead. It's been a privilege for me to have raised you and guided you all these years. More than you will ever know, you have been a blessing to me."

Now the tears burst forth in a flood, and it was all Jason could do to keep from bawling like a five-year old. "Whatever goodness is in me, I got from you, Dad," he choked. "I'm just sorry I—"

"No, wait, there's more," Mal said, shaking his head feebly. "You must listen. I'm almost out of time. I know you will feel guilty about this day, about what has happened. But you must realize that this was part of God's plan. You may never understand why, because God will not explain Himself. Just remember His

promises, though . . . you can lean on Him. And on Mitch, too."
He looked over and winked at his brother, then looked up at Jason
again and smiled, and his eyes, which had become glazed and
unfocused as he had been speaking, became bright and clear for just
a moment, and the depth of his love for Jason was never more
recognizable than in those final few seconds. Then his eyes clouded
over again, fluttered, and closed for the last time.

⚔   ⚔   ⚔

Jason and Mitch arranged to have Mal's body flown with
them back to their home in Sioux Falls, and somehow, once they got
there, they managed to attend to the remaining funeral details as
well. Yet most of the events between Mal's death and his visitation
four days later would always be like a dream to them, for they were
in a state of shock the likes of which few people ever experience.
And there was something else that occupied their thoughts as well,
something that neither one of them wanted to be the first to bring
up. But it was something that needed to be hashed through, and
finally, Jason threw it out on the table.

"Uncle Mitch," Jason said while they were eating breakfast
on the morning of the funeral, "there's something I've been
wondering."

"And I'll bet it's the same thing *I've* been wondering," Mitch
replied, suddenly anxious to talk about it. "You're wondering why
Mal didn't see this coming. Why it wasn't part of the dream."

"Yeah, that's right. Do you have any theories?"

"I've got one, though I'm not sure how plausible it is. In his
journal, Mal didn't go into any detail about the training missions,
saying that, aside from the ones that were not revealed to him, he
didn't care to go into the graphic descriptions of those he did see,
and also didn't want to provide you with any information that might
reduce the effectiveness of the missions. And then after that, he
described the very beginning of what presumably would have been
the final battle between you and the creature, when the two of you

177

jump out of the vehicle and approach the man lying on the sidewalk, the creature's first victim. He obviously could not have been with you in that final scene if he were already dead. So here's my theory. What if Mal *did* see himself get mauled by the bear? If that were the case, then it would make sense that he would have glossed over the scenes where you fight the animals. More specifically, it would have made sense that he omitted the very scene where he himself was killed. If he had included that in his journal, then you and I both know that we would not have allowed him to go on that trip. And though a minor deviation from the events as they were revealed to Mal might have seemed trivial to you or me, Mal would not have agreed. He would have been afraid that messing with the timeline even slightly could have had serious consequences."

Jason was nodding as he listened to Mitch's theory. "I was thinking along the same lines. The dream, and thus Mal's written account, came to an end shortly after he references the training missions involving fights with animals. He might have cleverly inserted himself into that last scene to eliminate any question in our minds that something might have happened to him prior to that. Maybe it was just *me* who got out of that vehicle. And not only that, but we know for a fact that Mal omitted at least one other detail from his journal, which was that he had shot me on the day he revealed to me my true identity. If he did it once, he could have certainly done it again."

Now Mitch was the one nodding. "It makes sense," he said. "Do you have any other theories?"

"No, that's all I could come up with."

"Okay then. Mal was taken from us unexpectedly, but we have a pretty good idea why. We also know that he died for what he believed in, and in trying to protect the human race. That makes him a hero. I guess I can live with."

"Me too."

"Then let's go give him a proper sendoff."

I f it were possible, the grief they felt at the loss of Mal was made even worse on the day they returned from Alaska, when they learned that their friend and neighbor, Garrett Blue, had passed away unexpectedly on the very same day that Mal had died. Garrett had been aptly given the nickname "Navy" shortly after graduating from high school and enlisting in the U.S. Navy, spending most of a 25-year career as an officer aboard a number of different carriers, including the *Kitty Hawk, Forrestal,* and *Constellation,* among others.

Because they had trusted Navy on account of his military background, and the fact that his was the only home within view of theirs and they were concerned that he would sooner or later take notice of Jason's extraordinary physical abilities and mention it to others, they had shared Jason's secret with Navy many years before. After that, Navy dropped by frequently to watch him work out and to offer pointers, and he had even accompanied the three of them on a few of Jason's training missions. Navy was always great fun to talk to because of his inexhaustible supply of heart-stopping, heartwarming, or just plain hilarious stories, but he was also a virtual fountain of wisdom and unique perspective that Jason had come to value almost as much as the guidance he received from Mitch and Mal. And so it was doubly devastating when Jason and Mitch were told of Navy's sudden death due to head injuries he suffered after falling down his basement steps. The old farmhouse he lived in had never had a basement handrail installed, and it was surmised that Navy had caught his heel while descending the steps, pitched forward, and having no handrail with which to catch himself, tumbled headlong down the steps and died almost instantly from a fractured skull.

As fate, luck, or divine intervention would have it, the visitations of Mal Anderson and Navy Blue were to be held concurrently at the same funeral home.

⚓   ⚓   ⚓

The day of Mal's visitation and funeral was one that Jason had been dreading since their return from Alaska. He knew that seeing his father's casket for the last time, even though it would be closed due to the severity of Mal's injuries, would force him to finally accept the fact that Mal was never coming back. On each of the last three nights, before he went to bed, he managed to convince himself that when he awoke, this would turn out to have been just a terrible nightmare, and there would be Mal sitting at the kitchen table sipping his morning coffee. And despite the fact that on each of those next three mornings when Jason awoke and there was no Mal to be found, he had managed to deny the reality of Mal's death. That was, until today.

Mitch and Jason arrived at the funeral home just minutes before the visitation began. They were not expecting a large turnout, just a few friends from church, most likely, since the two of them and Mal had had to live in relative seclusion during the past fifteen years in order to avoid drawing attention to Jason. Thus, Mitch and Jason had decided to have only a one-hour visitation, followed by a brief funeral service and then the interment. There would be no luncheon or fellowship time afterwards. Neither of them wanted a long, drawn-out process, preferring instead to finish it quickly and try as best they could to move on with their lives.

As they entered the building, Jason's heart began to beat faster as he anticipated facing his father's casket, the reality of the situation finally gripping him, as he knew it would. And yet, at the same time, there was still a bit of surrealism in the air, a hint of dreaminess, which he supposed was one of the body's defense mechanisms that God had designed in order to prevent us from being completely overwhelmed by the suddenness and devastation of tragedies like this. It was this battle between reality and surrealism, between despair over the loss of his father and hope for Mal's future in paradise that had Jason so focused on his thoughts that he did not notice a young woman standing in the hallway in front of him, next to the coat rack. He proceeded to blunder right into her, the collision nearly knocking her off her feet.

Jason snapped out of his trance instantly, and was mortified by his own carelessness. "Oh! I'm so sorry!" he said, holding her by the arm as she gathered herself. "I'm *terribly* sorry, miss! Are you all right?"

The woman took a moment to gather herself, and when she turned to look at him, even with obvious annoyance smeared across her face, Jason was struck by her beauty. She had wavy brown hair that cascaded across her shoulders, penetrating dark brown eyes, sensuous lips, and slightly rosy cheeks that were sunken just enough to make her appear trim and healthy, without the emaciated look of so many of the day's top models.

When she saw the sincere remorse on his face, as well as the sadness in his eyes, her expression changed immediately to one of sympathy and understanding. "That's okay," she said softly. "I'm fine, thank you for asking." She paused for a moment, then said, "I suspect that happens a lot in places like this, you know, with so many distraught people. It's very easy to get wrapped up in your thoughts."

Mitch had been standing next to Jason and the young woman quietly, but realizing that he was not needed here, and not wanting to intrude on what he sensed might be a rather lengthy conversation, he excused himself and walked down the hallway toward the chamber where Mal's casket now rested.

"Yes, I uh . . . I was just thinking about my dad," Jason

responded to the woman's comment without meeting her eyes. He was still ashamed at his own clumsiness. "He . . . he passed away. We were just going to his visitation and funeral."

The young woman gasped. "Oh, I'm so sorry! Is there anything I can . . ." She paused, realizing too late the silliness of her question, but not knowing how else to finish. ". . . do for you?"

Jason, aware of the fact that they had now both embarrassed themselves, could not help but smile faintly. "No, but thank you for asking."

The woman blushed and returned his smile. "My name is Julie," she said, extending her right hand. "Julie Brighton."

"Jason Anderson," he said, feeling both delicateness and strength in her hand as he shook it. "It's nice to meet you . . . even under the circumstances."

"It's nice to meet you, Jason," Julie said warmly. "And again, I'm very sorry about your father."

"Thank you," Jason replied. "That's very kind of you."

There was a moment of awkward silence, and then a thought occurred to Jason.

"Oh, I'm sorry!" he exclaimed. "You must have been here to see someone as well. And since you don't know my family, it must be Navy you are here for?"

"Yes!" she said, surprised. "He is . . . . was . . . my great uncle. You knew him as well?"

"I'm sorry to hear that," Jason said with genuine sympathy. "He was our neighbor, not to mention a very good friend. Were you close to him?"

"Uh . . . no," Julie said, hanging her head. "I'm sorry to say that I wasn't. I know he was a wonderful person, but being a *great* uncle . . . I'm afraid I just didn't make the time to go visit him, at least after the first couple of months. You see, I moved out here from Omaha two years ago, and I visited him a few times early on while I was missing my family. But after that, with a new career, finding a place to live, getting settled in . . . " She didn't finish her sentence, perhaps for fear that the reasons she had cited might seem like a poor excuse to justify what some might regard as essentially using, then abandoning, her own relative.

"I understand," Jason said, as reassuringly as possible. "It's hard to stay in touch with our more distant relatives. And it does sound like you've been busy for the past couple of years. If it's any consolation to you, I do recall him mentioning a while back that he had received a visit from a great niece who had just moved into the area, and how delightful she was. He didn't give us many details about the visit, but it was clear that he really enjoyed that time with her . . . . with *you*. The other thing you should know is that he was perfectly content living by himself in that old farm house of his, with only Sherman – his German Shepherd, as I'm sure you recall -- to keep him company. Not that he was antisocial, or anything like that. He came by to visit us quite often, at least once a week, and invited us over now and then as well. What I meant was, he was someone who liked spending time with others, but whose happiness did not depend upon it. He simply enjoyed life, period."

Julie smiled. "I'm glad. That eases my guilty conscience a bit. But can I ask you something else about him?"

"Absolutely, anything!"

She paused for a moment, searching for the right words. "Well, I'm not sure what your own personal religious views are, so if you feel uncomfortable or unqualified to answer this question, then please don't feel obligated to. I was just wondering, did my uncle go to church regularly? Would you say he was a . . . godly man?"

"Well, to answer your first question, he went to church occasionally. There is a church over in Brandon that he enjoyed going to, but it is so far away that most of the time he didn't like making the drive by himself. But don't worry, because the answer to your second question is yes, he was a very godly man. I know that he read his bible and prayed every day, and when he did get the occasional visitor, if it was someone he didn't think was saved, he had no fear of sharing the gospel with them. So, to your *third* question, the one you didn't ask but which I suspect was really the one you were getting at, there is no doubt in my mind that he is in heaven right now, as we speak."

She smiled again, and released a literal sigh of relief. "Thank you for sharing that," she said. "And I take it you are a Christian as well? And your father was too?"

"Yes, to both," he answered. "Though I have to admit that losing him like this has shaken my faith a bit."

She looked up at him, her dark brown eyes exuding compassion. "Don't feel bad about that. I'm sure it's normal. I mean, I can't tell you that from experience, as I've never lost anyone really close to me, but I am sure God understands if we go through a period of doubt when we experience tragedy. After all, Jesus Himself asked His Father why He had forsaken Him, as He was dying on the cross. So don't beat yourself up, okay?"

Jason nodded, grateful for her words of comfort and wisdom, though of course she could not possibly be aware that his anxiety, fear and frustration were not the typical sort felt by those who had just lost a parent. For he had lost not only his father, but also his mentor, his coach, and his best friend.

"If you don't mind my asking," she continued, what happened to your father? I mean, you're so young, so your father must have been young also. I'm sure that is the main reason you feel your faith is being tested. I don't think people typically feel that way when a loved one dies at an old age and has lived a full life."

"Yes, he was only forty-eight," Jason answered, then hesitated, unsure of how he should answer her question, even though he had answered it several times already in the past few days. "It was a . . . . hunting accident," he finally said.

"Oh, I'm so sorry, that is terrible!" Julie said.

And then, ever so slightly, almost imperceptibly, her eyes narrowed, and her body tensed, as suspicion suddenly filled her. It occurred to Jason that she must be remembering an episode of *CSI* or some other such crime drama, or perhaps even a real life news story she may have heard, about a person dying from a gunshot wound out in the woods somewhere, and the only witness is the friend or family member in accompaniment, who claimed it was a "hunting accident." And upon investigating, the police end up charging that friend or family member with murder. To relieve her suspicion, Jason hastened to elaborate on his initial explanation. "He was actually attacked by a bear. On a trip to Alaska. That's why the casket is closed."

Any suspicion Julie felt was instantly replaced with shock and renewed sympathy. "Oh my, that's horrible, Jason! I can't even imagine! You were with him when it happened, then?"

"Well, sort of. We were all three on the trip together, me, my dad, and his brother Mitch. That was Uncle Mitch you saw me with when we came in. I got separated from Dad and Uncle Mitch, and that's when the bear attacked. I heard Dad screaming, and Uncle Mitch yelling, but by the time I got there, it was too late to help.

She shook her head. "I can't even conceive of losing someone that way, seeing it happen almost in front of you. Again, I am so sorry. And please give my condolences to your uncle as well."

"Thank you, I will."

She nodded, and a brief silence ensued. "Well, I should excuse myself and let you get to your friends and family. It was nice talking to you, Jason."

"It was nice talking to you, Julie," he said, taking her hand again. He wished he could hold it a while longer, feeling its physical warmth and softness, in addition to the emotional tenderness that flowed through it. "And thank you for your kind words," he added.

warmth and softness, in addition to the emotional tenderness that flowed through it. "And thank you for your kind words," he added.

"You're welcome, and thank you as well," she said, and turned to walk away. But at that moment it occurred to her that while they had been talking, not one person had entered the building to attend Jason's father's visitation, which struck her as very odd. She could also see inside that chamber from where she was standing, and Jason's uncle was the only one present. This meant no parents and no grieving widow of the deceased. Jason had either lost his mother and grandparents as well, or was estranged from them for some reason. She had a sudden sense of being *needed* here, that this brief encounter with Jason was not mere coincidence but was in fact orchestrated. And of course, since God Himself was the conductor of all things, their meeting must be part of His plan.

"Excuse me, Jason?" she said, turning to face him again.

"Yes?"

"I was, uh, wondering . . . ," she paused, acutely aware that what she was about to say might be construed as a come-on, despite the circumstances, "if you would like to meet me later on today to talk. Or if you're busy, then anytime you could use a shoulder to cry on, so to speak."

For a moment Jason was taken aback by the boldness of her question. But after he considered it for a few seconds, he realized that it might actually be quite normal for women to ask men out on dates, perhaps even at funerals. After all, he had been completely removed from the dating scene his entire life, so he did not exactly know how things like this worked. In any event, he saw nothing but the same earnest compassion in Julie's eyes, and in fact, her question now seemed strangely fitting and reassuring, as if she were an old friend who simply wanted to be there for him to lean on.

"Yes, I'd like that," he finally replied, with a smile. "I'd like that very much."

"Let me give you my cell phone number," she said. "You can call me later and we'll make plans to meet somewhere." She removed one of her business cards from her wallet – Jason was impressed to see that she was a partner in a CPA firm – and handed it to him, then dropped the wallet back into her purse.

Jason slid the card into his shirt pocket. "I'll call you this afternoon. And thank you again for your kindness."

Julie returned his smile and responded, "I'll be looking forward to it." She turned and walked down the hallway, into the chamber where Navy Blue rested.

L ater that day, after receiving assurances from Uncle Mitch that
he would be just fine by himself for a few hours, Jason dialed
Julie's number on his cell phone. She answered on the second ring
in a very professional tone.

"Good afternoon, Julie Brighton."

"Oh, I'm sorry Julie, it's Jason Anderson, are you still on the
clock? I should have waited until this evening to call you."

"No, not at all, Jason! When you're a partner in an
accounting firm, you're pretty much always on the clock. Never
know when a client might be stressing out over an IRS notice, or a
cash flow projection, or whether he should proceed with an
acquisition or not. It comes with the territory."

"Are you sure? I can call you later if you're busy?"

"Honestly, it's fine. I had actually cleared my calendar for
today, since I didn't know what time I'd be returning from Uncle
Garrett's visitation. Anyway, I'm more concerned about you. How
are you doing? Not great I'm sure, as this must have been one of
the roughest days of your life. But are you hanging in there?"

"Hanging in there, yes. It finally hit me today, that it was
really goodbye, you know? I'm sure there will be plenty of days
ahead where it will feel like it just can't be possible that he isn't
there. I guess we'll just have to get through one day at a time. But
we will. We'll be okay."

"Well, at least you and your uncle have each other," Julie
replied, then nearly slapped herself at the cheesiness of her words.
"Uh . . . I see it's almost four o'clock, getting close to 'Miller Time',

as they used to say. Would you like to meet somewhere for a drink, maybe an early dinner?"

"Yes, that would be . . . very nice." Jason had been about to say "great", but decided that would sound a bit too enthusiastic under the circumstances.

"Oh, and what about your uncle? I realized it was very rude of me not to mention that you should bring him along as well. After all, losing a brother has got to be just about as bad as losing a parent."

"Again, thank you for your thoughtfulness, but I'm sure he would graciously decline. He's doing okay, all things considered, and he's already busy sifting through some of Dad's personal stuff, trying to keep his mind occupied. I'll be sure to let him know that he was invited. He'll appreciate that."

They made plans to meet at a popular bar and grill that served the best and most unique burgers in town, both of them figuring that a quiet, romantic restaurant would be a little too weird, considering that this evening was to be, officially anyway, not so much a date as a therapy session. While Jason was looking forward to the conversation with Julie, what he also needed right now was to be around people . . . because where there were people, there was life. Mal's absence tomorrow, and the next day, and the day after that, and every day from now on, would serve as a constant reminder that death would sooner or later find them all. Their faith gave them hope for a glorious eternity, but in this lifetime, there was no escaping the prospect of pain, grief, and loss.

After they were seated and had each ordered a beer and one of the establishment's signature burgers, Jason began to pepper Julie with questions about her family, friends, education, career, and hobbies, among other things, in an effort to keep the conversation focused on her. It had occurred to him as he drove to meet her that she would want to know all about *him* as well . . . but of course, knowing Jason Anderson was unlike knowing anyone else in the entire world. He certainly could not divulge his secrets to someone he had just met, which meant that he would either have to be vague in his responses to her questions, or even flat out lie to her. He hoped that this was the start of a beautiful friendship, perhaps more than that, in which case he might eventually tell her the whole story. But definitely not tonight. That much information so soon, if she even believed him, would certainly scare her away.

Mal learned that Julie was twenty-four years old, eighteen months younger than him, and that she had a younger sister named Maria and an older brother named Tyson. She was originally from Omaha, Nebraska, and had attended the university there on a volleyball scholarship. She had been an all-around athlete in high school, but volleyball was her best sport, and after leading her team to two consecutive state championships, had attracted the attention of several mid-major universities. As UNO was one of the schools that offered, and because Julie preferred to stay close to home, it was a perfect fit for her. Julie graduated from the accounting program at UNO near the top of her class, and had numerous job offers to select from. But the fast-track partnership offer from Cahill & Sterns, a relatively small but growing and reputable accounting and consulting firm in Sioux Falls, South Dakota, was the one she found most intriguing. Though she had missed her parents, siblings and college friends terribly for the first few weeks after her move, a handful of visits to her Uncle Garrett (she never felt as though she knew him well enough to call him "Uncle Navy") helped to ease her homesickness. She quickly came to love her new surroundings and had not looked back in the two years since then . . . though as she had mentioned to Jason earlier that day, if there was one thing she could change, it was to have spent more time with her great uncle. Julie also made it a point to mention – to Jason's delight, before he had even worked up the courage to ask her – that she was not currently dating anyone. In fact, she had been reminding herself of that repeatedly over the last few days since Uncle Garrett died, as a way of helping to ease her conscience just a bit. Had she been neglecting him while allowing herself to be wined and dined by a prospective suitor, the guilt would have been overwhelming. But that had not been the case; she really *was* married to her work at this stage of her life, as the old saying went.

Julie politely answered all of Jason's questions, though he could sense an underlying anxiousness as she waited her turn to learn about him. Finally, due to a combination of running out of things to ask her, and a growing sense of guilt about making the conversation so one-sided, Jason could delay the inevitable no longer, and he allowed Julie to begin her own line of questioning.

"I couldn't help but notice there were no other visitors at your father's showing today, besides you and your uncle," Julie began. "I would have thought that meant you had just moved into the area, away from other family, but you also mentioned that my great uncle was a good friend of yours, which tells me you must have known him for a while. Now I know this question will seem a bit more intrusive than the ones you've been asking me, so if hits a nerve then please don't feel obligated to respond. Where is the rest of your family, your mother, for example?"

"Mom left us not long after I was born," Jason answered. "Dad always said she realized she couldn't handle the reality of being a mother. We've never heard from her since then."

Julie gasped and shook her head. "That is just awful. You really have had more than your share of tragedy."

Jason shrugged. "Someone has always got it worse."

"What about siblings? Extended family? And what about friends? You seem like such a nice person, I would think you'd have had a lot of friends supporting you at the visitation today."

"There were a few people from our church who came just after you left. As for siblings and extended family, that is certainly a fair question, though I'm somewhat hesitant to answer, for a couple of reasons. For one thing, my life is extremely complex. It

191

would be hard for me to know exactly where to begin. And for another, believe it or not, I've never had to answer these questions before. I've never been close enough to anyone for them to have asked me."

Julie's expression was one of shock mixed with mild doubt. "Well, that's okay," she said, after a pause. "You can tell me as much or as little as you want. That's why we're here, after all, for you to share whatever you feel led to share. Nothing more, nothing less."

Jason nodded, then paused. He opened his mouth to speak -- once, twice, three times -- but nothing would come out. He was caught between a proverbial rock and a hard place. He could not yet reveal his purpose in this life, but there was very little he did, day in and day out, that did not have something to do with that purpose. And though he wanted desperately to change the subject, he was having difficulty even doing *that*. He had far fewer interests than the average young adult, for he simply had not had time to develop any during the past decade. What could he possibly talk about that would give her a glimpse into the world of Jason Anderson, without revealing too much too soon?

"Well, I'll tell you one thing about myself," he finally began, "I like . . . uhhh . . . ."

"You like . . . what?" she prodded.

"I like . . . animals. You know, wild animals. Exotic ones, to be more precise. We've traveled all over the world to find animals, big, dangerous ones. I've seen lions, hippos and rhinos in Africa, tigers in India, great white sharks off the coast of South Africa, alligators in the Louisiana bayou, and as you know, grizzlies in Alaska. I love nature in general, but seeing those kinds of animals in their native habitats is really something special. Besides providing an indescribable thrill, you feel like you're closer to God in those situations."

"And yet you hunt them," she replied coolly. "I find that

interesting, if not contradictory. It's not like hunting deer or rabbits, which are plentiful. Aren't some of those animals on the endangered species list? I realize that's a human standard, not one established by God, but I suspect that if He were sitting here next to us, He'd express His disapproval at seeing some of His creatures hunted to the point of extinction."

Jason wanted nothing more than to vanish like a shadow in sunlight at that very moment. Why had he told Julie they had been on a hunting trip to Alaska? Though it was absolutely true, it was not the kind of hunting trip she thought it was, and neither were any of the other trips he had just mentioned. He wished he had simply told her that they'd been on a hiking trip when Mal had been attacked. He should have realized there was a possibility that it would strike a nerve with her, which it obviously had.

"Look, Julie, it's . . . it's not what you think. Believe me when I tell you that I have great respect for all of God's creation, and I would never do anything to exploit it. But you have to understand that it's . . . well, it's very complex, like I said before."

"Complex? How is it complex? You're a big game hunter, that's all. I'm not necessarily saying that makes you a bad person, but neither do I think you can truly have the kind of love and appreciation for nature that you say you do. To me, loving nature means it would never even occur to you to kill a part of it for sport. But you, on the other hand, can somehow reconcile loving with killing. I'm sorry, but I just don't get that."

Jason sighed, leaned forward on his elbows and massaged his temples. How could this have gone south so quickly? "Look," he said, "I hope that I can eventually explain it in a way that you will understand. But for now, can we talk about something else?"

"Sure, we can do that." She paused for a moment as she took a bite of her burger and a sip of her beer. "So tell me about your family."

Jason slumped in his chair, defeated. *Dear God,* he thought, *this is hopeless. Either I tell her everything, or I get up and walk out of this place, and out of her life forever. There can be nothing in between.* He kept his gaze fixed on Julie as he slowly chewed a steak fry, mulling over the pros and cons of his two options. And in doing so, it occurred to him for the first time that the loudest, clearest voice of reason in his life – Mal – was no longer there to keep him on the straight and narrow. It was Mal who, ever since revealing the truth of Jason's identity and purpose on the day after his tenth birthday, had warned him repeatedly about the danger of getting emotionally attached to a young lady until after Jason's training was complete. It would undoubtedly be a significant distraction to him, one that might mean the difference between victory and defeat given the prowess of his foe.

In Mal's dream, he had seen the arrival of the creature take place when Jason was a young man, perhaps in his mid-twenties, though it had been agreed upon that Jason would continue his training until he was thirty years old. This would all but guarantee that the creature would eventually be sent back to a date that would fall within Jason's training period, if in fact this turned out to be the original timeline. But in the span of just a few hours, everything had changed. Jason had never before, and might never again, meet a woman as beautiful, intelligent, compassionate, interesting and just plain desirable as Julie. The thought of waiting another five years before pursuing a relationship with her – assuming she was still single five years from now, which was highly unlikely – was one that he simply could not bear. And so at that moment, he decided it was time to put his own wants and needs in their rightful place – alongside of, rather than subordinate to, those of everyone else.

"Okay," he said finally. "You win. I'll tell you all about my family. In fact, I'll tell you my entire life story. But first, there's something I have to show you, because unless I do, you'll never believe what I have to tell you. We'll have to go somewhere private, because it's something that no one else can see. Right now, though,

I'm going to order another burger, and another beer. Then I'm going to order a large chocolate milkshake, and maybe a big slab of bread pudding for the road. That okay with you? No need to answer, it was a rhetorical question. Just sit back and enjoy the show. We're going to be here a while."

Jason instantly regretted having spoken those words with such sarcasm and bitterness. He realized he was angry about this monumental decision he had come to, but whether it was with Julie for having forced him into it so suddenly, or with Mal for having shielded him from it for so long, he could not say.

10.

There was very little discussion during the next ninety minutes, as Julie was too busy gaping at the enormous number of calories Jason was consuming, and he was too busy thinking about how and where he was going to reveal his most guarded secret to her. He decided he was not going to delve into the story while they drove to their destination, because there was simply too much to it to try to condense into a ten- or fifteen-minute drive, and because, as he had told her a few minutes earlier, seeing was the only thing that would lead to believing. Ultimately, he decided on three simple feats -- one of strength, one of speed, and one of regeneration -- that should prove his superhuman abilities to her beyond any doubt. But that was the easy part. The hard part would be proving to her that he was not just some freak of nature, as she would no doubt conclude, but that he had been ordained as one who would save the human race from the hellish product of an enemy who would not even come into existence for more than sixty years, and who would utilize technology that was currently thought to be nothing more than science fiction. And so a possible future with this woman would come down to whether or not he could convince her of the truth. That was his mission tonight. It was ironic that this mission may prove to be more difficult than any he had faced during the past fifteen years, the absence of life threatening circumstances notwithstanding.

While Jason voraciously tore into his dinner, Julie, on the other hand, barely touched hers. She had been surprised, almost shocked, by his revelation that he had killed – no doubt illegally, at least on occasion – some of the most beautiful and exotic animals on the planet. And then she had been stung by the way he angrily resigned himself to sharing the personal details of his life with her, implying that she had somehow manipulated him into it. She suddenly did not know what to make of this man, and she was not even sure she still *wanted* to know anything more about him. It was strange, and a bit unnerving, that he could not just *talk* about himself; he had to show her instead. What exactly was he going to show her? Was he some kind of Norman Bates, a guy who was really kind and gentle and who a girl could see herself ending up with, as long as she could avoid any run-ins with the desiccated corpse of his long-dead mother? She desperately wanted to trust her intuition, which told her that Jason was, in fact, the man she had first judged him to be when they had met at the funeral home today. And if that were true, then the potential rewards that a budding relationship may offer were worth the risk of accompanying someone who was, in all honesty, still a virtual stranger, to some unknown destination. Besides, she had a can of pepper spray in her purse, so she was confident she could take care of herself if it came to that.

⋏ ⋏ ⋏

It was about six o'clock when they left the restaurant, so there was still enough daylight left on this pleasant September evening. Jason had formulated a plan for displaying his abilities to Julie, and had decided that the best location to carry this out would be a series of seldom used private trails that he had once discovered near the Mickelson Trail, the primary path that snaked through the Big Sioux Recreation Area. Once there, they would take a walk on one of these trails, away from any potential witnesses, and he would then show and tell Julie everything. Meanwhile, as he did not want the twenty-minute drive to consist of nothing but awkward silence, he endeavored to repair the damage that had been done earlier.

"Julie, I'm sorry for reacting the way I did to your questions. You offered to meet me somewhere if I wanted to talk, and I willingly took you up on it. It's not as though you forced me into it. If I wasn't interested in opening up to you, then I should have politely declined your offer. And as for what I said about our hunting trips, believe me when I say that I understand exactly how you feel. I would never kill something just for the fun of it, or even for legitimate sport. There's a bigger purpose, one that I couldn't possibly explain to you with words alone. That's why I need to show you. After tonight, I promise, it will all make sense to you. The hunting trips, the reason so few people came to my dad's visitation, and everything else you want to know about me but haven't had the chance to ask yet."

She silently stared out the passenger window of Jason's Yukon Denali for a few moments before putting him on the spot yet again. "Why? I mean, why tell *me*, and why *now*?"

Jason felt his heartbeat accelerate and brow prickle with sweat at this question. She was tricky, this one, subtly trying to force him into revealing his rapidly mushrooming feelings for her. But it was not clear to him yet what her reason was for wanting to know; whether to reciprocate, or to run away. He suspected, though, that he was about to find out.

"I'm not a believer in love at first sight," Jason replied. "But just like you can have a reaction instantly when you put two chemicals together, I think when you're talking about *human* chemistry, it can work the same way. If two people are right for each other, there can be an immediate reaction, a sense of belonging together, from the very first time they meet. That's how I felt when we met this afternoon, for my part, anyway. I know people always say that you shouldn't enter into a relationship while you're dealing with tragic circumstances, but to me that advice is rather silly. If you meet someone and feel like you have that chemistry, and the timing coincides with a tragic situation, do you just calmly and unemotionally conclude that it's unhealthy to pursue that relationship under the circumstances? Do you just shake that person's hand and say, 'Thank you, but I regret that I cannot reciprocate your advances at this time as I must attend to the business of mourning. Good day to you.'? Or do you instead recognize that this is a reaction that you may never experience again as long as you live, and that the prudent thing to do is to see the experiment through to its conclusion, so to speak? I choose the latter, and that's why I want to show you, and tell you, everything."

Those who are training for a career in sales are told that once you make your pitch to a prospective customer, you sit back and shut up. The silence that follows is a powerful thing, and the first to break it is the one who usually ends up losing. If the salesman is unnerved by the period of silence, he eventually brings up some additional features of the product in an attempt to close the sale, only to talk the prospect out of it altogether. On the other hand, if the salesman has the intestinal fortitude to simply shut his mouth and wait, no matter how long it takes, the prospect will often grudgingly end up buying the product because he does not have the nerve to look the salesman in the eye and say 'no'. Jason's admission was not terribly unlike a sales pitch in that, upon its completion, the proverbial ball was placed well within the boundaries of Julie's court, and the best course of action would have been for him to simply shut up and wait. And he did – for all of about two minutes. But then he could not wait any longer.

"So was I right about the reaction? Did you feel it too?"

"I may have felt something," she finally responded. "But then again, it may have been the greasy sausage patty I had for breakfast. That *always* gets a reaction from me. I'll let you know after you've told me everything."

Jason swallowed hard and tightened his grip on the steering wheel, his nerves jangling. It was clear that closing this sale was by no means a foregone conclusion.

When they arrived at the Big Sioux Recreation Area, Jason was relieved to see only a few cars in the parking area. It was not a large park by any means, covering only about ten square miles, but the Mickelson Trail was long enough that it was usually possible to find deserted stretches of it. With any luck, they would not have to venture off the main trail, which might alarm Julie to the point where she refused to go any further. All he needed was a few minutes out in the woods with no one else around to be able to demonstrate his physical abilities to her.

"What, you want me to walk through the woods with you dressed like this?" Julie asked when she realized what Jason had in mind.

"Crap! Sorry Julie, I forgot you were still wearing your business attire." Jason himself had changed into a pair of khakis, a navy blue golf shirt, and well-worn loafers after he and Mitch had left the cemetery earlier in the day.

Julie shook her head and sighed. "Well, at least I'm wearing flats and not pumps. Just don't expect me to go very far."

"Fair enough. We just need to get far enough away from the parking area that no one will see or hear us. Then it should only take a few minutes, and we can head back."

They were separated from the vehicle by about ten steps when Julie hear the words "no one will see or hear us." She froze, looked at him with unconcealed fear now, and began to back away from him.

Jason could not help but laugh at her reaction. "Relax, I said '*we* can head back', remember? That should be an indication that I'm not planning to do something like rape you, kill you, and cut you up into little pieces, don't you think?"

She stopped backing away from him but did not proceed forward again. "You said you needed to show me something. You didn't say it would require us to completely separate ourselves from the rest of humanity."

"Really? I'd hardly call venturing a few hundred yards from a parking lot, in a state park that you can walk across in a couple of hours, 'completely removing ourselves from the rest of humanity'." He stood waiting for her to rejoin him, but still she did not move. "Come on, Julie, enough of this nonsense! I'm sorry if I wasn't clear as to exactly how and where I would go about explaining everything to you. But the fact is, I'm about to share a secret with you that is known by only one other person on this planet, now that my dad and your great uncle are dead. The risk I'm taking by telling you this . . . well, let's just say it's unimaginable. There are a whole lot of people, both good and bad, who would dedicate their lives to hunting me down if they knew about this . . . . about *me*. Now you've trusted me enough to come this far. If you trust me enough to go just a little further, you'll have the answer to every question you could ever think to ask me. So what do you say?"

Julie searched Jason's eyes for a few moments longer, and apparently found something that convinced her of his sincerity, or at the very least, piqued her interest enough that she was willing to take a chance on accompanying him. She approached and then fell in beside him as they set off down the nearest trail that led into the woods.

As they walked away from the parking area, Jason noticed that there was a group of people using the covered picnic area nearby, possibly enough to account for most of the cars that were in the lot. If luck were on his side, he and Julie would find the trails to be empty, at least for the few minutes he would need for a demonstration. That is, if his heart did not fail him before he even got the chance; the way it was hammering away at the walls of his chest, he was not entirely sure. Even after all of the deadly creatures he had faced in his lifetime, he did not think he had ever been this terrified. He was about to expose himself to someone he had just met a few hours before, someone he judged to be pure of heart but who, he had to admit to himself, he was already falling in love with.

And that meant that he was not thinking objectively, which led to downplaying of risks and exaggeration of rewards. He was in trouble, and he knew it. But he had made up his mind that he was going through with this.

The trails and woods were as Jason had hoped they would be – quiet except for the usual occupants. A variety of birds flitted through the trees, while squirrels and chipmunks by the dozen scampered around playfully through the leaves. To their left, not fifteen yards off the trail, they passed two deer nibbling contentedly at the undergrowth. They had obviously seen so many human beings traipsing through these woods that they had become disassociated with their natural instinct to run from such potential threats. This was a good thing in that it meant people were respecting the park as a nature preserve, but would spell certain doom for the deer if they were ever to venture outside of its boundaries. Fortunately, as their normal diet was no doubt supplemented with lots of tasty treats that park goers left behind, they probably would never have a reason to leave.

After they had walked for about five minutes and had encountered no one else on the trail during that time, Jason decided it was now or never. He waited just a bit longer, until they rounded a bend in the trail and came to a section that was straight for a distance of about two hundred yards, and then he stopped.

"Okay, Julie, I think this is as a good a place as any. Now I'm going to show you something, a skill that I possess, and which no one else on this planet possesses. I'm concerned that you're going to be afraid of me when you see this, but you have to promise me that you'll control your fear, at least enough to ensure that you'll stay here and not run away, or start screaming as though someone were attacking you. There may be other people close enough to hear a scream, and what I absolutely cannot risk is for anyone else to discover the truth of who and what I am. I promise you, I won't hurt you, so there's no reason to be afraid of me. And when I have shown you what I am, I will tell you the whole story of how and why it came to be. Do you understand?"

"No, you haven't shown or told me anything yet. Only then will I understand."

"I mean, do you understand about not running away or being afraid? That's all I need to know for now. The rest will make sense later, after I tell you the whole story."

She nodded. "Yes, I understand and will not run away or scream. I can't promise you I won't be afraid, because that depends on what I'm about to see."

"That's good enough. Now, I want you to look straight down the trail, to where it bends again up ahead. Do you see the large tree down there right at the bend? Don't look at me for right now, just keep your eyes on that tree."

Julie turned slightly so that she was facing directly down the straight section of the trail.

"Are you ready?"

She nodded, and a moment later, a blurry streak of blue and beige color came into her view peripherally, zipped along the edge of the trail, and two, maybe three seconds later, Jason stood, impossibly, just in front of the large tree at the bend in the trail, waving at her.

"What the . . . how did he do that?" she asked herself.

"Don't move, I'm coming back!" Jason yelled.

Suddenly he seemed to disappear, that same blob of blue and beige color hurtled back along the same route she had seen it a moment ago, and then Jason stood next to her once again. Julie could do nothing but gape at him, not yet in fear as he had warned her, but only because she did not believe what she had just seen.

"Okay . . . .so you're the world's greatest illusionist," she finally said. "I'm sure you'll have people wanting to *hire* you, but *hunt* you? That's a little dramatic, don't you think?"

Jason laughed heartily at her sardonic witticism. He could

imagine hours of playful banter with her, if indeed this relationship became what he hoped it would be.

"I didn't expect it to be that easy," he said. "But that's okay, I've got a few more tricks up my sleeve."

He scanned the trees alongside the trail, found one that he thought would be suitable, and walked over to it. It appeared to be about forty feet in height, but it was the trunk diameter that he was interested in, and that he estimated to be about twelve inches. He had successfully attempted this feat before, with trees as large as sixteen inches in diameter at the base, but he chose one smaller this time to make sure that it was well within his range. Even at twelve inches, it would take the strength of at least ten ordinary men to achieve the same results.

"Okay, here we go," Jason said. He squatted down, placed one shoulder against the tree and his head alongside of it, then wrapped his arms around the trunk. It took a few seconds of grunting, gasping and straining before the tree relinquished its grip upon the earth with a cacophony of popping roots. Jason released the tree and it fell into the woods with a crash.

Again Julie stared at him, her doubts having dissipated slightly but by no means vanquished altogether.

"And now for my final act," Jason said, still standing at the edge of the trees. "But I'll warn you, this one may cause you to lose your dinner."

He picked up a fallen tree branch, roughly two inches in diameter, from the ground, and snapped off a piece of it that he judged to be about three feet long. He walked back onto the trail and stood about eight feet away from Julie.

"I don't want to stand too close to you in case the blood sprays."

Julie's expression of bewilderment suddenly changed to one of fear and confusion. "Blood? Wait, what are you going to do?"

"Just trust me, okay?" Jason said with a smile. He knelt

down on his right knee, so that the thigh of his left leg was parallel to the ground. "This would be easier if the branch had a sharper end, but it will have to do." He gripped the branch with both hands near one end, with the other end pointed downward, raised it up above his head, and then plunged it down into his leg. Because he had used a good deal of strength to compensate for the dullness of its tip, he successfully rammed the branch all the way through his thigh and out the other side.

Julie desperately wanted to scream with horror at this shocking and gruesome sight, but she was a strong woman, and she remembered her promise despite the feeling that her faculties were about to desert her. Instead, she covered her mouth with both hands, just in case a scream managed to slip out against her wishes.

Though the pain was horrendous, it was certainly not the worst that Jason had ever experienced, so he waited a few seconds for the images to become branded in Julie's memory: the branch protruding through his leg, blood dripping and pooling on the ground beneath the wound, the pain etched upon his face. He wanted to make sure there were no lingering doubts in her mind, that this was the real thing she was seeing and not an illusion. Finally, he yanked the branch upward and back out of his leg, which prompted a fresh explosion of agony, followed by a wave of nausea. He reached into the front pocket of his khakis and removed a handkerchief he had brought with him, then sat down and lay flat on his back to allow his body to work its amazing regenerative magic.

"Come over here," Jason called to Julie.

She had not moved from her spot, and still stood with her hands covering her mouth.

"Don't worry, I'm okay," Jason said. "I need you to come over here and see this close up. Please, do it now. There won't be anything to see in a minute or two."

She hesitated for a few seconds longer, before willing her legs to obey and carry her forward four steps until she stood next to

Jason.

"Take this and kneel down next to me," he said, offering her the handkerchief. "Now pull the flap of fabric back where the branch went in, and wipe the blood from around the wound so you can get a good look at it."

Julie winced at the thought but then proceeded to do as Jason had instructed.

"Okay, now just watch for a minute. The rate of healing depends on several different things, one of them being the severity of the wound, of course. But it also depends on how much food I've got in my stomach. My metabolism kicks into overdrive whenever I'm injured, as my body needs a huge amount of calories to heal itself at an accelerated pace. The more I've got in my stomach, the faster I heal, all other factors being equal. That's why I ate so much food at dinner tonight. Once I made up my mind that I was going to show you this, I wanted the wound to heal as quickly as possible in case someone else happened to come by. The last thing I need is for some well-meaning stranger to call 911 and have cops and paramedics showing up. They would discover the secret of my regenerative ability, if not my other physical abilities you just saw, but that might be enough to bring the government into it. They'd want to lock me up and make me a human lab rat for the rest of my life. I would escape, of course, but they would never stop hunting me after that."

By the time Jason had finished speaking, the ragged wound in his leg had completely knitted itself shut, leaving only a faint pink splotch behind.

With the show now over, Julie sat down on the gravel of the walking trail, oblivious to the dirt and dust getting on her wool slacks. She stared speechless at Jason with a combination of disbelief, shock, wonder, admiration, revulsion, fear, and probably a few other emotions as well.

"So now you know about me, or at least, the things I can do,"

Jason said. "But there's a whole lot more to the story, like how I got these abilities, and what they are to be used for. Then there's Mal and Mitch, who I've always thought of as my father and uncle, but are in fact no relation to me. Even your Uncle Garrett played a small part in this epic tale, which began when Mal was twelve years old and may very well continue on until long after you and I are both dead. I know what I just said doesn't make any sense, but it will. As I promised, I'll tell you everything. It will take some time, though, and I think we've covered enough for tonight. My wound may have healed on the outside, but on the inside, my body is still recovering from the shock. I need to go home and rest. Can I see you again tomorrow night? I have something else to show you, a narrative that Mal wrote many years ago, when he first became aware of my existence, my abilities, the role he was to play in helping us get to this point, and a whole lot more. I'll bring a copy of it with me tomorrow so you can read it. And then I can tell you about my life, from my earliest memories up until the moment you met me."

Julie hesitated before answering. A part of her was so overwhelmed by what she had just seen, the part that relished a safe, predictable, more or less uneventful life, and that part wanted nothing more to do with Jason Anderson, his freakish abilities, or outrageous tales. That part of her knew that if she continued on with this relationship, her life from this point forward would be anything but safe, predictable or uneventful. But she also had an adventurous side to her, a side that did not often get the chance to indulge itself, given her choice of career and lovable but rather unimaginative circle of friends. It was this daring side of her that quickly overruled the cautious side, and her decision was made.

"All right, you can come to my house for dinner tomorrow night. I'll send you a text message with my address."

"Perfect, I'll bring the wine. Now let's get back to the car before someone comes by, sees me soaked with blood and starts asking questions."

They were both quiet on the drive back to the restaurant, she because her brain was firing on all cylinders as she processed dozens of theories on how Jason obtained his incredible powers, and he because there was nothing to talk about except his own fantastic story, something he did not want to get any deeper into until tomorrow.

Darkness had arrived by the time they reached their destination.

"Well, I guess I'll talk to you tomorrow," Julie said.

"Good night," Jason said, for lack of anything better to say.

Julie leaned over, kissed him on the cheek and glanced into his eyes. It was just a momentary glance, but it was long enough to convey a message that said, "I trust you, and you can trust me. We are about to embark on an amazing journey together."

11

Jason arrived at Julie's house at 6:00 sharp the following evening, toting a copy of Mal's dream narrative, and a bottle of his favorite Moscato. He knew very little about wine in general, but what he did know about Moscato, aside from the fact that he enjoyed it very much, was that it was low in alcohol content, which he felt was important on a night such as this. A certain amount of alcohol would help both of them to relax and talk openly, but too much would make it difficult for Julie to process all that he was going to share with her tonight. What he had revealed to her the night before, as disturbing and incredible as it may have seemed to her, was nothing compared to what she was about to be told.

They dined on Irish dishes that included Shepherd's Pie, Purple Cabbage and Pecan Salad, and for dessert, an Irish Cream Bundt cake. Julie explained that she was of Irish ancestry on her mother's side, and when she and her two siblings were in high school, their parents had taken them there on a two-week vacation. She had quickly fallen in love with the people, culture, history, scenery, architecture, food . . . pretty much everything about the country. Ever since then, and especially during the last two years after she had moved to Sioux Falls from Omaha and had to start cooking her own meals every day, she had made it a point to cook an Irish dinner at least once a week. She was constantly experimenting with new recipes, but on this night, as she did not want to make Jason a guinea pig, she selected dishes that she felt she had perfected.

Jason was in total agreement – everything was absolutely

delicious.

"So you've done a bit of traveling yourself, then," Jason commented after hearing Julie rave about Ireland.

"Here and there, though that was certainly the trip of a lifetime," Julie answered. "Other than that, I've been to several major U.S. cities and some of the national parks. The usual stuff, I guess. Nothing compared to the places you've been."

"Maybe, but there are lots of places in our own country that I'd like to see but have never gotten the chance. And as far as I'm concerned, the more you travel the world, the more you agree with what Dorothy said in The Wizard of Oz: 'there's no place like home.' That has always been especially true for me personally, because of the fact that I hated doing what I had to do on those trips. You know, killing those animals."

"What do you mean? You mentioned something like that last night, about never killing animals for fun or for sport. Why would you hunt animals if you hated killing them? Did your father and uncle drag you along on their hunting trips?"

"No, no, it was nothing like that. I'll tell you all about the trips when I get to that part of the story, but for right now, believe me when I tell you that I *did* despise them, every one of them, and furthermore, they were not hunting trips in the traditional sense. They were training missions, intended to help me fully develop my skills through hand-to-hand combat with the world's deadliest animals. Unfortunately though, when you pick a fight with an alligator, a lion, or a bear, it ends up being a fight to the death. It's either going to be me, or it's going to be them."

"My God," Julie said, shaking her head. "This is just getting more and more bizarre. So you actually fought these animals with your bare hands? Why wouldn't you use a weapon? And what were you training for that required those kinds of confrontations?"

"At first I carried knives and battering weapons, like steel batons, because I wasn't strong or fast enough to win without them.

But I never once carried a gun. That would be too easy. My strength and speed are enhanced through direct, close quarter's engagement with my opponent. Likewise, my regenerative ability becomes stronger only when I sustain injuries that are severe enough to push me to my limit . . . in other words, to the very brink of death. It's like when you lift weights to try to build muscle. You first have to tear the muscle down in order for it to add new tissue when it repairs itself, thus making it larger. Because of all the serious injuries I have sustained during my training missions, my body's ability to heal itself has developed to the point where I can regrow entire limbs in a matter of minutes, maybe even seconds if my life depended on it. As for what I'm training for, well . . . let's not get ahead of ourselves. I brought the narrative that Mal wrote, the one I mentioned last night. I'll let *him* tell you that part."

They made small talk throughout the rest of their dinner and while they cleaned up the kitchen. Afterwards, they each poured another glass of wine and made themselves comfortable in the living room, settling in for a long evening of reading and discussion.

"Do you believe a person can have psychic abilities?" Jason began.

Julie considered the question for a moment before answering. "I think it is possible, yes. You hear about people in the news who are contacted by police departments to ask for their help in locating a missing person or solving a crime. Police detectives strike me as being naturally skeptical, so for them to enlist the aid of a psychic means they must be pretty sure that that person can help, either because they have witnessed it firsthand previously, or they have heard it from trustworthy colleagues."

"So you've never known anyone personally who claimed to be a psychic?"

"No. Why do you ask?"

"Because Mal was one of them. Not some phony like you might see on a cheesy reality show or infomercial. He was the real thing. He saved lives because of his ability, when he saw terrible tragedies occur in advance and was able to convince the people involved to avoid the circumstances that would have cost them their lives. He helped police detectives on several occasions as well, in situations like those you had just mentioned. Though he probably had the ability his entire life, he had his first meaningful and memorable vision when he was eleven years old, during some crazy adventure that he had with a friend of his when they discovered a private lake tucked away in the woods a few miles behind the church their families attended. He told me they were chased and nearly attacked by a vicious goat that his friend always thought was simply rabid, but which Mal recognized to be something much worse. He saw its eyes start to glow red, and heard it make some kind of a shrieking sound that no normal goat could have ever made. At that point, he had a vague awareness that it represented some sort of looming evil, but it wasn't until his next vision, over a year later, that it began to make more sense to him. He was sitting in church listening to the pastor's message when the second vision came to him. He saw everyone in the church being mauled by some invisible animal, one that he sensed had a malevolent purpose, as opposed to being instinctive or defensive like animal attacks on humans normally are. Meanwhile, the pastor was quoting the scripture verse from Jeremiah and Matthew about Rachel weeping for her children, and seconds later, the goat incident, which he had almost forgotten about, came vividly back to mind as though it had just happened the day before. Piecing it all together, he realized that someday, some sort of monstrous creature, unleased by a person possessed of almost unprecedented evil, would destroy the entire human race. Or at least attempt to."

Julie was utterly enraptured by the story she was hearing, scarcely able to contain herself when Jason paused for a moment. "So you're some kind of a hero then, is that it? That would explain your abilities! You've been chosen to fight this creature, haven't you!? Where is this creature now, and when is this supposed to happen?"

"Whoa, hold on a second! You're right about me being chosen to fight the creature. Whether I'm a hero or not depends on who wins the fight. But as for the where and when, those questions are a whole lot more complicated. That's why I brought Dad's journal. He wrote it when he was twenty-two, the next time he had an apocalyptic vision that was related to the previous two. Why don't you read it, and afterwards we'll discuss it. I brought a second copy that I'll be reading at the same time. I've read it a couple of dozen times already, but I read it again every few months to refresh my memory and to see if I pick up anything that I may have missed before."

Jason handed Julie a copy of the journal, and they both read in silence for the next two hours. By the time Julie finished, she could scarcely stand up, or even lift her arms. Reading the journal had produced such an incredible adrenaline rush that coming down from it weakened her muscles in a way she had never experienced before. "Incredible," she mumbled, and then sat in a kind of stupor for quite some time. Jason said nothing, either, for he knew she needed time to process everything.

"So I see now what you meant," Julie said at last, "when you said that whether or not you'd be a hero depends on who wins the fight. You don't know the outcome of the battle with the creature, because your dad's dream ended prematurely. But isn't it safe to assume that you will? After all, God wouldn't have chosen you for this role if He meant for you to fail, and for basically the entire human race to be destroyed."

"You wouldn't think so, but the question that always nagged at Mal was whether it would make a difference that he didn't see the entire dream. Was that part of God's plan? Mal told me several years ago, after I had almost been killed by a great white shark, that he was very concerned about not seeing me kill the creature, and more importantly, exactly *how* I manage to kill the creature. He said that that missing scene had 'haunted' him over the years. That was the word he used. He had this feeling that despite all of my physical abilities, that it would not be enough. He felt that for me to win, it would take something more, some kind of untapped skill."

"Like something supernatural?"

Jason shrugged. "Mal couldn't even wager a guess. But if it's true, then it begs the question of whether things are unfolding the way God intended them to. If Mal was meant to see the entire dream so that he could pass along all of the knowledge I would need to defeat the creature, does that mean that because the dream was interrupted, that I am now destined to fail?"

"I don't buy that," Julie countered. "If your success or failure hinged upon Mal seeing the entire vision, wouldn't God have ensured that no one would interrupt it?"

"Not necessarily. Maybe God only ensured that there was adequate time available, but it was up to Mal to utilize that time wisely. Remember, Randall warned him not to procrastinate because there would be people coming to get him. Granted, Mal did not know precisely what he meant at first, but the words 'you'd better get moving' ought to have been enough without having a complete picture. Yet later in the dream, after the death of Zintak's parents, Mal's fortitude wavered, and he went back to see Randall for a little pep talk. Had he not done that, there would have been time for him to see the entire vision, and that might mean the difference between winning and losing."

Julie considered this for a moment, then nodded. "I see your point. You can't be sure of how this thing will end. I guess the only thing you can do is continue your training until the creature arrives, then pray you have everything you need to get the job done."

Jason hesitated before responding. "Well . . . . see, the thing is, there's only a 50/50 chance that the creature will arrive in our lifetimes. We don't know if we're on the original timeline, in which case we'll live full and normal lives, or the altered one, where the creature may show up at any second. But either way, as for the training, I've made up my mind that it's over. I'm done. Now that Mal's gone, it's time for me to live for myself and not for everyone else in the world. He pushed me for fifteen years, getting me out of bed early every day, forcing me to sacrifice friendships, family, athletics, college, career, all the things that any other kid would be able to experience. Not that I blame him, of course, because I do understand why it was all necessary. But it has to end sometime, and I feel like now is the time. Why would God have brought you into my life right now if that were not the case?

Julie was surprised by these words, and was silent for several minutes as she considered them. "What if He is testing you yet again?" she finally asked. "You've certainly been tested like few other people ever have, but what if this is just another part of the same test? To see if you'll maintain your focus even after the death of your father, and after meeting me? Had you considered that?"

"Yes, I had," Jason admitted. "And if that's the case, then I guess I fail the test. My heart's just not in it. If I were to square off against a bear, or a lion, or a shark right now, I'd almost certainly get torn to pieces. Those encounters require supreme focus, something I don't have any more and probably never will again."

"No one is saying you have to jump on a plane for Alaska or Africa tonight, or tomorrow. Of course you need some time to mourn the loss of your father and get your head on straight again. But to give up completely? You don't strike me as a quitter, or as someone who makes irrational decisions. I mean, think about it. You might be at the very top of your game right now, maybe the best you can possibly be. But what if the creature shows up a year from now, or two, or three? Can you honestly say that you'd be as prepared then as you are now?"

"Who's to say?" Jason replied with a shrug. "Maybe my abilities would not regress even if they aren't continuously honed, like they would with a normal person. But even if they did, I can't go on with it if I just don't have it in me. And besides, I . . . . I don't want to lose you."

"Why would you lose me?"

Jason glanced at her with raised eyebrows. "Really? You're kidding, right? We're talking about five more years of this. That's what Mal and I had originally decided, that I would train until I was 30. I can't imagine that you'd be willing to wait for me that long."

Up to this point, it was Jason who had lowered his guard and exposed his inner self to Julie. He had been the one to share his secret, to trust her with information that many people would kill to possess. She knew it was time for her to reciprocate, to reveal to him what she, too, had been feeling since the moment they had first, literally, bumped into each other. That had been less than 36 hours ago, but it felt more like 36 months. She turned sideways on the sofa seat to face him, took his hands into hers, and looked him directly in the eyes.

"Jason," she said tenderly, "I'll be totally honest with you. One of the reasons I want you to continue your training is purely selfish. The thought of that monster tearing me and everyone I care about to pieces is utterly horrifying. Since we don't know if that will happen in this lifetime, I want you to be as ready as you can possibly be, just in case it does. But there's something else, something deep down in the pit of my stomach, that's telling me you need to fight through this adversity and finish your training. I'm no psychic, of course, so call it plain old women's intuition. I just have this feeling that there will be a terrible price to pay if you quit now. And as for losing me . . . that won't happen. You were right about what you said last night, that it felt like we were right for each other from the moment we first met. I will wait five years for you, if need be, because I am falling in love with you. However this timeline is going to end, we will see it through together."

Upon hearing this, Jason's head began to spin as though he

were intoxicated (in fact, the Moscato may have played a role in it as well). The room began to take on a dreamy, surreal quality, with everything in his peripheral view disappearing, and only Julie remaining visible to him. He leaned over and kissed her, and the smell of her hair, the warmth of her skin, the taste of her lips made the world melt away completely. Her presence, her aura, seemed to wrap itself around him like a blanket, and he knew nothing else for several minutes, until the kiss inevitably came to an end. Afterwards, they stretched out on the sofa and simply cuddled for a while, Julie purring like a kitten while Jason caressed her arm and sprinkled kisses upon her neck and shoulder.

"So is there anything else you want to know about all of this?" Jason finally asked.

"Yes, there's something I was wondering. How many of these training missions have you been on? How many animals do you think you have fought?"

"I don't know," Jason admitted. "I lost count a long time ago. I would say several dozen."

"And when you've gone on these trips, have you always encountered the type of animal you were looking for?"

"Yes, as far as I can remember, I always find the animals. Or they found *me*, however you want to look at it."

"Every single time?"

"Yes, every single time. Why do you ask?"

"Because I have to think that's incredibly unlikely. Animal attacks are pretty rare, when you consider how many people are out there experiencing nature on any given day, whether it's hiking through the forests, swimming in the ocean, going on safaris, visiting national parks, whatever. Unless a wild animal is sick, protecting itself or its offspring, or just really hungry, I guess, they almost always *avoid* people rather than attacking them. And yet you've been attacked each and every time you've gone out into a wilderness-type of environment. How do you explain that?"

"I can't. It just happens. Your Uncle Navy asked me this same question once, and all I could tell him was that I assume it is just part of God's plan. It's *His* creation, after all, so He can use any part of it in any way He sees fit."

Julie considered this for a moment. "Yes, I suppose that must be it." But she had this feeling that there was more to it than that, that there were connections to be made among the different variables and unknown pieces of the puzzle that they were overlooking.

They snuggled together for several more minutes before Jason willed himself to glance at his watch. "Well, I'd better get going," he said. "I'm sure we can both use some sleep."

"I'm sure I can *use* it, the question is whether I can *get* any of it, with all of this in my head now."

"Believe me, I know exactly how you feel. I'll never forget the day that Mal told me everything. And you're a grown woman. Imagine how that kind of revelation would affect a ten-year old kid."

"Yes, I can only imagine," Julie said. "As much as this has blown me away, it's nothing compared to the life you've had to lead. I'm sorry I doubted you."

"No, not at all. Who *wouldn't* have doubted me? At least you were able to set aside your doubts long enough to hear the whole story. Most people wouldn't have done that. Of course, we've pretty well established that you're not like most people."

She looked over her shoulder and smiled playfully at him. "Oh, you have no idea. Remember, you've known me for less than two days. I'm no superhero, but I've got a few tricks up my sleeve, too."

"Oh yeah? Would you like to share a few of them?"

"In due time," she said with a laugh. "Come on, I'll show you out."

At the door, they enjoyed another long embrace and kiss.

"Call me tomorrow?" Julie asked.

"And the next day, and the day after that," Jason said with a grin.

12

Original Timeline – April 2021

Five years came and went. Most of Jason's days were spent running, lifting weights, and employing whatever creative methods he could come up with to help sharpen his skills. There were dozens more training missions along the way, as well, and while these trips helped to stave off boredom, they were, as always, abhorred because of the bloodshed that resulted. And on every one of those trips, as before, Jason never came home with the mission unaccomplished; there was *always* an encounter, no matter where, or when.

During those five years, two things continually happened. One, Jason and Julie grew closer every day, bound together by the secret they shared, by Jason's need for encouragement to fight through the constant desire to simply be done with this lifestyle once and for all, and by Julie's desire to provide that support. They loved each other beyond words, and they longed for the day that they could begin to live the kind of normal life that others enjoyed, but which they had had to postpone. The second thing that happened was that, despite the energy that Julie gave him, the way she made him *feel* young, Jason was undeniably getting, and *looking*, older. He was still several months away from his thirtieth birthday, but the salt-and-pepper tint that his hair was taking on, and the fine lines that were developing at the corners of his eyes made him look several years older. Jason noticed this one day as he was shaving . . . that he no longer looked like that "young man" that Mal had seen engaging the creature. And while Jason certainly did not relish this, neither did he dread the changing of his appearance, because he realized that his training, finally, could come to an end.

For the first couple of years after Jason had met Julie, they had, figuratively, held their breath as they wondered whether this would be the day the creature arrived. As time went on, however, they thought about it less and less frequently, until at last that fear was downgraded to a mere possibility, and was confined to the back of their minds as the focus became more about grinding through the final stages of Jason's training. On this day, as he studied himself in the mirror, it dawned on him fully that they were finally in the clear.

He was planning a trip to the Rocky Mountains to tangle with a cougar or two, and to strengthen his endurance a bit through some intense workouts in the thin mountain air. He called Julie to break the news to her.

"Hey, it's me," Jason said when Julie answered the phone. "I've decided it's over."

Julie did not have to ask what "it" was, since "it" had consumed their lives for the past four and a half years. "What made you decide this?" she asked.

"Because I'm old," he replied.

She burst out laughing and said, "You are *not* old, and you know it. You're as hot as ever, baby."

Jason himself could not help but laugh at this. "Well, maybe I'm not old, but I'm not young anymore, either. You know what I mean. I'm old enough that I don't have to do this anymore. I've done my time. The creature will have certainly arrived by now, whether on this timeline or on the altered one."

"Yes, I would have to agree with you. There's no way we can be absolutely sure, but as you said when we first met, 'it has to end sometime.' It wasn't time then, but I think it is now. After you fly home from Denver, we'll have a party and officially celebrate our new life together. How does that sound?"

"Sounds like the best thing I've ever heard. And maybe you'll pull another of those tricks out of your sleeve for when I get back."

"Well," Julie said with a laugh, "I'll see what I can do. Be safe."

"I will. Love you."

"Love you, too."

⅄   ⅄   ⅄

Jason rented a 4 x4 at Denver International Airport and drove west toward the mountains. He had been out here numerous times before and knew of several dirt or gravel roads leading up into the mountains that were used by hunters, fishermen, hikers and photographers to reach secluded lakes, rivers and prime hunting areas. He chose one of his favorites, on account of the unobstructed views it offered on the way to a beautiful little waterfall just a couple of hundred feet below the peak of the mountain, and headed up the narrow, boulder-strewn lane.

About thirty minutes after leaving the main highway, Jason reached the small, makeshift parking area alongside the waterfall and was glad to find it deserted. Not that there was a significant risk of anyone ever witnessing one of his animal encounters, since he always ventured far from the main trails and deep into the backcountry in search of an opponent. Nevertheless, the fewer people he crossed paths with along the way, the better.

Jason got out of the vehicle and locked it. He scanned the trees and ridges all the way around him, making sure there were no backpackers who might have ventured this far up the mountain on foot. Seeing none, he sprinted across the open area adjacent to the waterfall and sprang from the ground, reaching the mountaintop in just a few giant leaps. Just like that, he was in the backcountry, safe from potential discovery and free to roam the isolated peaks and

222

valleys until he found what he was looking for. He walked along casually, not being noisy but then again, not being especially quiet, either. That was another odd thing about these trips that he had realized years ago – stealth was by no means a necessity, as one would expect it to be when in pursuit of a reclusive animal that could hear and smell a human being coming in plenty of time to make its retreat.

It usually did not take long for Jason's opponent to make its appearance, and sure enough, after about ten minutes, he spotted a large cougar crouched on the slope opposite the one he was currently descending, probably about two hundred fifty yards away. But the cougar had apparently not yet seen or otherwise detected Jason, for it was looking away from him, and in fact, based on its crouch and the way its tail was swishing from side to side, it appeared to be ready to attack something else. What was strange, though, is that it seemed to be looking down upon its prey, as though it were lying on the ground right at its paws. Perhaps it had spotted a mouse or other small rodent and was about to pounce upon it?

Jason continued his approach toward the cougar, indifferent as to whether or not it would turn to attack him once it became aware of his presence. If it turned out to be more interested in the prey it was already stalking than it was in him, no matter; another one would come along shortly. When he got to within twenty-five yards of the animal, it finally heard him and whirled around, startled. It sat frozen for a few seconds, a trademark low-pitched growl emanating from its throat as it attempted to warn Jason off. And then it seemed as though it was sizing him up, assessing whether he might be a more desirable meal than the one it had been about to partake of. It looked down at the ground again, then at Jason, down at the ground, and again at Jason, trying to make up its mind. And that was when Jason noticed that the cougar had not been looking down at some small critter upon the ground, but rather was standing alongside a narrow crevice and peering down into it. He was too far away from the crevice to see into it himself, but there was clearly something in there that had drawn the cougar's attention.

Jason could have probably drawn the cougar away from the crevice and enticed it into attacking him, but his curiosity had now gotten the better of him. He started shouting at the cougar, waving his arms and walking toward it to try to frighten it away. At first, the cougar refused to give ground, and its growl intensified as it attempted to win this showdown by establishing itself as the dominant predator. But of course, Jason had no fear of the animal and continued forward until he was within a few yards of it, at which point the cougar reluctantly turned, leaped across the crevice and bounded away amongst the boulders and scattered pine trees.

Jason approached the crevice expecting to see a young mule deer, perhaps even an elk wedged into the narrow gap. Instead, when he looked down into it, he found not an animal, but rather, a man.

ᴧ   ᴧ   ᴧ

The crevice was about four feet wide at the top, plenty wide enough for any human being to fall into, and it was extremely deep – so deep that the bottom was shrouded in darkness. Fortunately, it narrowed gradually to a width of about two feet at a point roughly twenty feet below the rim, and the man had fallen that far before getting stuck. It had undoubtedly been a nasty fall, but the man was actually lucky that he had fallen that far, for he had been well out of the reach of the cougar. The animal had been studying him, pondering how it might get down there and make him its next meal, and eventually it might have made such an attempt.

"Hello!" Jason called down to the man. "Sir? Can you hear me?"

There was no response, nor any discernible movement. Jason feared that the man had been trapped here for several days and had died of exposure or dehydration, if not from any serious injuries he might have sustained during the fall.

"SIR!" Jason yelled at the top of his lungs. "CAN YOU HEAR ME?"

"Uhhhhh," came the reply at last.

That was a relief. The man may very well end up dying, anyway, but he was alive for now, which meant there was a chance to save him. The question was *how*. The easiest and most logical way to rescue the man would be for Jason to lower himself down into the crevice with a rope, tie a second rope around the man's chest, then climb out of the crevice and pull him up from the top. That would also allow Jason to conduct the rescue without any noticeable use of his superhuman abilities. But he had not brought any rope with him, nor did he have any in his vehicle. Furthermore, he had no cell phone signal up here, and he could not risk driving all the way back to the nearest town to go for help, or to bring rope back to rescue the man himself, for he might die while Jason was gone.

Jason came to the inescapable conclusion that he could not use conventional methods if he were to save the man. So, hoping that the man was not conscious enough to see or understand what was about to happen, Jason sat down on the edge of the crevice, stretched his legs out across the gap and planted his feet against the opposite wall. He began to work his way down into the crack, pressing his back against one side and his feet against the other. But he was only about halfway down when the crevice became too narrow, and he had to lower his legs in order to continue his descent. That was not the issue, however, for there were plenty of finger and toe-holds in the face of the crevice wall to allow him to climb down the rest of the way. The problem was going to be figuring out a way to get the man up out of the crevice while simultaneously climbing out of it himself. That would most *certainly* require a superhuman feat.

Jason continued the downward climb until he came to a point just above and to the side of the man. He was positioned almost vertically, facing towards the crevice wall, and was wearing a daypack on his back. Again, it was to his good fortune that he had worn this pack, for it gave his body enough girth to allow him to get stuck at the narrowest point in the crevice. At approximately two feet, the gap was wide enough to allow the man to have slipped through had he not been wearing the backpack, and now that Jason had climbed down this far, he could see that the crevice widened dramatically beginning at a point just about where his feet were now. Had he fallen below the narrow point, the man would have dropped into the blackness and either died instantly when he eventually hit the bottom, or would have never been seen or heard from again.

Jason inspected the visible areas of the man's body, and it was clear that his injuries were fairly serious. His right arm was not visible, as it was wedged between his chest and the crevice wall, but his left arm dangled freely, and Jason could see that it had deep cuts on it, probably from scraping against the rough walls of the crevice as he fell. There was a gash on the side of the man's head as well, and he had cracked lips, papery skin, and sunken eyes, all symptoms of extreme dehydration. Attempting to rescue the man immediately, rather than going for help, was clearly the right decision, for it appeared as though he did not have much longer to live without water and medical care.

The man seemed to have slumped back into unconsciousness, so Jason decided not to try to revive him until he had gotten him up out of the crevice, for he was about to utilize a measure of strength that would likely surpass that of any normal person, and he did not want the man to be aware of that. Of course, if the man was delirious and hallucinating, it probably would not matter if he were conscious or not, but Jason could not be sure of that.

Jason found a solid foothold for his left foot, turned his body so that he was facing down the length of the crevice, then found another foothold for his right foot on the opposite wall. He inserted the fingers of his left hand into a crack that ran horizontally along the face of the crevice, then with his right hand, he removed the hunting knife that he had noticed was hanging from a sheath on the man's belt. He used it to slice through the left shoulder strap of the man's backpack. He could not reach the opposite shoulder strap to cut through it, but he expected the backpack to simply slide off the right shoulder once he began to lift the man up by his left arm. Jason returned the knife to its sheath, reached down again and grasped the man by his left wrist. He then began the extremely difficult task of climbing the wall using just three of his limbs while also tugging a two hundred-or-so pound man up with him. His plan was to ascend the first ten feet or so using this same straddle position, keeping one foot on each of the walls, and then when the crevice became too wide, revert to pressing his back against one wall and his feet against the other.

Jason had climbed about three feet up the wall when he reached the point where the man's arm was fully extended, and he then began to gently pull upward to free him from the vice he was caught in. He did not want to pull any harder than necessary, for fear of exacerbating any internal injuries the man might have, as well to avoid dislocating the shoulder. But the man was wedged in tighter than Jason had expected, and as he pulled up on his arm, he was also pushing down heavily on the footholds that he was using on each of the crevice walls. And suddenly, this downward pressure caused all hell to break loose; there was an ear-splitting *crack!,* and on both sides of the crevice, enormous chunks of granite gave way just about at the level of Jason's waist and collapsed into the dark void below. The crevice had turned out to be just a tiny gash at the top of a huge underground cavern!

As the opposing sections of the crevice wall calved off and fell to the cavern floor far below, they took Jason's footholds with them. Were it not for the fact that he had established a firm grip on a tiny ledge in the wall with his left hand, he and the man – or at least, the man, anyway – would have fallen to their deaths. But now, he found himself clinging to what was left of the crevice wall, his feet dangling in empty space, and with his right hand, holding onto the man's left wrist while he, too, hung suspended in mid-air.

The sounds of the crevice walls splitting off and crashing onto the cavern floor instantly brought the man back to full consciousness. His backpack finally slid off his right shoulder just as he opened his eyes, and he was confused for a moment as he saw it disappear into the black void below. But then he looked up, saw Jason holding him by the wrist, and furthermore, saw the predicament that Jason *himself* was in with no way to climb the wall one-handed, and screamed. In the process, he reflexively pulled on his left hand and nearly yanked it out of Jason's grip.

"HOLD STILL!" Jason yelled at him. "You've got to stay calm, or I might drop you!"

The man stopped squirming, but he could not hold his body entirely still, for he was now trembling with terror.

Truth be told, Jason was terrified as well. He had never felt so helpless in his life, as though he were trying to take on a polar bear with both hands tied behind his back. There were not exactly a lot of options at his disposal for saving their lives. Had they been near a trail or a popular scenic overlook, someone might happen to come along shortly and discover them. But such was not the case; they were not only deep in the backcountry, but also twenty feet underground and hidden from the view of anyone who might be in the area.

"Are you with anyone?" Jason asked the man. "Is there anyone who would be out looking for you?"

"My family," the man said hoarsely. "I was with my family."

Jason felt a glimmer of hope for just a moment. He knew that he could hang here for hours, perhaps even a day or more, before his strength gave out, and the fact that the man had clearly been stuck in the crevice for at least a couple of days apart from his family meant that his wife would have certainly notified authorities by now that her husband was missing.

The man seemed to read Jason's mind. "But I . . . I wandered off the trail without telling them. I saw some bighorn sheep on the opposite slope from where I was hiking, and I left the trail to get a better view of them. They won't be looking for me here."

Just like that, Jason's hopes were dashed. He would have to come up with a plan B. He took a deep breath and forced himself to focus, and then a thought occurred to him. "I want you to squeeze my wrist with your hand," he said to the man. "I need to see how much strength you have."

To that point, the man had simply been allowing Jason to hold him by the wrist without attempting to bolster their connection by gripping Jason's wrist in return. Now he attempted to do so at Jason's command.

"Is that as hard as you can squeeze?" Jason asked.

"Yes."

Upon hearing this, Jason's fear and dismay increased to new levels, as he realized that plan B was not going to work, either. He had hoped the man would have enough strength left to wrap his arms around Jason's waist, thus freeing Jason's right hand and allowing him to climb the wall. But as weak as the man's grip was around Jason's wrist, there was no way he could hold on for the two or three minutes that Jason estimated it would take to climb up out of the crevice.

And so on to plan C. There seemed to be no getting around it now; Jason would have to reveal his supernatural strength to this man – if it was not already apparent -- in order to save both of their lives. He looked down at the man and saw that he was trembling more violently than before, and his breathing had become rapid and shallow, a sign that he was going into shock. Combined with the effects of advanced dehydration, it would certainly result in his death in short order. Jason had no choice but to act now.

"Sir, listen to me," Jason said. "I'm going to start swinging you back and forth. When we get enough momentum built up, I'm going to throw you up through the gap. You can see that it's narrow right above my head, but then it starts to widen out. When I release you, I'll try to throw you at an angle, so that you land on the edge of the crevice instead of falling directly down into it again. Do you understand?"

The man looked up at Jason with a blank expression that made it clear he did not, in fact, understand. "Throw me? Did you say *throw* me? But how—"

Jason was expecting those questions, and had been about to interrupt the man and tell him not to worry about that right now, but rather to focus on the instructions he had been given if he wanted to survive this ordeal. But the man actually cut *himself* off before Jason had the chance, while at the same time, a strange expression appeared on his face, one of . . . . recognition? Jason could not see how this was possible, for he was sure he had never met the man before. But right now, it was of little consequence.

"Do you understand?" Jason asked again.

"Yes, I understand," came the response.

"All right then. I'm going to start swinging you now, and when I feel like we have as much momentum as we're going to get, I'm going to count to three and release you. When I do, you need to keep your legs tight together, your right arm tight against your body, and your left arm directly above your head like it is now, so that no body parts catch against the opening on the way up. Do you follow me?"

"Yes."

"All right, here we go."

Jason began to swing the man back and forth in a motion that aligned with the direction of the gap above his head. Despite the instructions he had given the man, Jason could not help but worry that he would not pass through the opening cleanly but rather scrape against it. If that were to happen, it would probably negate enough of the upward momentum that the man would not reach the surface, but would instead tumble back down through the gap and fall to his death. Allowing for this possibility would require Jason to hurl the man upward much harder than he would have liked to, but it was either that or bet all of his chips on the hope that the passage through the gap would be a clean one. He decided that the first option was the better of the two.

"I'm ready!" Jason said, when he had the man swinging in a wide arc below him. "One, two, three!"

Jason flung the man upward towards the gap on a slight angle with not all, but a considerable portion of, his strength. His aim was true; the man sailed through the opening without so much as a flap of his clothing touching the edges. He soared up, and up, and up . . . well above ground level before gravity finally curled its fingers around him and pulled him back down, at which point he disappeared from Jason's view. A second later, there was a sickening *thud!* that could be heard even from twenty feet below ground.

"Hello!" Jason called. "Are you okay up there?"

Silence.

"Oh, crap," Jason said aloud. "I pray to God I haven't killed him."

With both hands now free and feeling significantly lighter, Jason was able to pull himself up with his left hand, reach higher up and find another horizontal crack with his right hand, and so on until he had reached a point where he could use his feet as well. From there he was able to quickly scramble up the wall and out of the crevice. He found the man lying on his side a few feet away and knelt down beside him.

Jason nudged the man's shoulder gently, worried that he may have suffered more internal injuries, in addition to those he might already have. "Sir, are you okay? Can you hear me?"

The man groaned as he had when Jason first found him trapped in the crevice, and seemed to have returned to that same semi-conscious state. It was not necessarily a positive sign, though at least he was not dead. But now Jason faced the same dilemma as before: whether to go for help, or to try to save the man himself. On the one hand, if he left the man here and went for help, he could bring back paramedics who would have the proper equipment for transporting him safely, and Jason would not have to take the chance of exacerbating any internal injuries the man might have if he were to attempt to move him. On the other hand, the man had already been in bad shape due to a nasty fall, dehydration and exposure, and now shock and a second fall on top of that, thus leaving him out here any longer might just finish him off. While Jason could not treat the man's injuries, at least he had water in his vehicle and could perhaps get him somewhat rehydrated on the way to the hospital. Furthermore, leaving the man completely defenseless would almost certainly get him killed. There was at least one cougar prowling nearby, and probably a few others as well, not to mention bears and coyotes.

After considering both options, the choice seemed clear to Jason: he would have to evacuate the man himself, despite the risks that such action would entail. He hooked his arms under the man's knees and upper back, carefully lifted him, and began to work his way down the mountain toward the gravel parking area. He could not utilize the same method for getting down the mountain as he had in getting up – a series of forty- or fifty-foot leaps – for that kind of jarring impact would undoubtedly be too much for the man. So he had no choice but to weave his way down through the trees and over the boulders, albeit at a much faster pace than any normal person could have managed.

The man was still semi-conscious when they arrived back at Jason's vehicle about fifteen minutes later. Jason opened the door of the 4 x 4 and set the man down on the passenger seat. He removed a bottle of water from his cooler, tipped the man's head back and poured a small amount of liquid into his mouth. The man was definitely still out of it, but his body so craved water that he swallowed involuntarily. Jason waited several seconds to make sure the man did not choke on or regurgitate the water, then poured a little more down his throat. He also took a towel that he had brought along, saturated it with the water from a second bottle, and wrapped it around the man's head, hoping that some of the moisture might be absorbed through his skin and help speed the rehydration process. Unable to think of any other way to immediately assist the man, Jason closed the water bottle, placed it in the man's lap, got in behind the wheel of the vehicle and started back down the mountain.

The drive down seemed excruciatingly slow. The dirt road was full of rocks and holes, so Jason had to keep the 4 x 4 in low gear and his speed under fifteen miles an hour all the way down. And every few minutes, he stopped and poured more water down the man's throat. Thus it took over an hour to cover a distance of twelve miles, but finally they reached the main highway. Jason punched the gas pedal as soon as the tires touched pavement, for it was another thirty miles to the nearest hospital, and he figured he would not only have a good excuse if he were stopped for speeding by a policeman, but that he might even be offered an escort as well.

The good news was that Jason's treatment of the man, amateur though it was, seemed to be working. The man gradually returned to consciousness, until finally, as they were nearing the hospital entrance, he had become fully awake and coherent.

"I guess that'll teach me," the man said hoarsely, "to watch where I'm walking."

Jason glanced at him quizzically.

"I was lost, like I told you, and was looking down at my cell phone to see if I had a signal, so I could find my location on a map. My foot was out over that giant crack before I saw what I was stepping into, and down I went. Thank God I got stuck and that you eventually came along. If I had slipped through that narrow spot in the crevice, no one would have ever found me."

"How long were you down there?" Jason queried.

"I remember three sunrises, for sure. But by then I think I was either hallucinating or unconscious most of the time. So it could have been longer. What day is this?"

"It's Thursday."

The man thought for moment, then gasped. "It was Sunday morning when I left my family to go hiking. I've been gone for four days! They'll be out of their minds with worry!"

"Yes, but it all worked out. Now that you're awake, you can use my cell phone to contact your family. When you see them in a couple of hours, it'll be the greatest reunion you've ever had in your life."

This seemed to calm the man down a bit, as he recognized that this ordeal would soon be over, for both himself and his family. "Thank you," he said, turning to look at Jason, "for saving my life."

"You're welcome." Jason hesitated for a moment, then said, "You seem as though you have all of your faculties about you. Do you remember how I was able to get you out of that crevice?"

"Yes, I remember."

"But you haven't asked me how I was able to do those things. Aren't you curious?"

The man looked at Jason again and smiled. "No, I'm not. I know exactly how you did it. And I know exactly who you are, Jason Devine. You see, my name is Randall Wilhelm."

13

Original Timeline – August 2021

F our months later, Jason and Julie were married during a small ceremony in Sioux Falls, alongside the cascades of the Big Sioux River that the city was named for. Though Julie had always dreamed of having a huge wedding while she was growing up, her stance on this had softened significantly during the last five years after she had met Jason. They were five *long* years, with Jason's training, and of course, the possible arrival of the creature, having been the focal points throughout. Now that that was over, the anticipation she felt of them finally moving on to the next phase of their lives, not to mention the sound of her biological clock ticking, trumped all of those childhood fantasies. So they planned their wedding rather quickly, with no caterer, disc jockey or wedding cake, one flower arrangement on either side of the minister, and a very short guest list (Mitch and the Wilhelm family on Jason's side, Julie's immediate family on her side). Afterwards, they all went out to dinner at an upscale Italian restaurant, and once the dessert was eaten and the gifts were opened, the small group parted ways. Just like that, their big day was over, and they began their lives as Mr. and Mrs. Jason Anderson.

Though Randall was eleven years older than Jason, they had become best friends following their harrowing experience in the Rockies. Jason's abilities and purpose in life could not afford discovery by an unscrupulous or untrustworthy person, so he had no choice but to avoid developing close friendships (Julie and her Uncle Navy having been the exceptions) until his training years were over. And even *after* his training had ended, he had to be careful not to be seen by a stranger displaying his talents for fear of the government finding him out. Thus, there could have been no better friend to Jason than Randall, for not only did he already know Jason's secret, he could be trusted to keep it that way.

For Randall, the uncanny coincidence of meeting Jason the way he had not only brought back the *memory* of that dream he had shared with Malcolm all those years ago, but also the *faith* in it as well. Over time, he had come to convince himself that the dream, as vivid and realistic as it may have been, was nothing more than that – a dream. But when he realized the kind of inhuman strength it would take for Jason to rescue him as both of their lives hung in the balance, Randall understood that the dream had been real and that he had come face to face with the man who was to one day save the world.

The friendship was initially fanned by Jason's desire to glean any additional information that he could from Randall, aside from what Mal had recorded in his journal. From his perch on the mountaintop, Randall had seen everything, just as Mal was seeing it ("spatial relationships don't mean much inside a dream," Randall had told Jason when asked how he was able to see everything from so far away). Randall had not gone so far as to write everything down as Mal had, but even so, knowing there was a second eyewitness to the events made Jason tingle with excitement at the prospect of gathering even a tidbit or two that Mal may have forgotten or overlooked. Or fabricated. That was the thing Jason *had* to know first; was the theory that he and Mitch had come up with as to why Mal had not recorded his own death in the journal accurate?

"No," Randall had said to Jason's surprise, after Randall had read Mal's journal. "He did not die from a bear attack in that version of the timeline. It's true he left out the details of your various fights with deadly animals – and yes, the part about him shooting you -- but I'm assuming it was for the reasons he provided. The only scenario in which he did die was the one where he chose to do nothing and was eventually killed by the creature. But obviously he was never going to choose that path, because it would have certainly brought about the end of the human race. You would have never discovered the truth about who you really are, and the creature would have had no worthy opponent to challenge it. So he chose the other alternative, the one in which he took you from your family and trained you to be that worthy opponent. And now the human race has a chance."

"But if that's true, then why? Why didn't he see his own death in the dream?"

"I believe," Randall responded, "that it must have been because God chose for him not to see that, in order to preserve his faith and courage. Imagine if you knew the precise time and place of your death well in advance, and that you could take steps to prevent it if you wanted to. That's exactly what you would do, isn't it?"

"If the survival of the human race depended on my preordained death, I'd like to think that I'd have the courage to go through with it."

"Yes, we would all like to *think* that. But thinking it and actually doing it are two different things. Jesus proceeded through His ministry knowing exactly how it was going to end, but not many others have His resolve. Even soldiers, policemen and firemen who risk their lives for the sake of others do so with every hope and intention of staying alive. To actually know for certain that you are going to die, and still have the fortitude to complete the task is something that I think would be pretty uncommon."

"It might be uncommon but not unheard of. Mitch and I had surmised that Mal had seen his own death in the dream, and had intentionally omitted it to prevent *us* from stopping him. Now you're telling me that he would have actually chickened out if he had known in advance? I don't buy that. Mal was a hero in my book."

"Mal *was* a hero, yes, for trusting in God's plan for him. Just because he didn't know about his own death in advance doesn't make him any less a hero. Do you see what I'm saying?"

After thinking this over for a moment, Jason recognized the wisdom in Randall's words. If things were happening exactly as God had planned for them to happen, including Mal's death, then what would it have mattered if Mal had known about it ahead of time? Why should God have placed that burden on Mal, allowing him to have that kind of knowledge? It would have served no purpose, and would have only caused Mal a tremendous amount of anguish, especially as the years went by and the day of his death drew nearer. And so, for the second time, Jason came to be at peace with the fact that Mal's death had taken them all by surprise.

The other question that Jason had for Randall was, of course, whether he had some clue as to how the dream was supposed to have ended, and what hidden skill Jason might have employed in order to defeat the creature. He explained to Randall how the dream had ended prematurely when Mitch had called the police and asked them to check on Mal after he had been unsuccessfully trying to reach him by phone for three days. And then Jason went on to explain how, years later, following his battle with the great white shark off the coast of South Africa, Mal had shared his concerns about having missed out on the conclusion of the dream, and specifically, how Jason was to have defeated the creature.

"Yes," Randall had said. "I figured that was why the dream had ended so abruptly and why I heard someone calling out 'Mr. Anderson! Mr. Anderson!' just before I woke up. In fact, as you recall from Mal's account, I warned him multiple times that someone would be coming to get him. Of course, when I first said those words, I didn't know what they meant any more than Mal did. I only repeated what was being piped into my head. Eventually, as the dream progressed, I think we both became aware that it would not last forever, and there were a lot of things that needed to be seen within a limited amount of time. But by the time we started to feel a sense of urgency, it was too late, and the dream was going to have to end prematurely. Anyway, I guess I just answered your question about whether I had any additional insights into how the dream was supposed to end or this undiscovered skill, talent, or weapon that you would have used to defeat the creature. After all, the dream ended at the same point from *my* perspective as it did from Mal's, meaning neither one of us could have seen anything more."

"That's what I figured," Jason said with a sigh. "But what do I do? If I need some secret weapon to kill this thing, and I don't know what that weapon is, then how do I kill it?"

Randall looked at Jason, puzzled. "Why is this such a concern to you now? You've already concluded that we're beyond the point where the creature would have arrived, and based on your appearance now, compared to what you looked like in the dream when the creature actually did show up, I would have to agree with you. So what are you worried about? It's the Jason on the *altered* timeline that ought to be concerned."

"I don't know," Jason admitted. "I understand what you're saying, but I guess I just wanted some closure, that's all."

"You'll just have to have faith," Randall counseled. "You must believe that either you already have what you need, or if you need something else, then God will reveal it to you when the time comes."

After this exchange, it was now Randall's turn to grill Jason. He wanted to hear all about Jason's training missions, his stories of hand-to-hand combat with lions, tigers, bears, and sharks. Of course, Randall had already seen some of these encounters himself, those that were revealed in the dream, but he wanted to hear about all of them, as well as the intimate details, from he who had actually experienced them. Jason was not comfortable recanting all of that, for he would never be proud of his many victories in those battles no matter how essential they were. But he agreed to humor Randall, figuring he owed it to the man who, aside from himself, now that Mal was gone, was the most important person alive today in connection with this unfolding drama. And in the end, Jason was glad that he did, because he found that disclosing the guilt and remorse he felt over killing all of those animals was unexpectedly therapeutic. It was something that Julie had never wanted to hear about, notwithstanding her acknowledgement of the necessity of Jason's training methods.

The other significant development that, while devastating to Jason and Julie, served to strengthen their friendship with Randall, was when they discovered that they could not have children. Jason, as it turned out, was sterile, probably a result of his body having been ravaged so severely on so many occasions. It was a steep price to pay for being the savior of humanity, especially when added to the sacrifices that had already been made. But the disappointment that Jason and Julie felt about not being able to have children of their own was softened by the joy they felt whenever they were with Randall's family. Randall had been married for ten years to an amazing woman named Mindy, whose life story was no less dramatic than Randall's had been. Mindy's first husband had died of a brain aneurism just three months after she had given birth to Jacob, their first and only child. Jacob was now fourteen, and had a kid sister named Jocelyn who had just turned five. These two quickly became the apples of Jason and Julie's eyes, and the feelings were mutual; within a matter of months, the kids were referring to them as Uncle Jason and Aunt Julie. And the fact that all four of them – Jason, Julie, Jacob and Jocelyn – shared the same first initial was something they liked to imagine gave them a bond like that shared by any true blood relatives.

The Wilhelms lived in Bunting, Colorado, which was over 650 miles from Sioux Falls. For that reason, Jason and Julie were not able to spend as much time with them as they would have liked, but they still made plans to visit each other several times a year . . . just enough to give the Andersons their "Jacob and Jocelyn fix" before they began to miss them too terribly. And when Jocelyn was eight, an annual tradition was established where she would spend an entire month with Jason and Julie each summer until the year she graduated from high school. Jacob was almost eighteen when this tradition began, old enough to have begun to think it was uncool to spend excessive amounts of time with grownups, though he, too, would always love his "aunt" and "uncle" dearly for the rest of their lives.

It was hard to imagine that sheer coincidence alone had brought Jason and Randall together that day on the mountain. But as the years went by, that was certainly how it appeared to them. Following their initial discussions after Randall had left the hospital, they spoke little of the dream or the events that were to come. At this point, there was nothing they could do to affect that. The foundations had been laid, and their roles in this lifetime were now fulfilled.

14

Original Timeline – July 2081

Julie slipped away peacefully one night in her sleep, not long after her 89th birthday. Despite her age, her death came as a relative surprise to Jason and all who knew her because she had been vibrant and healthy up until that day. It was a bittersweet way for Jason to have to part with her; on the one hand, we all want to have our loved ones around for as long as they remain happy and healthy, but on the other hand, if we do not want to see them deteriorate slowly and indignantly, we must necessarily be willing to part with them while they still cling to vitality and love of life.

As Jason stood alongside Julie's casket at the interment ceremony, the closing remarks and prayers of the minister hardly registered with him. He was thinking back on the discussion he had had with Mal, over eighty years ago, when Mal had first revealed to him his true identity. They had pondered the question of whether or not they were on the original timeline: would the creature appear within their lifetimes, or would the birth of Brian Zintak not take place for many decades and thus not prevent them from pursuing their dreams of happiness once they had gotten through twenty or so years of grueling physical and emotional toil? On the day Jason had met and rescued Randall, before leaving for the airport that morning, he had realized the answer to that question. And God, how incredibly grateful he was! To have shared sixty-five wonderful years with his best friend and soulmate, despite the fact that they had not been blessed with children of their own, was more than he felt he deserved. Furthermore, the fact that they had both long ago put their trust in Jesus Christ as their Lord and Savior meant that their parting in this lifetime was only temporary; they would soon be reunited for all eternity.

Jason knew that that reunion was fast approaching. Not because he intended to simply give up and wait for his own death, now that Julie was gone. He had always been of the mindset that every day was a gift, even those that were a struggle to endure because of loneliness, pain or grief. No, it was because he knew his own body better than most other human beings knew theirs. During his years of training, all of those devastating injuries he had suffered, and the healing that had always followed, had given him a unique feel for the inner workings of his body. He always knew, for example, the instant that he contracted an illness such as a cold or the flu, long before he began to actually experience the symptoms. He could feel, somehow, the battle inside of him between his white blood cells and the intruding pathogen, from the moment it began. That was one of the reasons, he believed, that Julie had always been healthier than he had, because he would immediately quarantine himself in the guest bedroom and thus minimize the chance of passing the illness along to her.

Given his acute sensitivity to even the minutest changes within himself, Jason had known for a while now that his body was beginning to shut down. That was the other reason, aside from Julie's good health, that he was surprised at her death – he had come to believe that he would go before her. And he was glad that he had ended up being wrong, for he would rather be lonely himself than for Julie to have to go through it, especially when his body was telling him that it would only be a matter of days or weeks before it would finally run out of gas.

For that reason, he would need to act quickly. There was something he needed to do, an urge that had been growing inside of him for several years now. He would have never acted upon this urge as long as Julie was alive, but now that she was gone, he felt compelled to do so. It was fueled by that old, unanswered question, that nagging doubt that had first haunted Mal, and then Jason himself once he learned of it. How was he to defeat the creature? What was that undiscovered weapon or ability that he would need to utilize in order to ensure a victorious outcome? Without it, would he not lose his fight with the creature, resulting in the removal of the only obstacle that stood between it and its mission to destroy the human race? He just could not seem to push these thoughts out of his mind; they seemed to always lurk there in some shadowy corner, and he dwelled upon them often enough that it came to be an obsession. This obsession led him to begin toying with an idea that, while loathsome, would make the unknown skill irrelevant by destroying Zintak's insane plan before it was even conceived. Jason would do this by killing Brian Zintak while he was still a child.

λ　　λ　　λ

Jason knew from Mal's account of future events that Zintak would be born sometime during the year 2079, which had been two years ago. So at the beginning of that year, Jason had started doing internet searches for "Brian Zintak" every few days, looking specifically for a child by that name born to Carl and Sherry Zintak. In July of 2079, it happened: Brian Carl Zintak came into the world, just as Jason knew he would. But what came as a complete shock to Jason, at least initially, was the town that the Zintak family hailed from; none other than Bunting, Colorado, where the Wilhelms had resided. It seemed like yet another ridiculous coincidence at first, like so many others he had experienced throughout his lifetime. But the more he thought about it, the more he came to believe that this time, it was *not* a coincidence (maybe *none* of them were, in fact?). There was some connection between Randall and Zintak, or at the very least, something about Bunting that encompassed multiple facets of this story. What that connection was, and its degree of significance, could not be determined on this timeline, though Jason had no doubt it would become clear on the next one.

⅄   ⅄   ⅄

Following the interment, there was a luncheon provided by the church where Jason and Julie had been members for decades. It was a large and somewhat boisterous gathering which included their neighbors and church friends, along with the remaining members of Julie's immediate family. Uncle Mitch had been gone for over twenty years, Randall and Mindy had passed on a few years before, as had Julie's older brother Tyson and his wife Marla. Tyson and Marla had had one child, Julie's nephew Philip, who came with his wife Cassandra. Julie also had a younger sister Maria who was still alive, and she attended with her husband Paul, as well as their two children, Julie's nieces Morgan and Natasha, and their spouses. And of course, Jacob and Jocelyn were present along with their families. Jason was sincerely touched by the turnout, though he had a difficult time focusing on the conversations he was obligated to engage in as a steady stream of people stopped by to offer their condolences. By then, the wheels inside his head were spinning at maximum RPM as he considered how to best go about enacting his dark plan.

When he arrived home after the luncheon, he wasted little time making preparations for the trip to Bunting.

⅄   ⅄   ⅄

Jason crept quietly down the hallway of the Zintak home, having successfully gained entrance by using a small laser torch to slice through the deadbolt lock on the garage service door. There was a nightlight glowing in the bathroom at the end of the hallway directly in front of him, and it cast just enough light for him to pick out the child's room from the coloring book pages that were taped to the outside of the door. Left open just a crack, the door swung noiselessly inward when he pushed on it. He tiptoed over to the child's bed and stood next to it, gazing down at the small figure sleeping peacefully upon it. This was it – the moment he had been pondering for over five years now. An opportunity to save the world, just as he had been chosen to do, though in a very different way than what had been revealed to Mal in his dream, and what Jason had trained for decades earlier.

Was this not a better way? After all, it was guaranteed to work, unlike going the route of engaging the creature in a battle to the death, which given the information he was missing, seemed more likely to end in failure than success. He reached down, unsnapped the sheath on his belt, and removed the eight-inch hunting knife that he had selected for the task. It would be easy and virtually soundless; a quick, downward thrust directly through the boy's heart, which would kill him instantly.

Jason held the knife over Brian's heart, gripping the handle with his right hand and placing his left hand over its butt to help guide the direction of the blade on its way down. A minute passed. Then another, and another. His shoulders began to burn, and his arms began to tremble, as he continued to hold them out over the boy's body while trying to work up the courage to finish the job. He kept telling himself that this was for the best, that even though it was *possible* for him to defeat the creature, it was better to be safe than sorry. Better to take one innocent life than risk the loss of billions.

But even as he repeated these arguments in his head, there were contradictory thoughts that were battling for his attention as well. He had, after all, spent twenty years of his life preparing to battle the monster that this child would one day create. He had made enormous sacrifices in order to be ready for that confrontation, including separation from his biological family, the premature loss of the man who had raised him, and the inability to ever have children of his own. And most of all, there were the words that Randall had spoken shortly after they had met, when Jason had expressed his concern about not having discovered the particular skill that would be needed to defeat the creature. Randall had said, "You'll just have to have faith. Either you already have what you need, or if you need something else, then God will reveal it to you when the time comes."

Jason had not realized at the time, or during the decades that followed, just how wise those words really were. But now, at last, he did. While he still did not know what the final outcome would be, he recognized now that having paid such a tremendous price, it was time to trust in his destiny, in God's plan for him. It was time to stand down. He slipped the knife back into its sheath, and retreated from the Zintak home as quietly as he had entered.

Jason drove all the way back to his home in Sioux Falls without stopping. It was a ten hour drive, but it felt like little more than ten minutes, for as he drove, he felt his mind and spirit reaching a plateau of peace like he had never felt before. The air swirling through the slightly opened windows seemed fresher, the colors of the sky and passing landscapes seemed more vivid, than he had ever noticed before. It was a strange feeling, for even as he experienced these amazing sensations, at the same time he sensed his biological clock very rapidly approaching midnight. And that was perfectly okay with him.

He arrived home around one o'clock in the afternoon. It was a glorious midsummer day, the temperature warm enough to soothe the various aches that had steadily taken hold of his joints throughout the years, but not so warm as to be unpleasant. He decided to order a pizza from his favorite Italian restaurant in town, and had them really do it up right with double pepperoni, feta cheese and banana peppers. After he ordered the pizza, he sent a text message to Pastor Pearson at the church, asking him to stop by sometime this evening, and to come around back as he intended to spend the day out on the patio, watching the birds and enjoying the fragrant smells of his flowers. He told the pastor he could use some company and perhaps a bit of spiritual guidance, but that was not really the case. Indeed, the way he felt right now, he was less in need of spiritual guidance than he had ever been in his life.

The pizza arrived about a half hour later, and after receiving it from the delivery boy, Jason sent him on his way in a state of shock with an extra $500 in his pocket. He grabbed a few napkins, along with a cup, a bucket of ice, and a two-liter bottle of diet cola, and headed out to the patio. The pizza was delicious, the best he had ever tasted (well, probably not, but on this day it seemed that way), and he savored each bite before washing it down with a swallow of cola.

When he finished his lunch, he stretched out on the patio sofa and lay there contentedly, enjoying the sunshine upon his face and all of God's beauty that surrounded him. He felt himself getting drowsy as the afternoon wore on, and for a while he fought it, reflecting back on his life over the last ninety years, the places he had been to, the people he had met, the blessings he had enjoyed. Thinking of all of this brought to mind the words of Captain Woodrow Call, the character played by Tommie Lee Jones in the classic TV miniseries *Lonesome Dove* that Jason had watched as a boy. It was at the very end of the series, when a reporter who had heard about Call's legacy as a Texas Ranger confronted him and made the statement, "People say you are a man of vision." Call thought back on a lifetime of shootouts, harrowing escapes, buried friends, and hanged enemies. After a long pause, he responded to the reporter by saying, "Vision? Yeah, hell of a vision." And then he headed off into the sunset as the show ended. Jason smiled as he fancied himself something of a Woodrow Call, a modern day Texas Ranger who had packed about ten lifetimes' worth of adventure into just one.

At last, with evening drawing near, the pastor probably on his way, and the beckoning of sleep now irresistible, he closed his eyes and headed off into the sunset of his life.

PART THREE

REAPER

Altered Timeline – June 2016

J ason, wake up!" Mal shouted into Jason's ear.

"What the . . . . what are you doing? What's going on?" Jason asked groggily. It was ten days after they had returned from a trip to Africa, where Jason had once again gone toe-to-toe with a ferocious predator, this time a lion, and he was finally feeling like himself again. He was not particularly happy about being awakened from the first truly restful sleep that he had had since before that trip.

"I've had another dream! I saw the creature arriving, as I did the first time, but this time I saw something I had missed before."

That got Jason's attention in a hurry, and he bolted up out of his bed. "What? What did you see?" he demanded.

"I know where it's going to arrive! There was a delivery truck parked in the driveway of one of the houses along the street where the creature appeared. On the side of the truck was a logo with the words *Wetzel's Bakery, Bunting, Colorado.* And then I looked in the other direction, and saw there was an intersection nearby. The street sign said River Drive, and the crossroad was Main Street. That's where we need to go, the intersection of River Drive and Main Street in Bunting, Colorado!"

"Is that all you saw? Was the dream extended beyond where it ended before?"

Mal knew what Jason was referring to and shook his head.

"I'm afraid not. The only new information I got from this dream was the name of the town and the exact spot where the creature arrives."

"Well, that's important, too," Jason said as he slumped down onto the bed again, disappointed that there was not more revealed in this latest dream of Mal's. "So where is Bunting, Colorado?"

"It's a little town at the eastern edge of the Rockies, about forty miles southwest of Denver."

"Okay, but why couldn't this wait until morning?"

"Because it's coming! I don't know the exact time, but I know it's only a matter of hours. We have to leave right now!"

Jason shot out of bed a second time. "Why didn't you say that in the first place?"

A   A   A

Twenty minutes later, they were on Route 115 heading towards the Sioux Falls Regional Airport. They had spent a few minutes debating their various travel options before deciding the only viable one was for them to board a plane to Denver. They certainly could not drive from Sioux Falls to Bunting, as that would take about nine hours to get there traveling at eighty miles an hour. The second option was for Jason to travel on foot, as he could now reach a speed of over 150 miles an hour, which would allow him to arrive in Bunting in about one-third the time it would take to drive there. But that would require a significant expenditure of energy, something he could not afford if he were to immediately engage the creature upon his arrival. That left them with the third option – flying. There was a flight leaving for Denver in two hours, and the flight time was about an hour and a half in duration. Then they would have to rent a vehicle and drive to Bunting, which might add yet another hour. That meant a total of approximately four and a half hours before they arrived in Bunting, about the same amount of time that it would take Jason to travel the distance on foot. But Jason would now be at full strength when they got there. There was also the option of flying to Denver, and then Jason traveling on foot from there, but again, it would mean his strength would be reduced, though to a lesser extent. They felt it was a risk they could not afford to take.

So, like it or not, they were in for a four-and-a-half hour wait. At least it would mean that Jason could eat several meals along the way, allowing him to build up energy reserves that would be crucial in the event that he did, in fact, have to engage the enemy immediately upon their arrival. Additionally, they could review Mal's journal and the results of all these years of training one more time. Maybe they would have an epiphany, some kind of strategy they had not thought of before. Then again, maybe that was just wishful thinking.

R andall Wilhelm had been praying for the second coming of Christ since the day he was saved and baptized five years earlier. It was not that he was unhappy or in any way dissatisfied with his life. In fact, while he was by no means a wealthy man, he considered himself to be richer than any man could ever hope to be . . . in particular himself, in his "former" life, when he was a well-known model and millionaire several times over. Now, instead of millions in the bank, he had thousands; instead of an 18,000 square foot palace and several vacation condominiums, he owned a modest 1,800 square foot home and rented a cottage on a small lake one week a year; instead of driving a Porsche, he drove a Prius. And most importantly, instead of nightly sexual escapades with stunningly beautiful actresses and heiresses who meant nothing to him, he was now committed for life to a pretty-but-not-gorgeous intensive care nurse whom he adored and would give his life for.

Though Randall had at one time possessed great material wealth, he had certainly not been born of it. In fact, his life had taken a very circular path, as his origins had been quite humble. His parents were a devout Christian couple who survived by running a small print shop and office supply store in Cottonwood, Arizona. They never took fancy vacations, rarely went out to dinner, and drove their cars for at least ten years before buying new ones. And yet, they were as happy as a family could be, for they understood that the purest form of joy came through the pursuit of deeper relationships with each other and with Jesus Christ, rather than fame or fortune. Randall had even dreamt of attending a seminary one day and becoming a minister, something that never failed to bring forth a fresh burst of pride from his parents when he spoke of it. They knew they had raised him well to that point, and could not wait to see how God would use Randall in the years to come.

But something happened when Randall was eleven years old that would set him on an entirely different course in life. He went to bed at around nine o'clock one night as he normally did . . . but woke up in the hospital three days later to find his parents and the associate pastor from their church praying fervently alongside his bed. His parents had tried to awaken him for school on the first morning, but he simply would not wake up. They shook him, yelled his name repeatedly, and even doused him with water, before rushing him to the hospital. The doctors acknowledged that Randall had slipped into some sort of coma, but they were at a complete loss to understand what was causing it. There was no head trauma, no indication of stroke, no toxins or infections, oxygen and blood sugar levels were normal, and no evidence that he had suffered a seizure. All of the CTs, MRIs and various other neurodiagnostic tests the doctors performed showed that Randall's brain was functioning at a very high level of activity . . . much like a person who was simply dreaming.

And in fact, he was doing just that. But it was like no other dream that Randall had ever had before, because from start to finish, he *knew* that he was dreaming. A lucid dream, he later found out while doing some research to try to figure out what had happened to him. In the dream, Randall's role might best be described as a prepubescent sage, offering wisdom and guidance to a real-world psychic who was having the very same dream at the very same time. The psychic was shown future events that would affect the fate of the entire world, and what he must do to save it. The events took place over a period lasting more than a century, and included an evil genius, a time travel machine, an unimaginably horrific creature developed in a laboratory, and a man of tremendous strength, courage and character who was chosen by God Himself to save humanity from total destruction. When Randall finally awoke after his three-day slumber, he started spouting off like Dorothy in *The Wizard of Oz* about this incredible dream he had and how real it was. But unlike Dorothy, Randall would not backpedal, at least for a while anyway, on the reality of his dream, and instead relentlessly insisted that he had seen the future and that the events would one day come to pass.

Up through Randall's junior year of high school, he was relegated to hanging out with the *real* freaks in the class because he was labelled one himself. There was a never-ending stream of taunts and teases, things like, "Hey Randy, isn't it about *time* the creature showed up?" The jocks would puff out their chests or flex their biceps and say, "Randy, check out these guns, do you think I'm ready to save the world, or do I need another month in the weight room?" Even those who claimed to be Christians would get into the act, with witticisms like, "Randy, since you're some kind of dream master like Daniel was, how about we throw you into a lion's den and see how that works out for you?"

Little by little, the attacks eroded Randall's faith, until one day during the summer before his senior year, he finally realized that not only did he no longer believe in the reality of the dream, he no longer believed in God, either. And it was then that things turned around for him – spiritually, for the worse, socially, for the better. Once he relinquished his claim to have seen the future, his classmates no longer saw him as a whack-job or Jesus freak who should be avoided like the plague, and instead began to see more of his natural qualities – his physical stature, handsomeness, athletic ability, intelligence, and charisma. That year, Randall tried out for the football, basketball and baseball teams for the first time, and became the star player in all three sports. When his picture appeared in the newspaper after being named first team all-state in basketball, his uncommon good looks drew the attention of a modeling agency representative, who invited him to attend a photo shoot for a client who was publishing a sporting goods catalog. The camera, as the saying went, loved him, and in the span of just a few months, he had apparel and fragrance designers hounding him incessantly. He quickly hired an agent to handle his contract negotiations, and just a few weeks after graduation, when most of his friends were flipping burgers or roofing houses to help pay for college, he moved to San Francisco and deposited his first check for half a million dollars.

Naturally, along with fame and fortune came beautiful women and the occasional snort of cocaine, though he became addicted only to the former and not to the latter. There were nights when he had orgies with as many as three or four women, and he took great pride in being able to pleasure all of them long after the point where most men would have exhausted themselves. And when morning came and he had to get up for work, he felt as fresh and energized as if he had gotten a full eight hours of sleep.

In short, Randall Wilhelm had built a life that most people would have killed for. He had more money than he could spend, any material possession he desired, enormous popularity, all the sex he could handle, a job that took him to the most exotic places in the world . . . he believed he had everything a person could want. That is, until the fateful day when he realized he had nothing at all.

He visited a trendy club for celebrities one night, where he met a waitress by the name of Kendra Simmons. Although physically she fit in perfectly in a room full of women whose beauty all but defied description, Randall could tell that she was different from most of the other waitresses at this club, or any other celebrity club for that matter. Virtually all of the others were groupies, women who, at the very least wanted to boast about sleeping with a famous actor, model or athlete, or at the outside, were hoping to ensnare a naïve celeb in some sort of scandal that might involve financial gain. But not Kendra. She was shy, polite, and took obvious offense at being groped or propositioned by her customers, no matter how deep their pockets or how recognizable they were. He guessed that she was not native to the area, that she had been raised in a rural setting with good old-fashioned values, and had come here hoping to launch a singing or acting career. If that were the case, she was only working at this club because of the generous tips and the possibility of meeting a producer, director, or record company executive who would be willing to give her an opportunity to demonstrate her talent.

And so Kendra became a project for Randall, a mission. He began to visit the club more frequently, and would always request to be seated at one of Kendra's tables. He spoke to her very kindly, asking her how she was doing, how her job search was going (she was, in fact, an aspiring actress), and whether there was anything he could do to help. When she realized that he always sat at one of her tables and asked him why that was so, he used a bit of reverse psychology on her, saying that he was tired of waitresses who wanted only to sleep with him, that he could see the wholesomeness in her and that she would not throw herself at him like the others did. At first she was plainly suspicious of his response, but as the weeks went on and he made not a single sexually-oriented comment or innuendo, or even so much as asked her out for a drink, he could sense that she was beginning to lower the barrier she had put up around herself. And finally, when he was sure that she would not only be unsurprised if he were to ask her out, but that she would also be expecting it, he asked if he could buy her a nice dinner sometime. She accepted immediately.

Thus, the second phase of his conquest had begun. He took her out to dinner three times before she invited him to come inside for a drink. To her surprise, he thanked her for the invitation, but declined, saying that he did not feel it would be gentlemanly of him to come inside at this point in their relationship (he also made a point of emphasizing that he was by no means suggesting that she had invited him in for anything other than a nightcap, but that he simply felt they had a good thing going and that he wished to enjoy her company slowly and to the fullest as they moved forward, much like one sips, not gulps, of a fine bottle of wine). At that, her apparent disappointment turned to obvious delight, and leaning over, she stroked his face gently while they shared a long goodnight kiss. In truth, however, the reason he had declined her invitation was that, while he felt confident that they would have had sex had he gone inside, he had no intention of ever setting foot inside her apartment -- which was modest at best -- much less having sex in her bed. It was, quite frankly, beneath him. Instead, he planned to bring her back to his own house, and have sex in his own bed, after which he would take her back to her apartment and never contact her again.

A week later, when he called her on the phone to make plans for that evening, he asked if she would like to come to his house for dinner. He would have his chef prepare them something incredible, something unique, something she would never forget, and after that they would go for a walk on his private beach. Kendra was thrilled and accepted his invitation, saying that she had something special to share with him that evening.

Randall picked Kendra up around 7:00 and brought her back to his house, where they feasted on an incredible meal prepared by his chef, Marty, and then went for a walk on the beach as they had planned. Afterwards, stretched out on the plush carpet of his living room floor, in front of a roaring fire, Randall made his move and leaned toward Kendra to kiss her. But she stopped him momentarily, saying she wanted to share that something special with him.

"I wanted to tell you, Randall," she began, her eyes filling with tears, "that these past couple of months have been the most wonderful time of my life. I had determined a long time ago that I would never get involved with a man who was a famous actor, athlete, or in show business of any kind, even though it's what I dream of doing myself. There are just so many greedy, shallow, selfish people in the business that it never really occurred to me that there could be one who is honest, kind and generous. But now that I've met you, I realize I was wrong. You've been so good to me, and so sincere. I know that you must really care about me, that you're not just trying to get me into bed, because if that's all you wanted, you wouldn't have wasted all this time with me. If it was just sex you were after, you can get that from hundreds of women anytime you want, yet you've chosen to spend time with *me* and have not tried to do anything more than kiss me. And for that, I wanted to tell you that. . . I love you."

Randall was stunned by her admission, figuring that the "something special" she wanted to share with him was simply a night of good sex. He had known for weeks that she was becoming more and more fond of him, but he did not expect her to drop the "L" bomb on him already. Not that he had not heard it before; in fact, he had heard it many, many times, but when it came from the mouth of a groupie during a night of kinky sex, you learn pretty quickly that it does not mean a thing. But that was not the case with Kendra. He could see that she actually meant it, that she actually *felt* it . . . and it startled him so much that he nearly recoiled from her as she was speaking the words. The mere *thought* of a monogamous relationship at this point in his life nearly sickened him, and he felt a hot flash of anger towards her for what he perceived to be an attempt to tie him down, to disable the thrusters on a career that was rocketing forward.

Yet as quickly as these thoughts were entering his brain, he was pushing them aside, for he knew that if they were visible on his face or in his body language, she would realize immediately that he had completely fooled her, and that in fact, he had no feelings for her whatsoever. And if that were to happen, there would be no sex with her tonight, or any other night for that matter, and all of his efforts during the past two months would have gone for naught. So, maintaining his composure, as well as his façade, he gazed at her with warm, solemn eyes, and opened his mouth to respond with something he knew she would want to hear.

But she held up her hand to his mouth and stopped him. "It's okay," she whispered. "You don't have to say it yet if you're not ready. I was, so I said it, but I want you to wait until you truly mean it before you say it."

He smiled at her and nodded, as if to say, "thank you for saying that, I'm almost there, just give me a little more time." She returned his smile, then without saying another word, she took his hand and led him upstairs to the master bedroom. Project completed; mission accomplished.

⅄   ⅄   ⅄

The next morning they had another fantastic meal prepared by Marty, during which Randall gave Kendra no indication that this would be the last time they would see each other outside the club, as he did not know what her reaction would be and did not want her going postal inside his house. She was clearly oblivious to his intentions, chatting happily and making plans for the two of them during the coming weeks – romantic dinners, adventurous day trips, relaxing strolls on the beach, etc. Seeing her like this, Randall actually regretted, in his own limited way, what he was about to do. But of course, it had to be done.

And so, after breakfast, he drove her back to her apartment, and almost before the vehicle had come to a stop, he broke the news to her, figuring it was best to do it quickly and not delay the inevitable. "Listen," he said, "the last couple of months have been great, and last night was just out of this world. But what you said after dinner, about how you love me, it really freaked me out. I guess I gave you the wrong impression, and for that I apologize, but the truth is that I really can't get involved in a serious relationship right now. I'm just too busy, and my career may very well end up taking me somewhere else, somewhere far away from here. So it's better if we just call this off right now, before it goes any further."

Not wanting to be cruel, but at the same time recognizing the importance of being firm, he turned away from her and looked straight ahead, his hands on the steering wheel, to communicate to her that the conversation was over and that he was waiting for her to get out of the car. He waited for about thirty seconds, during which time she never flinched, and he finally turned to look at her again. She was staring at him in obvious shock, her mouth hanging open, perhaps wondering, and no doubt *hoping*, that this was some kind of ill-conceived joke.

"I'm sorry if this sounds harsh," he said in a slightly gentler tone, "but I have an important shoot today and I really need to get going. I wish you the best of luck in your acting career . . . I think you'll do great, honestly." He paused for a moment, and when she still did not move, he said, "Goodbye."

Without taking her eyes off him, as if she were in a trance, she reached down and picked her purse up off the floor, then groped for the door handle. It was not until she had swung the door open that she finally looked away from him and stepped out of the car. Even then, as she walked up the sidewalk toward her apartment building, she stumbled along as though she had no conscious thought of what she was doing.

Randall watched her long enough to make sure she reached her building safely, feeling whatever pity for her that his selfish nature would allow him to feel, then sped away without looking back. Within thirty minutes, he had forgotten all about Kendra . . . and it remained that way until she showed up at his house three days later.

λ   λ   λ

Randall was eating breakfast when the doorbell rang. Marty, who besides being the chef was also a quasi-butler as well, answered the door.

A moment later, he came into the dining room and informed Randall that Ms. Simmons was here to see him. "I told her that you were very busy this morning preparing for your workday, and that you did not have time to speak to her, but she said she would not leave until you do. Would you like me to call the police?"

Randall suddenly wished he had followed the advice of his agent and hired a team of security guards to keep out reporters, obsessive fans, or in this case, jilted lovers like Kendra. But he had decided against it, thinking that he would feel like a prisoner in his own home if it had to be protected by a small army. "No," he said with a sigh, "I'll talk to her."

He wiped his mouth with his napkin, walked through the spacious dining room, then turned the corner to the foyer where Kendra was waiting for him . . . and gasped when he saw her. She looked absolutely terrible. Her hair was a tangled, frizzy mess, her clothes were wrinkled and dirty, she was not wearing any makeup and had dark, puffy bags under her eyes. And judging from her red eyes and nose, it was obvious that she had been crying, probably for quite some time.

"Kendra?" he asked hesitantly. "Are you . . . are you okay?" It was a dumb question, because obviously she was not okay, but he did not know what else to say.

She stared at him for a few moments, appearing to size him up, perhaps trying to gauge by his current demeanor whether he had had any regrets as to how he had ended their relationship three days earlier. "Tell me just one thing," she finally said, her voice noticeably hoarse, "and tell me the truth. Were you honestly surprised by what I said to you, about how I felt, or did you realize it before then and just pretend you didn't know?"

"No, Kendra," he said, shaking his head emphatically. "I really didn't know. You have to understand the type of women I'm used to being with. They don't care about me, and I don't care about them. We have fun for one night, sometimes for a week or two, then it's over and we both move on. That's the way they want it, that's the way I want it. I don't know if it's right or not, but that's my life, and I like it that way."

She nodded. "I see. So your plan was to have one night of fun with me, and then move on, is that right?"

He stared at the floor, surprised that he felt ashamed to meet her gaze now that she understood his true motive, and wondered whether he should attempt to save face with a lie or simply acknowledge the truth. "Yes," he finally admitted. "That was my goal all along. Although, for what it's worth, I really did enjoy the time we spent together, not just the other night, but the last few weeks as well."

"And yet, you still have no feelings for me whatsoever?"

He shifted uncomfortably, then said, "I like you, Kendra, but I just can't give you what you're looking for. I'm sorry."

She sighed deeply and nodded again. "I'm sorry, too. But it's over now, and it will never happen again."

At first, he thought she meant that she was putting all of this behind her, and that she would not bother him again, but seconds later, he understood the true meaning of her words when she withdrew a handgun from her purse, placed it against her temple and blew her brains out all over the floor of his foyer.

ᛉ   ᛉ   ᛉ

For the next two years, Randall's life was mostly a fog-shrouded odyssey of drugs, depression, remorse and emptiness. The knowledge that his actions were directly responsible for the death of another human being gave birth to an agony that was unlike anything he had ever felt before. *Someone* died *because of you!!* He would scream silently at himself, over and over and over again. *You might as well have put that gun to her head and pulled the trigger yourself!!*

His modeling career collapsed almost immediately, but he did not care. In fact, he did not care about anything anymore. He realized that, despite all of the money, possessions, and fame, he had never really had anything to begin with, at least nothing of *true* value. He was completely devoid of compassion, of love, of any desire to do anything for anyone besides himself. And that, he now understood, made him truly bankrupt, no matter how many millions he had in his investment accounts.

Weeks and months went by, and all Randall wanted to do was snort his fortune away in a desperate attempt to escape the memory of that horrific day – the day he knew for the first time that he was damned. And when the money finally ran out, he turned to a cheaper form of fix – alcohol. Eventually, his home was foreclosed upon, and he became a drifter, wandering about the western half of the country, sometimes waking up in an entirely different city without remembering how he got there. He would stay for a short time, pilfering coins from fountains, begging for money on street corners, working odd jobs when someone would hire him, and always, as soon as he had a few dollars in his pocket, he would head straight for the nearest bar. It was a miserable life, and he knew it, but he did not have the courage to do what Kendra had done and end it himself.

After two years of this pathetic existence, he found himself in the town of Bunting, Colorado, and was crossing the street at an intersection one day on his way to the liquor store, when a careless teenager driving a beat-up old Mercury Capri zipped past the stop sign and mowed Randall down. He woke up in a hospital ICU ten days later, having been in a coma that entire period of time, and found that there was scarcely an appendage on his body that he could move. He was not paralyzed, just immobilized, as he soon learned, for he had broken over forty bones throughout his body and was in a cast from shoulders to toes. Additionally, he had a bruised kidney, a punctured lung, and his spleen had had to be removed.

Despite the excruciating pain of such extensive injuries, along with the prospect of being bedridden for months, followed by physical therapy for who knows how long, and the possibility of permanent debilitation, most people would have been happy to be alive after such a terrible accident. But not Randall. He had had only a half second, perhaps, between the time he saw the vehicle coming and when it actually struck him, but it was long enough for him to realize that it was finally over, that his misery was finally at an end, and that he was, at long last, about to face eternity, whether that be heaven, hell, or simply nonexistence. Regardless, he was ready.

But to his shock, it was *not* over. And he wondered whether it ever would be. Perhaps he was destined to live like this forever, as punishment for what he had done to Kendra . . . his own personal hell on earth. Indeed, how could hell be any worse than this? He did not even have the means to withdraw from the pain as he once did, since hospitals typically did not serve alcohol, especially to alcoholics.

The day after he had fully emerged from his coma, the stark reality of his situation sinking in, he was contemplating whether it would be possible to commit suicide simply by holding his breath, when one of the nurses came in to check on him. Two years ago, he would have been instantly aroused at the sight of her -- medium brown shoulder-length hair; full, sensuous lips; sparkling brown eyes, and slender, athletic figure. She was not exactly beautiful, more like pretty or attractive, but there was an enigmatic aura about her that somehow made her exude sexiness. But Randall's libidinous desires had apparently followed Kendra to the grave, for since that day he had had no interest in women whatsoever.

"I was a big fan of yours," the nurse said, with a warm, genuine smile. "In fact," she giggled, "you might say I even had a crush on you." She smiled at him again, then gasped as a thought occurred to her. "Oh! I'm so sorry about my choice of words! You know . . . *crush*. Given your current condition, I mean. I'm very sorry."

Despite himself, Randall returned her smile, or at least he thought he did. He was not sure yet which of his body parts were working, including his facial muscles. "It's okay," he rasped. "No offense taken."

"My name's Mindy," she said. "I'm one of the ICU nurses, as you probably guessed. I'm here from seven a.m. to seven p.m. on Mondays, Wednesdays and Fridays. Let me know if there's anything you need."

"How about a double shot of whiskey, straight up?" He was still smiling when he spoke, to give her the impression he was kidding, but the truth was that he would have drank an entire bottle right then and there if he could have. He had gone eleven days without a drink – though of course, he had been unconscious for ten of them -- and not being able to quench his thirst was like having a godawful itch that you could not scratch.

Mindy could see right through his attempt at humor, and studied him with evident concern. "Mr. Wilhelm," she said, "I may be overstepping my bounds by saying this, but I see your accident as a blessing to you. You are going to be in this hospital for a long time, during which there will be no alcohol, and no drugs other than the ones we give you. I hope and pray that by the time you leave here, you will have not only conquered your addictions, but also figured out why it is that God chose to keep you on this earth, when by all rights you should be dead right now. I can't imagine what you've been through these last two years after seeing that poor woman take her own life in such a violent way, and I can understand how you would react to that by wanting to throw your own life away. But make no mistake, there is a reason you are still here, and I hope that one day, you will learn to trust God to reveal that reason to you, and then follow the path He has laid out for you. Now, is there anything I can do for you before I go?"

"No thank you," he said, though he was not even aware of having spoken the words, for he was already deeply reflecting on what she had said. It had not occurred to him since he was a boy that he had a purpose in life other than to make teenage girls scream and swoon, to pleasure and seduce as many beautiful women as he could, to accumulate such ridiculous wealth as to last a hundred lifetimes, to cram as much fun into a twenty four hour day as humanly possible. And as for God, He was just a myth, right? The product of the absurdly hopeful whims of a handful of delusional wackos?

For the next two days, Randall pondered Mindy's words nearly every waking minute. He found himself longing for her next shift so he could talk to her again, ask her the thousand questions that he had been storing in his brain since she last spoke to him. *Why did she believe in God? How had He revealed Himself to her? What was her purpose in life, and how did she recognize it when God revealed it to her?*

Finally, Wednesday came and Mindy returned. She entered the room with that same warm smile, that same mysterious energy that she had had two days before, almost as if she had simply left the room, then turned around and came right back in. "Good morning, Mr. Wilhelm! How are you today?"

Though he knew she would ask that question, he was not sure how to respond to it. "I don't know," he said quietly. "I guess it depends. Can you . . . can you tell me about God?"

She looked at him with something akin to pride, as though she were pleased that he had the courage to even ask the question. "I'd be happy to," she answered. "But this could take a while. I'll come back after my shift ends tonight, and we can talk as long as you like. How does that sound?"

He smiled and nodded, then watched her as she left the room to check on the patient in the one adjacent to his. The next twelve hours were the longest he had ever experienced in his life.

人　　人　　人

Eight months later, two weeks after leaving the hospital, Randall was baptized at the small Baptist church that Mindy attended. Though he had long since left his former life behind him, as the baptismal waters flowed over him, he realized that it was now official; the old Randall was dead, and the new Randall was born. His God-given purpose that Mindy had told him about had also been revealed to him months earlier; to be a husband to Mindy and a father to her four-year old son, Jacob. Mindy's first husband had died of a brain aneurism just three months after Jacob was born, and the boy had never known what it was like to experience the love, protection and guidance of a father. When Mindy revealed this to Randall, on that first evening that she visited him after hours and shared her testimony with him, he was so moved with pity, and so humbled by her courage and unwavering faith, that for the first time in his life, he wept for another human being. Not even for Kendra had he cried, for that would have required a degree of empathy that he was not emotionally capable of at that time. All he had felt for the better part of two years was self-loathing. But on that night, with Mindy's help, he took the first step down the path of self-forgiveness, of accepting the same from God, and eventually, of living his life entirely for those around him, instead of for himself. Four months after Randall's accident, with his spiritual journey far from complete but well underway, after expressing his feelings toward Mindy and hearing her reciprocate, Randall asked Mindy to marry him. She accepted without hesitation, and their wedding was six weeks after Randall's baptism.

Now, some five years later, as Randall walked home from his job as a branch manager at a community bank, he reflected back on his three lives. As an eleven year-old boy who had witnessed something incredible, he had had a blind and naïve sort of faith in God as he waited for that experience to manifest itself or to be followed by others like it. Then, as an arrogant, self-centered philanderer, he would have told God to get lost if He had come calling at that point in his life. And now, having been re-introduced to God by a woman who had enlightened him about the wonderful things that God had in store for His followers, Randall actually longed for this life to come to an end . . . in a manner of speaking, that is. For he looked forward to the day that Jesus Christ would come back to rapture His church, thus ending a life that, for all of its wonders, joys and delights, was nothing compared to the life promised to those who put their trust in Him.

Randall had worked late this evening, helping to finish up the bank's month-end closing process with this being the start of a new month, and it was dusk as he covered the last two hundred yards to their home. Most days, during the warmer months of the year, he would walk to and from work, as they lived just a half-mile from the bank, and since their daughter Jocelyn had been born five months before, he did not have much time to exercise. He could see the lights of their home twinkling up ahead, and he smiled at the thought of spending a wonderful evening with his family.

Suddenly, directly in front of him, a faint, shimmering circle of light appeared, suspended in mid-air about a foot above the sidewalk. There was nothing in front of him that could be reflecting light, just open space, which gave the appearance that the light was actually *self-created*, or without any discernible source. Randall stopped abruptly and stared at the light with a mixture of confusion, fear and curiosity. The light was round, more or less, approximately ten feet in diameter, and as he studied it, it seemed to increase gradually in brightness. Then, incredibly, the center of the circle began to recede, giving it a quality of depth, as if it were actually a . . . a tunnel! It seemed impossible, but as he continued to observe it, he could discern the smooth walls, and eventually, a much brighter light at the far end of the tunnel.

Terrified, yet utterly fascinated, Randall continued to watch as the characteristics of the tunnel became more and more defined. Finally, after what seemed to be several minutes, a figure appeared at the far end of the tunnel. He could not make out who or what it was, for it was silhouetted by the bright light behind it, but there was no doubt that something was there . . . and it was now moving toward him.

And suddenly, the answer just popped into his head. It was so simple, so obvious. "Oh . . . my . . . God," he whispered. "It's *Him*! It's time!"

He wished he could run to the house and get Mindy and the kids, so they could all welcome Him together, but there was no way he was leaving this spot now, not when He would be here in just a few seconds. Besides, Randall knew that when Christ came back, He would be coming for all of them, no matter where they were, and they would all be together in paradise very soon. So he waited.

The silhouetted figure moved toward him slowly, until it had traveled about half of the tunnel's length, and then it shot forward as if from the barrel of a gun, covering the remaining distance to Randall's end of the tunnel in virtually the blink of an eye. Before he could even think about reacting, Randall found himself lying on his back, staring straight up at the darkening sky, with a wickedly sharp pain piercing his legs just below his groin. He tried to sit up so he could determine what had happened, but found that he was unable to, and he wondered if he had injured his spine in the fall and was paralyzed from the waist down. But then he became aware of not just an inability to *move* his legs . . . but of the *absence* of them altogether. He slid his arms, which had been extended out perpendicular to his body when he came to rest on the sidewalk, down to where his thighs should have been, and confirmed that his legs were, in fact, gone.

Despite the excruciating pain, and the shock at discovering his missing legs, Randall remained oddly alert and clearheaded. He understood immediately that whatever had come through the tunnel was not who he thought it was, and it occurred to him that if indeed it had been Jesus returning, instead of being silhouetted by the light at the far end of the tunnel, He *Himself* would have been emitting the light. This was something different, something evil, in fact . . . . and that something suddenly loomed over him, teeth and claws gleaming in the yellowish light of the sodium streetlamps. He could see that it was not something born of this earth but was instead some horrific patchwork of various members of the animal kingdom. It was like something out of a horror movie, one produced by Satan himself.

And then the memory suddenly leapt from the recesses of his mind to the forefront – the dream! It had been twenty-six years since he had had it, and twenty since he had stopped believing in it. But now, as the beast looked down upon him, he could not help but recall its hideous face, its evil origins, and its monstrous intentions. He had been wrong to dismiss the dream as merely an unusually vivid nightmare, and the three-day coma as an unrelated phenomenon. But the fact that the creature had arrived *here*, in his own town, and in fact, *right in front of his own house*, was what he found most disturbing. How could he not have recognized this neighborhood when he and Mindy had moved here after their wedding? Had he so vigorously suppressed the memory of the dream that it would not resurface even though he had, on countless occasions, walked directly over the spot where the creature would arrive? And if that was not enough of a shock to the system, he realized, too, that the man who had been killed the moment the creature emerged from the time tunnel was none other than himself! That was the clincher; he knew then, if there had been any doubt in his mind up to that point, that he was about to die.

The creature hovered over him for a few seconds, as if contemplating whether the damage it had inflicted was enough to finish him off. Then, apparently satisfied with its efforts, it left him, moving away so quickly that it seemed to vanish before his eyes.

ᛉ　　ᛉ　　ᛉ

To this point, it has known only confinement, the inside of a prison cell. But suddenly, it is thrust into a new world, a world with no boundaries, no restrictions. A world where its instincts are unharnessed, where it can finally pursue the purpose for which it was created . . . to hunt down and kill everything on two legs. It must eat frequently to fuel its racing metabolism, and will sleep one or two hours a day. But aside from that, it will spend the next nine decades doing just two things – either pursuing its prey, or killing its prey.

The creature enters its new domain and immediately attacks its first victim. It hesitates for a moment before moving on . . . it is, after all, an infant, one that has not had the benefit of a mother teaching it to kill, as do its distant relatives in the animal world. But then its instincts, its genetic programming, take full charge, and it focuses its attention on the houses surrounding it, sensing that there are multiple kill opportunities available. It streaks across the front lawn toward the nearest house, a virtual blur to the human eye, crashes through the front door as if it were made of balsa wood, and begins its systematic destruction of humanity.

Dusk had arrived by the time Jason passed the "Welcome to Bunting" sign on Route 285 doing better than 100 miles per hour. The day had been an utter disaster from the minute they had left home. It started when they were t-boned by a drunk driver at an intersection just a quarter of a mile from the airport. Neither Jason nor Mal was injured, but Mal's vehicle was totaled, and the man who had hit them was seriously injured and had to be transported to the hospital by helicopter. By the time the scene was cleared and the police had taken their statements, they had missed their flight to Denver. They waited another three hours for the next one, but shortly after they had boarded, the captain came on the radio saying that they had found some mechanical problems with the plane and that the flight was cancelled. So they waited *another* three hours for the flight after that, which finally did get them to Denver but only after it, too, was delayed for yet another hour. They also had to wait at the baggage claim area for the cases that contained Jason's .45 caliber handgun, ammunition, and preferred handheld weapon, a machete, since these items could not be brought into the cabin of the plane. Ultimately it had taken them twelve hours to reach Bunting instead of the four-and-a-half that they had anticipated, which gave them more than enough time to discuss every possible detail and strategic approach they could think of. There was one constant, however, one thing they agreed upon no matter what else might occur. When Jason first came face-to-face with the creature, it would see him as just another prey item rather than as a dangerous opponent who could potentially harm it; therefore, it would attack him as it would any other human being. That would be the only time that Jason would have the element of surprise, and since the creature could fly while Jason could not, he must seize that opportunity to damage its wings to the point that it could never fly again. Of course, the hope was that Jason would not merely *injure* the creature but actually kill it on their first encounter, but at a minimum he needed to level the playing field.

Jason continued on Route 285 for another half mile, then slowed to around 40 miles per hour so he could make a hard left turn onto Main Street. From there, River Drive was just a quarter-mile ahead. Part of him, the part that dreaded taking on the creature by himself, hoped that a police officer would have spotted the speeding vehicle, called for backup, and the entire Bunting police force, small as it probably was, pursued them until they reached their destination, then helped him engage the creature once it appeared. But another part of him, not necessarily the more courageous part, but certainly the more protective, hoped he would encounter no one, neither along the way nor at the scene of the arrival. For he knew that no human being aside from himself, whether armed or not, stood a chance against this thing.

A few seconds later, with the moon rising in the eastern sky, Mal and Jason spotted the small sign for River Drive. Fifteen years of grueling physical and mental preparation, of incessant sacrifice and secrecy, of sweat and blood (*lots* of blood), and now, suddenly and almost unexpectedly, the time had arrived; the most important battle in the history of the planet was about to begin.

On River Drive now, Jason and Mal scanned the deserted street and the modest but well-maintained houses on either side for any signs of unusual activity. They saw the delivery truck with the words *Wetzel's Bakery, Bunting, Colorado* parked in the driveway of someone's home, and knew they were close. Seconds later, Jason saw someone lying on the sidewalk to his left, slammed on the brakes of the car and leaped out to investigate.

"Oh God, we're too late," Jason said, mostly to himself as Mal was still getting out of the vehicle some thirty yards away.

He approached the mutilated man and knelt down beside him, his mind reeling, trying to take it all in, while at the same time reluctant to accept that it had finally come to this. He had hoped that they would reach the intersection of River Drive and Main Street before the time portal opened to admit the creature, and that Mal could then direct Jason to the very spot where it would arrive. Then just as the creature set foot into this world, Jason would surprise it and deal it a lethal blow before it could ever get close to its first victim. Naïveté, perhaps even arrogance, had given birth to such an absurd wish, for that was not how Mal's dream had gone. Indeed, actual events seemed to be unfolding just as Mal had foreseen them, though he realized that having reached the point where the dream had ended, they were now in uncharted waters.

Jason stood up and turned away from the dead man, focusing his keen senses on the neighborhood surrounding him, assuming that the creature would commence a systematic, house-to-house extermination plan. The slowly expanding pool of blood beneath the man, along with the steam rising from it into the cool night air, were indicators that he had missed the creature by only a couple of minutes. So there was still time to keep the casualties to a minimum, as long as he could locate his enemy quickly. And then, to his shock, he heard a weak, raspy voice behind him say "You . . . are . . . . the one." Jason spun around and looked down, seeing now that the man's eyes were open. He could not be sure, but he had thought that they had been closed a moment ago.

"You're . . . alive," Jason said, as he knelt down again next to the man, feeling foolish as the words left his mouth, but not knowing what else to say. Even as those words left his mouth, he remembered the last few sentences of Mal's journal, when he had spun around in surprise after hearing the man on the sidewalk mutter a single word ... *You...* "Of course you're alive. How did I forget that?" Jason asked rhetorically, for there was no way the man would know what he was talking about. He quickly unfastened the man's belt and yanked it through the loops on his trouser waistband, then wrapped it around his thighs and cinched it tightly. It would slow the loss of blood somewhat, but Jason knew that unless help arrived immediately, which was very unlikely, the man would not last more than a few minutes.

The man arched his back and groaned with pain as the belt was tightened just above where his legs had been severed, but then relaxed again momentarily. "Thank you," he said, "though it won't matter. I'm a . . . . dead man walking." In spite of his imminent demise, he laughed hoarsely at his own ironic humor.

"I'm . . . . sorry that this happened to you," Jason said. "This won't make any sense to you, but this is my fault. I should have gotten here sooner."

The man shook his head again. "No. It's not your fault. You are the one. The one who can stop this, not the one who started it."

Those words again. *You are the one.* They had not registered with Jason at first. He had been startled at hearing the man speak any words, period, so the fact that they actually held meaning had been lost on him. "You . . . . you *know* me?"

"Yes, I know who you are," the man replied, his voice a bit weaker now. "I know *exactly* who you are, Jason Devine. You see, my name is Randall Wilhelm."

Mal had arrived just in time to hear Randall's words, and he and Jason let out a collective gasp.

"Randall Wilhelm!" Mal exclaimed. "My God, you're a real person! I never knew if you existed in real life, or if you were just an imaginary character in my dream!"

"As real as you are, Malcolm," Randall responded. "It's been twenty-six years since I last saw the two of you. It's nice to officially meet you both, even under the circumstances."

Jason and Mal exchanged glances, the shock still visible on

both of their faces.

"We're glad to have met you as well, Randall," Jason said. "And again, I'm sorry this happened."

"Like I said, it's not your fault."

Jason knew he should leave Mal and Randall behind and go after the creature, but now he was glued to this spot. To meet Randall in person, when for years they were not even sure if he existed, was probably the biggest shock he had experienced since the day Mal had shot him in the leg.

"You live here, Randall?" Mal asked.

"Yes, for about five years now."

"Then tell me something. In the dream, when I came back to talk to you on the mountain, after Zintak's parents had died, you said you had been watching the events unfold just like I had. Which means that you knew this was his hometown, the place where he would not only grow up, but also recruit his master race, build his time machine and send the creature back to this very spot. So why did you come here? Sure, you didn't know *when* the creature would arrive, but just knowing it would happen right here, why didn't you stay as far away from this spot as you could?"

"Because I didn't recognize it," Randall said. "As you recall, the name of this town was never revealed to us during the dream, and by the time I moved here five years ago I had long since convinced myself that the dream was just a dream and not a vision of the future. I had buried it so deep by the time I came here that it would have just about taken a hypnotist to get me to remember. That is, until I saw the creature face to face a few minutes ago. And then I remembered that the two of you would be right on its tail."

Randall turned his head to look up towards his house, but the outer twenty- to twenty-five feet of the front lawns along River Drive dropped steeply down toward the street, and the homes sat far enough back that they could not be seen by someone laying on the sidewalk. " Up there. My family. Did it . . . did it get them? " he asked with trepidation.

Jason and Mal looked up at the house, saw the front door smashed in, and what appeared to be blood trickling down the inside of a window in a lighted upstairs room. They exchanged knowing glances before Jason responded.

"I think they're okay, the creature went further down the street," he lied. Apparently Randall had not yet remembered *every* detail of the dream, like the fact that the very first house the creature had entered after attacking him was the one he and his family lived in. That being the case, there was no reason to break the news to him, as he would be dead within minutes.

"Thank . . . God," Randall said with a faint smile. His breathing was very shallow and rapid now.

"Randall, I need to ask you one more question," Jason said. "Mal told me a couple of years ago that he thought I would need to use some sort of skill that I had not yet discovered in order to defeat the creature. Presumably it's something that you and Mal would have both seen if the dream had not ended before it was supposed to. But is there anything you can tell me, anything at all, even if it's just a gut feeling, that might help me to defeat this thing?"

Randall thought for a moment before answering, now in little more than a whisper. "I'm . . . afraid not. You'll just have to have faith. You must believe that either you already have what you need, or if you need something else then God will reveal it to you when the time comes."

Jason sighed and nodded, disappointed but not surprised at Randall's response.

"It's time . . . for me . . . to go," Randall said, looking at Jason, his breathing now so shallow that he could scarcely get enough air in his lungs to speak. "But I want . . . you to know . . . something. When I saw . . . . the tunnel . . . opening . . . I thought it was . . . Jesus . . . . coming to . . . take us . . . all home. I realized . . . too late . . . that it . . . wasn't Him. But then . . . I saw it . . . and

I remembered. I knew then . . . the dream . . . was real. I am about . . . to meet . . . the One who . . . saves . . . human souls . . . and I have now had . . . the privilege of meeting . . . . the one who will save . . . human lives. All in all . . . . not a bad day. May God . . . be with you, Jason."

And with that, Randall Wilhelm died.

⚔   ⚔   ⚔

Jason and Mal were silent for a moment, both feeling, strangely, as though they had lost a loved one, even though they had known Randall for all of about five minutes. There was no time for reflection, however, as seconds later, they heard a tremendous crash and an ear-piercing scream come from one of the houses down the block. The nearest ones were in a condition very similar to Randall's – eerily quiet and with smashed doors or windows evidencing the creature's ruthless and rapid entries, assaults and departures. But Jason could see people moving around inside the homes further down the block, so there was still an opportunity to intercept the creature before the swath of blood it left behind became a veritable river.

"Get in the car and drive away from here!" Jason commanded Mal. "It's on *me* now!"

Mal opened his mouth to protest, his fatherly instinct telling him to stand and fight alongside this courageous young man who was the closest thing he had ever had to a son. But he realized how utterly foolish that proposition was, and indeed, he had never intended to provide Jason with anything more than logistical assistance on what they both knew would be the final confrontation, the training mission to end them all. He threw his arms around Jason, then spun around and stumbled back to the truck, wiping tears and trying in vain to swallow the lump in his throat that felt like it might choke him to death.

Jason did not return Mal's embrace nor watch him grope his way back to the car, afraid that if he did, he would be unable to

279

control his own emotions. There was no time for that, as he heard a dog yelp, then seconds later another crash a bit further down the block. The creature's speed was shocking; it had taken only a few seconds for it to dispose of the inhabitants of one house and move on to the next, apparently encountering and destroying a dog along the way. He withdrew the machete from its sheath, and the .45 caliber pistol from its holster, and sprinted off in pursuit.

⚔ ⚔ ⚔

After killing its first victim, the creature moves along the street toward the first structure that emanates light. Its instincts tell it that there is more likely to be prey available if there are lights on inside. It crashes through the door and indeed finds the house occupied by three inhabitants, a grown female of the species, along with two young ones, a male and a female. It quickly dispatches all three of them, exits the structure and moves on to the next one, and the next, and so on down the block. Within minutes, however, it begins to feel weak. Its journey through time, followed by successive encounters with numerous prey items, has accelerated its metabolism even more than usual, and it must find food quickly to replenish itself. It hears growling coming from the rear of the next enclosure, and veering off in that direction, quickly devours a small domesticated animal. Its genetically enhanced physiology rapidly responds to the infusion of nourishment, and within seconds it returns to full strength and focuses once again on its mission of annihilation.

⚔ ⚔ ⚔

Jason moved in the direction of the dog yelp and the crash that followed. He stopped in front of the last house on the street that had clear signs of damage to the exterior; those to the south were all damaged as well, while those to the north were unblemished. He knew the creature must be inside, so he leaped onto the porch and entered the house. Once inside, he heard heavy footfalls and thumps coming from the second floor, so he paused for a moment to weigh his options. He could point the .45 out in front of him and wait for the creature to descend the stairs to the first floor, where he would hopefully take it by surprise. He might be able to end this quickly with one well-placed shot between the creature's eyes. On the other hand, if the shot was not true, or if the creature sensed danger before he got the shot off, it would escape through a window or the rear door of the house and most likely fly away. If that were to happen, there was no telling how long it might be until his next encounter with the creature, as it could easily stay one or two steps ahead of him indefinitely. That meant that many more people would die.

The creature seemed to have finished its work upstairs, for Jason could hear the floorboards creaking as it approached the head of the stairs. He decided it would be better to lure the creature in by pretending to be completely vulnerable than it would be to openly brandish his weapons and risk scaring it away. From the way Mal had described this thing, it had such uncanny intelligence and survival instincts that it would not fixate on one target that it saw as a threat when there were billions more out there, most of which would not be capable of putting up a fight. In other words, it was designed to go after the low-hanging fruit first and leave the most difficult targets for last. So he slid the machete into the sheath that was strapped to his back, the .45 into the shoulder holster he wore outside of his Kevlar vest and beneath his jacket, and waited.

⅄   ⅄   ⅄

The creature clears another dwelling of its inhabitants and moves toward the exit at the bottom of the steps. Once there, it comes face to face with yet another target that had apparently just entered the structure. It takes one step towards its victim, then hesitates for just a brief moment. This one seems different from the others; he stands his ground instead of trying to escape. And while the others reeked of fear, the scent is present on this one but barely detectable. Yet his appearance is no different from the others. He walks on two legs, which means he is not built for speed, he has no exoskeleton and therefore no natural form of defense, and his arms terminate in small gripping devices rather than in claws or other weaponry. In short, though he seems to have an air of poise and determination about him, this target is no more a threat to the creature than any of the others. It attacks.

⚔   ⚔   ⚔

When the creature came into view, Jason was shocked at how grotesque and ferocious it looked, even after having read Mal's description of it dozens of times. If a picture of a monster was worth a thousand words, then having one alive and in the flesh right in front of you must be worth a million. Indeed, it was close enough that Jason could smell its fetid breath and see his own reflection in its birdlike eyes. And yet, he had come prepared for this moment, had *been* preparing for the last fifteen years, so even as the sight of the creature revolted him, he steeled himself against the avalanche of horror that would have crippled any normal human being.

The creature paused for just a moment when it saw Jason, then launched itself at him. He was ready for it. He dropped onto his back and drove his feet up into the creature's relatively soft underside as it sailed over him. Despite the fact that the creature was many times heavier than Jason, the force of his kick was strong enough to send it catapulting head over heels. It slammed into the wall behind Jason with such force that it disintegrated a section of plasterboard and snapped the wall studs like they were toothpicks. Even before it touched the wall, however, Jason had jumped to his feet, withdrawn the machete from its sheath, and was closing the distance between himself and the creature. He knew that the impact would not be enough to injure it, but he hoped that it might be stunned for just a few seconds, long enough for him to hack through one of its wings and permanently disable its flight capability. Then if it chose to flee rather than stay and fight, he would have a reasonably good chance of being able to pursue it on the ground. After all, though there was supposedly some secret skill or weapon that he had yet to discover, he highly doubted that it would involve the ability to sprout wings and fly.

Jason's incredible speed allowed him to reach the creature in less than two-tenths of a second. It was lying on its left side, with its exposed right wing tucked into the groove along its right side. He raised the machete high above his head and brought it down as hard as he could, but the creature, with its genetically enhanced reflexes, sensed the blow coming and rolled onto its stomach. The machete blade shattered like glass when it struck the armor plating that covered the creature's back and flanks. The wing remained intact; Jason had missed his opportunity.

Leaping to its feet, the creature counterattacked, slashing at Jason with its razor-sharp claws. He anticipated that maneuver and backpedaled away, now trying to buy himself a few seconds while he came up with a plan B. He did not want to pull out his .45 just yet, for fear that the creature might instinctively recognize it as a more deadly weapon than a sharpened piece of steel, and then decide that this confrontation was no longer worth the risk. So again, he baited the creature by keeping his .45 concealed. And again, the tactic was successful, as the creature barreled forward, its teeth clicking, its claws shredding the carpet like it was newspaper. Jason dealt it a crushing roundhouse kick to the side of the head, then charged in and pummeled it like a punching bag, blows that would have fragmented the skulls of most other animals. But though the creature had no armor covering its head, it had been engineered with enhanced ram DNA, giving it a skull that was nearly as tough as the plating on its back. It merely shook its head, snarled with rage and slashed at Jason again. This time, because he was in such close proximity, the claws found purchase and raked across his chest, leaving deep scores in the Kevlar material. Before Jason could react, it swiped again, and this time one of its claws caught him on the left bicep after it had passed across the vest. It sliced halfway through his arm, but the pain had not even registered in his brain yet before the wound had knitted itself shut.

Jason tried a different approach, kicking upward into the creature's more delicate throat area, and as soon as it connected, he knew he had met with a bit of success. It backed off a few feet and broke into a fit of hacking and choking, its throat traumatized and its air supply cut off momentarily. Jason seized upon the opportunity and hurled himself full-speed at the creature's side. Though it weighed upwards of 4,000 pounds, there was enough momentum generated by his own weight and speed that it knocked the creature off its feet and onto its side, again exposing its vulnerable underside. He kicked furiously at its chest and belly, hoping to drive the wind from it and incapacitate it long enough to do some real damage to it, possibly even kill it. The creature roared with pain and slashed at his legs, delivering deep lacerations to his right calf muscle, which again healed almost before they could bleed.

Though the creature was in pain, it still did not seem to be seriously injured, and again it leaped to its feet and stared at Jason with fury. This time, though, it did not charge him, but instead circled him, growling menacingly, pondering its next move.

⅄ ⅄ ⅄

The creature stares down its opponent. He cannot be called "prey" anymore, for he has proven to be as strong, fast, and cunning as the creature itself, meaning they are virtually even at the top of the food chain. Anything that is not below it on the food chain cannot be considered a prey item, and must be considered an opponent. An enemy to be wary of. The creature was bred for one purpose – to kill human beings. As long as it is not threatened, it will kill without stopping, for days, months, years, decades, until the day its heart stops beating. But when a threat does materialize, its survival instinct will supersede its urge to kill, and it will look to make its escape. Now, as it faces off against this opponent, having not only been unsuccessful in its attempts to kill him, but also being on the receiving end of his unexpectedly powerful blows, the creature has begun to sense that it must retreat or put itself in jeopardy. It must live to kill another day.

ᴧ　　ᴧ　　ᴧ

The creature suddenly whirled about, bolted through the open doorway and out onto the sidewalk. Jason took off after it, his sense of desperation now escalating rapidly. He knew that he simply *must not* allow it to fly away. Once it reached the open street, out from under the canopy of trees above the front lawn, the creature spread its wings and lifted off the ground. It rose quickly to height of fifty feet, then seventy-five, then higher still. Jason sprang from the ground to meet it, fearing that was it already out of reach. But just as he arrived at the apex of his leap, he managed to stretch his hands out and grab the creature's left wing just below the shoulder, causing instant immobilization of that appendage. Both man and creature plummeted to the pavement below.

Jason heard bones snapping as he and the creature tumbled onto the asphalt surface, and he knew that many, if not all of them, were his own as he felt agony explode throughout his body. Even so, he maintained his grip on the creature's wing, though he could do little more than that until his bones mended themselves.

The creature lay silent and dazed for several seconds before it revived and again howled with pain, but was not injured so badly that it could not rise up and begin to thrash about like a bucking bronco, trying to shake Jason loose. Despite being slapped repeatedly against the pavement like a dirty rug, however, Jason would not let go of the wing. Victory depended upon it, plain and simple. And yet the creature's efforts to rid itself from Jason were relentless, and after several minutes of this, he began to grow fatigued. The broken bones and lacerations were mounting faster than his body could repair them, and it would not be much longer before the creature was able to tear away from him. He needed to do something, and do it right *now.* So he concentrated on the rhythm of the creature's incessant thrashing, which was extremely difficult, since it did not always stick to a regular pattern. But when he felt he had the timing down, or was as close to it as he was going to get, he waited until the precise moment when the creature descended and touched the pavement, then yanked downward with all of his strength just as its powerful legs were beginning to push upward again. His strategy worked; the combined effect of two tremendous forces moving in opposite directions allowed him to rip the creature's wing completely free from its upper flank. Then came an unearthly screech like no one had ever heard before.

А   А   А

The creature felt two things it had never felt before; unimaginable pain, and fear. It had been designed so that it would never experience these things, but it now faced an enemy that it never expected to meet. Its prey was supposed to have been like cattle, each one of them easily hunted and easily killed. But this one, though he looks and smells like the others, is different. He not a prey item, he is a predator, like itself. Something to be feared. Something to be avoided, at all costs. It flees.

А   А   А

Jason tossed the bloody, detached wing aside and tried to struggle to his feet, but found that he could not yet do so. His damaged bones, tendons and muscles were still healing themselves. Somehow the .45 caliber pistol had not been dislodged from its holster while Jason was being whipped about by the creature, so he withdrew it, took aim and began to fire. But the creature darted off just as he fired the first shot, and he missed. The second and third shots missed also. But on the fourth shot, the creature squealed and tumbled across the pavement just as it reached the cul-de-sac at the end of the street, where the sodium lighting terminated, then immediately got up and disappeared into the darkness. He fired two more shots into the spot where it he had last seen it, but heard nothing. Now he *had* to go after it, whether his body was ready or not.

Forcing himself to stand up and gritting his teeth at the pain, Jason began to hobble down the street after the creature. It was slow going at first, but with each step he took, the pain steadily subsided as the fragments of bone in his legs fused themselves back together. By the time he reached the cul-de-sac, he was back at full strength. He removed a small LED flashlight from a pouch on his belt and directed its beam into the darkness.

Just outside the cul-de-sac began the forested foothills that led up into the mountains. Jason could see the broken branches indicating where the creature had entered the forest, and on the ground he saw a trail of blood that he could easily follow. But he knew there was not much time before the creature's wounds would scab over and the blood trail would be lost, for it had been engineered with rudimentary regenerative abilities. It could not regrow entire limbs, like he could, for its abilities were of scientific origin, not divine, but they were enough to allow the creature to survive injuries that would kill any other animal. He slid his pistol back into the holster and plunged into the dense forest in pursuit of his quarry.

4

Jason felt confident about his chances of defeating the creature, having not only survived a close encounter with it, but having also dealt it a pretty good beating. He had even managed to injure it, and if he could injure it, he could kill it. The creature had proven to be strong, fast and ferocious, but by no means was it indestructible. But at the same time, he felt something else, something that had spawned the tiniest seed of doubt in the back of his mind; the very early stages of fatigue. He had expended a significant amount of energy in his initial fight with the creature, and his unique physiology required him to replenish spent calories frequently. For now, he still had plenty left in his fuel tank, given the massive quantity of food he had consumed on the trip to Bunting, but a prolonged chase or another intense battle with his nemesis would certainly burn through most of what he had left.

After about ten minutes, the blood trail disappeared, but fortunately Jason was able to continue tracking the creature using the path of broken branches and disturbed leaves and underbrush that it left behind. Still, he picked up his pace, hoping to close the gap between himself and the creature, for he knew that as they steadily moved up the mountain, they would eventually reach the upper tree line, above which it would become more difficult to stay on the creature's trail.

Jason had maintained the accelerated pace for about ten minutes more, when he halted suddenly, thinking he had heard something up ahead. As soon as he did, he knew he had been right, for he could hear the sound of twigs and branches snapping at a distance of what he judged to be about seventy-five yards ahead. He sprinted forward again, oblivious to the noise he himself was making, or the slapping, gouging and scraping of the branches against his face as he charged through them. He was determined to destroy this thing right now, before it could slip away from him, out of the mountains and back into populated areas.

The minutes ticked steadily by, and as they did, Jason could hear the sounds of the creature getting louder. Eventually, he saw flickers of movement at the far reaches of his flashlight beam, and he pushed himself even harder to overtake his enemy. It was close now, maybe fifty yards away. Close enough that it was in full view. He could see it limping ever so slightly as it ran, hampered by the lingering effects of a .45 caliber bullet to the leg. Even so, it was moving incredibly fast, probably at least seventy miles an hour. But Jason was moving faster; not nearly his top speed, which could only be achieved on open, flat terrain, but fast enough so that the gap continued to close. It was now forty yards. And now twenty-five. He removed the pistol from its holster, did his best to aim at the creature's hindquarters despite running, dodging trees and leaping over stumps and logs, and fired twice. Two little puffs of dirt exploded inches from the creature's right rear leg. Upon hearing the shots, it veered to the left, momentarily creating separation between itself and its pursuer. But Jason closed in again, this time getting to within fifteen yards before firing his next shot. It was a bit too high, and ricocheted harmlessly off the creature's armor-plated back. That was nine shots fired, by his count, leaving one more bullet left in the clip. He had more clips in another pouch on his belt, but if he needed to reload, then he would probably have to stop for several seconds, as it would be too difficult a task to accomplish on the run. With his last shot, he hoped to bring the creature down long enough for him to pop a new clip into the gun, and then pump all ten rounds into it from point blank range. If that did not kill it, nothing short of a missile strike would do it. So he got even closer this time, close enough to almost hitch a ride on the creature's back. He pointed the gun and fired.

⅄   ⅄   ⅄

The creature was supposed to have been the fastest animal on the planet. It was designed that way, to ensure its superiority over all other life. To ensure its conquest of the entire planet. Instead, it had encountered something even faster, even stronger, than itself. Something fearless, something relentless. He was right on the creature's heels now, close enough for the creature to smell him, close enough to feel the vibrations of his pounding footfalls. And he carried a weapon, something the creature had not seen when it first faced this enemy inside the house, an instrument that could hurl deadly projectiles faster than the creature could run. It senses that its pursuer is about to use the weapon again, and that this time he would not miss. It reacts instinctively, instantaneously, not with thought or premeditation but merely with a primal urge to survive.

⅄   ⅄   ⅄

As Jason fired the last shot in the clip, the creature unexpectedly twisted its body, dropped, and skidded to a halt, and the bullet sailed harmlessly above it. Jason's momentum carried him forward into the creature, his legs slammed into its side and he flipped headfirst over the top of it, losing both the gun and the flashlight in the process. The creature wasted no time in resuming its escape, and was gone almost before Jason realized what had happened.

The flashlight was still lit, and Jason recovered it instantly. The gun, however, was a different matter; he did a couple of 360-degree sweeps with the flashlight but could not immediately locate it. As he searched for it, he debated whether he should leave the gun behind and continue his pursuit of the creature, for every second that passed by allowed it to separate itself from him even further. But he decided not to go after it without his gun, because he had no other weapons with him, and though he had been able to *hurt* the creature with his bare hands, he did not think he could *kill* it. So he painstakingly walked back and forth along a series of parallel lines about three feet apart and about thirty feet in length, scanning every inch of the forest floor within that area. After about four minutes, he saw a metallic glint alongside his foot, bent down and found the gun mostly buried in the leaves. It took another minute for him to find the creature's trail, and when he did, he took off after it again at top speed.

ᴧ   ᴧ   ᴧ

The creature had paused briefly to consume a small, furry animal it had encountered as it fled from its pursuer. It resumed its flight, then captured another small prey item, and then a third. It continued on this way through the mountains, alternating between running and feeding. Precious seconds were sacrificed each time it stopped to feed, but it was a worthwhile exchange. Though its enemy had superior strength and speed, the creature had one significant advantage; its razor-sharp teeth and large, powerful jaws enabled it to consume large meals very quickly. Its digestive system was also highly advanced, allowing it to process food into fuel in a matter of seconds. It was therefore able to remain re-energized, rejuvenated as it hurtled through the darkness, while its pursuer, on the other hand, steadily consumed his energy supply even as he closed the gap between them. Thus emerged the creature's strategy; it would defeat its enemy not by outrunning him, but by outlasting him.

ᴧ   ᴧ   ᴧ

The black canopy above Jason was morphing into shades of gray, pink and green. Dawn had arrived. He had been hunting the creature for hours, pursuing it first up the mountain, then down again, through valleys and meadows, and now back towards the summit. Two or three times, the creature had managed to briefly throw him off its trail by climbing a tree, then leaping to the next one like a squirrel, before dropping to the ground and running again. It cost him only a minute or two each time, but it helped the creature to continue to stay ahead of him. He stopped occasionally to listen, and could hear its telltale signs – swishing through leaves, splashing through streams, or snapping of branches. And while he knew he was getting closer, for some reason it was taking a lot more time and consuming a lot more energy to close the gap than it did when the chase had first begun.

The creature was definitely moving faster than before, probably because the bullet wound in its leg had fully healed, while at the same time, Jason's fuel tank had been steadily approaching empty. But as long as there was anything left at all, he was not going to break off his pursuit. If worse came to worst, and he collapsed from exhaustion before he could overtake the creature, he would go back, refuel and re-equip himself, and then he and Mal would have to find a way to pick up the creature's trail again. He wanted to avoid that if at all possible, however, because it might take days or weeks for them to zero in on it again, which would mean the deaths of thousands of people during that time. And so on he went, pushing himself like never before, intent on finishing this once and for all.

⅄   ⅄   ⅄

The creature can hear its pursuer's breathing becoming more labored with each passing minute, his once almost inaudible footfalls now pounding heavily on the forest floor. The enemy is near exhaustion. And yet, the creature senses, instinctively knows, that even though it may win this battle, the war with this particular enemy has just begun. This opponent is relentless and determined. It will not be long before he finds the creature again, and when he does, he will once again be at full strength, and with more powerful weapons. As long as this enemy breathes, as long as blood courses through his veins, the creature's mission, and indeed its life, will be in peril. It must evolve its strategy from defensive to offensive and seize this opportunity to destroy its opponent now, while his strength is diminished, and he is vulnerable. To do this, the creature will lure the enemy in. It will set a trap for him. And just when the enemy thinks he has won, the trap will spring.

⚔   ⚔   ⚔

Jason knew he was drawing nearer to the creature, because its sounds were getting louder. Perhaps, finally, it was beginning to tire. Jason himself was nearly running on fumes now, but that would be enough. He was mere minutes away from overtaking it, and then he would kill it. After that, he could eat a horse and sleep for a month if he wanted to. But right now, there was business to attend to. He willed his body to move even faster, beyond anything he ever imagined he could do.

Moments later, he burst out of the forest and found himself standing on a broad overlook, a wide valley a few thousand feet below him and the mountain range stretching out beyond that. The creature stood facing him about twenty feet away at the edge of the precipice, its eyes wide with terror, having unwittingly run itself into a corner; on one side a sheer cliff that it could not possibly negotiate even with its enormous claws, and on the other side a merciless, unceasing pursuer that was about to destroy it. Its rear leg had apparently not healed from the gunshot after all, for it held that one off the ground as it stood on the other three. It panted and swayed from side to side, as though it scarcely had the energy left to stand up.

Seeing it now in a much different light, Jason almost felt sorry for this pitiful thing. After all, it could hardly be blamed for the evil intentions it harbored, as that was entirely unnatural among animals. Even the most deadly and aggressive ones only killed for two reasons; for food, or to protect themselves, their offspring, or their territory. Until now, the only thing on earth that killed for the sake of killing was human beings. And in fact, that was still the case, for this thing, this abomination, was the work of human hands. It was no animal, it was a weapon created by humans, to destroy humans. In short, to do what humans have always done. Nevertheless, Jason had no choice but to kill the creature. It could not be caged or otherwise contained. It certainly could not be domesticated. If allowed to live, it would continue to hunt people, as it had been designed to do, until every last one of them was dead.

When Jason removed the handgun from its holster, the creature recognized it and began to whimper and mewl like a giant kitten. If it could speak, it would have undoubtedly been begging for mercy. He pointed the gun at it, hoping he could kill it from a safe distance, but it dropped to its side with its armor plating toward him and tucked its head, arms and legs as tightly into its body as it could, effectively shielding all of its vulnerable areas. Jason fired three shots at its back, but as he anticipated, the bullets ricocheted away. He would have to get close enough to reach over its back and fire the shots from point blank range into its head or torso, below the armor plating. He was wary, though confident, as he approached, believing the creature to be too exhausted to put up much of a fight, if it still had a mind to.

⅄   ⅄   ⅄

The creature had deliberately slowed its pace, allowing the enemy to gradually catch up. It had been skirting the edge of the forest when it saw the overlook -- the perfect location to set the trap. It moved away from the trees until it reached the edge of the cliff, then turned and waited. To mislead its pursuer, the creature had feigned terror, injury, and exhaustion. And when the enemy came out of the forest, saw the creature and where it was standing, he clearly believed he had won. Now he brings forth the weapon and fires it three times, but the creature drops to a defensive position, and though it feels the projectiles strike its armor with tremendous force, it is not injured. The enemy now has no choice but to approach. Cautiously, but steadily, he comes toward the trap, closer and closer, not knowing, not expecting, closer still. And then – snap!! – the trap springs.

⚑ ⚑ ⚑

Jason was three feet away from the creature when, in a blur of motion, it flipped itself over and lashed out at his legs with its front claws. A second later, he was staring up at the blue sky above, a searing pain just below his left knee. He had lost enough limbs during his training missions to know without even looking that his leg had been severed. He felt his regenerative motor kick in, though very sluggishly, and the leg began to regrow. Then the same pain exploded in his right forearm, and he knew the creature had severed that hand to separate him from his weapon. He held up his right arm, saw it stubbornly regenerating, and then spotted his severed hand and forearm, still holding the gun, lying some distance away. He tried to sit up, but was slammed onto his back again, and the blue sky above disappeared, obscured by the hideous face of the creature looming over him. He barely had time to get his arms up to protect his face and head before its raking blows rained down upon him. It slashed ruthlessly, repeatedly, at his arms, hands, head and chest. Its talons gouged deep into his Kevlar vest, threatening to pierce it or tear it away altogether. Knowing he had to fight back, Jason kept one arm over his face and extended the other one out to the side, then rammed his fist against the creature's jaw. Its head snapped sideways, and blood and teeth flew from its mouth, but it hardly seemed phased by the blow. It resumed its vicious assault, slicing away at his appendages.

The creature's intentions were now clear; it was not merely trying to disable him so that it could escape again. No, this time it was going to kill him. It had appeared to be injured, afraid, and exhausted, but Jason now realized it was none of those things, and that it had lured him in close to it so that it could strike at him unexpectedly. Panic gripped him like at no other time in his life. Somehow, he had to get away, concede this battle for the sake of preserving his chance of winning the war. He rolled over onto his stomach and got to his hands and knees, aware that he was exposing the back of his head and neck, but knowing he had no choice. He tried to get to his feet, but the creature hammered him down again, now raking at the back of the vest and across his legs. Then one mighty swipe finally tore the vest away completely, and the creature set to work on his exposed back. He desperately tried to crawl away, but knew it was useless. His body was still trying to heal itself, but new gashes and gouges were being opened up by the second, and there was no more fuel left to drive the regenerative machinery within him. The creature slashed at his legs again, this time severing both of them between the knees and ankles. It clamped its teeth onto the back of his head, then released and bit again, and again. Blood poured down the sides of his face and into his eyes. His life was literally gushing forth from his body now, bits and pieces of him flying in all directions, but still the creature continued to hack away at a feverish pace, intent on completely eviscerating him.

Jason was entirely spent. He could not believe that the thought even crossed his mind, but he was ready to give up. He wanted this to be over, for the pain to end, and to just be able to sleep for a long, long time. He was about to fall onto his face and let the creature finish him, when through the red haze that blurred his vision, he saw something to his right, a few feet away – a narrow gap between two large boulders, just wide enough for him to slip through. The two boulders butted up against a third one on the opposite side, creating a shelter that was large enough for a man but too small for a mutant creature. If Jason could reach that shelter, there might be a chance he could hold out long enough for his body to recover. There was only a glimmer of hope that it would work, but it was all he had. Reaching deep down within himself, Jason found one last surge of energy and darted toward the boulders on his hands and knees, slipping through the gap as the creature's jaws snapped shut behind him.

Once inside the shelter, Jason found it to be shallower than what he had hoped it would be, only about seven feet from the opening to the boulder on the backside. He scurried toward the back, turned sideways and pressed himself tightly against the huge block of stone. The creature jammed itself into the gap and extended its talon-tipped paw as far as it could reach, a distance of about four feet from its shoulder to the tips of its claws. At its widest point, across his muscular upper back and shoulders, Jason's body spanned a distance of over two feet, leaving less than twelve inches of clearance between himself and the creature's razor blade claws. There was no room at all for him to maneuver, but for now, he was perfectly fine with that.

When the creature realized it could not get at its enemy, it roared with anger and leaped atop the boulders, trying to get at him from a different angle. The boulders were relatively round at the top, which created a tapered opening directly above Jason that was larger at the top and narrower at the bottom. The creature slipped down between the boulders until it reached the narrowest part of the opening, and again extended its arm down toward him. Jason feared for a moment that it would be able to reach him and finish him off by slashing through the top of his head, but fortunately it again came up just short. Again it bellowed with fury, a deafening sound that could be heard echoing through the valley below. It jumped off the boulder and again tried to reach him from the ground, but with the same result. The creature circled the entire formation of rocks, searching for yet another opening to get at him, but there was none to be found. Again it leaped atop the boulder and tried in vain to reach him, then from in front again, then around the rock formation. Up and down, back and forth, around and around it went for several minutes, working itself into a frenzy, but refusing to give up.

Jason, meanwhile, examined the gashes on his arms and torso and the stubs of his legs, trying to will the wounds to knit themselves shut, the missing appendages to grow back, as they always had before. But this time, his body simply would not respond. The blood continued to flow, and as it did, his life steadily ebbed away. Darkness crept in at the edges of his vision, his eyelids fluttered and became increasingly difficult to keep open. At some point he became aware that the creature had stopped its terrible shrieking, and he now heard a different sound, a kind of scraping, scratching, soft chopping noise, like someone hoeing weeds in a garden. With great effort, he lifted his drooping head up, turned it in the direction of the sounds, and saw that the creature had begun to dig a tunnel just outside the gap between the boulders. It had already dug deep enough so that its head and shoulders were below ground, while its torso and hind end were still visible. In just a matter of minutes, it would tunnel beneath the boulders, up into his shelter, and finally end his life. That is, if he did not bleed out before then. He vaguely hoped that his heart would stop beating before the creature got to him, but frankly, he no longer cared much at this point. Once again, he was ready to die.

As he waited for the end to come, one way or another, Jason was dimly aware of just how much he had underestimated this thing. It was cunning in a way that he could never have imagined, that even *Mal* had never imagined, though in his vision he had seen it destroy the entire human race. It made sense, in a way; for in that version of the altered timeline, the untrained Jason was not a formidable enough opponent for the creature, and therefore it never had to reveal the full extent of its abilities. What was never revealed could obviously never be seen. Even so, he could not understand *why* he had failed this test. What did God expect from him? He had spent fifteen years of his life preparing for this day, and when it finally arrived, he did not run from it but instead charged boldly into the fray, just as he had been expected to. If there was something he was missing, some weapon or skill that he needed, how was it *his* fault that it was not revealed to Mal in the dream? With all of his physical abilities, what more could he possibly do? Shoot lightning bolts from his eyes? Laser beams from his fingertips? Those thoughts had never occurred to him before, but he was fairly certain that they were not the secret talent he had been searching for. Just to be sure, though, and since he had nothing better to do at the moment, he looked toward the opening again and imaged himself shooting lightning bolts from his eyes, liquefying the creature's hind end in a millisecond. But no, nothing. He strained to lift a hand and point his finger toward the creature. Again, nothing. So what, then? Maybe Mal had dreamed up the whole idea of a hidden skill. Maybe it was all in his head. And because of that, it had been stuck in *Jason's* head all these years.

And then the lightbulb came on. *In my head*, he thought. Not lightning bolts or laser beams, but *in my head*. Select memories came flooding back to him, pieces of the puzzle now assembling themselves in his head. Like the question that Navy Blue had once asked him, whether he thought it was strange, if not impossible, that on every one of his training missions, he had invariably encountered the animal he had set out to find. Jason had responded by saying that he assumed that it was all part of God's plan, that the animals were basically just puppets under His control and that He was directing them to attack Jason in order to prepare him for his battle with the creature. But what if that was not the case? What if the words that Mal had spoken after he and Mitch had pulled Jason from the water following his encounter with the shark – *"there is something inside you"* – were meant to be taken literally? A talent that came from within rather than one like speed or strength that are displayed openly and visibly for all to see? And one that, as Randall had counseled just hours before, *"God will reveal when the time comes"*?

That was the answer. It had to be. On some level, he had known it all these years, but it was at this moment that he became consciously aware of it. He closed his eyes and reached out yet again, this time not with his arms but rather with his mind. As he had never knowingly used the ability before, he did not know exactly what thoughts he should be thinking, or how to project them.

He simply tried to visualize what needed to be done, and the apocalypse that would come about if the task were not completed.

ᴀ   ᴀ   ᴀ

The summons was different this time. It went out to all of them, not just to one particular kind, as it had before. And there was something else that was different, a sense of urgency like never before. A sense of finality as well, as though this would be the last time. They all listened to the call, and they all heeded it.

ᴀ   ᴀ   ᴀ

Jason focused on the message intently, for as long as he possibly could, but the effort was monumental and drained the very last drop of energy that he could muster. Darkness, at last, closed in upon him.

ᴀ   ᴀ   ᴀ

Order is restored. The creature is no longer the prey, but has once again become the predator. Its enemy has been incredibly strong, fast, and resourceful, but in the end the creature will prevail. It is now tunneling beneath the rocks that shelters its opponent, and in a short time it will emerge within that space and finally end this confrontation. The creature has sustained permanent injuries and can no longer use flight as a means of transportation, but it will adapt and overcome this handicap, and any others it may sustain, and ultimately it will complete its mission.

Then it feels a sharp pain and intense pressure in its right haunch. Something is attacking it from behind. The creature lashes out with its right hind leg, hard enough to disengage from its attacker, then backs out of the tunnel to face it. As it spins around, the attacker lunges at it again, clamping down on its left leg above the knee. It is a large, powerful brown animal, almost as large as the creature itself, though with smaller teeth and claws. The creature roars and angrily slashes down along the animal's flank, opening up gaping wounds and causing it to once again relinquish its bite. But it does not back away, instead throwing its head back and issuing an intimidating roar of its own. The creature and the animal circle each other, growling, roaring, and posturing, each searching for an opening.

As the creature is about to engage the animal, something else slams into its side and latches onto it. This second attacker, another animal, is much smaller, sleeker, lighter in color, and with a long tail. This animal is nearly as tenacious as the first one, but based on its size does not appear as though it can pose as serious a threat. The creature tears itself away and whirls to face the second animal, but before it can deliver a lethal swipe, a third attacker, this one winged, swoops down from above and lands on the creature's head. This animal is smaller than even the second one, but sports a hard, sharp snout that it uses as a weapon. It tries to pierce the creature's eye with that weapon, and nearly succeeds before being sliced in half with one swipe of the creature's talons. But it is enough of a diversion to allow the second animal to attack its flank again. The creature slashes at it, but it ducks away and then comes in again.

The first animal now resumes its attack, blindsiding the creature and clamping its jaws down on the back of the creature's neck. Again it jerks itself free, a chunk of its flesh being torn away as it does so, but now the creature is in a rage like never before. It delivers three slashes in rapid succession to the animal's huge head, tearing away the top of its skull and most of its brain. The animal drops dead instantly, but at that moment, another one just like it comes lumbering out of the forest. Behind it come more like the second animal, as well as various other species the creature has not seen before. More of the winged variety swoop down from above, each of them diving in and then retreating, trying to stab at the creature's face and eyes.

The creature fights frenetically, slicing through flesh, muscle and bone, biting and tearing, destroying attackers with every swipe and with every turn. But still they pour out of the forest, still they rain down from the sky, and many of them inflict injury upon the creature before it can kill them or detach itself from them. And each time the creature does kill an attacker, another one takes its place. Minutes pass by, the creature expending massive amounts of energy just to stay alive. Eventually it tries to run, but is overwhelmed by the sheer mass and number of foes. Steadily it weakens, and as it does, the animals inflict more serious injuries, which sap the creature's strength even faster. At last it has no fight left in it at all, and its horrific mission, and unnatural life, both come to an end.

5

After driving out of Bunting and pulling off the road several miles away, Mal had begun following Jason's movements on his tablet using a sophisticated tracking program they had purchased a couple of years before. At that time, they had had a small chip implanted in Jason's neck, the location of which could be tracked using the software. They had chosen to have it placed in Jason's neck, rather than in an arm or leg, due to the likelihood of his limbs being severed during his training missions or when he eventually squared off against the creature. But if his *neck* was ever separated from his body, then obviously his head would be, too, and that would be the end of him.

When Mal had first turned on the device after getting clear of the town, he was surprised to see that the small blip on the screen was already well up into the mountains, meaning that the creature must have fled the town with Jason in pursuit of it. And then during the night, Mal had watched the blip pinballing throughout the mountain range as the chase wore on. Occasionally the blip would move very slowly for a short time, but then the frantic pace would resume. Despite having watched Jason train and develop over the last fifteen years, Mal was amazed at how fast he and the creature were moving, and for such a long period of time.

It was now just before 11:00 a.m., and what had Mal concerned was that the blip – Jason – had not moved in nearly two hours. Jason had either killed the creature and then stopped to rest, or he was seriously injured, or . . . Mal did not want to think about the other "or". He convinced himself that Jason was perfectly okay, that perhaps the creature had eluded him, or that he *had,* in fact, killed it and was using the opportunity to heal and re-energize himself. In any event, as much as he dreaded the thought of trekking through the woods alone, it was time to go look for Jason. The good news was that he did not appear to be too far away, maybe five or six miles. At one time, the blip had been well to the north and west of here, a hundred miles or more into the heart of the mountain range, but the creature had apparently circled back and was approaching Bunting again when the blip stopped moving.

Mal turned the vehicle around and drove back toward Bunting. It occurred to him that if something *had* happened to Jason, the creature may have returned to the town to finish killing off its residents, in which case, it might still be there. However, despite the direction it was heading in when the blip on Mal's screen had stopped moving, he doubted whether the creature would have returned. It no longer had the element of surprise, and by now, Bunting would likely be a circus of paramedics, reporters, and most importantly, policemen, which would pose a much greater risk to the creature if it did return. So, though he approached the town limits with caution, he was reasonably certain that he would not find it to be a ghost town. It did not take long before his assumptions proved to be accurate, and he breathed a sigh of relief when he saw people walking and driving cars, trying to go about business as usual even though their town had probably made the national news by now.

Following the signal, Mal drove as far as he possibly could through Bunting, until he reached the west end of town, and parked in the lot of a small factory in an industrial complex. The edge of the forest was just off the rear of the property. He removed a daypack from the backseat of the car they had rented, and placed five bottles of water, several protein bars, a first aid kit, a blanket, a small butane torch, lighter fluid and two flashlights inside the pack. He then walked to the edge of the forest, took a deep breath, and left humanity behind.

Without benefit of a trail, it was slow going through the dense forest. The thin air, steep terrain and weight of the daypack made progress even slower, but little by little, the blip on the screen, which still had not moved, got closer to the point that marked his own location. Finally, at around 3:00 in the afternoon, Mal walked out of the forest into a small clearing at the edge of a cliff . . . . and nearly dropped the tablet from shock and horror at what he saw. It was an absolute slaughterhouse. Dozens upon dozens of dead animals, all kinds of them. Bears, mountain lions, eagles, hawks and other birds of prey, coyotes, raccoons, foxes and a handful of other species. Mal knew immediately that this was not the work of humans, for these animals had been mauled to death. Either they had killed each other, or something bigger or stronger had.

And that was when he saw it. He had glanced at it once and had not recognized it, because it had been torn to pieces to a greater extent than most of the other animals, so much so that there was not much left of it aside from a skeleton. Even then, as he was no expert on animal anatomy, he might have thought it was simply the remains of a very large bear, except for two things that he recognized. One, there was a huge, tattered wing lying near it, far bigger than any eagle or hawk wing. And two, the armor plating that had covered its back and flanks was still attached to its skeletal system. There could be no doubt about it – the creature was dead. Thank God for that!

But now, where was Jason? The image on the tablet screen indicated that he should be right here. Mal wandered about the carcasses for several minutes searching for him, wary of anything else that might still be alive, but he could not find Jason. He even looked for a skull or other bones that might appear to be human, and was grateful that he found none of those, either. But his alarm grew with every passing minute, as he tried to avoid coming to the conclusion that Jason was not only dead, but that his body had been completely consumed, bones and all, by the creature or by other scavengers that would have been attracted to the carnage. It seemed unlikely, but without a body, intact or otherwise, what else could have happened?

"JASON!" Mal yelled finally. "IT'S DAD! CAN YOU HEAR ME!?" He had been avoiding that, in case there were other large predators in the area, even though the sound of a human voice was more likely to scare them away than to draw them in. But now he was desperate to find his son.

He listened for several seconds, heard nothing, then called out again. This time, he thought he heard something, a faint whisper, though it could have been the wind or just his imagination. He was about to call a third time, when he heard it again, still very faint but this time more distinctly.

"Here," said the voice.

Mal looked around and for the first time noticed the narrow gap between the two boulders, the tiny sheltered area behind them, and the large hole that had been partially dug just outside the gap. He rushed over, took off his daypack and stepped down into the hole. He was then able to wriggle his head and shoulders into the space between the rocks. Jason was alive and in a sitting position, but was in maybe the worst condition that Mal had ever seen him in. His body was covered with dirt, dried blood and deep, crusted gouges, many of them down to the bone, and both of his legs had been severed below the knees. As Jason had apparently been here most of the day now, without being able to heal his cuts or regrow his legs, it was clear that his regenerative ability had been overwhelmed by the sheer number of injuries he had sustained, on the heels of what was undoubtedly a grueling, hours-long chase. But thankfully, there had been just enough of it left for his wounds to scab over, which had stopped the bleeding. Otherwise, he would certainly be dead right now.

"Jason! Thank God you're alive!"

"Is it . . . is it over?" Jason rasped. "Is it dead?"

"It's dead. I don't know how it happened. It was attacked by . . . well, you can see for yourself. Let's get you out of there."

Jason barely had the strength to turn his body and lie down with his head toward the opening, much less crawl out of the shelter under his own power, but positioning himself in that way allowed Mal to reach in and pull him out. Mal wrapped the blanket around Jason and then started pumping him full of water and protein bars, praying that the infusion of liquid and energy would kickstart his healing abilities. Nothing happened immediately, though Jason did begin to revive slowly as the hydration and nourishment worked their way through his system.

Mal debated whether he should try to contact the authorities and ask them to fly in and evacuate Jason, but seeing that he was not getting any worse, and in fact seemed to be growing steadily stronger, Mal decided against it. For one thing, when the rescuers arrived and saw the horrific slaughter than had taken place, they would launch a major investigation and possibly detain the two of them for days, maybe even weeks. They would not stop until they received satisfactory answers to every one of their questions. And what would Mal and Jason tell them? The truth? Even with the bizarre, never-before-seen remains of the creature to support their story, there was no way anyone else would ever believe that it had been sent back in time to destroy every human being on the planet. They might also point to Jason himself as evidence, if his legs were to grow back right in front of the authorities, but then he would be taken into custody permanently and turned into a lab rat. So all things considered, it seemed best to just wait for a bit and see what happened.

After he had eaten, Jason fell into a deep sleep. He had a dream about being in a strange sort of prison, a place he had been born in and where he had lived his entire life, and from which he emerged one day to discover new places, meet new people, and experience new things. As he walked through the barred gates out into the world beyond, he felt as though he had been born again, dying a prisoner's death, then living a free man's life. It was a fresh, new feeling, but comfortingly familiar as well, and he would have been content to remain inside the dream for a while longer, but something awoke him -- that tingling, itching sensation that he felt whenever his body began to produce new tissue, bone, and muscle. He looked down and saw the gashes on his arms and chest closing, saw the stubs of his legs extending downward, followed by the formation of new ankles, new heels, new arches, and finally, new toes. His body was now whole again.

About two hours had passed while Jason had slept, during which Mal had been looking out across the valley, first admiring the view, and then studying it more closely as he began to feel as though he had seen this before. The town of Bunting stretched out across the valley floor beneath them, a place he had returned to today for the first time in twenty-five years, the day he had seen it in his dream. And that was when it occurred to him: this overlook was the *very spot* where he had met Randall in his dream! He did not know why this surprised him. After all, why should there *not* be one final twist to this whole bizarre drama?

"A full circle," Mal said, when he noticed Jason had awakened.

"What was that?" Jason asked.

"A full circle. Well, in a manner of speaking. Physically, I was in Illinois when I had the dream. But in it, I walked out of the forest right over there, in virtually the same place I did today. This rock I'm sitting on is the very same one I sat on as I spoke to Randall, just before he pushed me off the cliff. And now, here we are, twenty-five years later, and this is where the story ends. A full circle."

"I see," Jason said nodding. "Do you think there's some significance to that?"

Mal thought for a moment, then sighed. "If there is, I say we figure it out later. I'm whipped, and I can't even imagine how *you* must feel."

"Like I just got my butt kicked by a mutant monster from the future," Jason said with a smile. "But I'm ready to go home now. Help me find my boots."

6

W hen they arrived back home in Sioux Falls, Jason practically cleaned out the refrigerator and pantry. His energy reserves had never been so depleted, and it required an unprecedented number of calories to restore them.

He had also never been so tired. After his massive meal, he slept for thirty hours, and when he awoke, he felt completely rejuvenated, and as usual following his recoveries, stronger than he had ever felt before. But the one unique thing about this recovery, as compared to all of the previous ones, was the faint scars that crisscrossed his flesh, and that would serve as a lifelong reminder of the epic battle that had been waged – and won – for the preservation of all humanity. Jason was not really surprised at seeing this, however, for he alone knew just how close he had come to stepping off the precipice of physical life and into the eternal realm beyond. He had never before, nor would he ever again, face such a lethal foe, and in the end it was not his physical abilities that had enabled him to defeat the creature, but rather his mind and his faith.

That morning, for the first time in a decade and a half, Jason had nothing to do and nowhere to be, so after he awoke, he lay in bed for a while, thinking about all that had happened. He was comforted by the thought that humanity, for the most part, would go about its business as it had before: every morning, there would be coffee brewing, bacon sizzling, men and women heading off to work, children dashing out the door just in time to catch the school bus; every evening, kids doing homework, families gathering at the baseball diamonds and soccer fields, eating dinner, watching the new episode of *Duck Dynasty* or *Game of Thrones*. Births, deaths, laughter, sadness, weddings, graduations, retirements, vacations, triumphs, disappointments . . . for most people, it would all continue on as it had for thousands of years.

But of course, there were those few who were impacted by the creature's arrival, and whose lives had either ended, or would never be the same. It was truly a tragedy that a courageous man such as Randall Wilhelm, who not only had a family that adored him but was also a positive influence on everyone who knew him, had been one of the victims. His life story, his testimony, was one of the more powerful ones that Jason had ever heard, and it was no surprise that it had helped to transform the lives of numerous people who had heard it. Well, at least his wife Mindy and his children, Jacob and Jocelyn, would not have to live without him, for though they, too, had been tragically killed by the creature, they were now together in paradise. Indeed, Randall –

Jason instantly and almost involuntarily jerked upright into a sitting position. How did he know all of that about Randall? He had only met him briefly, just before Randall had died, and the only personal details he had shared were that he had a family (he did not mention their names), and that he had moved to Bunting just a few years before. And yet somehow Jason knew not only the names of Randall's family members, but his entire history, from his childhood, through his young adult life as a partying, happy-go-lucky celebrity, to the day he was run over by a car and nearly killed, and on to his salvation, marriage, family life . . . right up to the moment Jason had met him as he lay dying on the sidewalk.

But that was not all. Jason saw even beyond that . . . *far* beyond that. At that moment, the memories came rushing back to him, things he had seen along two different timelines, one original, one altered, after he had summoned the animals to attack the creature and had lost consciousness. During that time, he had walked the very boundary between life and death, a place few had ever been to, where he stood above time itself, the events of two lifetimes clearly visible as though they were merely numbers on a tape measure stretched out upon the floor. That was how he knew about Randall's life, first a happy one as a child, then an artificially contented one as a young adult, then a miserable one after causing the suicide of a young woman he had rejected, and then ultimately a truly joyful one as he basked in the glow of his lovely wife, children, and most of all, his Creator and Savior.

All of those events in Randall's life had occurred before the creature had arrived and altered the timeline (actually, that was not entirely true, he now realized. The timeline had been altered at the point where Mal had his *second* dream, the one in which he was alerted of the creature's imminent arrival. That did not happen on the original timeline, for it would have sent them scurrying off to Bunting for no reason. Since the second dream must have been of divine origins to have happened at exactly the right moment, it might be argued that God Himself was responsible for altering the timeline). But Jason's knowledge of Randall's life came not from that brief encounter on this, the altered timeline, but rather because of the friendship they had shared on the original timeline, and which had been revealed to Jason while his life had hung in the balance up on the mountain above Bunting.

This was indeed a bizarre feeling, for a twenty-five year old to have sixty-five years of memories, things he had experienced only on the original timeline, suddenly funneled into his brain all at once. That instantaneousness made it seem as though he were actually living out those events right then and there, and he even felt the same emotions he must have had at those very moments. He remembered the day of his last training mission, the day he found Randall stuck in the crevice up on the mountain, very near dying from dehydration and exposure. He remembered the fear he had felt when the walls of the crevice collapsed, and both of them had nearly plunged to their deaths. He recalled the shock he had felt afterwards, when

Randall had revealed who he was, and that he knew who Jason was – just as he had done on this altered timeline when he lay dying on the sidewalk.

Jason also relived the joy and warmth of the bond that had developed with Randall and his family, one that remained strong for the rest of their lives. He remembered how grateful he had been for Randall's counsel and wisdom throughout the years they had shared together, and it occurred to him now how ironic it was that the most sage and prophetic advice Randall had ever offered him, *"God will reveal it to you when the time comes,"* was something he had said to Jason on both the original and altered timelines. The words were of great importance in both instances, though for very different reasons. On the original timeline, they came to mind just as Jason was about to plunge the knife into young Brian Zintak's body, and thus prevented him from committing that horrific crime. And of course, they came to mind on the altered timeline as well, as Jason was staring death in the face and desperately needed to unlock the mystery of the undiscovered ability that had caused him so much anxiety.

Yes, Jason missed Randall now that he had these memories to reflect upon. It grieved him to know that the friendship would never happen on this timeline, and that the world was a lesser place without Randall. He should have been able to walk the same path as he had before, bestowing his various gifts on those around him, but that path had been blocked by something that had no God-given right to be there, something that had never been destined to be born, but was instead created in a laboratory.

After reflecting upon Randall for a bit, Jason's thoughts turned to Mal, his surrogate father in fact, but his flesh and blood parent in essence, who had once been taken from him but had now been returned. It struck Jason how ironically opposite the twists of fate had been for both Randall and Mal. Though they had both been poster children for being in the wrong place at the wrong time,

Randall had once lived a full life, then an abbreviated one due to the arrival of the creature, while Mal, on the other hand, had lived an abbreviated life, then a (hopefully) long and full one . . . . also due to the arrival of the creature! Jason recalled the discussion he had had with Mitch after Mal had been killed by the bear, when they had posed the question as to why Mal not seen foreseen his own death in the dream. Their theory had been that Mal *had*, in fact, seen his own death coming, but had kept it a secret in order to prevent them from altering the sequence of events that God had intended. But five years later, Randall had quashed that notion by stating that the events had played out exactly as they had in the dream. He was of the opinion that it was God who had excluded Mal's death from the dream, in order to protect all three of them from the temptation and anxiety that may have come from such knowledge.

But now, Jason realized that Randall's theory, too, had been incorrect. Mal's vision had begun when Zintak was a six year-old boy. It continued on into his adulthood, when he devised his maniacal plan to send the creature back in time to retroactively wipe out humanity. But at that point, the vision offered two possible versions of an altered timeline; one beginning in the year 2016 that showed what would happen without Mal's involvement (the creature's unobstructed rampage across the world and ultimate success of Zintak's plan), and the other beginning a year prior to that, showing the events that would transpire if Mal carried out the role intended for him (the kidnapping and training of Jason that would allow for humanity to be saved). Of course, the dream had been interrupted partway into the second version of the altered timeline, but even if that had not happened, Mal would not have witnessed his own death, because as it turned out, Zintak had sent his evil creation back to a point in time that was three months *before* that fateful training mission to Alaska.

Yet even though Mal was alive and well now, there was a shock to Jason's system as he realized he had been responsible, in a way, for his father's death on the original timeline. When he had stepped out of the vehicle in the Alaskan backcountry, Jason had, as always on his training missions, though unbeknownst to him until he finally figured it out just in time to kill the creature, telepathically summoned his desired opponent . . . in that case, a grizzly bear. It was not long before a bear indeed arrived, but what Jason now recognized is that the second bear, the one that had attacked Mal, had also responded to his summons, though it was a bit further away and therefore took longer to arrive on the scene. But when the first bear reached its destination and commenced the attack, Jason's telepathic transmitter automatically switched itself off. At that point, the second bear, which was moving in from the opposite direction, no longer felt the irresistible pull toward Jason, and instead attacked the first prey item it had encountered – that being Mal. Knowing this, Jason could not help but feel an intense wave of guilt for what had happened. After all, there was no escaping the fact that the Mal he knew before, the Mal on the original timeline, had suffered horribly for a short time before death mercifully claimed him. *That* Mal was gone forever, and nothing, not even the second chance that this altered timeline afforded, could change that.

After reflecting and agonizing upon the bear incident for a time, Jason's thoughts next came around to Julie . . . the woman he had married on the original timeline, but had yet to meet on this one. He remembered the love he had felt for her, almost, it had seemed, from the first time he saw her. Her small, tender, yet surprisingly strong hands; her long, shimmering brown hair; her big, dark brown eyes, full of compassion, wisdom, mystery, and a thousand other intricacies just waiting to be discovered. And of course, her amazing intuition, which she had used to convince him to continue his training after Mal had died, though his heart was no longer in it. If not for that, Randall would have died alone when he fell into the crevice on the mountain, for Jason would not have been there to save him. What would their lives have been like without the companionship of Randall and his family? The disappointment and pain they had felt at not being able to conceive a child would have been greatly exacerbated without their dear friends there to comfort them. Yes, Julie was a treasure, from the day Jason had met her until the night she died peacefully in her sleep. Thankfully, he had joined her just a few days later, after he had nearly made the colossal mistake of murdering young Brian Zintak. Jason had been sure of his salvation, whether he had committed that heinous act or not, but he could not shake the notion that Julie would have been ashamed of him when he met her again in heaven, if he had actually gone through with it.

As he thought of Julie, Jason realized suddenly, with a bizarre mixture of both horror and delight, that he was still destined to meet her in this lifetime, at the same time and place as he had before . . . . but *only* if he did not intervene to prevent Navy Blue from falling down his basement stairs to his death. That tragic event was still three months away, and if Jason were to allow it to happen, he would bump into Julie, literally, at Navy's visitation. The circumstances, and that very first conversation they had had, would be somewhat different this time around, since Mal would now stride through the doors of the funeral home alongside Jason, rather than lying lifeless in the room next to Navy's. But no matter, for the mutual attraction they had felt was virtually palpable, and the details of the conversation were, and would again be, inconsequential. The point was that they would have the same life together as they had had before . . . maybe even better, now that the first five years would not be consumed with training missions and creature preparations. But of course, his conscience would never allow him to stand idly by while Julie's great uncle tumbled down his own basement steps and died alone in a broken heap. No, he would soon pay Navy a visit and put up a basement handrail for him, which would most likely prevent a repeat of the fall that had claimed Navy's life once before. And somehow, he would find another way to meet Julie.

As Jason thought more about the life he and Julie had once shared, and God willing, the life they would share again, his mind came to rest on a topic they had discussed occasionally throughout their lives, which was whether or not he should seek out his real parents. She was always in favor of him doing so, for not only did it seem like the natural thing to do, but there was also the written promise that Mal had made to James and Katrina Devine: that one day, Jason would return to them. There had been a time, prior to Mal's death, when Jason had felt the same way. But he had begun to feel differently after Mal was gone, fearful that if he were to search for his biological parents, he might find that they, too, were now dead, and he dreaded the additional heartbreak that would go along with such a discovery. Furthermore, the love he felt for Randall, who was as much like a father and brother as he was a best friend, served as a reasonable proxy for the relationship that could potentially be available from his blood relatives. Thus, he had no great motivation to seek out the Devine family. He also had a certain fear that if in fact his parents were dead, he might find a way to blame himself for their deaths, regardless of how they had come about. After all, their lives would certainly have taken an entirely different turn if Jason had been a part of them, so whatever it was they were doing, and where ever they happened to be when they died, they would have almost surely been doing something else, been some*where* else, if Jason had been there. So he had concluded that if his real parents were dead, there would be no getting around the fact that it would have been, indirectly at least, his fault.

But now, for whatever reason on this altered timeline, he regretted his decision to remain dead to his real family, both for their sake and for his own. To contact them now, however, was not as simple a thing as it might seem. On the original timeline, he had feared reaching out to them only to find that they had died, but the opposite could also happen if he *did* contact them. What if, by him entering their lives, it somehow *caused* their deaths? What if, for example, they were driving to his house one snowy Christmas Eve and their car slid off the road and they died in the crash? Maybe nothing so dramatic would happen, but at a minimum, their destinies would certainly be *altered* if he became part of their lives, and if the right of revisionism did not belong to Brian Zintak, though his motives were far more sinister, then why should that right belong to Jason himself?

He could think through the possible scenarios all he wanted, but ultimately he knew this was something that would require him to follow his heart and not his head if he wished to find the answers to his questions. And his heart told him to seek out his family . . . but not just yet. There was something he had to do first, someone he had to see.

⅄   ⅄   ⅄

A week later, on a fresh, sparkling morning in early July, Jason backed his Yukon Denali out of the driveway of their house on Lockwood Avenue and set off in the direction of Julie's office in downtown Sioux Falls, six miles to the southeast. He wore a brand new charcoal gray Armani Collezioni suit, a light gray, trim fit John Varvatos Star USA shirt, a yellow Salvatore Ferragamo silk tie with gray diamonds, a pair of black Allen Edmonds Oxford shoes, and Ray-Ban sunglasses. In short, he looked like someone wealthy, or important, or both.

His plan was simple: he was going to walk through the front door of Julie's accounting firm, and politely ask the receptionist if he could meet with her. The receptionist would, of course, ask him if he had an appointment, to which he would reply that he did not, but that he was in need of a good accountant and she had been recommended to him by a friend. This was not entirely untrue, for despite the substantial wealth possessed by the Anderson family, they had never sought the services of any professionals in town. For one thing, there was never a dire need for them, because they already had trust advisors, lawyers and accountants in Chicago, and for another, they had kept their relationship-building to a minimum while Jason was advancing through his developmental years, as they felt the need for privacy was paramount. So now, after all these years, it was finally time to hire the local accountant that they never had . . . and in the process, make a connection with the woman he had once been married to, in another life, and who he felt he was destined to marry again. Of course, she would not recognize him now, so his only hope was to secure the appointment, start off the conversation with his chosen pseudo topic, and then see where things progressed from there. It was, admittedly, a foolhardy plan, but at twenty-five, he still retained enough of his youthful naïveté as to believe that when he met Julie, it would spark something inside of her -- not a memory, of course, maybe something more like *Deja vu* -- that would open the door to the past . . . . and to the future.

Altered Timeline – September 2017

On a late Friday afternoon in early fall in Grayling, Michigan, with warm sunshine streaming through the windows and a pleasant breeze distributing the mouth-watering smell of freshly baked beer bread throughout their modest but impeccably clean home, James and Katrina Devine sat reading their books at the kitchen table. In the living room, their son Chase was making the most of his daily one-hour allotment of video game time, playing one of his beloved Xbox battle games. James was now fifty years old, Katrina forty-nine, and Chase was a highly energetic seventeen year-old who was about to enter his senior year of high school. They were waiting for the other member of their family, Madison, to arrive home from college, as she did every Friday around this time, where she would spend the weekend with her family before heading back to school on Sunday afternoon. She was now twenty years old, their oldest surviving child.

"So what kind of beer did you use in the bread?" James asked.

"Cherry wheat," was Katrina's reply.

"Mmmm . . . my favorite."

Katrina looked up at her husband and smiled. "As if I didn't know that, babe."

"Guess you've learned a thing or two about me over the years," James said, smiling back at his wife. "And what's the main course?"

"Ritz chicken casserole."

"Seriously? You know I can't stand that stuff!"

Katrina playfully cocked her arm back as though she were going to hurl her book at him, then resumed her reading. Ritz chicken casserole was, in fact, a favorite of not only James, but of the kids as well.

James Devine looked more like thirty-five than fifty. His hair was thinning a bit, and its original shade of dark brown had all but given way to salt and pepper hues. But aside from that, his chiseled handsomeness, athletic build, limitless energy, and boyish charm never ceased to cause amazement when people learned his age. Likewise, Katrina Devine, despite having borne three children, had a figure that most twenty-five year old women would envy. She had shoulder-length sandy blonde hair, styled in a contemporary fashion that suited her perfectly, and with facial features that were so refined and youthful, she and Madison were often mistaken for being sisters. This was by no means an affront to Madison, for she was regarded by most to be the most beautiful woman in the city of Grayling, with her father's athleticism, dark brown eyes and poignant countenance, and her mother's golden hair, porcelain skin, and satirical wit. Chase Devine, though being the last member of the family, had been spared none of its enviable genes. He was every bit as handsome as his father, was the strongest and fastest athlete in his class, and was on pace to be class valedictorian if he kept up his grades throughout his senior year. By most accounts, including their own, the Devine family would have been considered the most richly blessed family in Grayling.

But there was a hole in their lives that had been there for twenty-six years, and would remain there for as long as they lived. Those years, though they had brought healing to their broken hearts, had also brought a keen awareness of the absence of memories that they would have enjoyed had their firstborn child not been stolen from them. At certain times, especially on holidays and birthdays, James and Katrina would each, secretly, create a mental picture of their son Jason, as they imagined he would look now, and insert him into the scene before them. Perhaps him opening a gift, perhaps laughing at whatever joyful occasion they happened to be celebrating, perhaps just sitting quietly and contemplating the life that should have been his. And of course, aside from that small, dark compartment of their hearts that harbored the sadness they had felt all these years, adjacent to that there was also a perpetual glimmer of hope that one day, they might somehow be reunited with Jason, and those imaginary scenes would become real. After all, the person who took Jason from them had promised in his or her letter that Jason would be safe and would return to them one day, and while they knew they might be naïve to believe that promise, neither could they think of any reason to disbelieve it.

A short time later, they heard a car door slam in the driveway, and momentarily, the back door opened and Madison Devine entered the kitchen. She smiled and was about to say something, but instead drew in a deep breath of the wonderful aroma that filled the house. "Ahhhh!" she sighed. "I wonder if those beer bread mixes release some kind of airborne narcotic when they start to bake. The smell alone is addictive!"

James and Katrina both laughed, then each stood to exchange hugs and kisses with their daughter as they always did upon her return.

"Hiya, sis!" Chase called from the living room, though the physical portion of his greeting would have to wait until he finished his game of *Assassin's Creed 27*, or whatever it was that he was playing on his Xbox.

"Hey Casanova," Madison called back. She was always kidding her brother about the dozens of girls at his school who were swooning over him at all times.

"So what's new at the U?" James asked Madison. "How did

that philosophy exam go?"

"A-minus. It was pretty brutal."

"You'd better cut back on the partying and study harder, girl," Katrina said sternly.

Madison smiled and rolled her eyes, fully aware that her mother was teasing. There was no one who worked harder at studying than Madison, so on the infrequent occasions that she earned anything less than an "A" on an exam, they all knew that it *must*, in fact, have been brutal.

"Any new developments on the dating front?" James asked.

Madison laughed and shook her head. "It took you all of two minutes to ask me that, Dad. Are you that eager to walk me down the aisle and give me away?"

"Just the opposite," James said with a smile. "I need to know who's pursuing my daughter, so I can run him out of town before he can steal your heart."

"Dad!" Madison protested. "That's terrible!!"

James laughed and held up his hands. "Now you know I'm only kidding. I truly am praying you'll meet the right man someday, someone who will love and honor you all the days of your life, though I have to be honest and say that I hope it won't be until after you're out of school. But then again, whenever God decides to bring that person into your life, and you into his, that will be fine with me."

"Thanks Dad," Madison replied. "But don't worry, I happen to agree with you about school being my top priority right now. If someone interesting were to come along and ask me out, I would not be opposed to a few dates, but I am certainly not sending out any invitations or broadcasting my availability."

"Smart girl," James said, patting her arm. "Just like your mom."

Now it was Katrina's turn to roll her eyes. "Dinner's already in the oven, and you know you can have me anytime you want me, so there's no need for flattery."

"Awww, Mom!" Madison complained. "That's gross! I did *not* need to hear that!"

As the three of them were laughing at this, the doorbell rang, and only Chase heard it. He came in a moment later and said, "Mom, Dad, there's a lady at the front door who wants to talk to you."

They all four went into the living room, James and Katrina walking to the front door while Chase and Madison stood behind, their curiosity having been piqued by this unknown and unexpected visitor.

"Can I help you?" James asked the woman pleasantly through the screen on the storm door. She was a strikingly attractive young lady, about 5'-3" in height, with wavy dark brown hair that hung to about the middle of her back; large, thoughtful eyes of the same color as her hair; concave, slightly rosy cheeks; and a curvy but athletic figure. He judged her to be a few years older than Madison, though she gave the impression of being older than that due to her professional appearance; she wore a charcoal gray business suit with a white blouse, and a stylish pair of glasses with black frames and small rectangular lenses.

"Are you Mr. Devine?" she asked, though her tone and manner suggested that she already knew the answer to that question. Indeed, it seemed to James that there was actually a hint of recognition on her face as he had approached the door, though as far as he could recall he had never seen her before.

"Yes. And you are . . .?"

Instead of an immediate answer, the woman looked at Katrina and said, "And you must be Mrs. Devine?"

"That's right. Miss . . . .?"

The woman smiled apologetically. "I'm sorry, I know I have you at a disadvantage. My name is Julie Brighton. Please excuse me for being so forward, but I wondered if I might come inside, as there is something very important that I need to talk to you about, and it will take some time to explain." When the Devines hesitated and glanced at each other uncertainly, Julie added, "I should have mentioned right away that I am not a salesperson, a Jehovah's Witness, or a deplorable, in case you are wondering." She offered as disarming a smile as she possibly could, and a moment later, James Devine opened the storm door to admit her.

Julie sat down in the love seat in one corner, while James and Katrina sat on the sofa. Chase and Madison were still standing in the open doorway between the living and dining rooms, their body language and expressions clearly saying to their parents, "Can we stay? Can we stay?"

Their father glanced at them and had to fight to suppress a smile. "In case you were not formally introduced," he said to Julie, "this is our son Chase. And this is our daughter Madison. Is it all right if they stay and listen, or would you prefer they leave the room?"

"No, please stay! It's very nice to meet both of you! We wondered if there were other children, but we had no way of knowing unless we had gone snooping around behind your backs, which of course we would never have done."

The Devines all stared blankly at Julie for several seconds.

"Excuse me?" Katrina finally said.

Julie could not help but laugh. "I'm sorry, I'm getting ahead of myself. This is just so exciting, I can hardly contain myself. But let me start at the beginning. The *very* beginning." She suddenly became very serious. "Mr. and Mrs. Devine, do you recall the words of the letter that was left by the person who kidnapped your son Jason twenty-six years ago? Or perhaps you still have the letter itself, if it was returned to you by the police after their investigation was unsuccessful?"

James and Katrina Devine gasped, and all four of them stared at her in utter amazement.

"How do you know about that?" James demanded. "Who *are* you?"

"Please," Julie said gently, "just bear with me. I know I just gave you a shock, which is why I wanted to come in and have you sit down before I started. This will all become clear to you in a few minutes, I promise. Now, as I was saying, do you have the letter, or do you recall its words?"

"Of course we do," Katrina said, her tone now curt as she eyed Julie suspiciously. "The police gave us a photocopy of it. They have kept the original in their evidence file all these years. And we can tell you word for word what it says, because we have read it hundreds of times since Jason was taken from us."

Julie nodded and gazed at them solemnly. "I, too, know what the letter said, not necessarily word for word, since I have never seen it, but I know what its message was."

"And how exactly do you know that?" James repeated, becoming more agitated by the minute.

"Because I know the man who wrote it very well. His name is Malcolm Anderson. You might say I am his future . . . stepdaughter-in-law."

James and Katrina were silent this time, perhaps too horrified to speak having just learned that the woman sitting before them was closely connected to the monster who had stolen their son.

"I'll get back to how I came to know this man shortly," Julie continued. "But first let me switch gears for a moment." She reached into the pocket of her suit jacket and removed a folded-up piece of newspaper. She unfolded it and passed it to James Devine. "This is an article from a Denver newspaper. I'm guessing the subject of the article is something you're familiar with, as the incident made worldwide news last year."

James and Katrina both glanced at the article and nodded.

The article headline was "Unknown Assailant Slaughters Seven Families in Colorado Town." It was about a series of gruesome attacks that had occurred in Bunting, Colorado, apparently by some sort of wild animal. Twenty-four people residing in seven different homes, all on the same street, had been killed within minutes of each other. Authorities were speculating that the attacks were perpetrated by an animal of some kind that had wandered into town, and indeed there were three eyewitnesses who stated they had seen a large creature – a "one-winged monster", as one of them described it, fleeing the area. The animal had purportedly been chased into the forest by an unidentified man and had not been seen since.

"Now I know you're both wondering what this has to do with you, or your son, or the man who kidnapped him. Well, as you recall from the letter, Mal . . . uh, that's what everyone calls him, so please excuse me for using such an endearing term . . . Mal stated that Jason was an extraordinary person who had been chosen for a mission of great importance. That mission -- and here's where the story gets really incredible, so again, please bear with me -- was to save the entire human race from being destroyed by the unknown creature that was described in that article."

The look on the Devines' faces was now a mix of shock and indignation, the latter at having their intelligence insulted with such an outrageous story. James Devine opened his mouth to speak, but Julie held up a hand to halt him.

"*And*," she continued, "Jason did, in fact, accomplish his mission, for he was the unidentified man who not only chased the creature off following those attacks, but then killed it a few hours later."

Again, stunned expressions around the room, along with a healthy dose of skepticism.

"Now I won't go into details about what exactly the creature was and where it came from, we'll save that for later, but what you should know for now is that it required superhuman, and in fact supernatural, abilities to kill the creature, and Jason was the only human being who has ever been born with those abilities. Mal knew that -- exactly *how* he knew that I will also defer till later -- but the fact that he knew that about Jason was the reason he kidnapped him. When Jason was ten years old, Mal revealed to him his true identity, as well as his destiny. Had it not been that way, had Jason remained unaware of his own abilities and how he was meant to use them, the preconceived notions that all human beings have about their own physical and mental limitations would have prevented him from ever reaching his maximum potential. And that would have meant certain doom for every one of us, except for those who would have been lucky enough to die of something else before the creature got them."

Julie paused for a moment to assess the mindset of her audience. They were definitely engrossed now, though she could not ascertain what they might be thinking or feeling.

It was Katrina who broke the silence. "I am not saying I believe any of this, but I have to know . . ." In her tone there was a dawning recognition of the implications of Julie's story, and her voice cracked with rising emotion. "Where are you going with this? You said you knew this Mal Anderson, and that you are going to marry his stepson. And if he did kidnap Jason and raise him as his own son, then does that mean . . . . does it mean . . .?" She was too terrified, too excited to finish the sentence.

Julie smiled and stood up. "Yes, the remaining details of the story can wait. Let's skip to the good part. Please, don't get up yet. Just give me one moment." She walked to the front door, looked out toward the driveway and motioned.

James and Katrina both turned around and looked out the picture window behind the sofa. When Julie had arrived, they had not noticed that there was a man sitting in the driver's seat of the vehicle. Upon seeing Julie motion from the door, the man got out of the vehicle and walked toward the house.

"You see," Julie continued, "we thought it would be too much of a shock to you, or too unbelievable, if he were to simply knock on your door and announce himself. So we decided to take this approach, to have me come in and give you a bit of background, try to mentally and emotionally prepare you, if only a little."

The man had reached the front door now, and stood looking into the living room and grinning at each of them in turn. The Devine family all stood up and nearly ran each other over trying to be the first to reach the door. But there is no force on earth that can keep a mother away from her son, especially when she has not seen him for nearly twenty-six years, so it was Katrina who emerged first from the scrum and stood face-to-face with Jason.

"Oh . . . my . . . . God," she whispered, as she stared at him through the screen. "It's true." While she fought hard to keep her composure, she could feel it rapidly slipping away, for she knew in an instant that he was, in fact, her long-lost son. His hair color, his playful smile, his compassionate eyes . . . there could be no mistaking who he was, for aside from the faint scars on his still-handsome face, he looked exactly as James had twenty-five years ago. Her eyes welled up with tears, and her arms and legs suddenly felt like they weighed a hundred pounds each. She began to reach for the door handle, but had not the strength to even do that.

Jason, seeing his mother overcome, and needing no further invitation, opened the door and let himself in. He threw his arms around her and held her tightly, just as her legs gave way entirely.

"Hello Mom," he whispered into her ear. "I'm home."

Altered Timeline – April 2079

Bunting, Colorado had grown steadily over the decades and was known for its culture and broad array of activities, but was by no means a "city that never sleeps" kind of place. There were a handful of bars open past midnight, but the community's young people were mostly educated professionals such as lawyers, software designers, and engineers who arose early for work each morning and were therefore typically in bed by 10:00 p.m. on weeknights. Those out roaming the streets beyond that time were generally your obligatory winos, prostitutes and assorted riff-raff. That being the case, it was not surprising that at 3:30 on a Wednesday morning in early April, the city was a virtual graveyard, at least outside of the downtown area.

Jarrett McVicker drove slowly but purposefully through the residential area on the west side of the city, thankful that his mission had not brought him to a place such as Las Vegas or New York. The job would have been much more difficult in a city with more lights, more people, and all-night police patrols. Bunting was like a retirement community compared to those places, and thus Jarrett's primary concerns centered more on what he would encounter *inside* the Zintak home rather than outside of it. Concerns such as noiselessly entering the house, locating Brian's bedroom using only a pen flashlight, lifting the baby from his cradle, and exiting the house, all without waking the parents. He also prayed that there was not a dog in the house. There had been no mention of one in Mal's journal, but his dream had begun in the year 2086, nearly seven years from now, so it was possible there could be a dog present now but not later.

Still, it was not a fear of being caught that was causing the queasy feeling in his stomach, or the cold sweat that prickled his forehead and the back of his neck. It was the self-loathing he felt for the act he was about to commit – the stealing of a helpless baby from his parents. Jarrett knew that this child, if allowed to follow his original path of destiny, would eventually grow into a brilliant, yet wicked and insane man who would nearly destroy the world. Yet even this knowledge was not enough to convince Jarrett that he was not a baby-snatching monster, but actually a hero who might just be saving mankind. So strong were Jarrett's feelings of remorse, in fact, that he nearly wished he had not been born with the same awesome psychic abilities that his grandfather had had.

Two years after the creature had been destroyed by Jason Anderson, who later reclaimed his birth name Jason Devine, Malcolm Anderson, at the age of 50, had married a 32-year old psychology professor whom he had met at a seminar on psychic abilities and phenomena. The couple had had four children, all girls, none of whom had inherited their father's abilities. But those abilities did not disappear from the family altogether, they simply skipped a generation, for Jarrett, who was the firstborn child of Hannah, Mal's second-eldest daughter, had begun to demonstrate psychic powers at a very young age. Those powers increased steadily throughout his childhood and adolescent years, until they eventually exceeded those of his grandfather.

Jarrett became aware of this fact when he one day discovered he had an ability that even the amazing Malcolm did not possess – the ability to see into the future. Not simply through the receipt of random visions that he could not create or control on his own, as Mal had been limited to, but by actually *choosing* to look into the future. Very seldom did he use this power, however, for two reasons: (1) he did not *want* to see into the future for fear of what might lie ahead; and (2) it was incredibly difficult for him – both physically and mentally – when he did look into the future. In fact, it made him so violently ill and exhausted that it took weeks for his body to recover.

Unfortunately for Jarrett, he never had the pleasure of knowing his grandfather, for Mal passed away a few months after Jarrett was born. But he heard all about Mal from both his mother and from his "Uncle" Jason, though Jarrett did not see much of the latter since he and "Aunt" Julie lived six hundred miles away, as the crow flies, in Traverse City, Michigan. They had moved there from Sioux Falls two years after Jason had defeated the creature, in order to be close to his birth parents and siblings. Jason and Julie, now in their late 80's, had been unable to have children of their own. For that reason, though Jason was also very close to all of his nieces and nephews on both sides of the family, he and Jarrett had always had a special relationship. Jason said that Jarrett reminded him of Jacob Wilhelm, the son of Randall, Jason's best friend on the original timeline. Jacob had become like an adopted son to Jason, but because he had died along with his family over sixty years ago on this, the altered timeline, there had been a strange void in Jason's life, a sort of echo from the original timeline, that Jarrett had filled when he had been born.

Though Jarrett saw Jason infrequently over the years, they talked regularly on the phone. Jarrett had read Mal's journal about the dream, and had also heard the story from Jason more times than he could count. Plain and simple, the events fascinated Jarrett, and he loved to talk about them with Jason. It was during one of these discussions several years earlier, as they pondered all of the "what if this" or "what about that" scenarios that might have changed the outcome from good to bad, that Jason revealed to Jarrett that he had almost murdered Brian Zintak near the end of his life on the original timeline, because he was afraid of facing the creature without knowing what special talent or skill he would need to defeat it. At the last minute, however, he had remembered Randall's words about believing that when the time came, God would reveal whatever Jason would need to know, and so he did not kill Zintak after all. A sort of divinely inspired stay of execution, one might say. And of course, God *did* reveal to him the means to kill the creature, right when he needed it, and just as Randall had predicted.

But Jason went on to say that he felt things were different this time. The history books that Brian Zintak would eventually read on this altered timeline were not the same ones he had read originally, Jason reasoned. They now included accounts of a number of families who were murdered in Bunting, Colorado – Zintak's very own town -- in the year 2016. Eyewitnesses to that incredible event stated that the people had been killed by some kind of "monster" which, after its initial attacks, was apparently chased off into the mountains by someone and was never seen again. While most people at the time had dismissed the story as something akin to a Bigfoot or UFO sighting, it was part of history nevertheless, and Jason felt that it would be foolish not to think that Zintak would learn of it. Initially, the event would be of no consequence to him, but later, it would take on *enormous* significance after discovering the letter under the rug in his living room, the one that leads him to believe that his mother had deceived and betrayed him by having an affair with a stranger. That belief causes him to abandon his original plan and to come up with the idea of engineering a creature that can destroy mankind. At that point, assuming he had learned of the Bunting "monster" attacks during his history studies, he would certainly deduce that it was his very own creation that had somehow been defeated, whether by the mysterious man mentioned in the article, or some other unknown cause. Zintak would then endeavor to make the creature even stronger, faster and more intelligent than he otherwise would have, to increase the chances that it would be successful. And despite Jason's faith (or perhaps because he still did not have quite *enough* of it), the thought of facing an even more powerful creature terrified him. Given how close he had come to dying before he finally realized how to defeat the creature, he now feared that any deviation from its original design would tilt the playing field just enough in its favor that it would come out victorious on the next timeline.

The possibility of this turn of events compelled Jason to make a special request of Jarrett -- to use his ability to see into the future to determine whether his theory was correct or not. And as much as Jarrett dreaded the aftermath of its use, he had to admit that Jason's concern had merit, and thus needed to be validated or nullified, one or the other. If he did not, he would worry and stress over this until it drove him crazy.

And so, one Saturday morning, after Jarrett's wife Linda had taken their three children and left to do the weekly grocery shopping, he lay on their bed, closed his eyes, and stretched his mind and consciousness out across the next two decades to spy upon the greatest villain in the history of the world. He listened in on the very same conversation between Zintak and Millenkamp that Mal had observed some 90 years before. And yet, as Jason had feared, it was *not* the same conversation. For Zintak had indeed done his homework and discovered the newspaper articles about the "monster's" brief appearance, and was impressing upon Millenkamp the need to fortify his genetic design to increase the chances that their plan would succeed. From there the discussion became a jumble of technical jargon and scientific theory that Jarrett could not follow, but it did not matter. He had learned everything he needed to know.

ᚠ   ᚠ   ᚠ

When Linda returned home with the children and found Jarrett drenched in sweat and hunched over the toilet bowl vomiting up his breakfast, she knew immediately what he had done, though she did not yet know why. He never told her when he was going to use his ability to see the future, because she would always try to stop him. But she never got angry with him afterwards, because she knew he would not use his power unless he felt it was absolutely necessary. And as always, when he explained to her why he had done it and what he had seen, she understood completely. *Especially* this time.

Later that evening, when Jarrett was feeling a little better, he called Jason to tell him what he had seen.

"So what do you think we should do?" Jarrett asked Jason. "Does this change your views on whether it's okay to murder an innocent child?"

"Of course not," Jason responded. "And I know *you* are no more capable of murder than I am. So that option is out."

"What about killing an adult? Is that any less immoral than killing a baby?"

"If you're talking about killing Sherry Zintak, it's every bit as immoral. That woman is a saint, as you recall. Besides, if I remember the dates from Mal's journal correctly, she is pregnant with Brian as we speak. So we'd be killing both of them."

"Actually, I was speaking of Zintak's father, Carl. If we took him out of the picture, Brian would be raised only by his mother, who as you just pointed out is a saint. Wouldn't Brian then turn out to be a normal kid rather than the monster he will become due to his father's influences?"

"Possibly," Jason said, after a moment's pause. "But Brian obviously had an unnatural obsession with his mother. That is not likely to change without Carl around, and in fact, may actually be worse. And sooner or later, Sherry will get involved with another man again, and when she does, it may set Brian off just like finding the letter under the rug did on the original timeline. The only way we would know for sure if this option were to work is if we actually did kill Carl Zintak, and then you looked into the future again to see how Brian's life would unfold afterwards. And then what would we do if it didn't work? Would we *then* have justification to kill Brian? I think not."

"But what if it did work? Is the death of one really bad person such a huge sacrifice to make for the survival of humanity?"

"Not to you or me, maybe, but I suspect it is to God. I just don't think that's the way He would want us to handle this. Ultimately, though, it's your decision. I know *I* won't be the one to plunge the knife or pull the trigger. Will *your* conscience allow you to proceed in that manner?"

Jarrett sighed. "No, I guess not. But you were the one who brought this whole thing up. What would you suggest we do?"

"I think you have to follow in the footsteps of your grandfather. I think you have to kidnap Zintak from his parents and raise him as your own."

Upon hearing this, Jarrett nearly dropped the phone. "Uhhh . . . . come again?"

"You heard me. You and Linda need to raise that boy in a loving, Christian environment alongside your own children. You'll take him to church every Sunday, teach him the Word, and treat him with kindness at all times. Under your auspices, the boy could grow up to be a productive, rather than destructive, member of society."

"The key word being '*could*'. What if he has some sort of hereditary psychosis that causes him to follow the same path as before, no matter what we do?"

"That's certainly possible, but though I'm no psychologist, I don't think that will happen."

Jarrett considered this for a moment. "Well, I guess I could look into the future after the kidnapping and see if it altered Brian's course for the better."

"Yes, you could do that. But what if *that* didn't work, either? You'd be faced with the same dilemma of having to kill Brian as a last resort. My feeling is, you kidnap him, but don't look into the future beyond that point. Trust in God to take it from there."

"Sound advice, but who's to say we shouldn't trust Him right *now*? Leave it to Him to come up with a plan to deal with Zintak's beefed up creature."

"It seems to me that He *did* come up with a plan, and that plan is you. On the day Mal revealed my true identity to me, one of the questions I posed to him was with respect to this very scenario that we are discussing. That killing the creature would not be the end of it, because Zintak would realize he had failed and would simply make another attempt. Mal pointed out that God would no doubt anticipate any such developments, and that His plan to address them would involve other people, not just Mal and me. There is no doubt in my mind that you are one of those other people."

As much as Jarrett hated to admit it, Jason's logic was unassailable. He knew what he had to do.

        ⅄   ⅄   ⅄

Jarrett drove down Main Street until he reached the intersection of River Drive. The Zintaks lived on Williams Boulevard, on the other side of town, but since he was here, he was curious to see the infamous spot where the creature would be created, and where it would it be sent back in time. He drove north two blocks on River Drive, and there it was – the huge warehouse that Zintak would eventually acquire and turn into a laboratory and commune. Sixty-three years ago, this had been a residential district, and Randall Wilhelm's house had been located almost exactly where the warehouse now stood. It gave Jarrett chills to think about all that had happened here, and would happen again if he did not do what he was about to do.

The house numbers along Williams Boulevard were painted fluorescent yellow on the curbs, and Jarrett had no trouble locating the Zintak residence halfway down the second block. As he had hoped, there were no lights on, either inside or outside the house. There was also a row of hedges along the front of the lawn that would partially block the view of his car from the house. He had decided beforehand that he would park directly in front of the house, even if the front lawn was bare of trees or bushes, to ensure the fastest getaway possible. So the fact that there was a hedgerow along the front of the lawn was simply a bonus.

Jarrett eased his car to a stop in front of the Zintak house. He had purchased the car four months ago, and had chosen the color black explicitly for this mission. Furthermore, while he was normally very meticulous, and some would say obsessive, about keeping his car immaculately clean, he had avoided washing it for the past few weeks so that the accumulated dust and dirt would mask the car's usual gleam. He was careful, however, to keep the license plates clean so as not to arouse the suspicions of any passing law enforcement officers.

Having parked the car and turned off the engine, Jarrett paused before getting out, wondering whether he should leave the keys in the ignition or put them in his jacket pocket. On the one hand, he wanted to be able to make a quick getaway without having to fumble in his pocket for keys. On the other hand, what if he left the keys in the ignition and someone happened to come along and steal the car while he was inside the house? The prospect of having to escape on foot while cradling a baby in his arms would have been laughable were it not so terrifying.

His hesitation lasted only a moment, however, as he realized how irrational it was to worry about car thieves prowling the streets of this town, when he had already decided that many of its residents would feel secure enough to leave their house doors unlocked at night. In spite of the legitimate danger he was about to face, Jarrett chuckled at his own paranoia. He left the keys in the ignition, got out of the car and closed the door as quietly as possible.

A half-moon was suspended in the western sky above the jagged mountain peaks, providing just enough light so that he did not have to turn on his flashlight. He walked around the car and stood on the gravel shoulder of the road for a moment, then leaped across the drainage swale that ran alongside the road. Though the ditch was narrow and the water level low, he put all of the leg strength he could muster into his leap in order to gain as much horizontal clearance as possible. He did not want to risk slipping on the opposite bank and plunging his feet into the water, for to do so would have forced postponement of his mission. There was no way he could move quietly through the Zintak house in wet, squishy shoes, and to go barefoot would be foolhardy given the potential need for rapid escape.

Jarrett crept along the outside of the hedgerow to the corner of the yard, then darted along the edge of the property until he was even with the end of the house. Jason had informed Jarrett that the Zintaks' house had a standard floor layout that included an attached garage with a service door, an interior garage door leading to the kitchen, with a living room and dining area beyond that, and finally the bedrooms at the opposite end of the house. This should allow Jarrett to enter the house without being heard, in the same way that Jason had.

Jarrett darted quickly across the yard to the service door at the side of the garage, keeping low to the ground, then turned to see if he had somehow attracted the attention of the Zintaks' neighbors. No lights had come on in the house next door, and in the darkened windows there were no curtains drawn slightly aside indicating a curious onlooker within. He turned back toward the door, tried the handle and found it locked as expected, then used his handheld torch to slice through the deadbolt.

Once inside the garage he clicked on his penlight. Though there were windows in both the overhead and service doors, he was reasonably confident that no one would see the tiny light from the outside, especially since he held it at his waist, below the level of the windows, and kept the beam pointed down at the floor. He maneuvered around the car parked in the garage, tried the handle to the entry door, and found it unlocked.

Jarrett pushed the door open slowly, wary of the possibility of dry or rusty hinges broadcasting his entry. The door opened noiselessly, however, and he stepped into the kitchen of the Zintak residence as he had expected. He took a moment to thank God for his success thus far, and to ask Him to top off his tank of courage, for he had burned through a good deal of it just getting to this point. And the most difficult and dangerous part of this mission was about to begin.

Like most kitchens, the Zintaks' had a floor with a hard covering, in this case some type of laminate, so Jarrett took great care to tread very softly as he crossed the floor toward the adjacent rooms, which were likely to be carpeted. Of course, if the floorboards popped or creaked, which was a near certainty in a house that he judged to be forty to fifty years old, there was not much he could do about that. He made it as far as the living room before triggering the first significant pop in the floor, but the carpeting and underlying pad helped to muffle the sound. Aided by the natural light that came through the living room windows behind him, and his knowledge of the location of Brian's room, Jarrett turned off his penlight as he tiptoed down the hallway.

Jarrett entered Brian's room, clicked the light back on and directed the beam at the floor so as not to risk having it fall on the boy's face. Most babies, he knew from experience, were likely to sleep through just about anything, with the possible exception of having a bright light shone directly in their faces. He studied the small figure lying upon the mattress for a moment, to impress upon his memory exactly how and where the baby was positioned. He would need to turn the light off and put it in his pocket in order to free up both hands for picking up the child. He also needed those few seconds to summon one last bit of resolve, for as he now faced the culmination of months of planning, his legs became rubbery with tension, and his courage wavered. But there was no turning back now, and after another quick prayer and a few deep breaths, he clicked off the light, placed it in his pocket, and reached down toward the child. As gently as possible, he slid one hand under the baby's head, and the other beneath his tiny rear end, and lifted him off the mattress. The child's only protest was a soft grunt and a brief squirm, and then he was sleeping peacefully again even as Jarrett laid his head upon his left shoulder. The child was only three weeks old at this point, so Jarrett judged that he weighed no more than ten, maybe twelve pounds, and he could easily hold him with one arm as he reached into his pocket with his free hand and once again retrieved the penlight.

Jarrett exited the baby's room, and as he tiptoed past the parents' room, he could feel the tension and anxiety within him ease a bit, as he could see the end of this little scheme of his fast approaching. While there would be an omnipresent fear for many years to come that the police or FBI would track down the missing child and come knocking at his door, this single event, though he knew it would take no more than ten minutes from start to finish, had overwhelmed him spiritually, mentally and emotionally for the past seven months. And though Linda agreed with and supported him in this decision, it had taken its toll on her as well. But at long last, he could finally see the proverbial light at the end of the tunnel.

Jarrett reached the end of the hallway and entered the living room once again. He tried to avoid what he judged to be the location of the loose floorboard that had popped as he had passed through the room the first time, though he knew he could just as easily run afoul of others. Yet this time, the floor made no protest whatsoever, and his hopes reached new heights as he entered the kitchen.

Then came a soft *click* from behind him, and the living room was instantly bathed in light. "ROBBER!" a man yelled, and rather than running out through the open door in the kitchen that lead to the garage, Jarrett's instinctive reaction was to spin around and face the owner of the voice. In the space of perhaps half a second, he saw a tubular metallic object protruding from the shadows of the still-darkened hallway, held by a man wearing shorts and a t-shirt.

"No, don't shoot! I have —" But his words were cut off.

Without having heard a sound and with no awareness of the passing of time, Jarrett found himself looking up at the ceiling, an indescribable agony exploding in the center of his chest, and feeling warm wetness on his hands and face. A few seconds later he heard a woman somewhere nearby screaming "BRIAN, OH MY GOD, MY BABY BRIAN! CARL, WHAT HAVE YOU DONE?!?"

Then Carl Zintak loomed above Jarrett, his face ashen and his mouth open in shock. He was still holding the weapon at his side, and he tried to raise it again, but his hand, and indeed his whole body, was shaking so violently that the weapon slipped from his grasp and thumped to the floor.

Jarrett realized at that point that he was still holding the baby against his chest, but he chose not to look down, knowing the horror that he would see. There would be no need to look into the future now, even if he had intended to, for there was no longer any doubt that Brian Zintak would never pursue his genocidal plan. Furthermore, Jarrett's own plan had not materialized as he had hoped it would, and he feared what the future would hold for his family – the unimaginable grief they would have to endure until time eventually healed their wounds. Still, he understood and accepted the sacrifice that he had been asked to make, and that there was only one plan – God's – that was now complete. There was nothing left for Jarrett to do but walk down the lighted tunnel that opened up before him, toward the dazzling figure in white that now beckoned him home.

EPILOGUE

Altered Timeline – October 2120

I t had taken over three hours to power up the time machine and for the compression module to ever-so-gradually compact the matter used to create the singularity that replicated the effects of the black hole. As the process had continued, the event horizon had slowly crept outward from the device until it reached its maximum radius as precisely calculated by Zintak, a point just inches away from the inner cage that surrounded the machine. The inner cage had been built both to protect the machine from the creature prior to commencement of the process, and once the process had begun, to protect the creature from crossing the event horizon and being shredded into subatomic particles. The distance from the inner cage to the outer cage was seventy-five feet all the way around, an area that allowed the creature room to maneuver while at the same time ensuring that it would be within the temporal zone once the event horizon had reached its maximum radius.

Seconds after the event horizon reached the wall of the inner cage, the creature, which had been pacing relentlessly around the perimeter of the enclosure, suddenly froze as though it were a video recording on pause, then shimmered, faded and disappeared. Everyone who was watching from the control room erupted into applause and shouts of joy, all those months of stress, fatigue and mounting tension instantly forgotten in their moment of triumph.

All of them, that is, except Zintak. He remained quiet and

stone-faced, studying the instruments and computer screens, comparing the uptick in the readout on the time travel counter to the burnup rate of the nuclear fuel. The counter needed to hit at least 101.7 years – the creature's maximum life span once the synthetic casing surrounding the implanted virus had deteriorated – before Zintak could breathe a sigh of relief. And while he had personally calculated the fuel burnup rate hundreds of times, it was purely hypothetical until the machine was actually powered up for real.

The counter continued to rise – 66.0, 78.0, 84.0 – while the fuel gauge did as well – 81.0%, 83.0%, 86.0% . . . . When the fuel gauge surpassed 95.0%, it slowed down significantly, which in turn increased Zintak's stress level. They were not quite where they needed to be yet . . . 88.0, 91.3, 95.0. Almost, but not quite. 98.2%, 98.7%, 99. 1% . . . . and then, the counter clicked to 101.7, then 101.8, then 102.6. It finally came to rest at 105.3 years, within the margin of error that Zintak had calculated. Now, at last, he could celebrate with his team. He raised his hand to call for quiet.

"Thank you all for your commitment to this initiative, for your patience, endurance, and for the sacrifices you have made in order to become pioneers in a new and better world. Each and every one of you, regardless of your role here, has been an integral part of our project for the last eight months and now stand ready to reap the rewards for your contribution. I do, however, want to especially thank Dr. Millenkamp, my partner and friend, for all that he has done. His ingenuity and bold vision allowed us to create something completely unique and with all of the attributes needed to reshape the past in a way that will ensure an unimaginably bright future for each of us."

There were smiles and nods at Millenkamp, who proudly puffed out his chest and nodded back at them.

"Now then," Zintak continued, "let's go check out our new world."

They all filed out of the control room, abuzz with fresh speculation as to what they might expect when they stepped outside of the temporally-shielded building. Each and every one of them had, of course, been discussing this topic ever since they had first been recruited to join Zintak's team, but now that the moment of discovery had actually come, they were like elementary students going on a field trip.

They approached the enormous outer doors of the warehouse, and Zintak punched his code into the keypad. The magnetic bolts slid aside, and sunshine spilled across the floor as the doors opened to the outside world for the first time in eight months. They crossed the threshold and proceeded across the delivery platform toward the concrete wall that surrounded the perimeter of the property. They reached the gates, and again Zintak entered his access code into the keypad that controlled the hinged entry doors. The doors swung open as designed, and the master race flowed through the doorway and out into the access drive that led to the street. The adjacent property was also surrounded by a concrete wall approximately five meters high, so they could only see a small section of River Drive at the end of the alley directly in front of them. They paused there for a moment, watching and listening.

At first they saw and heard nothing . . . just as they had hoped and expected. More smiles and hopeful glances were exchanged. But then a hover car whizzed by . . . and then another. A moment later a terrestrial vehicle passed by (these were now somewhat unusual but not gone altogether), followed by another hover car. Then a couple of pedestrians came into view and continued on past the alley. The signs of trouble were mounting quickly, and another one came seconds later as they looked back towards the warehouse for the first time and noticed that the temporal shields were still concealed by the outer shell of the building. Changes made to the past should have wiped out the very existence of the building, causing the metallic shields to become visible from the outside.

In virtual lockstep, those members of the master race who had brought their electronic devices with them frantically brought them forth to check their date/time displays or their home webpages for current events. One quick glance confirmed their fear – that the world had not changed. Or if it had, the changes were not apparent, and probably not significant to Zintak and his group.

There was silence for a long time, as disappointment and despair overcame them. Finally, Zintak, his expression morphing from shock to rage, turned and pointed a trembling finger at Millenkamp.

"You . . . failed me," he said hoarsely. "You failed us all. The creature was defeated. *DEFEATED!* By people who were like Neanderthals compared to us!" He took a step towards Millenkamp, then another, as he continued his rant. "Primitive weapons and technologies, that's all they had! They should never have stood a chance! This should be an empty planet right now, with only us left to rule over it!"

As Zintak spoke, other members of the group began to encircle Millenkamp, their disappointment now giving way to anger and hatred as well.

"Wait, no!" Millenkamp protested. "How do you know the creature failed? It could have been the machine! Maybe it vaporized the creature instead of sending it into the past. Or maybe Zintak miscalculated and sent the thing thousands or even millions of years into the past, before people even existed. It would have died long before it ever even encountered a human being!"

Upon hearing Millenkamp's words, the group members halted their advance and looked around at each other with uncertainty. There was merit in what each of the men said, so how could they know who was right and who was wrong?

"YOU WILL NOT EVEN *CONSIDER* HIS ABSURD ALLEGATIONS!" Zintak screamed. "My design was flawless, a product of my unparalleled genius! *This* fool is to blame for our failure! We will replace him with someone competent, then make another attempt at purging the evil, decay and corruption from our society. And this time, we will succeed!"

"Think about it, Zintak," Millenkamp countered. "We observed the creature's development for months -- its ferocity, its abilities, its natural instinct to kill humans. And even though it could not be fully tested inside the cage, we knew it would be unbeatable out in the open, against people who would never see it coming, and that it could indefinitely evade any weapon or location technology of that time. The creature existed. We know this because *we* created it, and *we* turned it loose. But with your machine, on the other hand, we had no empirical evidence that it could work. It was built entirely on your theories. And what kind of theory? That a black hole could be *replicated* and used to send something back in time?!? Ridiculous! I should have laughed in your face and walked away from that very first meeting."

"I would have killed you if you had! Just as I am going to kill you now!" Zintak lunged at Millenkamp, but was intercepted by one of the other men in the group.

"Stop, Zintak!" the man commanded. "The fact is, you are both at fault. It was you who recruited us, who convinced us to leave our families to join your cause. 'Don't worry,' you said, 'they will not die, nor feel any pain whatsoever. They will simply cease to exist. And in their honor, we will create a new race, one without greed, hatred, or depravity of any kind. Even physical detriments will be all but eliminated from humanity, as we will select only those who are without disease or deformity and are in fact as close to being physically perfect as any person can be.' But it was all a lie. And you," he said, turning to Millenkamp, "were right there alongside him the entire way. His number two. Peddling the same false hope, perpetuating the same perversion of evil to good, and good to evil.

All because you both had to deal with tragedy. How many others, throughout history, have had to deal with tragedy in their lives? And how many of those bring about healing for themselves by building time machines and unleashing horrific monsters in order to destroy the entire human race? Yes, there is tremendous evil in the world, so much so that it has become an incurable cancer, as you both have often described it. Even now, I know this to be true. But what I am just now recognizing is that the two of you were never working on the cure, you were part of the disease itself. The rest of us are now going home to our families, if they will still have us. And since we have no desire to ever 'cease to exist', well . . ." The man glanced at several of his associates, communicating his message without the use of words, and each one confirmed his or her understanding with a nod.

There was time enough for just a couple of screams before a wave of vengeful humanity washed over Zintak and Millenkamp. Then a deep silence followed, broken only by a light breeze that whistled softly between the concrete walls surrounding those who remained . . . as though the world itself were exhaling with relief at the knowledge that past, present and future were at last secure.

ABOUT THE AUTHOR

Reaper is **TIMOTHY J. VANBRANDT**'s debut novel. Tim was born on September 19, 1966 in Toledo, Ohio. He attended St. Anthony Catholic School through the eighth grade, then graduated from Whiteford Agricultural Schools in 1984. He attended the University of Toledo, earning an Associate of Applied Science Degree in 1986, a Bachelor of Arts Degree in 1989, and a Master of Business Administration Degree in 1992. He holds a Certified Management Accountant designation and has worked in the finance and accounting fields for most of his career. He is currently a Regional Compliance Director for Bon Secours Mercy Health.

Tim lives in Ottawa Lake, Michigan, where he grew up, with his wonderful wife Teresa, their youngest son Mason and their dog Baxter. They also have two older sons, Trevor and Joshua. They are members of Bedford Alliance Church in Temperance, Michigan, where they are small group leaders. Prior to that, they were members of Fremont Alliance Church in Fremont, Ohio, where they were involved in numerous ministries including governing board and the church's annual Passion musical, among others. They have also participated in mission trips to Ecuador and Nicaragua.

Tim is a huge fan of Michigan Wolverine and Toledo Rocket football. He enjoys reading, playing softball, hiking and bicycling. He coached Mason's youth teams at Whiteford, including football, basketball and baseball, for several years, and he and Teresa are active in the school's Athletic Booster group. You can reach him at Timothy@VanBrandtbooks.com.